פֿאַרדוון

THE CONJURED WOMAN
A NOVEL
BY ANNE GROSS

מיטהַלט

Library of Congress Cataloging-in-Publication Data available upon request

For inquiries about orders, please contact:
Beaufort Books
27 West 20th Street, 11th Floor
New York, NY 10011

Published in the United States by Beaufort Books
www.beaufortbooks.com

Distributed by Midpoint Trade Books
www.midpointtrade.com

Printed in the United States of America

Gross, Anne
The Conjured Woman
ISBN:
Paperback: 9780825307980
eBook: 9780825307515

Design by Michael Short

Dédié à la memoire de ma grandmère,
Marie-Jeanne Laurier "Naninou"

THE CONJURED WOMAN

A NOVEL

BY ANNE GROSS

BEAUFORT
BOOKS

Table of Contents

THE FORTUNE

A light wind blew through the open French doors and lifted the diaphanous curtains, revealing a riot of blooming rosebushes surrounded by low boxwood hedges. Feeling the breeze on the back of her neck, Adelaide quickly placed her hands over the tableau of colorful cards spread carefully on the table. It wouldn't do to have them scatter. "This card here," she began when the curtains fell back to the floor, "in the Western cardinal position, represents the consultant. In this case, you."

"I know who I am, I do not need you to tell me." Napoleon Bonaparte squinted at the cards on the delicate table, seemingly unable to resist the urge to see if something in the illustrated symbols revealed a characteristic about him that he hadn't known, or a confirmation of what he already knew to be true. "The king of diamonds," he noted out loud.

The strongest men always bucked against her talent, Adelaide thought to herself. Wanting to assert their power, yet powerless to know their future without help, they pointed out the obvious and waited to be congratulated for their discovery. "Yes, I am not surprised that showed up for your reading." Adelaide gave him a conciliating smile while she considered her next move. If she ignored his thinly veiled boast of self-knowledge and continued reading the card, he would insist he already knew what she was telling him and force her to move on to the next cardinal point. She knew that skipping the King of Diamonds would help to move the reading forward, and that would be a relief, but she also feared that if she did so, he would later berate her for having given an incomplete reading. She sighed, either way was failure for her—interpret the card and be accused of pedantic lecturing, or skip forward as his tone suggested she do and be accused of skimming. She decided to call his bluff. "Let us move to the next card, since His Imperial Majesty knows his own strengths and failures."

As she expected, Bonaparte drew himself up in the chair with an affronted breath of air. "Mademoiselle Lenormand, I would expect that you interpret all the cards you pull. To do less is to steal from France herself."

Adelaide placed an affected hand on her breast, "Your Majesty, I beseech you, please pardon me for any unintentional affront I may have caused. I merely wish to humbly serve you." She made a florid gesture over the table. "Shall I then read the card?"

"By all means."

Adelaide closed her eyes to fight back her growing apprehension and trusted she looked merely meditative. The constant tightrope a person such as herself was forced to walk in order to maintain control of the cards was at odds with the modest servility her clients demanded.

Although her power in reading the cards was great, it was no match for the power of the society in which she worked. It was worse when she read for men who either misinterpreted the intimacy of the situation, or chafed at the reversal of gender roles. Reading for Bonaparte added even more layers of murk.

"The King of Diamonds, a man with strong character who is very successful in his business affairs." Adelaide opened her eyes when she heard her client snort derisively. Bonaparte had flung himself backwards deep into his chair and was now looking at the ceiling. "Yes," agreed Adelaide, "it does seem obvious, but please consider that this card was randomly chosen from a fifty-four-card deck. The fact that it should fit you so perfectly aligns with what you have heard of my reputation, no?"

"Josephine tells me you developed these cards yourself."

"I did. I spent my entire life studying mythology, numerology, astrology, the fundamentals of alchemy, and, of course, cartomancy before I developed the images you see on the cards in front of you."

Bonaparte huffed once through pursed lips, which was all the acknowledgement of Adelaide's accomplishment that he would deign to give. "Go on," he ordered with a flick of his hand.

"The King of Diamonds is but one symbol on this card, and a small one at that. I included the images from the standard playing cards in each left corner mostly to add organization and familiarity to the deck. The main scene, as you can see, is of Cadmus bringing an offering to Athena and informing her of the slain serpent. You know the story, do you not?"

"Of course I do. Cadmus slew the serpent and was instructed by Athena to bury the teeth. After the Spartoi were born from those teeth, they warred amongst themselves until there were only five left alive. Those last Spartoi helped Cadmus build the city of Thebes."

Bonaparte paused in his narrative and smiled. "Are you comparing me to Cadmus?"

"I assume, Your Majesty, you understand the consequences of slaying your enemy."

"The consequences of victory, you mean."

Adelaide looked at the Emperor and saw how his eyes glinted. She knew she must tread carefully. "From the serpent's teeth the five noblest families of Thebes were born. Cadmus, with the blessings of Athena, ruled them all. Yet the story does not end well."

"No," Bonaparte allowed, "the serpent was a favorite of Ares who was angry to lose his pet. Cadmus was beset with ill-fortune for killing the serpent and eventually was himself turned into a serpent."

Adelaide nodded. "A great soldier, a founder of cities, and in the end, a monster." She had his full attention now. He sat forward and caught her gaze with such self-confidence that she couldn't help but avert her eyes. He then bent over the table and looked just as intently at the card as if to force out its meaning.

"There are other scenes here," he said.

Adelaide exhaled. She hadn't realized she'd been holding her breath. "Yes, the rook dropping fruit that the hog gobbles up; the lady holding a scarab beetle on her finger. The cards reveal their stories in their own time. I cannot know what all the pictures mean immediately upon looking at them, they must be interpreted not only by their images, but also in relation to where they are placed in the spread and who is sitting across from me. Some scenes have no meaning on their own, but are merely revealed for the purpose of adding clarity to the card adjacent to it."

"How do you know when an image is to be interpreted only for another card?"

"No single card can be read alone, each one influences the others, just as in life there will never be any single event to define a person, but a series of events, one after the other, each adding or detracting so that in the end a person's wisdom and character is marked by multitudes of experiences layered, not linear." Adelaide paused before taking another tack, "The Empress convinced you to seek my counsel, did she not?"

"I agreed to meet with you; she would not let the matter drop otherwise."

"Do you trust her?"

"She is my wife," Bonaparte's eyes flashed dangerously. "I would trust her with my life."

"Just your life? You do not trust her judgment as well? You seem very skeptical of my talents. The Empress is not. I had hoped her opinion of me would sway you."

"Josephine is a remarkable strategist amongst the court and has a keen wit to suit her own purpose, but all her purposes are fickle. She is a woman, after all." The Emperor waved his hand dismissively and smiled, "Go on with your reading. I will behave."

Referring to himself as like a child who needed to behave served to remind Adelaide of her feminine duty to placate and soothe, despite the irritation she felt on Josephine's behalf. She doubted it was an intentional maneuver, but it was nonetheless effective. She continued the reading. "This card also speaks of receiving aid, as the rook aids the hog and the Lady aids the scarab. A person who is in a position inferior to yourself will come to you when you need help. I see that you wear a beautiful scarab as your talisman. The card's veracity is all the more strengthened by this."

The jewel was impossible to miss. The enormous emerald, cut in the form of the traditional Egyptian amulet and set against golden wings, had slipped forward on its chain from behind the Emperor's cravat when he leaned forward to examine the cards and Adelaide struggled to keep from staring. Her observation caused him to quickly drop it back down his shirt. "Merely a coincidence," he said dismissively. "I wear it to remind me of the great victory I led in Egypt."

"A coincidence? I don't believe in coincidences. I hope you'll forgive me for saying so, but I doubt you do either. It's common knowledge that you think yourself to be living under a lucky star."

"A figure of speech. My successes are due to my skills in diplomacy and governance," the Emperor corrected.

"Of course. But even a hero like Cadmus sought help from the gods. I caution you that your star, your gods, will be no help to you in the coming months. You will soon be under a great burden."

Bonaparte laughed. "You must be joking. I do not need to have my cards read to know that I have no end of burdens." He paused to glare into Adelaide's eyes. Again, she averted her gaze. "Talleyrand is tired of entertaining those royal Spanish idiots I've imprisoned in his home, and burdens me with his endless complaints. Spain herself burdens me with its insolent militias that prick me like irritating mosquitos. Fouché reminds me at every turn of my burden to produce an heir. This very hour with you is a burden my wife placed upon me. And now you are burdening me with vague and useless portents couched in mythology." He sat back in his chair again, shaking his head. The candlelight played on his features, darkening his eyes, deepening the lines around his mouth. Adelaide let him brood on his exhaustion so that her next words would be fully felt.

"That is what I'm trying to tell you—you have need for an aide fixed to you with loyalty beyond that of a valet, or a wife, or even a mother."

"A person like that does not exist."

"No, not a person." Adelaide felt her cheeks flush as she paused. She knew her next suggestion was radical and she feared the Emperor's reaction. "A golem, created for the sole purpose of carrying out your wishes; to protect France."

"A golem." Bonaparte echoed with a smile. He didn't even bother to sit back up in his chair at the suggestion. He casually looked at his nails and picked at them as he thought. Adelaide felt a trickle of sweat roll down her neck while she waited. "I think, Mademoiselle," he continued, "you would be much more entertaining to me if you would take off your clothes. You have strayed from telling my fortune to an even more ludicrous path so I am fairly certain disrobing would not sully your professional integrity. You may start by pulling the sleeves of your gown off your shoulders."

Adelaide stared at Bonaparte in shock and considered her options. Then she loosened the drawstring of her chemise. The cloth slipped open at her neck and she pushed it over her pale shoulders. She had no other option. "I was given the instructions for the ceremony when I was still quite young and have been studying those sacred words ever since. I can call it for you."

"Vous êtes toujours une petite fille, Mademoiselle." Bonaparte leaned forward and lightly drew the backs of his fingers down the length of her neck from behind her ear to the end of her sloped shoulder. He smiled when he saw her shudder. "A little girl who still believes in fairies."

"You do not think I could do it?" She was a woman in her early thirties, certainly not a little girl. It annoyed her that she was flattered by the comparison.

"There is no such thing as magic," he responded. "You could no more call forth a golem as you could shit a nosegay of dewy violets."

"If you do not believe in the supernatural, why wear that Egyptian jewel?" Adelaide challenged.

Napoleon reflexively put his hand to his neck and fingered the scarab under his collar. His face took on a distant expression and Adelaide wondered if he was remembering his ill-fated journey to

Egypt, but he composed himself quickly and said merely, "It is just a trifle. It accents my waistcoat."

"It accents nothing if you wear it under your collar." replied Adelaide, wishing she could see it again. "I am sure it is powerful. You must take care."

"Bof." Bonaparte waved his left hand dismissively. "It is no more powerful than this ring on my finger. A man wears the jewel; the jewel does not wear the man."

His cavalier attitude towards the power in his wedding band made Adelaide gasp. She looked down at the forgotten cards and blushed for the Emperor's sake. "I would like to help you," she said quietly, without looking up. "If you would allow it, I will call forth a golem for you."

"And why would you do such a thing for me?" Bonaparte laughed. He seemed to be enjoying himself much more.

"You can make France the greatest country in the world, but not alone. The cards tell me you need an aide."

Bonaparte smiled slyly and reached over the table to finger a lock of her black hair. "Why not you?"

"No, not me, your Majesty. I am corruptible. You need someone bound to you by something stronger than the ties of human loyalty. I can, however, provide that aide." Adelaide examined Bonaparte's relaxed pose and his crinkled smirk. He was barely containing his derision. Another breeze came through the doors, carrying the heady smell of Josephine's favored roses. Poor Josephine, thought Adelaide as she glanced at an adjacent card whose meaning was incontrovertible. There would be a divorce. She wondered how the roses at Malmaison would fare without their mistress. Adelaide hoped that Josephine would be allowed to stay for the sake of her beloved garden. The card blew off the table and landed on the parquet floor. Neither of them bothered to bend over to retrieve it. "Perhaps we should continue another time," she suggested.

"Tell me more about this golem first," the Emperor said indulgently. "Where is it now? Where would you call it from?" He resumed stroking her shoulder, pushing her gown just a little further down on her round white arm.

Adelaide braced her palms against her thighs as the sensation of his teasing touch coursed down her spine. She struggled to answer his question. "I have no idea where it is. Where do infants reside before they are born?" she replied.

Bonaparte stood suddenly and gripped her elbow to pull her from her chair. The light table tipped and the cards fell all about like flower petals before a bride as she was led to the divan. "That is a good question," he said, "and one I am sure I can help you answer."

As the Emperor dipped his head to taste her skin at that tender spot just behind her jaw and under her ear, Adelaide's last coherent thought was that her question had been meant to be answered philosophically, not probed for literally.

THE SEDUCTION

It was the combination of a pounding headache and the sound of some idiot honking in the street that woke Elise that morning. She lay on her side in the bed and squinted at the room, trying to clear her vision and locate her car keys in the swirl of abandoned clothes and empty bottles that littered the floor. A man's hot breath was steaming up the back of her neck and the sweat of him made her back slick as he curled closer against her. Her mouth felt like someone had pasted it shut with the contents of a soggy ashtray. She blinked hard to clear the film from her corneas and finally spotted her keys on the floor where she had dropped them as she came in.

Carefully so as to not awaken her companion, Elise removed the muscular arm that was draped over her side and untangled her feet from the sheet bunched at the bottom of the bed. Tentatively, she stretched her legs off the mattress and slid onto the floor where she fought a surge of nausea that accompanied her move to her knees. She paused to clamp her head in her hands and watched the dust bunnies float across the Saltillo tile under the bed.

When the spins stopped, Elise raised her pointed chin to peek over the top of the mattress at her lover. Emmett was ardent, but not overly intelligent, a combination of character traits she found convenient. It meant he was too love-struck to shake off easily, and too clueless to feel any shame when she stood him up. As a result, other guys came and went, but Emmett was always around if she had an opening. Elise watched his broad chest expand when he took a deep breath and his abdominals tightened beautifully as he coughed. The situation wasn't all bad, she thought lasciviously.

When he coughed again, Elise hurriedly reached out and grabbed her skirt, which was bunched next to her knees. To avoid having to make excuses for her quick exit, she would have to move fast to get out before he woke up. The disappearing act would be much easier on both of them. Without getting up off the floor, she pulled the skirt over her skinny legs and lifted her hips to impatiently tug the tight fabric over them. Then she crawled over to the armchair to contort herself into her bra and tucked her soggy, wadded thong into her waistband. She used the arm of the chair to pull herself to her feet and was delighted to find her blouse partially hidden behind the seat cushion. She snatched it up to drape across her shoulders, and thus partially clad, she staggered outside with her purse and keys tight in her hand, only to swivel and return to collect her forgotten heels.

The kiln-like heat of the Tucson morning caused Elise to blink, narrow-eyed, from Emmett's porch into the unrelenting sunshine. It was the beginning of the monsoon season, and despite the clear skies, it seemed as though the entire world was enveloped in the smell of rain.

In the yard, a palo verde tree spread its pale green branches over the wide expanse of gravel that substituted for lawn. Cicadas hid as best as they could behind the tree's bean-sized leaves and added their high decibel trill to the sounds of traffic coming from Speedway Boulevard. Over the roofs of the homes across the street, the Catalina Mountain range loomed in shades of violet and burnt orange spreading from East to West. She had grown up in the Midwest, but the desert was her home. In the desert it never mattered what had happened the night before because every morning was a fresh start. The thought caused Elise to sigh contentedly, which caused another wave of nausea to hit.

She fumbled in her purse and found her aviators, which she put on with relief, then pulled out a packet of cigarettes and knocked one out to dangle from her bruised lips. When she realized she'd left the lighter inside, she threw the cigarette at the tree in frustration. Anita would be finishing her night-shift at the hospital right about now, she thought as she dove back into her purse and looked for her phone. She could use a Bloody Mary and some female company.

The drive from the downtown Barrio to Fourth Avenue was thankfully short. Even so, by the time she reached the dark bar, Anita, still in her hospital scrubs, was already seated with her dinner—a long neck and a hotdog. A swath of her curly brown hair had fallen out of her ponytail and puffy dark circles ringed her eyes.

"Hey. How'd it go last night?" Elise asked. She could tell right away something was wrong.

Anita shrugged and took a bite of her dog. Elise knew enough not to press. She'd come out with it soon enough, and insisting on hearing the story before she was ready to spill would only cause the water-works to turn on. Instead, she ordered her drink and ignored the dramatic sigh from her companion.

"How 'bout you. What'd you do last night?"

"Emmett."

Anita rolled her eyes. "So where is he now?"

"Probably still in bed. We got pretty hammered."

"Yeah. I gathered."

Elise felt self-conscious when Anita's brown eyes took in the details of her sweaty outfit and smeared eye makeup. "Was it any good?" asked Anita. "Or don't you remember?"

"I'm getting flashbacks right now." Elise swirled her drink in her glass with her celery stick. "Do you want an interpretive reenactment of the night?" She half stood off her stool, threatening improvisation.

Anita laughed and playfully hit Elise. "God no, sit down. I bet he's already texted you, he's just that dumb."

"He hasn't yet. I'll give him until 10:30."

"Hopefully I'll be sawing logs by then," said Anita as she took another sip of beer, washing down her dinner. She sighed again. "It was a rough night. Room 410 passed last night."

There it was, thought Elise. "Which one was 410?"

"The GI bleed you sent up last Tuesday."

"Oh him." Elise studied her friend and wished she'd get a thicker skin. It had been just over a year since they'd graduated from nursing school together, and they were still trying to figure out how much of themselves to give to their patients. The amount of personal responsibility Anita took for the emotional welfare of others concerned Elise. Anita had entered the field to help people. Elise did it because she knew she'd need a job right out of college, and for the blood and guts. As a result, Anita worked the intensive care unit on the fifth floor, and Elise stayed behind the sliding double doors of the emergency room on the first floor. "He was already going when I had him. I'm surprised you didn't bag and tag him earlier."

"I think he was hanging on for his son to fly in to say goodbye. He had such a nice family."

"How many of them were bedside?"

"Just five, but still."

Elise nodded. Dealing with families that were holding vigil was a burden for sympathetic nurses who might run themselves ragged getting extra blankets or boxes of tissues for weepy relatives, all while maintaining the care of the patient. In the ER, however, none of Elise's patients stayed long enough for her to get to know them, much less their family. The anonymity of her patients suited her just fine since what kept her interested in her job was not the prospect of developing relationships, it was the adrenaline rush that came from never knowing what kind of medical issue was going to walk or roll through the doors. "You're not on again tonight, are you?" Elise asked.

"No, thank god. I hope I sleep for a week."

"I think my next shift is Wednesday."

Anita nodded. They wouldn't see each other, but it was nice to know they were in the same building at the same time. Nurses on separate floors didn't mix. During a twelve hour shift on a busy night even breaking for dinner would be done one hasty bite at a time between every patient visit. On a full moon in the ER, you ate a power bar for dinner. Wandering to a different floor to socialize for ten minutes with another nurse was a good way to lose your job.

Anita motioned the bartender over when Elise started crunching on her celery stick again. "My friend wants one of those," she said pointing to an enormous jar behind the bar and reaching into her purse.

"No really, I don't." Elise protested as the bartender dunked his long tongs and started fishing for a pickled egg in the pink, cloudy brine.

"Oh shut up, you alkie," Anita responded. "You've been eyeing them ever since you got in here. Besides, you could use a little protein to mix with all that tomato juice you're dribbling on your blouse."

Elise ate her egg and tried to ignore Anita's bemused stare. "You're disgusting, you know that right?" Anita asked.

"Here. I brought you a souvenir." Elise pulled her thong out of her waistband and dropped it into her friend's lap, who squealed and stood up quickly so that the thong dropped onto the floor under the barstool.

"I can't believe you just did that!"

"What? I thought you could use a little sex in your life."

"That's so gross. I'm going to have to burn my scrubs now." Anita furiously rubbed her pants with a cocktail napkin.

"My undies are the cleanest thing you've touched all night."

"Yeah, but I usually get paid to touch nasty shit, so you owe me." Anita sat back down and glowered at Elise. "You're not going to just leave them there, are you?" She pointed to the spent triangle of lace on the floor.

Elise shrugged noncommittally as she sucked egg brine from her fingertips. Wiping her damp fingers on her skirt, she got up to leave. "Thanks for the egg. I'm out of here. Sleep tight, Snow White."

"Aw, come on. So soon?"

"Seriously, I'm beat. I need to get back and shower."

Anita held her nose. "I didn't want to mention it but…" She ducked Elise's swat and grinned. "What are you doing tonight?"

"I don't know. I'll probably nap, and then go for a run before the rains come. Interested?" She always felt better after a run, cleaner somehow. Hair of the dog, and a long run were the best remedies for overindulgence, she'd found.

"I don't think so. I need to regroup; watch a little TV; drink a little wine."

Elise paused and tried to gauge her friend, "It was his time, you know? You shouldn't let yourself get so involved."

"I know. I'm okay; worry about yourself. You need to be more careful with the company you keep." Anita smiled teasingly, "Like Emmett, for example. Let me know what happens with your man."

"He's not my man," Elise grumbled, picking up her keys. At the same time, her phone beeped from her clutch announcing the arrival of a text. It wasn't even 10:30 yet.

Adelaide paused before entering the guest bedroom at Malmaison and took a bracing breath. The man was insatiable, she thought, but there was nothing she could do. Josephine had given her a bedroom much more centrally placed, with better furnishings and a big fireplace, but he had moved her to a more discrete location, insultingly insisting the new bedroom was more suitable to a woman of her social standing. The new room had two doors, the main one that exited into the hall, and a side door that exited to the maid's room.

"One, two, three…" she counted quietly to herself after she entered the room, unpinning the lace cap from her head and unwinding her long black hair.

"Four, five six…" She sat at the dressing table and checked her teeth in the mirror for bits of the evening meal before picking up her brush. Her head was swimming from the endless glasses of Bordeaux that Josephine favored. Mademoiselle Poulette had been so sweet at the dining table, and animated. It was too bad the girl had ruined her white gown with that final glass.

"Seven, eight, nine…" Adelaide pinched her cheeks to bring the color back into them. She felt drained of energy, the way she always did after a performance. Palm reading was always a welcome diversion, especially when done loudly so everyone in the parlor could participate. A good performance always took a great deal of preparation. No one appreciated that the fortune-telling portion of her visit was the final stage in a long effort of piecing together histories and relationships. She was exhausted. It would be just a few hours before the sun rose and all she wanted to do now was rest.

"Ten, eleven, twelve…" In the mirror Adelaide saw the door to the adjoining maid's room slowly open. Someone had finally greased the hinges, she noted. She would have to find a bell to hang on the doorknob.

It took Napoleon twelve seconds to appear after her arrival in the bedroom, a testament to the quality of his informants at Malmaison. His black eyes flashed in anticipation as he peered around the door to make sure it was safe to enter. Then it took one second more for him to start undressing her. It didn't take long after that for the Emperor's stomach to swing freely and pendulously against her. The rhythmic slapping of it against her back caused Adelaide to start counting again. She absently wondered about the number twelve when he stopped after twelve thrusts. Twelve seconds to appear in my bedroom, she thought, twelve signs in the zodiac, twelve hours on a clock, twelve apostles, twelve months in a year, twelve gods of Egypt, twelve Marshalls in the army—a strong number indeed. He pressed his head against her neck, still breathing hard. His hair was damp and left wet streaks on her skin. She willed her pores to open up and drink in his power, then crawled out from under the Emperor and made her way towards the head of the bed.

"Josephine tells me that invitations have already been sent," Napoleon growled as he rolled onto his back. "Is there nothing I can do to stop this nonsense? You have thoroughly bewitched my wife with your swindles."

"You need merely resume your affections for her. As long as she is emotionally compromised, she will be suggestible to anyone who lends her an ear."

Napoleon grumbled, but made no comprehensible reply. Adelaide pushed his head off her thigh, swung herself off the bed, and pulled out the commode. "I only have your good intentions at heart. I went to your wife because you wouldn't see reason." She pushed the commode back under the bed before setting a basin on the floor into which she poured fresh water from an ewer. Napoleon sat up at the head of the bed and watched as she squatted over the basin with a rag.

"You should be thanking me, or at the very least, paying me more handsomely," Adelaide said over the splashing of water. "I am doing you the service of keeping your wife too occupied to vex you."

"You must be joking. If anything she vexes me more. I can't find any peace. I now know that my wife's chambermaid is the great, great, great grandniece of a onetime Sumerian Queen, that one of my guests was convinced by you to swallow a paper on which you'd written the name of the man she admires most so that she may one day feel him inside her, and that Talleyrand will be cured of his limp if he eats the meat of an ostrich at every meal for a year. I also know, thanks to my dear wife, that my own secretary Monsieur Gaston has a strawberry shaped birthmark on his stomach and that Madame Delesgans ate a particularly juicy strawberry in his presence while looking at him in a most lascivious manner. That is something I would have been happy to never know. However, and this is most curious: I know that Madame Delesgans's husband is arriving tomorrow and that I am now short one secretary as Monsieur Gaston has packed his bags and disappeared. Did you not tell Monsieur Gaston he would be dead within the month? Yes, of course you did. You use every opportunity to create havoc. Thanks to you and Josephine, my head is filled with distraction." Napoleon paused to watch his paramour as she bathed. "That is Imperial seed you are so cavalierly washing away," he noted.

"Strewn across a barren landscape, I'm afraid." Adelaide had been preparing her tea every day since she'd left the convent school, and had been thankful for it every encounter since.

Napoleon sighed. "That seems to be my lot, as of late. Still, I can't believe you're doing that in front of me. Where did you say you were raised?"

"Alençon."

"Oh yes, now I remember. A barn."

"We are all citizens of France," Adelaide reminded the Emperor.

"Fouché thinks you to be a danger to France. He tells me you listen to everything and forget nothing. He's counseled me to send you away."

"A danger? I am just a woman."

"So which are you, a citizen, or 'just a woman'?" He smirked and then waved his hand dismissively in the air when it became obvious Adelaide wouldn't take the bait. "I'm not afraid of the gossip and innuendo you peddle, but I admit I considered ridding myself of you when I found out that you and Josephine were plotting to go ahead with the conjuring. Cross me again and I'll—" His threat was cut off when an insistent scratching was heard at the door to the maid's room. He leapt out of bed and snatched up his shirt. Ten seconds later, a soft knock came from the door to the hallway. His eyes flashed large and he swept up his shoes. "Useless," he said in an overly loud whisper to the hapless man in the maid's room. "You call that a warning?" He clapped the man on the side of his head before he made his escape.

Adelaide calmly put away the basin of water and wrapped herself in her peignoir. While it had never been her intention to lift her skirts during her engagement at Malmaison, she had quickly realized the advantage of being able to bend the Emperor's ear in ways not limited by the cards. Maintaining discretion about her developing relationship had its challenges, but she was accustomed to keeping other people's secrets. As a purveyor of hopes, she opened up the tightest lips by spooning in the sweetest dreams of the future. Romantic aspirations were easy for Adelaide to discover. The more difficult task was to glean future political maneuvers. She stepped to the door to admit the Empress into her room.

"Oh, I've disturbed you from your slumber," Josephine said after looking at Adelaide's disheveled appearance. "I thought we could discuss tomorrow's event. Did you receive your equipment?"

It is already tomorrow, thought Adelaide. "I received my trunk this afternoon. Thank you for sending your footman to fetch it."

"You are most welcome," Josephine smiled. "I trust you checked to make sure everything was in order?" She glanced over at the large wooden box in the corner.

"Yes, your Majesty."

Josephine's eyes lingered on the trunk. "I'm so glad. Perhaps you should look again? The cook can help you acquire more pig's blood if you haven't enough." The Empress couldn't suppress the shudder that overcame her and it caused her to lilt to the left. She overcorrected her stance by taking a few shuffling steps to the right. Indeed, the wine had been flowing freely that night. "Let's take a look inside your trunk, just to make sure."

Adelaide suppressed a smile. Having been raised in Martinique, Josephine knew enough of magic in the form of voodoo to be more curious than frightened. It had helped Adelaide in making her argument to proceed with the ritual. "That won't be necessary. I assure you I will not be needing any blood this time. But I should remind you that I will require at least an hour in the banquet room prior to the guests' arrival so that I may arrange the details. No one can disturb me at that time, not even the servants. I must be completely alone."

"Anything," breathed Josephine. "Just tell me and I'll have it done for you." She took one last look at the trunk in the corner. "I'm so glad you are here. My husband's been so busy of late, and you have been so entertaining. Everyone has been talking about my cartomancer since the invitations were sent. You are a sensation. Do you really think you can conjure an aide? An aide would be so helpful." She smiled. "I try so hard not to bother him with my own needs, but maybe with an aide he'll have more time to spend with me. We want so badly to have children."

Adelaide stepped to the Empress's side and took her hand consolingly. "I have said before that this ceremony will be conducted for the sake of France, but after this week with you, I must admit I feel it is as important to do this for your sake as well. You have been so kind. I hope with all my heart that the outcome of tomorrow's event will give you back the attentions of your husband. No one deserves him more than you." When Josephine's eyes filled, Adelaide patted the back of her hand in hers. "Courage, my dear. Courage," she consoled. Josephine took a shatteringly deep breath and pulled herself up straight. "That's it. No tears." Adelaide turned the Empress around and, still holding her hand, led her towards the exit.

THE RITUAL

"Everyone, please quiet down. It is time to begin." Josephine clapped her hands to get her guests' attention.

From the head of the long banquet table, Adelaide waited as conversations were slowly brought to a close in titters and whispers. There were about twenty men and women gathered around the table, alternately seated by gender and in degrees of importance with those being of less import farthest from Bonaparte, who sat opposite Adelaide. Mademoiselle Poulette, so far from Bonaparte that she was practically nonexistent, bounced in her seat and clutched excitedly at her escort. Adelaide stared at the girl until she rested her hands on the table in front of her and calmly faced forward. Without bothering to look at Napoleon down at the other end of the table, Adelaide felt confident he was slouched in his chair. A quick glance revealed he was affecting a blasé countenance by staring at the ceiling as he swirled a strong *digestif* in its glass. Seated next to him, Josephine alternated between trying to increase his interest in excited whispers and maintaining the hauteur of an Empress.

Malmaison was a far cry from her humble beginnings in Alençon, Adelaide mused. She hated to consider that she had reached the pinnacle of her career since she was still young, but having displaced the Empress from her spot at the head of the table so that she could be directly opposite the scowling Emperor was not something she had ever imagined she would do. As the faces of the Imperial couple's friends began to turn towards her in anticipation, it was hard to think anything in her life could ever be better. Certainly it would be worse if she failed to impress that evening. The thought of failure made it difficult to breathe, so she closed her eyes and blew out slowly through pursed lips.

When she opened her eyes again, the room dazzled. The table was decorated lavishly with silken cloth that shimmered with brilliant golden threads. Low vases were filled with red roses from Josephine's garden, the petals of which fell gently onto the table's surface adding a negligent grace to the decor. Three platters of carefully constructed pyramids of puff pastries were quickly losing their height as the guests licked cream from their fingers. Infinitely reflected in three enormous mirrors were golden candelabras holding ivory tapers that flickered like starlight while the chandelier above sparkled with the inner heat of the crystal teardrops. Adelaide carefully took inventory of everything and reminded herself that the combined value of all the items in the room could never trump her own worth. Nevertheless, it was hard not to look at the items from her trunk that she'd placed near at hand and not feel somewhat diminished in comparison to the wealth on display. There was clay she'd dug from the shore of the Seine, beeswax, a mortar and pestle in which she'd placed a mixture of herbs to be ground, a tightly lidded jar of salt, her athame, five black candles, and a matching silver bowl and chalice—nothing worthy of the intense interest the Empress showed the previous night. She would not be using her cards, but she kept them close, fanned tight across her chest under her corset.

The event was finally coming together, but it had been a difficult battle to maintain control over the details. She had solved the problem of Napoleon's reticence by appealing to Josephine's desire to maintain her position. However, telling the Empress that the ritual would strengthen her marriage and guarantee her husband's world domination hadn't been the convincing argument. What Adelaide had failed to take into consideration was the vain pride the Empress held in her ability to throw a party. In Josephine's imagination, the ritual had become the most important event of the century, seconded only by her own crowning, and attended by all of the best artists, politicians, philosophers, and military strategists of France and some of other nations as well, who would be properly amazed and delighted by the Empress's audacity in tampering with the metaphysical. Adelaide, on the other hand, desired the ritual to be completed with solemn dignity, with only the Imperial couple present. Keeping the event limited to twenty had been a long negotiation that led to an unsatisfying compromise. Furthermore, Adelaide had wanted to do the conjuring in the library, a room she already knew well, a small room, confined and controlled, but the Empress preferred the airy banquet hall. A table with corners was never ideal, but Bonaparte must sit at the head, thus Adelaide could not convince the couple to abandon their long mahogany banquet table for a more egalitarian circular one. Adelaide had asked for the mirrors in the room to be covered, the crystal chandelier to be removed, and the roses be replaced with the purple flowers of bee balm, but Josephine refused each request and complained that Adelaide was trying to make the room common and ugly, an observation which was not too far from the truth.

And so, seated in the Empress's own chair, a battle of placement which she'd barely won, Adelaide opened her eyes to scan a large tome open to a handwritten page helpfully titled, "Conjuring a Golem," and hoped she wouldn't forget any of the steps during the evening. The guests were all anticipating a *Grande Spectacle* of royal proportions—a show of magic and trickery, perhaps smoke, perhaps electrical zaps from hidden wires in their chairs, but she knew there would be none of the showmanship they anticipated. There would be chanting; they would sip herbed spirits; and they would hold hands. Adelaide could only hope that the end result would be interesting enough for the Empress to consider the event a success.

If anyone had noticed Adelaide's moment of self-doubt, it didn't seem to cause any worry. She looked down the table and saw only smiles. Had they been sober, the guests surely would have understood the seriousness of the powers that were about to be released, she thought. They would pay closer attention. The smiles made her nervous. She picked up the lump of clay and began to warm it in her hands. If the lump of clay were cold, it would be difficult to shape, however if she rolled it between her palms for too long, it would dry out and cease to be malleable. Adelaide could feel Napoleon's black eyes boring into her. He was a bit like her clay, she thought. She'd overly rubbed him and now he was drying out. Like his guests, he wasn't taking the event seriously; unlike his guests, he wasn't entertained. Adelaide put the clay back in the bowl, met his eyes, and saw his glare slowly dissolve to a jeering smile. He stood and confidently gestured to all present, taking on the personae of the gracious host. *"Ma petite Yeyette,"* he called to Josephine, using her pet name in a loud voice even though she was sitting right next to him, "please introduce our honored cartomancer to our guests so that she may begin showing us her tricks."

The Empress made a great show of standing, swishing her diaphanous skirt. The outline of her meaty thighs was teasingly shown for mere seconds through the thin white silk. "Dearest friends," she started, "rarely does Mademoiselle Lenormand venture from her own home. Those who are lucky enough to know of her talent, those like Madame de Staël and our very own Talleyrand, will draw their carriage into the queue outside her home on Rue de Tournon every morning to have our charming *sibylle* turn her cards so that they may go about their day with the confidence of knowing what the future holds." Josephine paused in her delivery to smile knowingly at her guests, none of whom had ever heard of Adelaide, but would, no doubt, be gracing her with their business at her home by week's end. "We are so lucky to have her here today as I had great difficulty drawing her away from her regular customers. 'My friends need me,' she said. 'I cannot turn away those who seek my council,' she protested. But I insisted. 'France needs you,' I countered." Josephine leaned over and placed her palms on the table to emphasize her words. "France needs you," she said again, her décolletage heaving with the heavily drawn out words. Her guests tittered and nodded and looked at Adelaide with new admiration. "Had Ropespierre listened to her wisdom when she read him her cards, had Marat heeded the dire warnings she saw in the bottom of his teacup, perhaps France would be a different nation today. So I beseeched her on my knees, 'Do it for France,' I said. 'Come to Malmaison for France.' And so she came." The audience sighed rapturously and applauded Adelaide's rare sacrifice. Josephine stopped them with a wave of her arm and then self-deprecatingly folded her hands over her cleavage. "Ladies and Gentlemen, I present to you the greatest *sibylle* of all time: Mademoiselle Marie-Anne Adelaide Lenormand."

Napoleon yawned loudly over his guests' cheers. He knew full well that all it had taken to convince Adelaide to leave her regular customers was a fat purse. He acknowledged her with a barely courteous nod as she stood and thanked the generosity of the Imperial Majesties. When Adelaide sat, all attention was on her. "Please help me to do the following," Adelaide projected in a voice that was more commanding than it should have been, considering the people she was addressing. The voice was more of a compensation for the butterflies in her stomach than it was a grab for attention. "Take up the candles from the table and place them on the floor behind you so that they form a circle around the table."

Mademoiselle Poulette giggled nervously as her gentleman friend stood with exaggerated importance to honor Adelaide's request, and motioned for the other gentlemen to help. Five candelabras were carefully placed on the tiled floors in as close to a circle as the room would allow, as Adelaide stood and walked clockwise around the table, trailing salt crystal from the jar to join each candelabrum into a circle. Before she took her seat again, she lit the black candles and positioned four on the table at each point of the compass and a fifth candle in the center of the table directly under the chandelier.

Now, within the protective confines of the circle she had just drawn, she felt her power come to her. She returned to the head of the table, but remained standing. *"Compatriotes,"* she began in a voice she deepened and lengthened for effect. "This night I anticipate much will happen that will be unexplainable. Many of you will be frightened, confused, and perhaps even angry. These feelings are normal, but I hope that you will also be delighted by the creative powers of this world, amazed to find founts of power within you never knew existed, and thrilled by the collaborative powers of hands held in friendship and love. Despite these emotions, both positive and negative, you may not," Adelaide paused for emphasis, "you must not," again, another pause, this time accompanied by a glare, "rise from the table and cross the circle of salt, for to do so is to risk the safety of your dear friends."

A man seated near Napoleon chuckled and Adelaide caught his eyes and held them until his smile disappeared. "Am I understood?"

She waited for the nervous giggles and the assurances to die down before she took up a tiny pouch filled with short strands of black hair, a collection of navel lint still damp from previous engagements, and the corner of a linen rag crusted with unmentionables. These ingredients she dumped into the silver bowl. Still standing for all to see, she kneaded the bits of Napoleon into a lump of beeswax and placed the soiled, hairy mass in the center of the warmed ball of clay. She finished by forming a rough model of a figure and stood it in front of her on the table.

"Is that a man or a woman?" Josephine asked.

"It's neither," Adelaide replied, thankful Josephine hadn't asked what had been placed inside her clay figure. "It's a representation of the golem."

"It looks a little feminine, wouldn't you say? Such gracefully thin limbs. It's even turning up its pretty chin coquettishly. Is it looking at me? I think it's looking at me!" Josephine exclaimed to the guests. Everyone laughed politely.

Adelaide irritably answered the question by placing a prominent and pointed nose on one side of the round head, showing it to be facing herself, not the Empress. "I now ask you for silence for the rest of the proceeding."

She sat back down to look at the open book in front of her, but the words in her grimoire swam. She closed her eyes again and steadied her breathing. As she sat there in silence, she slowly became aware of the breathing of everyone else. To steady her own nerves, she pushed her consciousness out to touch each participant, starting with Mademoiselle Poulette. When the young lady calmed, she moved on to the gentleman sitting next to her, and then the lady next to him and on down the table to Napoleon, where she paused to struggle with the doubting Thomas. When she had successfully gathered the Emperor, she spread her consciousness along the other side of the table. She knew she'd completed her blanket of spiritual influence when she heard twenty sets of lungs align to breathe as one animal. To test her control, she sped up her respiratory rate, and her audience lurched to keep up. Before anyone fainted she took four deep lung-shattering breaths and opened her eyes, watching two of the older women who still clung to the past fashions struggle against their tight-waisted corsets. At that moment, she knew she could climb onto the table, stand on her head, and fart in the air and no one would raise an eyebrow. She heard the pounding of her own heart slow and strengthen as she took up the hands of her neighbors. The energy of the circle flowed through her palms as hands were taken up all around the table. She began to call upon the Forces to draw them down.

Elise ran because every time she landed on her heel was a moment that jarred her brain, loosening the extraneous thoughts so that they settled into insignificance. Usually, when she began her runs, anxiety about her patients would float to the surface before slowly drifting off. Next would come the unfinished chores of life, like grocery shopping, buying batteries for the remote, or scheduling a haircut. Then she'd resolve, again, to hang her clothes up in the closet and take her vitamins. By the end of the second mile she wouldn't be thinking about much at all and would barely notice the landmarks as she ran past them—the rock where the lizards looked warily at her and practiced their pushups, the boxing saguaro that stood with arms up and head ducked, the little wooden bridge anchored deep in the banks of the dry and dusty creek. Her goal was to reach the point where her only concerns were the repetitive motion of her body as the blood pulsed to her muscles, where to put her feet, the heat her body created, her breath. It was Elise's moment of peace.

With the parking lot only thirty feet behind her, she hadn't yet reached that coveted moment. Instead, Elise had just finished being horrified by the amount of phlegm she'd coughed up and was now transitioning from the guilt of her failed attempt to quit smoking, to the text she'd received from Emmett. It had been simple and sweet. "Missed you this morning. Next time, coffee. Call me." After reading it she'd gone home, showered, and crawled wearily into bed, sleeping nearly another four hours without calling.

He was nice enough, attentive, and from what she remembered of the conversations they had together, he had a job, possibly even a good job. Elise tried to imagine having coffee with Emmett after a night of binging and screwing. It seemed like a huge amount of effort. What would they talk about, television show plot twists, or the state of the economy? Would she listen politely while he postured over his stupid political views? Would he be disappointed if she gave a contradictory opinion? Elise would rather chase two ibuprofens with a beer and go back to bed than have to work up the energy for a conversation.

Without realizing it, she had picked up her pace as though running from the very thought of Emmett's affection. "Fuck no," Elise said as she breathed out, kicking up the fine yellow dust in the trail. She wouldn't call him until she got bored again, maybe next week, but not for coffee. She enjoyed him on her own terms, and didn't have room for conversations over warm drinks. "Fuck," she said as she sucked in her next breath. "That," she exhaled. She concentrated on the rocky outcropping in the distance that was her halfway point. "Fuck," suck, "that," suck, "Fuck," suck, "that," suck—it was a drumbeat that paced her as she headed up the dusty trail. Soon she forgot the words as she concentrated on her breathing. The looming cliffs moved up and down to the rhythm of her lope. Only the slowly setting sun as it threaded itself through thin fingers of red clouds shook her concentration.

Elise had been running the trails in the lower foothills of the Catalina mountain range since college, and there was not much about the Arizona desert that surprised her anymore. So when the wind picked up, and the quality of the light began to change, she knew the rain was finally on its way. The desert always warned before it snapped; snakes had rattles, cactus spines shone like spikes of glass in the sun, and storms were seen for miles in advance of their arrival. She knew the storm was gathering, but felt confident she had enough time. Her goal was the sandstone ledge that thrust out from the low cliffs on the horizon and Elise was determined to get there. She wanted more than anything to sit for a while on the smooth outcrop and watch the world below.

As she continued higher into the foothills, boulders began to crowd the trail. Pebbles slid out from under her feet in the dust, so she slapped her palms onto the nearby boulders to maintain her balance as she climbed. The rock formations that sheltered the sandstone ledge appeared and then disappeared as the trail started its switchbacks up the terrain. The wind hit her in strong intermittent gusts as she pushed on, and the increasing humidity was heady with the scent of creosote and the yellow mounding flowers of brittlebrush. Finally, she came to an abrupt stop, cut left, and walked off the trail. After rounding a particularly mean-looking cholla cactus, she turned sideways to slip through a narrow crack between two massively tall matching boulders she liked to call the sister stones and found herself completely alone on a thrust stage of a rock. Elise bent forward in a bow to the world below to catch her breath. Then she walked in tight circles, which was all the outcrop would allow, to cool her muscles. When she finally stopped moving and looked out across the valley, she smiled at the unrestricted view. She felt exhilarated and gloriously empty; a small speck on an enormous landscape.

A transient cold breeze startled her out of her reverie. Her chest tightened as her senses sparked into alert. The weather was changing. Something was coming. In the distance, she faintly heard the sound of traffic. A single insect buzzed nearby. The rest of the desert was silent.

Elise panned from left to right, scanning the horizon, but saw nothing but clear skies from the Rincon Mountains in the East all the way out to the Santa Rita range in the South. A low flying carpenter bee distracted her for a moment as it flew clumsily towards her, drunk off ocotillo nectar. She ducked out of its way, letting the obese bug fly over her right shoulder. She turned to watch it disappear between the narrow opening in the sister stones. It was then that she saw it: behind her, a wall of clouds was rising over the Northwest ridge of the mountains, swiftly moving towards her while crackling with lightning. Elise stood frozen in place to watch as individual clouds were beautifully delineated every time a bolt of lightning backlit the mass.

With the first clap of thunder, she bounded away from the edge of the outcrop to hug the sister stones in an instinctual move to protect her back. The stones vibrated strangely under her palms as she pressed against their warm surface, as though announcing the advancement of a distant stampede of horses, or maybe it was her own echoing pulse. The strength and age of the rocks comforted her and made her reluctant to leave their protection, but when the first of the fat drops of rain smacked her shoulders, she slipped back between the matching boulders to start her sprint to the car.

She had just begun pounding down the trail when a deafening roar caused her to whirl around. She stood, blinking at the trail up ahead, every inch of her body alert. At first it was just a streak of brown on the horizon. Quickly it became a foaming and churning wall of water that descended towards her like a freight train. Elise had just enough time to realize with horror that the trail she was on had become a conduit for rain that had already fallen miles away. Flash flooding of dry creek beds could crush entire trucks with only a foot of water and churning stones. She knew this because every year someone would think their SUV was burly enough to cross a swollen wash and would end up a patient in her emergency room. But this was a rocky trail, not a sandy *arroyo*. This wasn't supposed to happen on the high trails.

Nevertheless, Elise couldn't deny what she was seeing. The sound grew louder as she turned back around and flew down the trail. She tasted blood as she strained to fill her lungs past capacity in order to run as fast as she could. She didn't have a chance. The swollen river roared towards her and in seconds, hit her in the backs of the legs, buckling her knees so that she fell backwards into the slick foam. As it carried her along, it flowed over her head like hell's baptismal water and into her mouth, gagging her scream. Then Elise felt a sudden and strange sense of weightlessness as the sound of crushing rock and churning mud faded away.

THE THEFT

Where only seconds ago there had been a lovely chandelier dripping crystals from the center of an intricately carved ceiling medallion, there was now a long black tunnel going infinitely upwards towards nothing anyone wished to see. The unfortunate guests seated near the middle of the table were instantly drenched by the storm that roared through the opening of the vortex. "Do not break the circle," Adelaide shouted. She struggled against the wind to rise to her feet while still holding the hands of those seated adjacent to her in a vice-like grip. Mademoiselle Poulette tugged to free her hand while the other guests, seated farther away from Adelaide, were free to do as they pleased to get away. One gentleman ducked under the table and three of the women ran out of the room.

At the precise moment that the first delicate toe of a lady's satin slipper passed over the salted ring that surrounded the banquet table, the circle was broken and the vortex's opening began to narrow and close. Adelaide held her breath as she watched the hole, and her hope for the success of the ceremony, grow smaller by the second. Just before her knees buckled with the crushing force of her failure, the golem's head crowned and her shoulders slipped through with a slippery squish. She landed on the table in a pool of red mud.

Where do golems reside before they are born? The answer was still a mystery to Adelaide as she watched it moan and writhe on the table, flinging clods of muck over the distinguished guests, kicking over wine goblets, and grinding gooey puff pastries into the silk tablecloth. Only the Emperor, accustomed to the gore of battle, remained cool in the face of such chaos. As his guests pushed away from the table in alarm and raced for the safety of the walls, he slowly rose from his chair and circled for a closer look. He stayed Adelaide in her place with a fierce expression and an outstretched hand.

She marveled at Napoleon's ability to focus during such a scene. The creature was stretched out on its back and he stealthily approached it from above its head to avoid its kicking legs. As he slowly bent over to conduct his examination, the guests caught their collective breath and watched as though still under enchantment. Napoleon squinted. He bent his knees to look at the golem from the level of the table. He drew his fingers through a clod of mud and rubbed them together. He cocked his head. Then he straightened, and turned to his audience to give them a sardonic smile. "It's a woman," he announced. "Why am I not surprised?"

"That's not possible," Adelaide whispered to herself. A woman? It couldn't be—golems had no gender. Why would the ritual have brought a woman? But when the creature arched its back and clutched its head with an agonized expression, there was no mistaking the slender round hips and small bosom. Woman or no, the golem was female. Adelaide was torn between feeling pride in the strength of her sex as represented by the creature that had manifested in front of her, and feeling that her accomplishment was undercut by having conjured such a feminine creature. Just as she had decided to accept the golem as a form of validation, Mademoiselle Poulette's high-pitched giggle broke the spell resulting in a smattering of nervous applause for her fantastic trick.

Despite what anyone else thought, Adelaide knew the truth of it. Having caused a vortex to open through which a creature was called was no mere trick. However, the idea of a gendered golem confused her. Adelaide's mind raced to find an explanation for why there was a woman writhing on the table. Perhaps the mirrors had caused the anomalous result, she thought. A common belief with regards to mirrors was that some of the powers would bounce away and become useless, so Adelaide had drawn down an excess of power to cover that which would be lost. However, she had been surprised to find the accepted theory not only didn't hold to be true, it actually had quite the opposite effect. The intense feedback created between the three mirrors was like sunshine trapped within a three faceted crystal. Adelaide had struggled for control as her power was intensified in the highly reflective banquet hall.

Perhaps it was because the young Mademoiselle Poulette had broken the circle mid-ceremony by dropping Adelaide's hand to reach for yet another sip of wine. "All this chanting has made my mouth so dry," she complained loudly. She was not the only one who had become restless—they had been chanting for forty minutes with no discernible effect and everyone's clasped hands had gotten soupy. In her attempt to take back the young woman's hand before irreparable damage was done, the goblet was knocked over and wine spilled onto the little clay figure. The gentleman sitting next to Mlle. Poulette unhelpfully upended half a pitcher of water over the clay golem to wash it off.

Perhaps it had been the fact that she had misspelled the Hebrew word for life when she'd scratched it into the forehead of the clay figure. She was going to use Rashi script, but at the last minute changed her mind and used the modern alphabet for the benefit of those at the table who were watching. As a result, she had accidentally written Emmett instead of emet, a mistake she noted only after the figure had been drowned.

Perhaps it was all of these things combined, or something else entirely that she hadn't yet thought of. "Perhaps she will give you an heir?" Adelaide hadn't meant to say the words out loud, and regretted them as soon as they had left her lips. Josephine gasped at the affront from the corner of the room, and the Emperor's eyes flashed.

"Am I to bed this mangy boy with breasts and present its whelp to the people of France? Is that your plan? Is this your hidden purpose for conjuring this creature?" Bonaparte grasped the golem by its hair and dragged it down the table towards Adelaide to drop it at her feet. A trail of muck remained on the table like snail slime. For its crime of defiling the room, the Emperor kicked the creature viciously.

"Please don't hurt her!" Adelaide cried and protectively bent over the golem. "I am not able to guess why the ritual caused a female to be brought forth, but as you can see for yourself, she is not of this world." She cast her arm wide in a grand theatrical gesture for the benefit of the others, inviting everyone in the room to take a closer look. They didn't.

The golem's garments clung to her skin as though they had a life of their own and revealed the strangeness of her sinewy muscles as she rolled in agony on the floor. All she was wearing was some sort of pink corset that ended just above her stomach, and bloomers that barely covered her hips. She might as well have not been clothed at all. Her dripping hair was caught up onto the top of her head in a long clump that resembled a horse's tail and a forelock was stuck with red mud to her forehead. Adelaide bent closer over the creature in the hopes of discovering something which would, without a doubt, reveal the magical breeding of the golem: a tiny nub of a tail perhaps, or yellow eyes.

"*Bougre d'idiote*," spat Napoleon under his breath in frustration. He swept forward and snatched the golem back up again, lifting her onto her feet by her hair while at the same time carelessly elbowing Adelaide and sending her sprawling backwards onto the floor. "This?" He stood imperiously over Adelaide and shook the creature. "Is this rattling bag of bones to be my aide in the campaign, or my brood mare?"

"Don't kill her," Adelaide begged when the Emperor shifted his grip from the golem's hair to her neck. At first the golem slapped frantically at the Emperor as she struggled to breathe but when he lifted the creature up onto her toes, her breathing grew ragged and her eyes closed.

Adelaide scooted forward to replace the golem's feet flat onto the floor in a defiant maneuver to save her progeny. Even with all that was happening, she couldn't help but pause for a second to study the strange quilted and garish shoes the creature wore. At the same moment that Adelaide righted the soles of the shoes onto the floor, Napoleon's heavy scarab slipped from behind his cravat and swung forward on its chain.

Instantly, the golem's eyes opened wide. They fixated on the swinging emerald and sparked as green and lurid as the jewel itself, as though recognizing a lost lover. The muscles in the creature's back and shoulders rippled taut like a wound spring as she found her footing, snatched the jewel into her fist, and twisted the chain. Now both man and creature struggled with equal difficulty for breath as both squeezed the other by the neck. With a snap, the Emperor's chain broke and the golem fell backwards out of Napoleon's grip, the scarab still clutched tightly in her fist.

Hacking coughs filled the room as both Emperor and golem bent at the waist and sputtered. Along the walls, the audience watched wide-eyed and silent with the exception of an older gentleman who struggled to keep the swooning Josephine upright. In stark contrast to the Empress's weak-kneed antics, the golem, fiendishly more able of body than any woman should be, recovered before the Emperor. She quickly stepped back into the shadows to look down at the prize within its fist. A candelabrum still standing along the salted circle lit her hand from below creating a green luminescence between her fingers. The light caused the golem's smile to seem savage, her eyes to look feral, and her nose to point sharply from the shadows that played across her face.

The golem straightened and turned, and for a moment seemed almost human as she took a haughty stance. Shifting her weight to one leg, she placed a hand on her thrust hip and tossed her head as she surveyed the room. The creature seemed about to say something when the same hole that had spit her out opened up again, this time in the floor under her feet instead of in the ceiling. "Fu...?!" was all the golem managed to say before she was sucked back in.

"Where did it go?" roared Napoleon when the swirling vortex closed with an anticlimactic blip on the golem's diminishing scream. He stepped towards his guests for answers and they shrunk away from his approach. They knew their Emperor to be steady and confident. This confounded and enraged Emperor was unpredictable, and no one had answers. They all looked towards Adelaide. Napoleon's hands curled into fists. "What was it was about to say?"

"Fu?" answered a gentleman who had been brave enough to step from the wall to interpose himself between the Emperor and his object of wrath. He offered his hand to Adelaide and helped her back to her feet.

"*Charletan!*" screamed the Emperor over the tall back of the gentleman. "*Scélérate!* You planned this all along. That is why you insisted on having the room to yourself for a full hour in advance. This is a trick. You have robbed me. I will have it back! Give me back my scarab!"

"Please," Adelaide beseeched with clasped hands, "you must believe I would never steal from your Imperial Majesty. This was not what I had planned. This was never as I had planned it."

"Who hired this woman?" Bonaparte demanded with his finger pointed at Adelaide. "Which one of you bewitched my wife to plant this thief in our midst?" He circled around the room, glaring at his cowering guests. Finally, he lifted a chair in frustration and threw it. It hit the wall where ladies were clustered against each other like hens and scattered them squawking.

With tears streaming down her cheeks, Josephine flung herself to the floor to clutch her husband's knees. "My darling, I beg you," she cried. "Don't ruin our party." Napoleon scraped her off his legs with one strong arm and she draped herself on the floor with a broken wail.

"You have plotted against me. You all have plotted against me," he shouted as everyone scurried to exit the banquet hall.

Adelaide took a deep breath and tremulously lifted her index finger in an attempt to salvage her position. "Allow me to explain what may have happened," she said in what she hoped was a rational and bold tone, her mind flying desperately to come up with a plausible excuse.

"I do not want an explanation, *Menteuse*," Bonaparte shouted. "I will not listen to your continued lies. I want action. I want obedience. I will have that scarab returned to me and the golem punished!"

June XX, 1808
Paris, France

My Dear Madame S.

    As the youngest member of la Société d'Isis, the successful delivery of the Aide was of the utmost importance to me. I felt the honor and responsibility of carrying out the task and was humbled to be allowed the chance to utilize the combined powers of the members of la Société during the ceremony. However, as you are well aware, I was unable to maintain control of the forces involved. I have, unfortunately, allowed the Aide to slip back through.

    I am writing to tell you that there may yet be hope. In the early morning after the ceremony, I awoke from a dream wherein I had been clutching at the Aide's tether. With the sun just barely dawning, and myself still in partial slumber, I maintained a connection for a few more hours and determined that the Aide is still within our reach. Although I know not where the Aide landed, I felt enough to know that she is nearby.

    I wish to thank you for allowing me to pull upon your powers on that fateful night. I am confident that you and the others, who were so generous in lending me their strength, can feel the Aide's presence as well. Thus it is with a determined and hopeful heart that I call upon you to conduct a search within your own sphere.

I am sending letters to all other members of la Société with the same request. I feel strongly that, together, we can locate the Aide and go back to the task originally set before us. Thus it is that I remain,

Your humble servant and obliged friend in common cause,

Mlle. M. – A. Adelaide Lenormand

Awakenings

Elise had the strangest feeling that her shell of skin and flesh was falling like a brick while all her inner organs floated like feathers. She looked down the length of her body to verify that all was where it should be but when she wiped some of the mud off her stomach, she wasn't surprised to see a loop of her intestines lift from her navel. Carefully, she pressed it back inside with her index finger, but as she did so, another loop popped out. She tried again and each time a bit went in, a bit would come out again as though there was a shortage of space inside her abdomen. Frustrated, she placed her two hands flat over her belly and pressed hard, certain that would return it all to where it belonged. Instead, her intestines shot from her navel like she'd just lanced an abscess. Streamers of small intestine slipped away from under her hands into the void above her head and floated delicately upwards into the blackness while she herself fell downwards like Alice in the rabbit hole.

In a panic, Elise started pulling her entrails hand over hand to tuck into her body, and as she pulled, a dark mass at the other end slowly approached. Soon the mass was close enough to identify as a black haired woman wearing a diaphanous black dress. Elise squinted for a better look while she pulled the woman closer. Despite the strangeness of her situation, there was something familiar about the woman's face—the way her dark brown eyes were framed with delicate lines, the slight tip on the end of her nose. Elise tried to place the woman within a different context, and considered whether she had ever been a patient, or maybe a nurse on a different floor. Then she realized the woman was busy coiling her small intestine over her arm like it was a lengthy vacuum cleaner cord.

Fear shot through Elise. She started frantically pulling, hoping to get a majority of the prize before it all ended up in the other woman's arms. As a result, the black-haired woman approached at a faster clip, still coiling intestine as she came. Finally, face-to-face, the woman smiled in a way that suggested familiarity and friendship, which threw Elise off completely. She had never imagined she'd be eviscerated, and certainly not by a plump woman with a pair of friendly doe-eyes and a sweet smile. Elise was about to feign a lunge to the right to attack from the left, but a memory lit up her mind in a paralyzing jolt.

A dark room filled with mirrors that gleamed with candlelight. A man with a hand like a vise on her neck ground his sharp teeth in a snarl as he squeezed her breath away. In the shadows, screaming women huddled together while high winds lifter their skirts and whipped Elise's skin. When the black-haired woman joined the chorus with her own full-throated scream, Elise was snapped back from the memory. The woman threw Elise's intestines into the air and was sucked back up into the tunnel overhead. Elise watched her zip away until the black-haired woman was nothing more than a tiny dot in an infinitely receding void. Then everything exploded out of Elise's abdominal cavity like pink fireworks.

Elise sat up in bed, gasping, soaked in sweat, and aching all over. In a panic, she threw the covers off her body to look down at her navel, and was relieved to see it was intact. The muscles of her stomach rippled and quickly Elise leaned to her side. Her vomit made a splat, distant and hollow, as it hit the floor. After she puked the second time, Elise heard a stream of curses from somewhere nearby. She laid her head back against the pillow and as she drifted into her fevered dreams, she squeezed her left fist rhythmically. Hadn't she been holding something beautiful, she wondered?

The next time she woke it was easier to clear away the fog. Something cold and wet against her forehead slowly drew her into the present moment as her strange dreams faded from memory. Water droplets rolled down off her brow and made frigid puddles in her ears. Her hair felt damp and limp around her face. She tried lifting her hand to pull the soggy item from off her brow, but Elise found her muscles unresponsive and weak. Instead, she struggled to concentrate on the two voices that seemed to float above her head.

"Dear God, Richard. Why must you insist upon bringing strays into our home?"

"She's not a stray, Mother. She's a girl. And she needs our help."

Elise sighed with relief as the rag was removed from her head. A slosh of water announced its return to what she assumed was a nearby basin.

"She's hardly a girl. Young woman, I should say. For that matter, it's hard to tell even how old she is, isn't it?"

"Does her age really matter?" asked Richard. "She needs our help, and we're in the position to be helpful. Where is your sense of Christian decency?"

There was the sound of splashing again, more vigorously this time, and then Elise felt the rag slap back onto her forehead.

"Don't talk to me of Christian decency. Is it decent to lose the income from the bed this woman is lying in, income that would pay our employees' wages? This woman is stealing food right out of the mouths of Mrs. Postlethwaite's grandchildren. How is that decent? I don't suppose you thought of that before hauling this wretch up out of the street did you? You always were bringing in strays all your life and it was always your father and I who were feeding them."

"Mother. A kitten here and there is hardly a burden. Besides, they've all been excellent mousers."

"And I suppose you think that when this woman is back on her feet, she'll keep the kitchen free of vermin. Do you remember that dog you brought home? Do you? It snarled at every customer that walked through our door and when it finally bit someone, it was your father as had to take it out back and get rid of it, not you."

"I was eleven. A boy. And it was hard of Father to kill poor Rupert without allowing me the opportunity to say goodbye, very hard. Besides, she's hardly a stray. I'd say she's merely lost. I've a notion her family will be very anxious to have her returned to them. Have you put a discrete advert about her in *The Morning Advertiser*, as I asked? Her family will be so happy to find her that I'm sure they'll repay our kindnesses."

"Repay?" Richard's mother hooted. "What on earth makes you think that?"

Elise felt cold droplets of water run down the side of her nose and off her jaw as the rag was once again removed and dropped into the basin.

"Oh look! Her nose twitched! Do you think she's waking up?" Richard asked excitedly.

"Well, you're no boy now," continued his mother, ignoring Elise's return from unconsciousness. "And when this woman, wealthy family or no, goes and bites our customers, you'll be the one to take her out back this time. Do you hear me? I don't care how much howling you do, it'll be you as takes care of the problem."

"For goodness sakes! I told you she's no dog."

"Don't be so sure, Richard, just look at her hair. The last time I saw a fringe over a brow like hers I was scratching a terrier bitch behind her ears."

"Mother!" laughed the man. "What ideas you have!" There was a pause in the conversation and Elise realized that mother and son were staring at her. "I must say she does have a most unfortunate nose. Quite like a muzzle." continued Richard in a thoughtful tone.

Elise struggled again to lift her arms. She was feeling less inclined to stay in bed and it was clear by the conversation she was not welcome by all involved. Suddenly the rag was sloshed back onto Elise's face. "Do be careful how you tend to your charge," cried Richard. "You've gone and soaked the pillow."

"My charge?" The woman sounded indignant. "You have some nerve! It was you who saddled me with this creature. Now you're critiquing my nursing skills?" The woman paused and Elise imagined she was fixing her son with a glare. "Well, I have better things to do. I must make certain that Thomas is at hand." A final slap of water punctuated her words as the rag was returned to the basin.

"Tom is always at hand," Richard muttered in a petulant voice.

"Yes. Well. At least he knows his duty and never chases a gamble, like some others I could mention."

Elise breathed a sigh of relief as the woman's footsteps terminated with the slam of a door. Then all she heard was Richard's soft breathing. In the distance, the murmur of a crowd of voices was as mesmerizing as the muffled buzz of a bee from deep within an orange trumpet flower. The sound soothed, making her think of oasis gardens as she floated back off into her dreams.

It wasn't finding herself in a strange bed with a pounding headache that caused Elise the discomfort and confusion she was feeling when she came around again. She was used to strange beds and pounding headaches. It was her inability to piece together the recent history that had brought her to her current locale. She had tried to play the association game, which usually worked for mornings such as the one she was experiencing. The trick was to find the most recent memory of a place where she'd been and start adding as many faces involved with that place as she could remember. The more faces involved, the more the past events would emerge and interlock events into a timeline. She first thought of the dark bar in Tucson and inserted the face of Anita with her serious eyes and sweet smile. Then she worked forward in time to the text message she had read in her car, her apartment where she'd taken a nap and a subsequent shower, and ended with the trail run in the desert. There were no more faces. Elise raised herself up onto her elbows and grit her teeth against the pain she felt every time she moved. There was something about the trail run that she was missing, she thought. She tried to concentrate on the feel of dust under her feet, the heat of the Arizona air soaking her bones, the smell of rain. The harder she fought to work her mind through the fog, she more she began to worry. There was no memory past reaching her rock and seeing the storm sweep across the valley.

Unable to ascertain where she had been, Elise tried to figure out where she was now. She looked out across the bed and saw her toes making little tents in the coarse, brown bedcovers. Beyond her feet, a privacy curtain was drawn around the end of the bed and up one side; the other side of the bed was pushed into a corner against the wall. A tiny window suspended in the wall over her left hip let a weak light through its grimy glass. Nothing about the heavy curtain on her right, the filthy wall on her left, or the crunching sounds that came from her mattress when she shifted her weight, gave Elise any clue as to where she was or how she had arrived there. She swallowed her rising panic and sought to clear her mind. Breathing slowly through her nose, she steadied herself to look at the situation clinically—a trick she'd first learned in nursing school. When at a loss for what to do, remember your ABCs: airway, breathing, and circulation. It was a guideline that was supposed to be used for assessing patients, but Elise found it worked better when she applied it to herself as a focusing tool.

Warily, she crooked one finger around the edge of the curtain and pulled it open a crack to peek into the room. There was a short expanse of hardwood floor, a rickety looking wooden chair, and a narrow table on which sat a white enameled basin. Pushed against the opposite wall was what she assumed was another bed—all she actually saw was another drawn curtain. Hung next to a closed door was a rather large and heavy looking wooden cross, which was the only ornament she could find in the dreary space. None of the familiar objects that usually greeted Elise in her morning-after landscapes were there to put her at ease. There was no cheaply made metal and plywood desk holding an expensive laptop computer, no box of Kleenex conveniently located next to the bed, no rinds of take-out pizzas or empty cans of beer or even a single dirty sock.

Elise felt her fear rise as she assessed and cataloged everything. The room lurched and heaved the second she sat up to draw the curtain all the way back. Swimming through her nausea, she kicked her legs over the side of the mattress and leaned forward to place her head between her knees in an attempt to make the room stop spinning. While she gulped and waited, she noticed something gleam under the bed. "Oh thank god," she muttered to herself, drawing the chamber pot out from its discrete hiding place. She considered her options for only a moment as her bladder pressed against her pelvic wall, then carefully lowered herself from the edge of the low mattress onto the pot while lifting her skirt. Absently she examined the hem of the skirt, noting the beautiful line of irregular tiny stitches and carefully crocheted lace. Someone had made the garment by hand. Then she sighed in relief at the hollow sound of water against ceramic and hoped she had been careful enough to keep most of the lengthy gown on the outside.

It took a good deal more effort to pull herself back up onto the edge of the mattress than she had anticipated; her sore body and weakness surprised her. Curious, she drew open the neck of her gown and peered under the white muslin and over her breasts. Lurid bruises in vivid purple and sickly yellow bloomed across her side. The crest of her left hip was crowned with a partially scabbed, excoriated scrape that stretched down her thigh as though she'd been dragged. There were also bruises on her arms and thighs on both sides of her body, and her knees and shins were skinned. Experimentally, she took a deep breath, expanding her ribcage as far as she dared, and cried out in shock at the searing pain.

Elise leaned back and rested her head on the pillow. The energy that she had felt only moments earlier had disappeared and now it was all she could do to snake her legs back under the covers and fight her nightgown as it bunched uncomfortably up around her waist. Any alarm bells she'd heard earlier had been replaced by an immobilizing lethargy. Sleep and an escape from pain was all Elise wanted, and when she closed her eyes it came to her quickly, if not soothingly.

In the darkness of night, she lay in bed and clutched her chest, taking shallow, painful breaths while trying again to clear her mind of the incessant dreams of falling. She had earned herself some narcotics she thought. Wistfully, Elise pictured all the IV drips she had started in the past year. That's what she wanted for herself—a morphine drip and a nurse call light. The fantasy made her wonder why no one had taken her to a hospital. Someone must have seen the road rash and bruising when they changed her clothes. There was no telling how long she'd been in bed and her weakness alone would have alarmed anyone with sense. If she could ignore the pain, she'd be fine, eventually. But at that moment she was in no shape to get out of bed. Elise wondered if she could make it out the door she'd seen earlier if she crawled.

Someone cleared their voice from within the room. Elise felt her body tense—her skin tingled, her ears strained. She wasn't alone. She turned to look out into the room but someone had drawn the privacy curtain closed again. She tried to call out a hello from her bed but could only manage a few croaks and a cough.

The sound of a chair being scraped across the floor alarmed her. When the bed curtain ripped aside, Elise gasped painfully and flinched to the protection of the wall. "What is it?" someone whispered loudly. "Tell me."

A man leaned in through the curtain and loomed so close he was impossible to focus on—a two-headed monster. Elise squeezed her eyes shut and rolled them around under their lids to loosen the film that mucked her vision. Then, fighting to keep her fear under control, she finally managed to vocalize her most pressing concern. "Where am I?"

"You're safe here," he assured without answering the question.

Escape

The mattress shifted when the man took his weight off the edge to lean back in his chair. Now further away, his face was slightly easier for Elise to focus on and what she saw was a huge relief. He was young, perhaps a year or two older than Elise, with an honest face and a strong jaw—far from a two-headed monster. The blonde hair that fell forward in waves like a curtain over his straight brows did nothing to hide the sincerity radiating from big brown eyes that were crinkled up from his large smile. "We thought you would never come back from that fever," he said. "Mother's been with you for two days."

"Mother?" Elise rasped. In the distance she heard a roar of cheers and was relieved to know there were other people nearby.

"Yes, Mother and I run the boarding house as well as the public house downstairs."

"Boarding house?" Elise was used to the lilting Spanish inflections she heard in South Tucson, but this man's British accent was anything but melodic. All his vowels were ripened in his sinuses before they slid through his nostrils. Reaching behind her head, she propped the pillow against the wall and slowly eased herself up to lean against it uncomfortably. Echoing her movement in parallel, the man leaned forward with his hands on his knees and studied her face. "You don't look well yet," he said. "But I am glad to see you sitting up. You had given us quite a scare."

"Why didn't you get an ambulance? Why am I still here?" Her throat hurt to talk. She put a hand to her neck and swallowed hard.

"A what? Speak up, dear. You're here because you haven't been well enough to go anywhere else. But it seems you're now on the mend."

"Who are you again?" Elise peered closer at him, trying to see if she could place him in a memory. The meager candlelight in the dark room didn't help.

"How rude of me. You've been here for so long now that I completely forgot you would have no idea who I am." He inclined his head elegantly in a little bow. "Richard Ferrington, at your service." He smiled again and it seemed to cause his whole body to relax into the act of turning up the corners of his mouth. He slumped back in his chair with his relaxed-body-smile. "I trust you're feeling better?"

"Maybe a little," responded Elise. It was hard to imagine feeling much worse than she did at that moment, but at least she was awake. Her dreams had mostly faded out of her memory except for threads of images that made her uneasy.

"I suspect you'll be recovering quickly from here on out—the worst seems to be over. You should know that all of us here wish to do what we can to help. Mother is even bringing the barber." Richard looked at the door. "Actually, they should be here by now, I'm not sure what's holding them."

Elise absently put a hand to her hair, and then was drawn to pay attention instead to the tightening she was feeling in her bladder. "Would you tell me where your bathroom is?" She pushed the covers down and prepared to get out of bed.

"Begging your pardon?"

"The bathroom," Elise repeated sitting forward. She was thankful not to feel the nausea and vertigo she had experienced the last time she'd sat up.

Richard stood nervously. "Of course. You'd like a bath. When Mother arrives, she can help you. She'll be here soon."

"No, no. I don't want a bath," Elise tried to sound more cheerful than she felt. "I just need to pee. Can you show me the way?"

"The way?" Richard's smile disappeared. "You want me to show you the way?"

"Yes please."

"Don't you know?"

Elise warily eyed the young man. It was likely she had already used his bathroom at some point in her near history. "I forgot. Show me again?"

"How to urinate?" Richard squeaked. He was blushing and backing towards the door.

Elise rubbed her temples. There was something wrong with him, she thought as she wracked her head for more background information. How did he fit into the picture of her recent past? Boarding houses with Mother—that was too much. She was thankful that he didn't tell her his name was Norman. She pushed the covers all the way down, being careful to draw the hem of her gown down with them so that Richard wouldn't see anything he shouldn't. She hoped it had been his mother that had changed her into the nightgown. Then again, she thought as she turned back to appraise him through eyes that still weren't focusing correctly, it could be that he'd undressed her himself with her permission. He was her type: blond, built like a Viking, and not very smart.

When she swung her legs over the side of the bed, Richard bolted towards the door. It was not the reaction Elise had expected.

"Right. Yes." He sucked in a breath and clasped his hands in front of him. "Well, the chamber pot is under the bed, as you know. You do know, don't you? I'm not sure if Mary's emptied it yet. But as I've mentioned, Mother should be here presently. I'll just step outside then, for the moment."

"No, wait. I don't want to use the pot," Elise called, but Richard had already left. She stared at the shut door and felt her chest tighten and her skin tingle. She'd been kidnapped, that much seemed obvious. She pressed her fingers against her eyes and thought of the scrapes and bruises on her body. What the hell happened? There was something hopelessly final about being alone again. With only the single candle lighting the austere room, Elise was surprised and angry with herself for missing the man's company, despite his awkwardness. Stockholm syndrome, she muttered to herself as she kicked the chamber pot out from under the bed. It tipped dangerously and then settled in front of her with a contained slosh. There was no sense in trying to make a run for it with a full bladder.

The distant voices swelled into a dull roar again as if applauding her effort as Elise squatted over her business and tried to work out the details of her situation. It had been Sunday afternoon when she'd gone for a run. Was it the weekend again? With so many people cheering, it had to be a weekend. Her stomach clenched when she realized she might have been languishing in the strangely crunchy bed for a full week. If that were the case, there would be a lot of people missing her; police would have been notified. Anita would be busting down her apartment door, she was sure of it. Elise rubbed her temples again, but her head still felt fogged. The only thing clear to her was that she had to gather her strength and get out. Even injured, no one could make her pee in a pan for long, she thought.

Just as she started lifting herself back to the bed, the door cracked open and a woman poked her head in. "All done? We've a visitor," the woman chirped cheerfully. She opened the door wider. Elise barely missed knocking the pot over as she grabbed her gown and quickly pulled it down over her knees. Then she raised her arm to the blinding light of two more candles carried into the room. "Oh good, you're sitting up. That will make this so much easier this time," the woman said stepping aside for Richard and another man to enter.

"I present to you Mrs. Ferrington, my mother, and Mr. Theodore, the barber," Richard said with a dramatic swoosh of his arm. Then swinging his arm in Elise's direction he said, "and this is…"

"Elise," said Elise. She deliberately didn't offer her last name. You never knew what people would do with that kind of information.

"We've already met, Miss Elise, but I doubt you'll recall that," Mr. Theodore said politely. He looked more like a butler than a barber. The tails of his short-waisted coat were just barely shorter than his pants, which ended at his knees.

"We have?" Elise felt confused and put a hand to her hair. "I don't need a haircut."

The barber turned to Mrs. Ferrington. "Is she simple?" he asked.

"I must say I have no idea. This is the first time I've heard her speak. Richard's spoken with her." She turned to her son, "Is she simple?"

Richard waved away the question with an irritated flap of his hand that caused Elise to notice the lace at his wrists. He addressed her in a slow and steady voice. "No one is cutting your hair. The barber is here for your bloodletting."

"My what?" The young man's strange ensemble of buff leather pants paired with a tightly buttoned double-breasted suit vest didn't seem quite so important anymore, faced with the prospect of having her blood drained.

"You've had a fever, dear," Mrs. Ferrington said by way of explanation. "So Mr. Theodore has been kind enough to make house calls. If our books are correct, this is the third time my dear son has called the barber to open your vein."

"Madam, I am certain my own skills have had only a small bearing on this young woman's health. Your gentle ministrations have obviously done her a world of good." Richard scowled as Mr. Theodore bowed self-depreciatingly over his mother's hand. "Would that all my patients have such a nurse as you."

"You are too kind," Mrs. Ferrington responded with a flutter of her lashes and a youthful blush on her cheeks. Her eyes were just as large as her son's, but hazel. The long braid that she wore twisted into a knot at the back of her neck was still more blonde than grey. "Then perhaps we shan't need your services today after all?"

"Of course we do, Mother. We can't let the poor woman fall back into a fever."

"Mr. Ferrington's quite right, I'm afraid. We really can't risk our patient's health. However, after today I will have no further reason to return, except for maintenance purposes, of course."

"Do you really think maintenance will be necessary?" Richard asked in a concerned tone.

"Surely not," said Mrs. Ferrington, quickly withdrawing her hand from Mr. Theodore's tight grip. "I'm positive she'll remain the very picture of health."

"One can never be too careful," Mr. Theodore cautioned. "I recommend maintenance bloodletting for everyone. As long as I'm here, I can draw a half pint from each of you as well." He scraped the table across the room to the side of Elise's bed and placed his briefcase on it. "Draw your sleeve up, my dear," he said as he rummaged through his case and pulled out a cloth bundle, which he untied and rolled open on the table to reveal a collection of lancets, each tucked neatly in individual pockets.

"Oh look how big her eyes just got," cried Richard with a laugh as Elise scrambled backwards on the bed and pressed herself up against the wall. "Don't fret, it will only sting for a moment. Come back here so we can reach you." He patted the edge of the mattress. "Shall I hold the bowl for you Mr. Theodore? How much will you be taking this time?"

"Honestly, Richard, you really should be downstairs. I can hold the bowl just fine," Mrs. Ferrington snapped. "I can't believe you're still here fussing with this woman when you promised you'd help Thomas." She twitched the shawl that was wrapped around her shoulders.

"Tom can manage. He's always at hand."

"Are you daft? Have you not been hearing the crowd down there?" As if to punctuate her words, the sounds of cheering swelled loudly again. Richard's eye twitched.

While mother and son argued, the barber occupied himself with tying a long black apron around his waist. Seeing that no one was paying attention to her, Elise quietly pulled herself onto her feet by gripping the windowsill behind her. Her ribs screamed at the effort, but she ignored the pain. She held onto the curtain rail for stability and edged her way around the bed, never taking her eyes off the trio. "Stay away from me," she warned as one by one they turned back to her in surprise. "I'm leaving."

"Nonsense," Richard said with a concerned laugh. "In that?" He pointed up and down at the thin gown she wore. "Have you any idea the hour? I cannot let you leave. Wandering about in the night is exactly how you came to be in this trouble. Absolutely not." He shook his head and walked to the door to stand in front of it with his arms crossed, emphasizing his determination in keeping her inside. "In your state, the night vapors alone would kill you."

"Give me my clothes."

Richard looked helplessly at his mother who shook her head. "I'm sorry," she said. "When Richard brought you to us, you were wearing nothing but mud and rags. Your clothes, such as they were, were not salvageable." She smiled thinly at her son. "You were so charitable to bring her to us, Richard dear; always extending the comfort of your mother's arms."

"Look here, I don't have all night," Mr. Theodore piped up. "Be a good girl and get down off that bed." He reached out and caught Elise's ankle to pull her towards him. "Some help if you please, Mr. Ferrington?" he called out over Elise's screams. "We'll have to tie her down."

"Tie her? For god's sakes, man, let her go," yelled Richard. He stepped from the door to grab Mr. Theodore's shoulders and pull him away. "You're frightening her."

Just then Elise kicked off Mr. Theodore's bruising grip. Her second kick caught him full in the face and he staggered backwards from the blow. With the help of a surge of adrenaline, she leaped off the bed and ran for the exit. Sensing that Richard was close on her heels, she yanked the heavy cross off the wall and swung it with both hands in a low arc. It struck him behind his knees. Richard roared a curse and buckled to the floor. Another loud argument between mother and son began as Elise darted out of the bedroom.

The blackness of the hallway startled her when she slammed the door shut, but she didn't wait for her eyes to adjust. Get out, move fast, stay small, she thought as she stumbled blindly away. She pushed one hand along the wall in front of her to stay balanced and nearly missed a long fall when the hall ended abruptly at a stairwell. Elise hesitated nervously, not knowing what kind of situation she would encounter if she ran downstairs. The sound of the crowd came more loudly from below. The view over the edge of the banister was a dizzying swirl down three-stories of spiral staircase to a dimly lit black and white tiled floor. Shaking off a weird sense of déjà-vu, she descended the stairs as fast as she dared, clutching the railing with one hand and the heavy wooden cross in the other.

The bottom step splayed wide into what seemed to be to be a narrow entrance hall lit by one lantern resting on a round central table. She turned to look behind her and into the blackness above. There were no sounds of pursuit. The only thing she heard was the hum of a crowd coming through a door on her left. Directly in front of her was a second door, which, due to the proximity of a coat tree and umbrella stand, Elise determined was the exit. Triumphantly, she raced to it and threw the door wide.

The cold and damp hit her face like a slap. The smell of wood smoke, manure, and rot punctured her brain. When Elise stepped outside, she staggered as her bare feet slid on wet cobblestones. She reached out behind her to hug the brick wall of the building she had just left. Where was the black asphalt warming the night like a battery cell of stored sunshine? Where were the stars, brilliant even against the streetlights? For that matter, where were the streetlights?

Elise didn't notice when she began shivering as the cold cut through the thin muslin of her gown and crept up through the soles of her feet. She was too busy trying to shake her confusion. As her mind rolled with a jumble of unconvincing explanations, a strange echoing sound caught her attention. She whipped her head to the right and crouched like a cat let out of a cage in a new house. A black buggy drawn by an enormous black horse turned the corner at the end of the block. The horse snorted and shook its mane and the tall decorative plume that stood between its ears waved like a red warning flag. It approached at a terrifying pace, as though the walls of the surrounding buildings were greased for the horse to more easily glide through the alley. Elise shrunk against the mossy building behind her. There was no room, she thought in desperation as she watched the mass of muscle roll towards her. The horse nodded his heavy head against the reins as though agreeing with Elise's assessment and jangled the bit in his mouth, honing his sharp teeth against steel as his eyes flashed red on either side of its head.

Pressing herself further against the wall, Elise tried not to scream as the massive animal passed. The smell of leather and horse sweat filled her nostrils. The horse saluted her by lifting his tail to drop steaming manure onto the cobbles. The driver touched his top hat. Through the window of the buggy, Elise caught a glimpse of a second man and briefly smelled pipe smoke. Then the entire ensemble passed, continued into the dark night, and was gone, while the sound of the hooves and the creaking of the wheels echoed back to her.

As the sound of the carriage faded away to the left, Elise heard the same sound coming again from the right. She whipped her head back around and saw, to her horror, another horse approaching. Wiping tears from her eyes, she turned to run but stopped when she noticed a second door adjacent to the one she'd left. A large wooden sign above the door creaked in the breeze. On the sign was a prominent carving of a buxom woman in a green dress. The woman was holding her bloody head in one hand, tucked in her elbow like a football, while cheerfully lifting a mug of beer in the other, as though toasting her executioner. Painted in black above the figure were the words, "The Quiet Woman."

A beer, Elise thought with relief. A beer would be nice. In her confusion, the idea of sipping a foamy pint was the most stabilizing force she could imagine.

Suddenly the door opened and Elise stepped back with a little scream as a strange man hung on the doorknob and swung out into the lane. Letting go of the door, he faced the wall, staggered to his left, then staggered to his right, and finally steadied himself enough to unfasten his pants. As a yellow stream arced against the wall, he tipped his hat. "Evening, Miss," he said with a smile.

"Close the bloody door," someone bellowed over the noise of a crowd inside. Elise hastily ducked through the doorway and the man flattened himself against the urine soaked wall to let the second carriage pass.

THE QUIET WOMAN

The smell of stale beer, tobacco, and wood smoke in the Quiet Woman drew Elise over the threshold like a powerful pheromone. She breathed a sigh of relief and hugged herself as the warmth of the room began to bathe her skin. A poorly drawing fireplace on her right was hot with sputtering damp logs. In an overstuffed armchair drawn near the fire, an elderly man sat sucking on a long-stemmed pipe. He glared at Elise and adjusted his coat as though drawing a blanket up to his chin. "Are you the angel of death come to freeze me?" he pointed at the cross Elise held tightly under her arm. Surprised, Elise stared at the cross, marveling that she was still carrying it. "I said," the old man said more loudly, "close the damned bloody door." Elise jumped and pulled it shut. It latched with a heavy, satisfying click of its iron knob.

The old man turned away and began smacking the head of his pipe against the heel of his shoe to dislodge the ash, satisfied that his life had been spared.

Three other old men were huddled around the hearth with pewter mugs clutched tightly in their fists. They didn't seem very happy either. Their attention was centered at the front of the room near the bar where a noisy crowd of men were grouped around something that was happening in their midst. Elise watched the men's backs as they jostled each other and cheered. Shoulder to shoulder, their bodies formed a single gland whose sole purpose was to pump virility. Elise sighed with relief. Boys and beer—finally something familiar, she thought.

She found a small table in the shadows, sat down, and looked around for a waitress. She didn't have any money, but she wasn't too worried. With so many men around she'd have her drink. As she scanned the room she noticed a door was ajar against the far wall. Through it she could just barely glimpse hexagonal black and white tiles on the other side. Elise realized with a jolt that the bar was attached to the entrance hall where she had stood at the bottom of the stairs only minutes earlier. She stared at the door. Part of her wanted to run back up to the room and demand an explanation. Would they still be there? Maybe Richard was already in the bar, Elise thought. The idea made her stomach leap in fear and she peered into the gloom towards the front of the room for a tall blond, but recognized no one.

Elise refocused her wheeling mind back to her quest for wait staff, but it was hard for her to concentrate on a single task through the surreal haze—even her own hand, as she pressed fingers to her temple, seemed out of place. Everything about the room felt heavy: the wooden bar that spanned the front, the smoke that hung from the ceiling, the wet fire, and the piles of tables and chairs that had been pushed against the walls towards the front of the room. It was as though the Quiet Woman had been designed to hug its patrons with weight.

A woman, looking as heavy as the rest of the pub, held a pitcher in one hand over her head and three pewter mugs in her other hand. Elise watched her slide between the men in the outermost circle of the crowd to disappear within the pulsating mob. Elise's ribs ached when she stood to look for another server. It was hard to believe there was only one. She caught sight of the same waitress as she slipped through the crowd again with empty hands then lost her in the shadows behind the bar. Thirty seconds later, the same server headed back into the crowd with a pitcher in each hand. Elise realized that if she wanted a beer, she would have to go and get one.

She took two steps towards the bar and then had to clutch the back of a chair as everything began to pitch and whirl. She wondered how much blood she'd lost to the vampire barber. A half-pint? Three pints? She would need to rehydrate while her body worked to build more red blood cells. Elise shook her head to try and clear the fog. To her addled mind, a pint of blood could easily be replenished with a pint of beer, and the fact that both beer and blood were measured in the same units had a certain poetic beauty. There's water in beer, she reasoned. With determination, Elise hitched up her skirt and began to move towards the bar.

She aimed for the last place she had seen the waitress and stopped when she reached her goal. It was the overwhelming smell of wet wool and perspiration that made her hesitate just outside the crowd, not the potential risks involved with pressing between inebriated men in her nightgown. She lifted the heavy cross she still carried to test its weight, shifting it from one hand to the other as she calculated her chances. Finally, Elise took the cross in both hands and used the top of it like a crowbar, prying it between the shoulders of the first two men she encountered in the outermost ring. After she slipped between them, the opening closed behind her, sealing her exit.

Suddenly pressed against men, the odor of the crowd became nearly overwhelming. The turnips, onions, and terrified barn animals that they had all eaten for dinner oozed from the men's pores and assaulted Elise's nostrils. Breathing through her mouth, she continued to use the cross, twisting it ruthlessly between shoulders, hips, and knees to create a path for her increasingly desperate quest to find the waitress. A good head and shoulders shorter than everyone else, she had completely lost sight of where to go and was now anxious to find the center of the circle and a little space where she could feel some air on her face. As she moved through the layers of the crowd, she collected men behind her who were unhappily clutching their bruises. Elise was only two thicknesses of men away from a fresh breath when she felt the inevitable heavy hand on her shoulder. She ducked under the hand, looked behind her and met a sea of glowering faces.

"I'll be taking that stick of yours, if you don't mind," said a man with pores the size of craters and whiteheads like smoking volcanoes. His polite phrasing belied the daggers that shot from his eyes. When he reached for her weapon, Elise pulled it sharply away and accidentally caught a man next to her in the ribs. He howled in pain and jumped sideways, knocking his nearest neighbor off balance. Fortunately, this gave Elise just enough room to squat low as the man with the acne lunged at her.

With one hand out for balance and the other clutching the shorter shaft of the cross like a billy club, she swung a low arc at her attacker. His ankles tangled under the blow and Elise stepped aside to watch him stumble into the foremost rows of the crowd. A cloud of profanity rose towards the ceiling. Men pushed each other to avoid being struck by the flailing legs and elbows of Elise's tumbling opponent. Elise followed the path he created through the crowd and emerged in a small clearing at the center. Only now, with all eyes on her, she wished she had never left the thick of it. And still the waitress was nowhere to be seen. "Buy me a beer?" she asked the acne scarred man sprawled at her feet.

It was more of an arena than a simple clearing in the center of the crowd. Two bare-chested men, one well over six feet tall with broad muscles and a healthy defending layer of fat, the other slightly shorter and a good deal leaner, stood in the center of the arena and faced off with their fists raised. They both wore pants that stopped below their knees, white stockings, and soft black leather shoes. Each had a different colored sash tied around their waist. When the smaller man turned to look at Elise in surprise his opponent took advantage of the distraction and clocked him with a massive roundhouse, sending him skittering off to be caught by the crowd. A roar of cheers went up and the men around Elise suddenly pressed back together, anxious to see what they had missed. The man at Elise's feet lifted himself off the floor and slunk away before anyone remembered that a skinny woman with a heavy cross had just bested him.

Off to one side of the ring, the slender boxer rested on one knee with his head bowed in his hands, recovering from his opponent's last punch. A referee stepped into the ring and began to count loudly while the crowd chimed in cheerfully. Elise counted along with everyone else, but choked on the number twelve when the crowd parted and Richard stepped through to kneel beside the fighter and talk into his ear. "Thirty!" howled the spectators. Richard slipped away into the crowd and the slender boxer stood back up on unsteady legs. The referee circled around the edge, calling "Behind the line, Gentlemen. Please step back behind the line." When no one moved he started pushing. "Get back you buggers," he shouted. Elise tried to take a few hasty steps backwards but was launched forwards by the men behind her who were pushing for a better view. She scrambled back to her place, receiving a glare from the referee as he passed.

"Knock him out, Mr. MacEwan!" came a scream from the other side of the crowd. Elise finally saw the waitress again. She had climbed onto the back of one of her customers for a better view and was now cheering wildly for the slender boxer. The crowd became loud with their various opinions on the matter. "Please come to the scratch line," the referee called, and the fighters met warily in the center. They lifted their bare fists in an upright stance and everyone hushed.

The feeling that she had fallen into a rabbit hole slowly crept back into the forefront of Elise's mind. She shook her head to clear it and hugged the cross tightly to her chest as her ribs throbbed painfully. Then, the bigger boxer's powerful arm swung out and she was swept back up into the excitement of the fight. From the back of the room, Elise heard the waitress scream, "Look out, Mr. MacEwan!" The slender boxer easily pulled away from the jab and took a step back. The bigger fighter tried again with a hook, which Mr. MacEwan easily slipped under before taking another two steps back. Again the big boxer swung, and again the slender boxer stepped back. They were moving out of the center of the ring and towards the edge of the crowd. "Steady on, you coward" the man next to Elise yelled. "Stand and fight." When the combatants reached the edge of the ring, Mr. MacEwan crouched down and pulled in tight against the ring of the shouting audience. His face took on a look of intense concentration while his opponent's eyes widened, uncomfortable with the proximity of the crowd. Although it looked as though Mr. MacEwan had been running away, Elise realized the retreat had been a deliberate maneuver to draw his opponent to the place where he was most insecure.

The crowd reached out to slap at the fighters' backs and give friendly pushes, completely oblivious to the danger of getting caught in a swing as the two men shuffled past them. Elise could see the psychological effect the proximity of the crowd was having on the bigger man as they approached from around the circle. Sweat was streaming down his face and his eyes were darting from his opponent, to the crowd, and back again. As he passed, Elise hauled out and slugged his shoulder in what she hoped would be construed as a friendly, sportsmanlike punch, knowing she'd never again get the chance to punch a boxer in a bare fisted boxing match. His flesh twitched, but he continued forward.

"How long have they been circling like this?" Elise asked the man next to her.

"Thomas has been ducking and dodging all night," the man responded.

"Thomas is the skinny one?"

"The smart money is on Jim. He'll win if he can ever land a punch. He's got more strength and weight behind his fists." The man nudged Elise with his elbow. "You did me a good turn earlier with that commotion—nearly got Thomas MacEwan knocked out."

"Thomas, is it?" Elise's eyes narrowed. She didn't share the man's view on bigger being better.

Just then, Jim attempted another right-handed jab. This time, the smaller Thomas MacEwan stepped forward under the swing, landing a strong upper cut to Jim's face. The crowd gasped. Elise's neighbor groaned. "Now I see what he's doing," he said, shaking his head. "It's damned unsportsmanlike, and if he's doing what I think he's doing, the match is nearly finished."

Elise watched as Jim tried to throw a couple of punches at close range but was obviously more comfortable with distance. His fists landed weakly on Thomas's torso before he darted out of reach. Nearly finished? It hardly seemed like it had begun, thought Elise. Aside from the few punches she'd seen, neither man had sustained much injury. Jim swung again, telegraphing his intention from miles away. Thomas slipped to the right and countered with a blistering cross. The big man roared in frustration and tried for an upper cut. Thomas pulled away and landed a straight jab before resuming his endless shuffle backwards.

Elise studied the two men and the cogs in her brain began to lubricate as they passed in front of her again. Jim carried his arms like they were a chore to lift. He dragged his feet. Thomas was blinking hard from sweat that rolled into his eyes, but he seemed focused. His movements were gracefully methodical. Jim suddenly reached out with both hands in a desperate lunge and tried to clinch Thomas's shoulders to stop the endless backwards movement, but Thomas easily shook off the clumsy grip and took two steps to the inside to start pounding. It was like the burst of chaotic fireworks at the end of a lightshow. Elise gasped as blood sprayed from Jim's nose. The smell of sweat surged and the crowd roared, pressing against her. Then Thomas calmly walked away to the other side of the ring to watch as his opponent threw hook after hook into thin air in an attempt to land a punch on what he could no longer see. Finally, he dropped his arms in defeat and put his hands on his eyes. They had swollen shut.

The man next to Elise grumbled unhappily. The crowd loosened. The referee came back out into the ring, to call Thomas the victor and lead Jim away. The waitress screamed from the top of the bar where she was now standing and clapped her hands over her head.

"That was the sorriest excuse for a fight I've ever seen," Elise heard a man mumble to another who nodded in agreement but still kept his hand held out. The first man hesitated before he fished for coins in his pocket and slapped them into the open palm. As the crowd thinned, she saw a pushing match start up near the bar that was quickly ended by a large woman who came roaring out of nowhere like an enraged bear. The woman seemed to disappear back into a cave when the threat was over. The tension was palpable. Elise decided it would be best to return to the back of the room near the exit until all money had passed into the correct hands.

Unused to walking in long skirts, she bunched the hem of her gown over her knees to quietly slip around the tables as they were being returned to their proper places from their pile in the corner. With the fight over and nothing else to centralize people's attention, eyes drifted and landed easily on her. Elise felt them on her back as she headed for the shadows. A man nodded as she walked by. Without trying to hide his interest, he let his gaze slide over her from top to bottom and lingered on her bare legs. Every inch of Elise's body tingled a warning. She dropped her cavernous gown and let it drag along the wooden floorboards. In three steps, it got caught between her toes and she stumbled off balance.

"Careful," said a gentle voice at her ear. Someone caught her elbow to steady her. Elise gasped and snatched her arm away while jumping two steps back. "You're as skittish as a rabbit, aren't you?" said the man, taking two steps forward to keep her near. It was Thomas, the slender man from the fight, only now up close he seemed more massive than slender. Elise craned her neck up to look at him as he stopped to casually button his white shirt over his broad chest and roll his sleeves with hands that were still bloody.

His expression was unreadable. A thin white scar cut through the right side of his upper lip, making the corner of it turn up in a smile, but the left side of his lower lip was swollen from the fight and drooped over a fast blooming bruise on his jaw. His blue eyes, framed with black lashes, were unflinching. His skin was pale against a shock of unruly dark hair. The heat of the room and his recent victory flushed his cheeks bright red. He loomed close in an obvious move to intimidate. "That's a heavy cross you bear," he said. "Let me help shoulder your burden."

Elise backed up again quickly to gain distance between them, but he anticipated her movement and caught her upper arm with a vise-like grip while keeping himself out of her swing zone. Having seen him fight, she knew he could have unarmed her easily without the sarcastic offer of aide, and likely would do it still if she refused. However, for Elise, conceding was a bitter pill. He waited for her decision with his hand extended for the cross and one eyebrow patiently raised. Finally, she hedged her bets. "I'll give it to you if you get me a beer."

Thomas straightened up and dropped his grip on her arm with a surprised look. Then instead of insisting, the hand that had demanded the cross swept widely and generously towards the bar. "After you," he said stepping to her side. While not actually touching her, he crooked his arm around her shoulders, allowing her to move forward without forcing the action. It was both a polite gesture, and a means to keep her slightly in front of him where he could watch her carefully. As they walked, Elise saw her new companion raise his hand slightly from his waist in a subtle signal. Like magic, the waitress appeared for his order. "Two," he said simply, and she rushed off ahead to the bar without a word, but managed to give Elise a nasty look.

They walked around men who were settling down at the tables to drink. Some eyed the champion fighter with malice, but many slapped him on the arm as he passed and lifted their drinks. Thomas stopped at each table to chat while Elise protectively hugged the cross to her chest when the men turned their openly curious faces towards her. No introductions were made, and none were asked for. Elise counted the ceiling beams instead of risking eye contact with anyone.

When they finally turned to resume their trek to the bar, the referee stepped into their path. With a light touch to the inside of her elbow, Thomas stopped Elise. "That was the damndest thing," the referee said as he shook his head.

"Glad you enjoyed yourself, Mr. Cooper," Thomas replied.

"Can't say that I did. Where did you learn to shuffle and curtsey like that? You looked like a bobbing hen."

"If I was fighting to entertain, I'd have done it different. But I fought to win." Thomas nodded towards a purse the referee held in his hand. "I'll take that now."

"That was a dirty trick, blinding him like that."

"Come now, it wasn't a trick. If you thought I fouled, why did you call the win the way you did?" His expression clouded as he stepped forward. "Who changed your mind?" Elise recognized the strategy Thomas had used against her moments earlier: close in, look down, raise the eyebrow, hold out the hand. The purse was given over.

"No one changed my mind. You just didn't do it proper is all."

"You did right proper in ending it when you did. I wouldn't have wanted to fight a blind man." Cooper didn't look convinced. "Look," said Thomas, "everyone knows Jim's got a good chin on him. If I'd have done it the way you wanted, he'd have easily knocked me down first and I wouldn't have liked that one bit." Thomas studied the purse in his palm as he thought. "Though it might make you happier to know I wont be fighting for you again. This money will likely make the Quiet Woman square with the brewery."

Mr. Cooper smiled and shook his head. "You're not square Tom. Your Mr. Ferrington laid his own path for squaring debts, and Jim was a sure bet."

Thomas looked up sharply. "Richard gambled on this match? Against me?" He ran his fingers through his dark hair and tugged it gently. It stood thick and wild when he let it go.

"The other lad was a sure bet, Tom," Cooper repeated. "But don't worry. That young Cribb I told you about will be coming through in a fortnight. We can set the next fight up proper, with ropes and a platform. Cribb will draw a right crowd to the Quiet Woman, you'll see." He paused to smile down into the waitress's cleavage as she handed him a pewter mug.

"The porter is for the lass." Thomas said, nodding towards Elise.

Cooper seemed to suddenly notice Elise standing in his prize-fighter's shadow and reluctantly passed her the beer. "I'll take that other one," he suggested reaching for the second.

"That one's mine. Hand it here Mary, if you please." The waitress did a neat pirouette from one man to the other and dark liquid sloshed out of the mug onto Thomas's hand. He barely flinched when the beer flowed over his battered knuckles. "If you'd like a porter, Cooper, you can pay for it. The Quiet Woman is not yet yours. We'll be paying our mortgage, so I'll thank you to pay for your pints."

After dismissing the waitress to her duties, Thomas easily swept the cross from Elise's grip while her attention was centered on her first sip of the cool alehouse beer that slid across her tongue. "No," he shook his head, picking up the thread of the prior conversation. "I'll not fight your Cribb. I'm tired of fighting. I'm a publican, not a pugilist. I'll find another way to pay our debts, Richard be damned."

WHAT TIME IS IT?

"Suit yourself," Cooper said with a shrug. "But you'll be hard pressed to find an easier means for making your mortgage."

"I'd prefer it if my nose stayed in the middle of my face," Thomas replied.

"Even if your nose gets hit to the back of your head, you'll still need to pay back the brewery."

As the two men continued arguing, Elise felt a wave of exhaustion flow over her. She had been able to maintain her focus since she'd escaped the bedroom, but now that the fight was over and a beer was in her hand, she began to feel the bruises in her body and a dull thud in her head. Despite a vision that was becoming blurred, she could see it was late enough that the wiser of the customers were avoiding trouble and starting to head home. Some of the less wise types, still nursing their beers, stopped their conversations to look at Elise when she leaned on their table and clumsily set her mug down.

"Next time there'll be no more dancing in circles like you did," Cooper continued behind her. "The lads don't like to see one of their own prancing around like the prissy French."

"I'll fight the way I want to fight. Or maybe I'll let the brewery know what kind of work you've been doing on the side? I'm sure they'll be delighted to hear how their compliance inspector has been setting up boxing matches in their public houses."

Elise blinked hard and shook her head. She spread her hands flat on the table's surface. Tiny newsprint on an open paper swam before her eyes. She ground her fist into her right eye until the letters stopped moving and she was able to read, *The Morning Advertiser, June 21, 1808*. Elise blinked again and felt her stomach knot. A tear rolled down her cheek. Though her rational mind screamed that it was impossible, her intuition catalogued all her recent experiences and came up with a clinical assessment based on the sudden weakness in her knees. It had to be a horrible dream, she thought as Thomas's angry voice faded away.

She listed sideways to the right and began to fall as her legs crumbled to the left. Falling was getting easier, she thought calmly as the ceiling receded. She reached for her beer, thinking she'd want it when she got to the floor, and it too fell, independent of the brown liquid that fell alongside it. She hit the hardwood with a thud, a splash of beer, and a cry of pain.

Elise wasn't sure how long she had been watching grey clouds of smoke drift across the ceiling before the ceiling was obscured by Thomas's looming face. His blue eyes were narrowed in an expression that could either have been concern, or irritation. "Hold my beer," he said gruffly to Mr. Cooper as he kneeled down. Elise caught a glimpse of a small vial in his hand seconds before it was waved under her nose. The smell was like a slap. She gasped and sat up straight, her heart pounding in her throat.

"What's this? Smelling salts in your pocket?" Cooper's loud voice cut through Elise's confusion.

Thomas shrugged. "A good publican always carries salts for the drunk sots that won't go home."

"That's very convenient during a fighting match."

"Are you accusing me of something, Cooper?" Thomas's voice took on a dangerous edge. The question was met with a petulant silence. "Go on. Give us some air." Thomas waved away the men who hovered. Then Elise felt his hands slide under her arms and he pulled her against his knees. "Rest for a minute," he said gently. "I suppose you'll be wanting another porter." Elise tried to turn to give him a thumbs-up to the idea of another beer, but only managed to lean dangerously to the left. "Steady lass," Thomas said. He gripped her more tightly in his arms and the increased contact alarmed her. When Elise looked up, she saw he was giving her as much of a reassuring smile as he could, but only managed to crinkle the corners of his eyes.

Cooper broke in. "So who's the Moll?" he asked as he eyeballed Elise warily. "Are the Ferringtons looking to make a little extra with the rooms upstairs? Best watch your coin. I came across a tiny little bunter last week that fell in a swoon at my feet like yours just did and when I picked her up, the ugly wretch swiped my handkerchief."

"Step back if you please, Cooper. You're in our way." Thomas offered his hand to Elise. "Let's pour you another porter, shall we?" he asked and pulled her to her feet. She swayed unsteadily until Thomas took her elbow to lead her towards the front of the room. Cooper followed and bellied up with the others at the bar, but Elise was drawn behind the counter with Thomas. "Mrs. Postlethwaite," Thomas bellowed through a door. There was some commotion of rattling pans before the bearish woman Elise had noticed earlier emerged from her den which Elise now saw was the doorway to a cavernous kitchen. "I could use your help. Might you keep this lass with you in the kitchen?"

Elise didn't like the sound of that, and apparently, neither did the woman, who put her fists on her hips. One of the woman's hands still held a butcher's knife and it jutted out dangerously at a right angle to her stout body. "Is this the one the Ferringtons have been fussing about?" the woman demanded.

"The very same," said Thomas.

"And where is Mr. Ferrington?"

"I've not the slightest idea. He asked me to watch over this one and then left."

"Well, if he asked you to do it, then I shan't step in. I saw the barber's bloody nose. He was none too happy, I can tell you that. Oh, no. I'll not be saddled with watching that one," she waved her knife in Elise's direction. "You can keep her yourself. It's time for me to go home."

"Now, Mrs. P., I wouldn't ask if I didn't really need you." Thomas started, but he was cut short by a careless wave of the sharp blade.

"I've got my own family to feed, Thomas; my own babes to put to bed. I won't stay here a minute longer than I have to just to look after vicious strays all night. It's bad enough with all those cats in the kitchen." She looked fiercely at Thomas. "That woman," she paused to point her knife at Elise, who had found a stool and was studying the bottom of her empty mug as she listened, "has already brought nothing but trouble." She gave a final huff to underline her point and then stalked into the kitchen. Thomas blew out a breath and looked curiously at Elise until Mrs. Postlethwaite returned with a shallow bowl filled with stew and a hunk of bread. "Eat," she commanded as she handed the food to Elise. Steam rose from the bowl and carried the smell of boiled beef and potatoes, making her empty stomach rumble.

"And another thing," Mrs. Postlethwaite continued as though she'd never stopped, "so help me, if you've lost another I'll whip you myself."

"I won the match, Mrs. P."

"Another tooth," Mrs. Postlethwaite corrected. "I don't care a fig about your matches."

Elise looked up from her meal in time to see Thomas's eyes smiling again—his mouth too swollen to perform the task. "I kept my teeth this time," he said, making Elise wonder how many molars he had left.

Mrs. Postlethwaite impatiently slapped a bonnet on her head and tied its ribbon around her chin. "You leaving already Mrs. P.?" The waitress approached the bar holding three empty pitchers in one hand and four empty mugs in the other. She didn't seem surprised when the older woman merely huffed and left through the kitchen door. "Where's that Johnny?" The waitress waved the empty vessels in her hand. "We've drained the second cask and I've customers waiting." She was flushed from running from table to table and her blonde hair curled prettily around her face where it had escaped the complicated braids pinned to her head. She rested her pink décolletage on the bar and leaned towards Thomas who maintained his composure despite a quick glance down her corset. A customer next to the barmaid was less polite and took a long look.

"It's dry," Thomas said, testing the tap.

"That's what I said, didn't I? We need Johnny to start running down to the cellar."

"I've no idea where he is, Mary. I could bring a cask up."

"The cask's dry?" Cooper nosed in. A couple groans were heard. "You can't bring up another one or you'll shake it all up. No one likes murky beer. You should have brought three casks up this morning."

"Did you look for Johnny in the yard?" Thomas suggested to Mary, ignoring Cooper.

"I've no time to be chasing that boy down, and I won't start running to the cellar to fill pitchers. I'd kill myself on those steps. Johnny's a useless bugger, isn't he?" She heaved a sigh and turned to scan the room again for the lost boy, and instead, noticed Elise staring at her. "What's she doing down here—did the Ferringtons let her loose?"

"More like she escaped, is how I heard it from Richard."

"Didn't get far, did she?" Mary's gaze dripped from the top of Elise's head to her bare feet, which were hooked on the bottom rungs of the stool. "So is this the latest in ladies' fashion then? How convenient. Dressing for dinner makes dressing for bed much easier, don't it Mr. Tilsdale?" She nudged the man on her left and laughed at her own joke. "Have you met our new tenant?"

A thin man with a patched coat half stood from his place at the bar to follow Mary's pointing finger. "Whom do you have hidden back there with you, Mr. MacEwan?" he asked, squinting into the darkness.

"No one to concern yourself with, Mr. Tilsdale," Thomas replied dryly.

"Why don't you make yourself useful and get me a beer," Elise said, waving her mug at Mary who looked at it disdainfully before ignoring it completely.

"Cold night for her to be wearing such a light gown, wouldn't you say, Mr. MacEwan?" Mr. Tilsdale leered, giving Elise the chills.

"Leave it be," Thomas replied in a warning tone.

"It certainly is a cold night, Mr. Tilsdale," Mary continued. Then she leaned forward conspiratorially, whispering loudly to be heard by everyone, "She's not right in the head."

Mr. Tilsdale nodded sagely. "I can understand if you like the simple ones, Mr. MacEwan, sometimes it's easier. Just make sure she's a gentle simpleton and not a lunatic. It's the lunatic simpletons you should take care with. Better she's one of the gentle types." He scratched his bald head as though he was thinking. "For myself, I'd not touch either, the gentle or lunatic; they're always talking to spirits and seeing things in the shadows," he shuddered.

"Oh, don't think Mr. MacEwan'll have her," Mary quickly corrected. "I honestly can't imagine any man sharing a bed with that one. She's always thrashing about at night. Thrashing and screaming and vomiting—I don't think I've gotten a lick of sleep these past few days. Besides, look at her," Mary pointed and her arm jiggled. "There's nothing to interest any man. Turn her sideways and you'd barely see her."

Elise's eyes burned red as everyone at the bar roared. She started to stand from the stool, but Thomas firmly pushed her back down. "I said leave it be, Mary, or I'll turn you out on your fat tail. You won't be so clever then, will you?"

"I hope I puked on your feet," was all Elise could think of to say.

"She's the lunatic type, aye, I see it now. They're all scrawny. Never think to feed themselves," said Mr. Tilsdale seriously.

Elise remembered the second bed and wondered if Mary had been sharing her room with her at night. She vaguely recalled someone cursing.

"There's our Johnny-boy," Thomas called out, changing the subject. A few customers waved empty mugs as a boy raced around the corner of the bar and nearly collided with Elise on her stool.

"Sorry Miss, I didn't see you there," he said with a grin. He was about to take off again when Thomas caught him by the collar. "Where have you been all night?"

"I've only been gone a few minutes, sir," Johnny protested.

"That's a few minutes longer for our customers to have to wait."

The boy shrugged off Thomas's grip and raced into the kitchen and disappeared through a dark doorway Elise hadn't noticed before. She squinted into the shadows, wondering where he had gone and if she could follow suit and perform her own disappearing act. Mary turned around and leaned against the bar, elbows now resting where her bosom had, to look at the crowd of people still milling in the barroom. She tapped at the counter impatiently. Thomas glowered at a customer who was twirling an empty mug on the bar. Then Johnny appeared again with two sloshing pitchers. "Be careful with that," Thomas scolded as he took one of the pitchers. He began filling empty mugs with one hand for those sitting at the bar, and taking coins with the other. Mary snatched the second pitcher to serve the tables and left the empty mugs on the counter for Johnny to clear. Then to Elise's great relief, Thomas filled her mug.

Now with the porter in hand, her meal was finally served correctly. Elise dipped her spoon into the stew and raised it to her mouth with eyes closed. No one had bothered to cut the fat from the beef before throwing it into the pot and it hung from the spoon in gelatinous globs. An assortment of white unidentifiable vegetables turned the dish into primordial ooze. Instead of chewing, Elise pressed her tongue against the roof of her mouth to mash her meal and as she did so, the flavors spread across her taste buds and melded with the porter. It eased the tension from her muscles and pushed a sigh from her lungs.

"Close the bloody door," the old man by the fireplace bellowed. Elise peered across the room and saw through the smoke and gloom the silhouette of a tall, wide-shouldered man. "Evening Mr. Ferrington," Johnny's childish voice called out, as Richard hung on the open door to greet his customers before making his way to the bar.

"She's still here! You caught her—I thought she'd be lost to us!" The lace at Richard's wrists fluttered with his enthusiasm as he lifted his arms towards Elise in an affectionate show of relief.

"I believe she's still lost," Thomas replied dryly. His battered hands were straining to complete the delicate task of filling a long stemmed pipe with tobacco.

"Don't be daft Tom, she's right there behind you." He slumped onto the stool Mr. Cooper graciously offered and rubbed the back of his bruised knee. "Mother will be so relieved to see her again." He motioned to Johnny who placed a mug in front of him and filled it from the heavy pitcher on the bar. "How did the match finish?"

"Well enough," mumbled Thomas between sucks on his pipe stem as he held a candle to the bowl.

"Looks like you caught a few hooks to the jaw."

"So I did," Thomas replied nonchalantly.

Mary arrived with a tray full of empty mugs and a bow and fiddle tucked under her arm. "We've had a very profitable night, Mr. Ferrington," she said enthusiastically and handed him the instrument.

"Wonderful. That's wonderful." He ground the bow across all four strings while turning the pegs up and down. Elise nearly dropped her stew to put her hands over her ears.

"Must you scratch at that thing every night?" Thomas asked. He pulled his pipe out of his mouth and glared while Richard pretended to be completely immersed in the task of tuning. The aural display had interested some of the patrons and a handful left their tables to gather near the bar. After nodding acknowledgement to the growing audience, Richard let his bow fly across the strings with a conviction that lent his arm grace, and a confidence that made Elise take a second look. There was a happy cheer as the patrons recognized the song's lively introduction and chairs were scraped back for better viewing. Just as quickly as he began, Richard stopped and whirled around to face Thomas, his fiddle still at his chin, the bow still poised over the strings. The men stared at each other for a split second and then Thomas opened his mouth wide to begin a raucous verse in a clear baritone accompanied by the screeching fiddle.

Elise was startled out of her growing stupor to see Thomas and Richard had formed a duo. The melody stretched Thomas's accent to such a degree that Elise could barely recognize the words. The song seemed to tell the story of Napoleon and a mammoth, but every time she thought she was beginning to understand the plot, the men in the alehouse would break in and bay like a pack of dogs. The song went on and on, verse after verse, with Thomas never seeming to falter in his poetic memory, and the men never faltering in their barking enthusiasm. Finally, Elise pushed her empty bowl down the bar and rested her head on its surface with her hands pressed over her ears. She closed her eyes and tried to pretend she was watching some highly overproduced period piece where it's always Christmas, and someone is either being rescued from the edge of starvation, or the life of a spinster—the one being barely different from the other in terms of tragedy. When the song was finished, Richard changed keys and slowed the tempo. Thomas hummed low to himself as the fiddle introduced a new tune.

"I love this one," Mary said softly, sidling up to Elise with another tray of empty mugs. Elise barely had the energy to move to make room for the waitress, and was irritated by the interruption as the two men started their song. Thomas's voice lilted like black oil as Richard coaxed cool water from his fiddle. When the song came to its end, Thomas started singing another song while Richard sat back to pick up his mug. "*Weep, weep for me, for my fortune is forsworn,*" sang Thomas.

"For Christ's sake, not this one again," Richard complained.

"*Let me mourn, let me mourn.*"

Mr. Tilsdale, asleep with his head on the bar, let out a great sobbing snore, while Thomas continued on with his dolorous verses.

"*Through the darkest night I toil,*" sang Thomas, "*my joys and aspirations spoiled.*" That seemed to signal last call. Mr. Cooper placed his hat on his head and said goodnight and Richard poured for the last men at the bar. "*Hark!*" burst Thomas before dropping back to a more ominous tone, "*you who would have me pale, shadowed, and worn. I reject your scorn. I reject your scorn.*"

"Damn his eyes," Richard mumbled before placing his fiddle back under his chin as Thomas replaced his pipe back into his mouth. Richard attempted the liven the mood again with a jig to retain the last customers, but soon lost his way, meandering on his fiddle through what sounded like an anthology of lullabies, some of which Elise vaguely recognized. The thread of sweet melody wrapped itself around her like a blanket and thankfully muted all other thoughts.

When she woke, the Quiet Woman was strangely still. Elise lifted her head and wiped her face with her palm where it was slick from the small pool she'd left on the surface of the bar. The only two people left were Richard and Thomas who were sitting at a table in front of the bar in deep conversation. Richard's face was pale, and he absently bent down to rub the back of his knee where Elise had clocked him with the cross. "Is that so?" he asked. "Well you are an experienced champion, aren't you? I'd no doubt in my mind you'd win."

"There's no need to lie to me. Cooper told me Jim was a surer bet. You had your doubts, Dick." Thomas lightly plucked a string on Richard's fiddle, which was on the table between them. He looked as though he was trying to find the right words. "I know it's not my place to say this," he began, "but you need to be more careful about your gambling. No one wants to see you end up in debtor's prison."

Richard laughed nervously. "You worry like an old woman, Tom. You're nearly as bad as Mrs. Postlethwaite. I'm not going to prison. I only gamble when the odds are favorable. And anyway, I'd choose the army before going to prison."

"You? A foot soldier?" Thomas shook his head disbelievingly.

Richard's ears reddened. "You're quite right, Tom." He pushed his chair back and stood. "You've forgotten your place." He wrapped his knuckles on the table, as though punctuating his authority. "Look, you can stop worrying. The Quiet Woman will be fine, even with the new girl. I know you don't think we can afford an extra mouth to feed, but she is not well, Tom. We can't just put her out. Think of her family! They'd be appalled to know we did nothing but send their daughter back into the street, and in her condition." Richard turned to look at her and Elise pretended to be still asleep.

"What family?" Thomas asked. "How can you be sure there is a family? And even if there is, how do you know they still want her? She may have shamed them to such a degree that they wish to forget her entirely. Did you see how quickly she drank her porter?"

"This lass is special, you said so yourself."

"I said she was strange."

"There will be a reward for finding her. Mother has placed the advert in the paper. We need only wait."

"So it's another gamble for you." Thomas sighed when Richard set his mouth in a hard line. "Fine then, but if she stays, she works. Tomorrow she'll go to the kitchen."

"Mrs. P. will be delighted to have some help, I'm sure," Richard smiled at having won the argument.

"Oh aye, Richard. Delighted." Thomas's sarcasm dripped as he got up to turn the heavy key to the front door and lock up. His expression was unreadable as he watched Richard leave the room. On his way back to the bar, Thomas pushed both chairs up under the table and then knocked his pipe on the heel of his shoe. The cold ash fell in a little pile on the hardwood floor.

"How much did you hear?" he asked Elise without looking at her.

"Nothing. I'm supposed to help Mrs. P. tomorrow."

Thomas tucked his pipe back into his pocket as he came around the bar. He stood so close that Elise could see the buttons of his shirt more easily than the expression on his face. "It's late. I'm heading upstairs," he said. He touched her elbow. "I'll walk you to your room."

A crash came from the kitchen and Elise heard Mary scolding Johnny. They were still washing up the night's dishes. "Should we wait for them?" The thought of being in a dark hallway with the glowering fighter made her uneasy.

"Mary will be a while yet." His hand gripped her elbow more insistently.

Elise nodded, feeling trapped. She pushed herself up from the stool to stand, and for the second time that night, her legs gave out as she shifted her weight to her feet. This time Thomas caught her and lifted her into his arms. The buttons of his shirt scraped into her sore ribs. "God, you stink," Elise mumbled sleepily before she rested her head against his broad shoulder.

THE BLACK QUEEN

Adelaide sat on the narrow ledge of the cold windowsill and looked down into the slick grey cobblestone street. Despite the rain, a boy was sweeping a path through the manure to the other side of the street. For his service, he held out his hand to a pair of well-dressed women who could now cross without soiling the hems of their skirts. The apartments in the building across the street were shut up tight and the iron rails that both decorated and protected the windows gleamed wetly. Today, as it had the day before, and the day before that, and the day before that, and perhaps the entire last few weeks, the rain slapped ceaselessly over Paris. Even wrapped in her thick wool shawl, Adelaide shivered. It was a cold summer and the gloom was as oppressive as her insecurity. At least she still had her home, she thought, looking around at her comfortable parlor. The fire burned cheerfully behind the grate. Her maid, Agnes, had left the *café* on the table near the divan and it scented the room pleasantly. Her home was bought and paid for, thanks to her many wealthy clients, and would always be there for her no matter how far she strayed from its warm familiarity. She took strength from that knowledge.

She sighed heavily and flicked her eyes over to her writing table where her cards lay scattered face down with the exception of one. The queen of spades smiled at her teasingly in profile from the top left corner of the card. Adelaide looked back through the window. She had been consistently pulling the Black Queen from the deck since that horrid night at Malmaison and was tired of thinking about it, but the card's significance was hard to ignore. She moved back to the divan where she picked up her knitting and forced herself to start a new row. It was a simple lace pattern with an easy combination of increases and decreases, but nevertheless she had somehow managed to offset the pattern when she turned the work. She could go to the market, she thought restlessly as she began undoing her row. Agnes should go, but Agnes was unused to picking the best cuts of beef and could never get a good price from the butcher. Adelaide considered walking to the wine shop on the corner where she went to hear the latest news, since Bonaparte began censoring the opposition publications. But if she went to the wine shop she would be obliged to buy a drink and she was trying to save money. She would need new clients soon. All her well-to-do customers had started cancelling their appointments.

Somehow, the Black Queen found her way into Adelaide's hand with her knitting piled loosely in her lap. She stood and walked to her writing desk and brushed the other cards off in irritation as though swiping crumbs from dinner table. As she had done countless times over the last week, she paced her parlor and studied the card's many symbols, the Queen of Spades being only one of many. In the center of the card, Isis was shown discovering the body of her murdered husband Osiris. The Egyptian queen held her arms spread out from her sides in surprise to see the Pharaoh's body half hidden under a bush. By itself, the scene suggested a woman newly widowed or abandoned, which was appropriate for Adelaide's frame of mind, preoccupied as she was by her banishment from the Emperor.

After the botched conjuring, she had sworn again and again that she had never plotted to steal his scarab. She promised that she would find the golem and return the jewel. She begged Napoleon to be patient and allow her to stay in his home while she located the errant creature, but he would not be swayed. He was convinced their entire affair had been simply smoke and mirrors to shame him in front of all his guests. The fact that Josephine had been able to persuade Bonaparte to allow her to prove her innocence was a testament to the Empress's feminine powers, waning though they may be. As a result, Adelaide was given a small window of time to locate the golem and make amends.

There had been no response from any of the members of *La Société* to the letters she had sent, but it had been foolish to hope that anyone would respond. For all she knew, the *Société d'Isis* was responsible for the disappearance of the golem. She looked suspiciously at Isis depicted on her card and wondered if the image intimated she was being abandoned by the powerful women she held in such high esteem.

While she had waited for a response to her letters, Adelaide spent many hours in meditation until she finally found the golem's tether. The feeling of pulling the creature towards her, hand over fist, had been one of the most profound experiences of her life—like giving birth in reverse. When the golem came into view, she swelled with maternal pride at the sight of it and instinctively attempted spiritual contact with her progeny by psychically reaching through the black miasma. She had expected to be recognized and loved, but the creature pushed her away with a startling power. Over and over, Adelaide had tried reconnecting with the golem, but the more time passed, the more difficult the task became. The rejection stung. Adelaide sighed and gazed out the window again. The Black Queen did not lie. Fortune, her one true love, had indeed abandoned her.

The only queen she had left was Josephine. What a generous soul, thought Adelaide, what tenderness of spirit. Josephine, still clinging to the idea that they were friends, had come all the way from Malmaison to beg forgiveness for having placed her in an untenable position. Her sensibilities, so naturally amiable and true, obliged her to seek out the warmth of her friends when the warmth of her husband was no longer available to her. "No matter how beautiful the ceremony, it wouldn't have pleased Napoleon," the Empress said. "No one pleases him. He is intolerable."

Sweet Josephine, thought Adelaide, her husband was neither malcontented nor intolerable. The bedroom activities were a thrilling and productive means for controlling the storm that was Napoleon. His body was compact and widening, his hair was lank and thinning, his breath rank, and his tongue probing, but there was no denying the appeal of his power. She should have known that no force of nature could be corralled for long but she had let herself get swept away with the idea that she could play a part in the history of France. Adelaide gave a quick, defeated wave of her hand in the air as though she was talking to another when she thought of her embarrassing naïveté. Now she knew that while she had whispered fevered suggestions for shaping the future of mankind, the Emperor was only listening to his own heavy breathing. While all of France was still fixated on the heady novelty of greeting each other as equals, Napoleon fixated on Austria, on Iberia, on England. She berated herself for her stupidity.

She had read the cards to Josephine when she visited to calm the Empress and stop her tears. It hadn't worked. The Black Queen had been drawn then as well. Abandoned or widowed, which would Josephine be? Perhaps both. Not wanting to further upset the Empress, Adelaide had instead concentrated on the other images shown on the card. In the bottom left hand corner, a man stood over a lantern, refilling it with oil. Darkness and solitude would ensue—the loss of a friend or confidante was inevitable. Adelaide had taken the opportunity to explain that the two of them would not be able to meet again in the future. Josephine wept anew at the news, but Adelaide had felt mostly sorry for the loss of Josephine's influence, not her company. In the bottom right hand corner, a young woman sat with a crone. That was the crux of the problem, Adelaide had thought as she smiled thinly at the aging Empress. In the face of Josephine's growing inability to conceive, the Emperor had become a rutting animal, bedding any woman he could in order to prove the infertility of his wife was not due to his own impotence. If only Josephine had gathered wisdom instead of quips during her marriage she might have been able to sustain her usefulness beyond her childbearing years with the provision of invaluable advice and calculated introductions. Instead, the silly woman thought she could help by introducing her husband to a fortune-teller. Adelaide snorted at the thought. It sounded ridiculous even to her.

Pressing the Black Queen to her lips, Adelaide thought again of the golem. It wasn't too far of a stretch to think the card could also be meant for that green-eyed creature, although she hesitated to believe she could read for the supernatural. Solitude, despair for lost loves and lost lives—if the creature could emote, these would be the emotions she would surely be feeling. The fact that the card's interpretation centered on an Egyptian myth couldn't be a coincidence, considering the significance of Napoleon's lost jewel. Adelaide's situation would be entirely different had the scarab remained around the Emperor's neck. So would the golem's situation, for that matter.

A loud knock on the front door made Adelaide jump. She bent down and started gathering the cards from off the floor. "Agnes," she called. "See who is there." She knew full well who it was. She saw a flash of her little maid as she rushed through the hallway and heard her soft shoes brush down the stairs to the entrance hall. The pounding on the door grew more insistent. With her deck tucked into her apron pocket, she arranged herself on the divan and waited.

"*Monsieur, s'il vous plait,*" she heard Agnes squeak in surprise. Then she heard a rushed and heavy scrape of feet up the marble steps before a thin man with sharp cheekbones outlined in black sideburns darkened her parlor door.

"*Ministre Fouché. Je vous en prie.* Please enter." Adelaide said. She made a graceful gesture of invitation and offered him the armchair opposite the fireplace. "Have you come for a reading? Agnes, pour our honored guest a glass of our best Madeira." Adelaide reached into her pocket to touch her deck, drawing the cards' strength into her.

The man smiled coldly as he seated himself and graciously took the small vial of the sticky wine. "I've no wish to know the future before it arrives," he said. "Nor am I afflicted with so much self doubt that I would need to hear my own desires echoed back to me for reassurance."

Adelaide withdrew her hand from her pocket and fought to control her emotions. If the Minister of Police knocked on her door and didn't want a reading, then there could only be one other reason for his visit. She felt his eyes, high above his long nose, boring through her. It was just as well, even if he had been interested in her cards, he would have still apprehended her. This way she was spared the torture of reading for a prideful man. "Then you've come to punish me for my mistake."

"A mistake, for a woman, is selecting the wrong color gown for the ball, forgetting one's gloves in a lover's boudoir, misplacing a stitch in an embroidery. This was no mistake. This was a crime. The Emperor was generous enough, given your relationship with his wife, to allow you the time to ameliorate your situation. But now your time is up. I have come to ask: have you found your errant partner?"

"Partner? I have no partner."

Fouché's eyes narrowed. He shifted forward in the chair as though needing to relieve the pressure of the seat from his sharp tailbone. Then he smiled slowly, pretending sympathy. "You must feel so humiliated to have been left behind, abandoned with all the problems and none of the rewards. How could she have done that to you? Partner? No, she's no partner. That much is true." The Minister paused to look into her eyes. Adelaide pulled her shawl closer around her shoulders as a chill shot down her spine. "If I had a partner like that, I would move heaven and earth to find her and make her pay for her betrayal. But I can see that you are a generous woman. You hesitate to give up the location of your former friend." He waited for Adelaide to respond, then continued when it became obvious she wouldn't. "But perhaps you protect her location from me only for the joy of punishing her yourself?"

"Oh no," Adelaide exclaimed horrified. "I could never hurt her. But you are mistaken—she is not my partner."

"Have you found her then? Have you even been trying?"

"Yes, yes, of course. And I almost did. I almost found her."

Fouché stood and loomed over her. "Where? Does she still have the jewel? Tell me and all is forgiven."

"On the astral plane. I found her on the astral plane." Adelaide cried out in alarm when the Minister slammed his fist down next to her on the divan. "Please understand. All is not lost. The vortex did not take her out of reach. She can still be retrieved."

"Retrieved from where?" His long fingers locked around her shoulders. "People do not reside amongst stars. Do not torture me with your ridiculous speeches. Where is the jewel?"

"I don't know," Adelaide gasped. "Not France. She's not in France. I need more time, and supplies. You must give me more time to find the golem. If the Emperor refuses to have me return to Malmaison, I'll need money so I can recreate the conjuring here in this room. Candles, mirrors, the roses, the pyramids of pastries—all of it needs to be present. I won't be able to recall her, but I may be able to locate her if the scene is correct."

"Now we are progressing." Fouché sat back down in the armchair and brushed the lint off his lap. The sudden change in his countenance was heartening. "And how much do you estimate you'll need?"

Adelaide stood excitedly. "I've already calculated the sums. I've been thinking about this for some time." She pulled a sheet of paper with carefully marked figures from out of a collection of books stacked under her desk and handed it to the Minister.

Fouché glanced at it quickly. "This is it? Surely you will need more than this? You cannot host the ceremony here in this hovel of a room. You must rent a salon. And how will you feed your friends? You should be hosting a party for the recreation to be complete. We will need to double this sum, wouldn't you agree?"

Adelaide felt a bit astonished by the sudden transformation of the Minister. "Having others present would help to recreate that night," she agreed.

"Tell me, where did you first find the creature?"

"Find her? I didn't find her. She was gifted to me like a babe is gifted to a mother."

The Minister's friendly countenance dissolved as he folded up the sheet of figures. He shook his head. "Not only are you unrepentant of your crime, now you attempt to fleece more from the Emperor's coffers. I will keep this page you've given me as evidence. I wish to know who your partner's friends are, her lovers, where she eats, where she sleeps. I don't care about astral planes. I don't care about your diabolical cards. I want details. What kind of fool do you think I am? Astral plane?" The Minister scoffed and grabbed Adelaide's arm. "I've heard enough. Either you don't know where the scarab is, or you know but you refuse to say and think to con a few more *sous*."

"That's not true," Adelaide tried to shake his grip off her arm. "I only wish to help the Emperor. A second revolution is nigh. The Bourbons will return to power if I don't find the golem. Don't you see?" Adelaide pulled *le Valet de Piques* from her pocket and waved it at the Minister. "Even you will be harmed. You will be replaced by a Duke."

"*Idiotte*, my replacement will come after I choose to retire." He opened the door and pushed her into the hallway. "Your prophecies are treasonous. Just tell me where your partner is and I will suggest to the Emperor that he use a light hand in your punishment."

They paused at the top of the stairs and glared at each other. Adelaide clenched her fists in frustration. "Have you not heard anything I've been saying?"

The Minister took up Adelaide's arm again and started marching her down the long staircase. "I've heard it all, Mademoiselle. I've heard it all," he said wearily. "You'll hear it too, whispered from cell to cell, and soon it will bore you as much as it bores me. But eventually the tedium of your solitude will convince you to forego telling your tired little stories." He stopped to peel away Adelaide's arresting grip from the staircase banister as she fought to slow their descent. "Then, you may be happier to tell the details. I like details. I'll listen more carefully then." He crooked her arm painfully behind her back to keep her in front of him. "Perhaps your partner's parents live in Nantes? Perhaps she has a lover who she meets regularly on the banks of the Seine?" He grunted and lifted Adelaide back onto her feet when she tried to sit down.

Near the bottom of the steps, Adelaide stumbled. She clutched at the Minister to regain her balance, but he took a step away and let go of her arm. She tumbled down the rest of the stairs and sprawled into the foyer. Her maid, holding her broom like a weapon, flew from the kitchen hallway to see what the noise was all about.

"Do not be alarmed, Agnes." Adelaide knew her smile wasn't convincing. She pulled herself back up to her feet. "There has been a misunderstanding. I'm sure it will work itself out. Please let my clients know I will return soon."

The little maid nodded slowly and lowered the broom, showing no confidence that anyone, even her powerful mistress, would be released quickly once taken. She turned to the Minister. "Is it true what they're saying?"

He replied with the practiced gasp that no gossip could resist. "I don't know. Tell me: what is it that they are saying?" Adelaide hissed in pain as the Minister's grip returned to tighten around her forearm.

"You've not heard?" Agnes looked pleased. When the Minister shook his head with anticipation and leaned in towards her, she continued. "They say the Emperor has lost a beloved jewel! His missing mistress has skin kissed dark by the sands of Egypt, eyes like glittering emeralds, and auburn hair as soft as spun silk. Is it true?"

His expression froze with the exception of his eyes, which rolled up to fix over the woman's shoulder. "There is and was no mistress. The Emperor is forever loyal to his wife Josephine."

The maid huffed in disappointment to hear the Minister's cold response. She turned to Adelaide. "And what of my future husband? Am I not to be married?"

"Oh Agnes," Adelaide breathed and reflexively clutched the cards still tucked in her pocket. "I saw him just last evening. He is no longer a shadow—you will meet him soon. Your days of being a simple maid are almost over."

Agnes smiled happily, as Adelaide was pushed out the front door.

The Reluctant Maid

After Thomas dumped her unceremoniously from his arms onto her mattress, Elise rolled over and stared at the wall without saying goodnight. The room was so dark she had to reach out and touch the wall to convince herself it was still there. It was only when Mary finally entered with a candle that she stopped obsessively moving her fingertips over the bumps on its surface, hoping for a chink to press that would magically swing the wall around and send her back to the 21st Century.

She listened to the quiet rustlings as her roommate undressed, slipped into bed, and blew out the candle. When Mary's breathing grew steady, she turned over onto her back and stared into the darkness towards the ceiling. Sometime in the early morning Elise shifted her obsessive thinking from the unanswerable puzzle of her strange situation, to the unbearably stuffy air in the room. She climbed onto her feet and reached towards the little window suspended over her bed. Moving her hands in the dark around the window's casing, she tried and failed to push the window open. It was only when Mary's shoe hit the wall dangerously close to her head that she stopped banging on the stuck sash. The barmaid's aim was surprisingly good, even in the black night. Knowing a second shoe might hit its target, Elise made a herculean effort to lift the window and it finally opened three inches with a horrible squeal that sent a tremor down her spine. A cold breeze laden with the smell of thick smoke, horse and human excrement, and various other rotting things Elise didn't want to think about or identify smacked her in the face.

"Close the damned window," Mary groaned from her bed. The second shoe hit the wall near Elise's shoulder. "You'll kill us all."

Elise whipped both shoes back at Mary as hard as she could and took satisfaction from the resulting screech. Quickly she drew the protective curtain around her bed before all out war started. Then she slammed the window shut.

When she woke, it took Elise a while to cut through her groggy fog and realize she wasn't in Tucson anymore. She pulled the scratchy wool blanket up to her chin against the cold and wrinkled her nose at the smell. Again, she stared at the ceiling and was tempted to stay in bed all day. Metaphysics was supposed to be real only for people who lived in Sedona with their crystal pendants and scented candles, and even then it was only real in their own minds. There had to be tons of other people who would be overjoyed to fall into a wormhole, or whatever it was she fell into, why couldn't they have done it instead of her? The injustice of it all put her in a black mood. Briefly, she considered what would happen if she refused to leave her bed. Either she'd rot slowly as she developed bedsores and starved, or everything would return to normal when fate got bored with her. She rolled back onto her side and wondered how long she would last on a lumpy mattress that crunched every time she moved. It felt strange to anthropomorphize fate, but it was easier than thinking her travel through time was the result of a random bit of unexplainable weather, like being struck by lightning. Who ever did this to her must really hate her. Why else would she get stuck in a time with no toilets?

Finally, she decided she had two choices: find a way to get back or accept her situation and conform to the new rules. If she had landed with more resources—money, for instance—she might have tried hiring a carriage and making for the sea. Wealthy people didn't need to worry about conforming to society. They could be as odd and off-kilter as they wanted as long as they were generous. But she didn't have money and, as a result, she would have to learn to fit in. The one thing the pub did afford her was a small sense of normalcy. At the pub, conforming to new rules would be easy since they were relatively the same as any bar in any time: play nice and you could continue to drink. With her eyes closed and a mug of beer in her fist, Elise could fool herself into thinking she was still in Tucson, which was a small luxury necessary for her continued sanity. She would stay, make the pub home-base, and learn how to maneuver in this new world until she could figure something else out.

Elise crooked a finger around the bed curtain and peeked into the room. Mary's bed was empty, which gave her the courage to pull the curtain all the way back for a better view. The heavy wooden cross had been returned to its hook next to the door. The white enameled basin was back on the rickety wooden table and a large matching urn rested on the floor next to it—her bath, Elise realized. She didn't hold much hope that the water would still be warm. On the chair was a pile of neatly folded clothes.

Although she itched to wash the yuck off her body and unfold the gowns to examine their style, she rolled over to face the wall, still stuck on the idea that if she ignored it all, it would all go away. She squeezed her eyes shut. Then the pressure in her bladder made her sit up. Biology always trumps metaphysics, she thought as she pulled out the bedpan.

It was late when Elise finally made her way downstairs and walked through the dining hall. The few men still seated in the room had already pushed back their breakfast plates. Self consciously, Elise smoothed her dress over her torso when they nodded at her from their tables and followed her with their eyes. It had taken some time to figure out how to put her new clothes on, and she still wasn't confident that she'd dressed correctly.

The Quiet Woman felt differently than it had the night before—the fire in the great fireplace was smaller and no longer flashed orange and blue; the smell from the kitchen was more sour milk and thin porridge and less beef stew. Elise walked around to the other side of the bar and ducked through the door. Unluckily, Mrs. Postlethwaite was just as large and animated as she had been the night before. "Where have you been?" she asked loudly as Elise stepped into the kitchen and began to look around. "Mary's done all your chores and her own too, and is gone already for the water."

Elise gave a shrug of apology. The effort of attempting a more sincere response didn't seem necessary, given the circumstances. It was all a mirage. Soon she'd be back in Tucson.

Mrs. Postlethwaite carefully set down the butcher's knife that always seemed to be in her hand. The gesture didn't look like a sign of goodwill and the kitchen was heavy with silence while the cook sized Elise up with a squint-eyed, head to toe glare. "Cat's got your tongue?"

"I've been sick," Elise said sullenly. "But I'm here now."

Mrs. Postlethwaite glared a little longer before trying to smile. "Well then. Never mind. Get yourself some breakfast." She pointed to a large jar resting on the top of a lidded barrel. Inside the jar, eggs and beets floated like medical specimens in cloudy pink brine. Elise breathed a sigh of relief and her stomach rumbled with the anticipated pleasure.

As Elise sucked on a pickled egg, she watched Mrs. Postlethwaite sink one hand into a large hunk of meat sitting directly on the wooden table in front of her to grasp what Elise guessed was a femur. Her other hand reached for the knife and flicked it skillfully around the bone. The heavy kitchen table rocked slightly on its uneven legs while Mrs. Postlethwaite's strong arms pulled and sliced, butterflying the thigh.

Even though the day had hardly begun, the kitchen was already unbearably hot from the fire that roared in the open hearth. Mrs. Postlethwaite's cheeks were pink from the heat, and her sleeves were damp and rolled up high on her strong biceps. A crumb of pink flesh, as big as an earlobe, seemed to eject itself into the air. Elise ducked and cringed. Mrs. Postlethwaite didn't seem to notice.

"Are you preparing something special?" Elise asked, not knowing what else to say. She felt stupid just standing there, but deliberately didn't ask how she could help.

The cook smiled but didn't look up from her work. "Folks do like the Missus's stuffed ham," she replied.

"That's a ham?"

The knife paused in the air for just a moment, hardly long enough to lose prep time, but long enough for Mrs. Postlethwaite to shoot Elise another look, obviously making judgments about her worth but politely remaining mute on the subject. She started to explain the recipe. "First I take out the bone and then I fill the hole with chopped apples, onions, chopped sage, and a cup of chopped parsley. Then I add two big hands full of bread rubbed small," she stopped again, this time long enough to rub her palms together to ostensibly demonstrate making bread crumbs and used the moment to roll her shoulders back in a quick stretch. "And salt and pepper," she returned to hacking at the femur. "Then I beat six eggs to frothiness and throw that over all and mix well and put the whole mess into the ham hole. It's then tied in a cloth and boiled all day." The cook beamed at Elise, her first sincere smile, demonstrating her pride in the cleverness of the recipe. "I've already done the one, the rest of the beast is over there waiting." She pointed to the other end of the kitchen through an open door that led to a courtyard. A huge mound was hanging under a bloody shroud. Flies were circling. "I'll be salting it later today," Mrs. Postlethwaite said. "You can save a good deal of money by doing your own butchering."

"That's good to know," Elise drawled. The day was already getting worse. Elise didn't know much about the culinary arts, but detected something odd about the recipe and was grumpy enough to allow her disbelief to be heard in her voice. "So, you're really going to boil that?" She nodded at the thigh.

"Yes. Boil. The cloth will be tied up tight so the stuffing don't fall out," Mrs. Postlethwaite repeated, her smile disappearing. "The stuffing cuts out of the meat very nicely after it's cold from the cellar. You'll see." She straightened up and placed her hands on her hips effectively ending the tutorial.

The idea of eating gelatinized cold ham stuffing later that evening caused Elise's eyes to dart around the kitchen for possible alternatives. She saw nothing but tools of the trade. Pewter plates, scrubbed shiny, were lined neatly on shelves. Ironware in various forms—cauldrons, hooks, pointy things, things for fireplaces, things for frying—were all organized and in their designated places. Linens were folded and stacked next to white enameled basins. Barrels with lids lined one wall; a ladle was hooked to the lip of an open barrel containing water. There were no boxes of mac and cheese anywhere to be seen, thought Elise with disappointment.

Two cats slipped into the kitchen from the open courtyard door and walked brazenly towards the table to rub their heads on Mrs. Postlethwaite's ankles. She absently shook her leg and they swatted at her skirts before skidding away sideways across the wooden floorboards. Mrs. Postlethwaite pulled out a basket from behind the larder door. "Can you peel apples?" she asked by way of an order and placed the basket on the wide kitchen table in front of Elise. Without waiting for an answer, the older woman went back to the larder to pull out two onions and added them to the basket of apples. "You can chop these too."

There was nothing worse than chopping onions, Elise thought, and noted the ones in the basket looked especially fat and juicy. She thought fondly of peanut butter and jelly sandwiches before reaching despondently towards the apples. "The paring knife is in that drawer," Mrs. Postlethwaite waved again carelessly with the butcher knife. "I'll need four peeled and chopped with both those onions."

The fatty beef she'd eaten the night before had practically made her eyes roll back with joy when she'd first spooned it into her mouth. Now the memory of it was revolting. Tonight she'd have gelatinous ham; tomorrow it could be anything—tongue, tripe, maybe even pigeon. Elise shuddered and dragged herself back to the table with the paring knife, making sure to stand as far away as possible from the cook so as to avoid any flying bits. She had to find a way to Tucson soon before she starved to death, she thought.

They worked silently together until Mrs. Postlethwaite asked suddenly, "What shall I call you then?"

"Elise," Elise responded.

"What's your family name, Elise?

"Dubois."

"Elise Duboys? That's sounds very French." After a long silence, Mrs. Postlethwaite huffed. "Thomas did say you had a strange way about your speech. I don't know as how he noticed, seeing as you're so conversational. But maybe you don't speak much English. We don't get French people at the Quiet Woman. You'll be hard pressed to find a place for yourself if you're looking to find other frogs around here."

Elise shifted uncomfortably. "I'm not French," she said.

"Not French? Then what are you? You're not one of us, that's sure. How do you come to be here?"

"I don't remember," Elise said. "I think it'll come back to me, but I just need some time." She hoped that claiming loss of memory wouldn't get her a visit to a nineteenth century home for the insane, but she figured it was a safer explanation than time travel.

Luckily, the opportunity for Mrs. Postlethwaite to pepper Elise with more questions ended when Mary came in through the courtyard door with two full buckets sloshing at her sides. "So the Queen decided to get out of bed?" Mary asked rhetorically. "She kept me up half the night banging on the window." She poured the buckets into the water barrel. "Won't the Missus be wanting to send her back soon?"

"Send her back where? She says she can't remember where home is. Besides, you know how Mr. Ferrington feels about strays." To emphasize her point she shooed a cat off the table.

"Well, doesn't everyone seem lively this morning?" Richard said as he headed towards the larder. He had come through into the kitchen from a side door Elise hadn't noticed before. Mrs. Postlethwaite threw her hand over her mouth in surprise and Mary blushed deeply. All three women studied Richard, but he seemed unfazed by Mrs. Postlethwaite's criticism, if he had heard it at all. "I'm so pleased to see how well you're adjusting this morning, Elise," Richard called from the larder. His voice was muffled by whatever he had managed to find for his breakfast. "Mrs. P?" Richard asked turning back towards the cook with a hunk of bread in one hand and another hunk stuffed in the pocket of his cheek. Mary closed the larder door that he'd left wide open. "Could you manage a cup of tea?"

"Of course, Mr. Ferrington," she replied. She motioned for Mary to start steeping the tea, and the young woman pushed roughly past Elise to retrieve the kettle from its place over the fire.

As Mrs. Postlethwaite went back to preparing the ham, Mrs. Ferrington walked in, yawning and rubbing her eyes. "My dear girl, what ever are you doing?" she asked Elise.

"Peeling apples." Elise dared a glance at the dining room door for an opportunity to escape what was becoming a crowded kitchen.

"How very strangely you go about it," replied Mrs. Ferrington, looking absently at the button-sized peels that had scattered across the table. Then her son caught her attention. "Why must you hide your chin in those awful cravats? You have such a nice, strong jaw, Richard. It's a pity to hide it in your collar." She reached over and started plucking at Richard's neck.

"Mother…" Richard cut his sentence short and waved a hunk of his bread defensively in the air while he ducked his chin further into billowy silk.

"Tea, Mrs. Ferrington?" called out Mrs. Postlethwaite helpfully.

"Oh yes, please," replied the older woman taking her tea from Mary without turning away from her son. "You must make sure those barrels are delivered today. Have you spoken with Thomas about the delivery?"

"No Mother, I haven't even had my breakfast yet."

"Just remember those barrels. And speak with Thomas." Mrs. Ferrington paused to look at Richard like she was studying a work of art, with her head tilted and her eyes narrowed. "Might you let your hair grow just a little? That way you could pull it off your forehead and into a queue. Have you begun to go bald, dear? Is that why you're combing your hair forward like that? I think Mrs. Aldren has a hair tonic, although I'm afraid it's much too late for her husband, may he rest in peace. Would you like me to get some for you?" she took a sip of tea. "Oh! This is much too strong," Mrs. Ferrington exclaimed, and turned towards Mrs. Postlethwaite.

Seizing his moment, Richard leaned over Elise's shoulder. "Like this," he whispered as he took her hands into his while his mother fussed at Mrs. Postlewaite about the wastefulness of too strong tea. Elise looked up in surprise as he embraced her from behind and briefly caught Mary's angry glare. A long, single apple peel emerged from her hand, guided by Richard. Once the peel broke, he pocketed an apple from the basket and snuck out of the kitchen.

While Elise was grateful for the five-second lesson, she couldn't help but feel irritated by Richard's disappearing act, knowing it would mean Mrs. Ferrington's attention would eventually turn back to her. She busied herself with the apple, satisfied with how the paring knife felt more secure in her hand. Then she realized there had been a pause in the older women's conversation. When she looked up, she saw them watching her while Mary banged pots in the fireplace. They smiled. Elise looked back down, feeling uncomfortable.

"Well, she seems to be doing fine with that apple now, but you're right, Mary should be in the kitchen more. Elise will go to the pump for water in the morning and afternoon from now on instead of Mary. And I see no reason why she can't start the fires, empty the pots, and sweep out the dining room too. She seems perfectly healthy now, don't you think?"

"She seems a little frail, Ma'am."

Mary piped up from her corner, "She's wearing her chemise over her stays, and has forgotten her petticoat. I'll not be washing her stays every week just because she's too daft to dress properly."

Elise looked down at her gown. The stack of clothing that had been left for her had been confusing. The stockings were obvious, as was the apron. Was the enormous bra with the tiny quarter cups and all the uncomfortable under-wires supposed to go over the slip? That was stupid, thought Elise. There seemed to be an extra skirt too, which she realized must have been the forgotten petticoat. Elise had also left a pair of knee length shorts draped over the chair in her bedroom. She didn't see the use in them since they were crotchless but she now realized there would be an uproar if it was discovered she wasn't wearing the oversized undies.

"Mary, please try to be kind," Mrs. Ferrington chastised. "Elise will dress properly tomorrow, I'm sure. You'll be glad enough to have her when you're not set to fetching water and tossing out the night-soil."

That seemed to perk Mary up quite a bit, but sounded ominous to Elise. She hoped night-soil wasn't what she thought it was.

"Where's Thomas?" Mrs. Ferrington asked. "I know the odds were against him last night, but I hope he managed to earn my congratulations?"

"Aye, he won again last night. He's already come and gone, Ma'am," Mrs. Postlethwaite replied.

"Oh that's wonderful," Mrs. Ferrington chirped. "I don't approve of gambling, but I'll always put a little down on our Thomas." She was practically rubbing her palms together, Elise noted.

Mrs. Postlethwaite's lips pinched into a thin line and Elise saw Mary glance anxiously at the two older women. "He'll likely be back in the afternoon. You can congratulate him then if you're here." Mrs. Postlethwaite said. "Have you not finished with those apples yet, Elise? I'll need them soon." She'd returned to whipping the eggs. Talk of Thomas had caused the eggs to move well beyond the point of being frothy.

Three naked apples sat in front of Elise in a line. She picked up the pace with the fourth in her hands. "I'm almost done," she replied.

"Which fine ladies will you be calling on today, Mrs. Ferrington?" Mary asked.

"Mary, would you please come away from that fire and help Elise with those onions," Mrs. Postlethwaite snapped. Elise smiled to herself and slowed her work on the fourth apple to a glacial pace. If she timed it right, the onions would fall off her list of things to do.

Mary's question caused Mrs. Ferrington to suddenly remember she was late. She called out final directions for the evening meal as she bustled her way through the dining hall door. Mary came and stood next to Elise and took up an onion to start chopping. When Elise tried to discretely move down the table and away from the fumes, Mary followed, staying close enough for them both to suffer. "Mrs. P doesn't like it when Mr. MacEwan fights," she hissed at Elise when the stout cook had stuck her head in the larder. "She thinks Mrs. Ferrington encourages him for her own gain. The Ferringtons raised him, you know, so Mrs. P. blames them."

"Does Thomas fight a lot?" Elise whispered back, taking three steps to the left and wiping her eyes. Her apple was nearly peeled.

"Oh, all the time. He usually wins too." Mary scraped the onions down the table with the blade of her knife and followed Elise's retreat, resolutely staying close.

There was something about Thomas that was at odds with boxing, she thought, unlike Mary who seemed to enjoy picking fights. She took a half step to the left and realized she'd reached the corner of the table as the last red peel fell from her apple. Elise pulled an edge of her apron up to press against her watery eyes. When she pulled the apron away to squint angrily at Mary, she was handed the second onion and given a sly, teary smile in response. "Onions won't be the worst of it."

"What's night soil?" Elise asked suspiciously.

"You really are a queen, aren't you?"

Elise sighed. It was going to be a long day.

Burdensome Strays

"Good morning Mr. Tilsdale," Elise said as cheerfully as she could, but it came out only slightly more friendly than a grumble. She was descending the steps from the third floor, where she had groggily stumbled out of her bedroom only moments before. The lanky old man emerged from the gloom of the passage on the second floor and stopped at the staircase landing to let her pass.

It was another day, and thus another trudge through life in a place she didn't want to be. The day before had indeed been a trial. She had been forced to endure it with Mary most of the afternoon until dinner when the customers started coming through the door. No one paid any attention to her when customers were waiting to spend money. Thomas was strangely absent, and with no one watching the bar, she was able to get a beer from Johnny and slip away to her room for much needed rest. She didn't mind skipping her dinner of the Missus's famed stuffed ham.

The meager light that leaked through the tiny bedroom window had enraged her when she had opened her eyes. She wanted to rip the weak sun from the sky and punish it in her fist. In Tucson the sun was everything. It vibrated the cicadas' song; it reflected metallic off hummingbirds' feathers and sent the sweet smell of baking sage into every crevice of the dusty town. Here, the sun crept fearfully through the window and into Elise's bedroom, apologetic, mincing. It could be morning or noon or late evening, it didn't matter, the light was always the same: ineffectual.

It would have been easy enough for Mary to wake her, but making things easy didn't seem to be Mary's style. Also contributing to Elise's foul mood was the distinct swampy smell that her dress was beginning to take on. When she'd asked about a change of clothes the previous day she'd, once again, been called a Queen—as if having two dresses was a luxury. It was clear to Elise that if she didn't get up before Mary in the mornings, there wouldn't be any water left in the ewer for a sponge bath. It didn't occur to her to go down to the kitchen for her own water, and reusing the water in the basin was out of the question. What's more, she still didn't have any shoes.

Her red polished toenails had made quite a splash, as did the size of her feet—a respectable eight-and-a-half. "I'll not spend my money to have a pair of shoes made for those," Mrs. Ferrington had said. "You'll have to wait for a suitable used pair."

"The only other woman I know as got feet like frying pans is Mrs. Williams," Mary had laughed. "I can ask her if she'd part with one of her old pairs. I hope you're not too proud to wear an old woman's shoes?"

And to top it off, Elise was sure she wouldn't be offered any coffee that morning, and would be lucky to get tea.

Mr. Tilsdale touched his forehead where the brim of his hat would have been had he been wearing it on his head instead of carrying it in his hand. "Morning Miss," he said with a smile. Elise smelled halitosis and damp wool. The scent moved back into the tenant's passageway where it waited to seep slowly outdoors through the walls, one molecule at a time.

There were five tenant rooms on the second floor and four of them were rented. Mary had described the tenants as single men of humble professions and small incomes. Her eyes had sparkled when she had pointed to the one empty room. "It could be anyone as takes that room," she had said. "We're due for a handsome one. We've had nothing but louts and old farts lately."

As Elise attempted to swing widely around Mr. Tilsdale— undoubtedly one of Mary's old farts—he grabbed her arm. "Aren't you Mr. MacEwan's little lunatic? I believe we haven't been properly introduced."

"I say, by George, I believe you're right, Old Chap." Elise snapped back with an exaggerated accent. Later that day she would be discovering what he had to eat in the last 24 hours and carry it in a bucket all the way downstairs, past the kitchen and into the cellar. She would, she thought to herself, become very familiar with all the tenants' digestive hygiene. She pulled her arm out of his grip and continued down the stairs.

The previous afternoon Mrs. Ferrington had presented Mary with a grand promotion to be the cook's assistant, but Mary remained wary. While the barmaid was delighted to forego the job of dumping dumps out of the pots and into the household septic tank, she wasn't thrilled by the potential competition of having Elise take over the chambermaid duties. Mary's anxiety only abated when Elise showed very little interest or enthusiasm for learning the job.

The sound of Mr. Tilsdale's footsteps following her unnerved Elise—there was something in the way he said "lunatic" that made her skin crawl. She could feel the man's eyes on the bare skin of the back of her neck and wished she hadn't swept her hair up with borrowed hairpins. Mary said he was a Barrister's clerk when she'd taken Elise into his room for training. She could tell he'd been at the Quiet Woman for quite some time by the amount of things he'd accumulated—a pocket watch with its back pried open for repairs, a small sewing basket that held socks that needed mending, saved slivers of shaving soap, and a large grease stain on the mattress. With Mary supervising, she had swept his room and made his bed tucking the sheets with tight hospital corners. Elise considered hooking all the tenants up to urinary catheter bags as she'd poured his chamber pot into the bucket Mary had given her to take to each room.

At the bottom of the stairs, Elise said good day as she opened the door into the pub and Mr. Tilsdale left to go to work. The dining hall was empty with the exception of the shivering old man in the wing chair. Elise wondered if he'd gone home the night before.

In the kitchen, Mrs. Postlethwaite was chopping turnips with a loud banging against the table. Instinctually, Elise glanced at the stack of linens on the shelf behind her for makeshift bandages. Thomas was sitting on the low stool in the corner near the fire. His bottom lip had almost returned to normal and would have looked nice had his pipe not been dangling from it. Everything about him seemed wilted. His eyelids drooped over his bloodshot eyes. His hair, normally thick and unruly, fell lank to his chin. His chest was sunken and even his taut stomach seemed to fold over his thighs. He pulled his pipe out of his mouth and yawned. Elise's eyes widened in appreciation as he stretched to his full length, transformed for mere seconds before slumping back into his former position. "Where were you last night?" she asked.

"What business is it of yours?" came a sharp reply from Mrs. Postlethwaite. The cook looked up to scowl at Elise while her knife kept cubing vegetables. "Mr. MacEwan was attending to other matters of importance. He was attending to matters," she reiterated, "and you'd do best to remember that and thank him in the mornings and not talk to him like an old wife."

Elise didn't know what to say to that and stared at Mrs. Postlethwaite with her mouth open. She was saved when Thomas started to choke and cough after an ill-timed deep inhale of tobacco smoke. She turned to look at him and could swear he was trying not to laugh. "Serves you right." Mrs. Postlethwaite shouted at him. "Just look at that blooming eye," she said, jabbing her knife in the air to point at Thomas's face. A small cut high on his cheekbone was scabbed over and slightly discolored by a bruise. The eye itself seemed fine.

"How can I look at my own eye?" Thomas replied around his pipe after he recovered.

"I suppose you'll be wanting a side of beef to put on it."

"If you've got a side of beef, it'll go in my belly, not on my eye."

"Well, there'll be no beef for you." Mrs. Postlethwaite's knife came down decisively on a hunk of turnip with a deadly kerchunk.

Thomas bent to take a glowing twig from the hearth to relight his pipe, completely unfazed by the threatening cook. Grey tendrils of smoke swirled gently over his head as he sucked rhythmically on the stem, and the smell of it made all Elise's pores open like nicotine landing docks. She sidled up as close to him as she could reasonably get without giving her addiction away to inhale his second-hand smoke.

"Have you ever seen such a laggard?" Mrs. Postlethwaite asked, her attention and her knife suddenly swinging in Elise's direction.

Thomas puffed his pipe in response and closed his eyes with apparent exhaustion.

"Standing about, doing nothing for nobody, listening to things that she's no cause to listen to. So glad you could join us this morning, your Highness. Have you even put the water on yet?" Mrs. Postlethwaite scraped the turnips into a pile with the edge of her blade and then started chopping onions. Without waiting for a reply she continued, "Look at her, wandering down here, pretty as you please, well after everyone else was up and about? Mary's got all the fires going and the hall swept already."

"I don't have the strength to beat her this morning, Mrs. P. It'll have to wait until this afternoon," Thomas replied with his strange, scarred smile. He pulled himself straight again and the fabric of his sleeves stretched tight over the muscles in his arms.

Grabbing the kettle from off the shelf, Elise hastily filled it with water from the barrel and set it over the fire as she'd seen Mary do the day before. When she turned back to the kitchen table, Thomas was again slumped on the stool with his pipe in his hand. He was digging in the bowl with the unlit end of his twig.

"Don't tease the lass like that Thomas," Mrs. Postlethwaite laughed. "Look at her! The Queen's going to wet her bloomers."

"Damned thing won't draw," he mumbled grumpily at his pipe.

"Have you let the cats in yet, your Highness?" Mrs. Postlethwaite demanded. Being told what she hadn't yet done in irate tones instead of told ahead of time what she was expected to do seemed to Elise like the most inefficient way to learn her job. She opened the back door to the courtyard and the scrawny shadows slinked in, meowing and circling her ankles. "There's a pitcher of milk on the thrawl. You can give them some." Elise looked at the cook blankly. "On the thrawl. The *thrawl.*" Mrs. Postlethwaite shook her knife at the larder door. "What are you waiting for? You'd think I was speaking French, the way she stares."

Following the pointing knife, Elise held her breath and opened the door. The smell that came from the basement staircase located in the back of the larder emanated like waves of heat over Arizona asphalt. She located the pitcher of milk on a cold stone shelf and left quickly, pulling the door shut against all vapors. She took the milk to the table and poured a small amount out into a bowl under the watchful eye of Mrs. Postlethwaite who guided her to add a bit more with a nod of her head.

"Only four cats?" Thomas asked, after Elise placed the bowl on the warm hearth. "Where's the fifth?"

Mrs. Postlethwaite finally set down her knife to stick her head out into the yard. "Kitty kitty kitty," she called loudly and uninvitingly. When the fifth didn't come running she turned back to the table and sighed. "The Missus won't be happy."

"I think it's the black one that's gone missing, poor bugger." Thomas leaned over to pet one of the cats and it turned to hiss at him.

"They're all the same to me. Cats shouldn't be in kitchens anyway, filthy things."

Elise wished she could point out that the cats washed their paws more often than anyone else in the kitchen, but wisely kept her mouth shut.

"There she is," Mary called out loudly, glaring at Elise as she banged into the kitchen swinging two buckets full of water. Everyone jumped and looked around at the floor, thinking she was referring to the fifth cat. "And what have you been doing all morning?" Mary demanded, pointing a finger at Elise.

"The blackie's gone," said Mrs. Postlethwaite to Mary with her hands on her hips and her lips thinned into a straight line.

"Blackie?"

"Yes. Have you seen it?"

"No. That is, I don't think so. What does it look like?" Surprised by Mrs. Postlethwaite's accusatory ambush, Mary retreated from her initial attack.

The cook frowned. "It's all black is what it looks like."

"Oh yes, of course," Mary replied, not understanding.

"The black cat." Elise finally clarified.

"I knew that," Mary snapped. "The cat the Missus calls Magdalene? No, I've not seen it. Did anyone look in the cesspit?"

"Oh god, Mary. Why would that be the first thing you think of?" Thomas asked. He blew vigorously through the stem of his pipe and ash flew out of the bowl.

"Cats is always falling into cesspits. The night-men would tell you that."

"I'm not in the habit of talking to night-men," Thomas said.

"Neither am I," Mary replied quickly, blushing. Thomas raised a brow and continued scraping out his pipe.

Mrs. Postlethwaite picked up a potato. "Why don't you take Elise and go down to have a look?"

Elise glanced quickly at the larder door and shuddered. The idea of visiting the cesspit one more time than was necessary was unthinkable. The smell had nearly knocked her over the day before and she'd refused to move any closer than four steps down into the cellar so that Mary had to dump the bucket by herself. "I already looked," she said quickly. "The cat wasn't there."

"It seems to me that you just got here through that door," Thomas pointed with the stem of his pipe to the dining hall. "And the door down to the cellar is right over there," Thomas swung the pipe towards the larder. "So how did you pass me by without my noticing?"

Mrs. Postlethwaite clucked her tongue. "The only thing worse than a bad liar is a good one."

"You're always seeing the sunny side of things, Mrs. Postlethwaite," Thomas said smiling. "It's good to know our little Queen could be worse."

"Come on then." Mary grabbed Elise's arm and pulled her along. "You can hold the lamp and I'll do the looking." Coming from Mary, the offer was fairly generous. Reluctantly, Elise followed the young woman through the larder door.

The stairway down to the cellar seemed to be cut out of the earth and part of an even older London history. Elise's fleeting feeling that the 19th Century was somewhat modern by comparison was oddly comforting. Each step she took was slick, and her toes reflexively gripped the edges of the cold stone. The dampness of the descent added to the unpleasantness of the air, making it seem as though it was the foul odor that curled the hair around her face and filmed her skin, not the humidity.

At the bottom of the stairs, Elise lifted the lamp and peered into the gloom. The walls of the cave-like room glistened wet and dripped over patches of green mold. Stacked against the walls were empty wooden crates, a few ceramic basins waiting to be repaired, and other kitchen tools too old or broken to be useful. The cellar stretched back under the dining hall, and Elise saw two casks, one tapped. "Shouldn't those be upstairs?" Elise asked.

"The porter finishes its fermentation down here, so we only take up a couple casks at a time, depending on how much we think we can sell. Whatever doesn't sell fast enough, the brewery takes back. We're low now. Mr. MacEwan's boxing match brought in a right crowd." Mary walked directly to the center of the room and flipped open the hatch to the cesspit while Elise set the lamp on the bottom step and lifted her apron to cover her face and nose. The apron didn't help. "Come closer," Mary complained. "I can't see inside."

Picking the lamp back up, Elise approached while loudly sucking air into her mouth through the muslin of her apron. She stood behind Mary, balanced awkwardly as she lowered the lamp into the hole in the floor while at the same time leaning as far backwards as she could away from the smell. The lamp suddenly flared hot with an odd swooshing sound and both women jumped away with surprised shrieks.

"There's no way a cat got in there," Elise stated with certitude. "Why the hell would a cat be suicidal? There's no such thing as a suicidal cat." Elise backed quickly towards the stairs. "That hatch is always closed isn't it? Do you really think a cat would lift the hatch and jump down in? That's just stupid. That's the stupidest thing I've ever heard."

"You never know with cats," Mary insisted. "The night men always find cats in cesspits."

"Because that's where people throw their dead cats, Stupid."

"Just bring that lamp closer."

"No way."

"For God's sakes, don't be such a ninny." Mary came and snatched the lamp out of Elise's hand and returned to the side of the pit. As she leaned forward over the hole with the lamp, the methane gas again reacted dangerously with the flame, causing Mary to do a quick shuffle backwards with the lamp swinging from her extended arm. "No cats," she sung out with a falsely casual voice.

"Are you absolutely sure? Maybe you should climb down in and take a good long look."

Mary left the lamp on the dirt floor to dart forward and flip the hatch shut. "Definitely no cats down there," she said decisively.

Elise picked up her skirts and started running up the stairs. While nursing had prepared her for human mud in general, nothing had prepared her for the nastiness of the cesspit. Mary, equally as eager to exit the basement, squawked in protest when Elise nearly slammed the larder door shut on her nose in her haste to lock out the fumes. The smell of boiling turnips was a relief.

Back in the kitchen, Thomas caught Mary by the arm and Elise by her skirt and pulled them near while glancing furtively over his shoulder at Mrs. Ferrington, who seemed to be having a heated discussion with Mrs. Postlethwaite over the cost of mutton. "Did you find it?" he asked. When Elise shook her head he warned in a hiss, "You two will not breathe a word to the Missus about her damn cat. You let me handle this." He locked eyes fiercely with each of them in turn to ensure understanding, then left.

The Beer Engine

There's a meditative aspect to sweeping that Elise had never appreciated before. The repetitive motion of swinging the long broom handle forward, the scratching swish of the straw bristles over the wooden floorboards, the pile of dust that gathers, then scatters, then gathers again larger as it moves, inch by inch, further down the hallway—it all felt strangely satisfying in a way that vacuuming never had. Elise had left all the doors to the tenant's rooms open so that she'd be able to see the dust motes dance in each square of light that fell onto the hallway floor. Five bedrooms, five windows, five squares of light mesmerized her as she waved her broom back and forth through the sunbeams. Sweeping was universal. Sweeping happened in all times. She could sweep forever.

Hours later, Elise trudged back downstairs with her reeking bucket filled with night soil sloshing at her side. Her ribcage ached slightly from the activity, but she hadn't exactly exerted herself, and was healing quickly. The kitchen was empty when she ambled in. She was surprised to see the great wooden table had been pushed against the wall and the doors to the larder and the courtyard were standing wide open. There were voices coming in from the open door, and the sound of a short, rolling snort followed by jangling chains. Curious, Elise absently set the bucket on the kitchen table and went to poke her head outside.

Two sets of horses' eyes flashed at her, wide and dilated, proof, to Elise, of their unpredictable nature. The matched beasts looked like two gleaming chestnut grand pianos turned on their sides. They were goliaths with sharp hooves and grinding teeth. The hot steam they blew from their nostrils did nothing to quell Elise's fear. She wanted to call out a warning to Thomas and Richard who were standing dangerously close to the beasts while talking animatedly to a third man. Mrs. Postlethwaite, three paces behind the wagon, wisely stood behind an overturned crate with the kitchen broom clutched tight in her fist. The cook's show of courage gave Elise the strength to step outside to see what was going on.

"You can't say a thing is inconvenient without first having tried it, Tom," Richard said. He held what looked like plumbing in his hand and was waving it towards his barman.

"I can, and I did. It's worse than inconvenient. It means I'll have to drill a hole in my bar," Thomas said testily. "Besides, what do we need a beer engine for? We've got Johnny." Elise was surprised to see that the little cut he had on his cheek that morning had become a green and yellow smear around his eye. He could have used an ice pack after all. Or a cold slab of meat, she thought, correcting herself.

"Potboys are a thing of the past, Mr. MacEwan " the stranger said. "There's changes going to be happening, you watch. They'll soon be sending all boys to school. Even them that's got no head for it. It's progress, and you can't stop it."

"There's nothing wrong with being a potboy," Thomas said. "You get your learning from the talk around the tables; learn respect for your community. Now, if you're speaking about making boys climb down chimneys to sweep, I'll listen to your talk of progress, but Johnny's got him a good job. He's treated well at the Quiet Woman. We don't need the pump machines."

"Now don't get agitated," Richard slapped Thomas on the back. "We can find other work for Johnny. He won't have to leave. There'll always be plenty of pitchers to deliver to the neighbors. Besides, we don't really have a choice in this, do we Mr. Kneeley?"

"The brewery is making all their licensed houses switch to the beer engines. You'll not be the only ones. Look on it as an investment in better service. Your customers will flock to have their beer poured through these engines."

"An investment? So I suppose you'll be expecting Mr. Ferrington to buy these contraptions out right?" Thomas shook his head and spat onto the cobbles. "And what if we don't?"

"We won't sell our beer to them that don't use the beer engines. It's as simple as that. You'll have to find another brewery."

"Another brewery? There is no other that'll deliver here. You're putting us over a barrel," Thomas shouted.

Richard clapped a steadying hand onto Thomas's shoulder. "Come, Tom. The Brewery is only looking out for our best interest. They need us as much as we need them. I think the beer engine is a grand change for modernity."

"It's true," Mr. Kneeley said. "The brewery values the partnership so much that it is willing to offer a loan which many other public houses have chosen to take. There's no shame in it."

Thomas was quick to shrug off Richard's hand. "Can't you see? The brewery will only trouble itself on our behalf when it's finding more ways for us to fall deeper into their service. The more public houses the brewery can tie to itself through debt, the more the brewery guarantees its own success. They don't care two farts about any of us. They're merely looking to secure sales." Thomas grabbed and tugged his forelock in frustration. "Don't you see what's happening here, Richard?" His arms flew out in exasperation. Elise caught her breath as the closest horse shook its mane and took two nervous steps sideways.

Mr. Kneeley drew himself up defensively and cut off any reply from Richard. "I beg your pardon. Our porter is the most popular in London. The Quiet Woman would be at great disadvantage without the opportunity to work with us."

"Your beer sells the most because most of London's public houses are mortgaged to your brewery. I wasn't born yesterday. The lads aren't buying it because it tastes good. They're buying it because it's the only one offered. Tell me: what are your men cutting the porter with this time?"

Richard slapped his hand against Thomas's chest and slipped between the two men just as Mr. Kneeley started rolling his sleeves. "Mrs. P. is watching," Richard hissed.

Next to Elise, Mrs. Postlethwaite turned red at having been caught eavesdropping. She stepped out from behind the crate where she'd been hiding and quickly shoved the broom into Elise's hands. "There you are," she said to Elise, fooling no one. "What are you standing around gawking for, Queen? Don't you have work to do?" The obvious embarrassment of the cook dispelled the tension between the men, and they turned to silently watch as Mrs. Postlethwaite stepped briskly across the yard, shooing Elise in front of her.

"What's going on out there?" Elise turned to ask as she stepped back into the kitchen.

"What's it to you?" came the sharp, knee-jerk response.

"It's payday," Mary trilled happily as she entered from the dining hall door, unaware of the argument that had nearly come to blows. "Every payday is always the same, it's always a scramble to get everything ready for all the lads as just got their wages." She could barely hide her excitement. "Everyone is in high spirits on payday."

"I can't believe that drayman picked today of all days to come with his delivery." grumbled Mrs. Postlethwaite. She suddenly straightened up in shock. "Which one of you left the night soil bucket on my kitchen table?" she bellowed.

Just then, Richard came through rolling a cask into the kitchen and Elise realized why the table had been pushed aside. Mr. Kneeley followed close behind. "How far south does your cellar go? Maybe it would be easier to drill up through that shelving in the back there," he pointed to the back of the bar as they walked through the kitchen. Thomas's glower, as he came through with a barrel hoisted onto his shoulder, silenced any further discussion on the matter.

Elise grabbed the bucket from off the table and followed the men down into the cellar where they stacked the casks. On her way back upstairs, Richard ascended behind her and took her elbow to help her up the slippery steps while Thomas growled that she was too slow. In the kitchen, she pretended to be hard at work sweeping the hearth and moving coals around the open range in order to stay and watch the men continue to store the beer. The way they moved in tandem was so routine that it made any words between them unnecessary. Up until that moment, Elise couldn't think of two men less alike - sunshine and shadow – but with both of them side by side with their shirt collars unbuttoned, it became easier to see how they reflected each other with similar gestures of face and body, forged from similar work. Thomas was shorter than Richard, and broader across the chest, but he carried his mass without the tightness of movement that usually accompanies great strength. Richard was smoother in his actions with a seemingly practiced grace. Between the two of them, it didn't take long for eight casks to be stacked in the cellar and four stacked behind the bar to be tapped for the evening's crowd.

After the kitchen table had been moved back to its place in the center of the floor, Thomas stormed out through the front door, avoiding the drayman. He left the component parts of two beer engines on top of the bar, waiting to be assembled.

It was nearing evening when Thomas finally returned for dinner. Elise and Mary had already started in on their apple pudding and looked up in surprise when he entered the kitchen. Thomas's left eye was now nearly swollen shut and fully bloomed in shades of purple and yellow, but his right eye was clear and twinkling with satisfaction. He was holding a purring, black furball cradled in one strong arm as he stood in the archway to the dining hall, waiting, it seemed, for the heralds to announce his return.

"A cat? Why on earth would you be bringing me another cat, Thomas?"

Thomas looked at Mrs. Postlethwaite with surprise. "It's Magdalene, Mrs. P. I've found her."

Walking over to examine the cat more closely, the cook lifted the tail out of Thomas's elbow. "That's a tomcat," she said flatly.

"Aye, so it is, but the Missus never knows the difference."

"Sure she does. Mrs. Ferrington would never go naming a tomcat Magdalene."

Thomas pointed to another cat sitting on his stool near the fireplace. "That one there, I'll be damned if the Missus don't call it Jacob. And it being a bloody calico girl." The black cat under Thomas's arm had stopped purring. It too had noticed the other cats in the room and started hissing. When its wiggling didn't loosen Thomas' grip on him, it impaled him in the arm with both paws. Thomas howled and dropped the cat. It slid down the length of his arms with both paws still attached to his flesh.

"Best not be kicking the Missus's cats, Mr. MacEwan," called out Mary.

Gritting his teeth, Thomas replaced his boot back on the ground just shy of swinging his foot. The black cat started slinking around under the kitchen table, staying safely in the shadows. In response, Jacob stood up on the stool and arched her back, hissing. Another cat in the opposite corner of the kitchen gave a low warning growl from deep in its chest. "Damn these cats," Thomas yelled. A second black cat jumped onto the table. "Where'd that one come from?" he demanded surprised.

"I found the poor wee thing stuck under an empty crate. It was yowling at the world when you was yowling at the drayman. It's a girl." Mrs. Postlethwaite looked at it coldly. "I'm sure it's Magdalene. She just got a crate knocked on top of her somehow," she said.

"There can't bloody well be two black cats in London named Magdalene," Thomas snarled, wiping blood from his arm and examining the long claw marks that ran from his elbow to his wrist.

"Mine's a girl," reiterated Mrs. Postlethwaite.

"So is Jacob," Thomas retorted. "It makes no difference. The one I brought is Magdalene. The one you brought ain't."

"We should choose one and put the other out," Mary suggested. "The Missus will never know the difference, you'll see."

Elise had moved to the corner of the table with her steaming bowl of pudding to better observe the scene without having to become a part of the action. She counted six cats in the kitchen, two on top of the shelves, the calico on Thomas's stool, one feisty grey in the opposite corner that was crouched low with its ears flattened back. Then there was the hissing black cat on top of the kitchen table, and a second blackie underneath. She'd already learned all their names: Jacob, Jericho, Jonah, Sarah, and Magdalene. "She'll know," she said.

Thomas shook his head and cursed under his breath. "The Queen is right. We have to choose wisely."

"The one under the table seems nice enough," Mary said. "Lets keep that one. It's not hissing and carrying on like the others. Look at the way it slinks around under there. Must be smarter than the rest."

"That's the one I brought." Thomas's smile returned with his small victory. He stepped forward to scoop up the cat Mrs. Postlethwaite had found to toss it out, but as he reached for it, it lunged onto the frightened blackie under the table. "Damn it!" roared Thomas.

"I've heard enough of your tongue," Mrs. Postlethwaite snapped as she shuffled backwards to avoid the spitting ball of fur and claws that rolled under her feet. Picking up the broom she started swatting at the cats, trying to corral the violence. "Elise, she barked. Get the door."

Elise jumped to obey and the bowl of pudding clattered dangerously on the table. She threw the courtyard door wide open just in time for Mrs. Postlethwaite to bustle past, her broom whirring and thwacking as black fur floated up in the air in great clumps. Thomas went behind as her rear guard, squatting low and waving both arms while shouting, "Shoo! Shoo, kitty." Once both cats were safely outside, the door was slammed behind them.

"There," Mrs. Postlethwaite said, breathless and smiling. "We'll let the two Magdelenes sort it out on their own, shall we? Whichever one comes back tomorrow is the one we'll keep.

"Hurry and finish your pudding," the cook instructed. "Here come the lads." Elise swung around to look across the dining hall, past the tenants who were already seated and finishing their meals, to the front door. The first five factory men stomped in with loud voices and filthy haggard faces. It was clear by the way they took their seats and slapped at the tables that their intentions were to be served beer and food immediately, in that order.

It didn't take long for the Quiet Woman to fill with men as they ambled in, exhausted by a week's worth of work and a full purse to show for it. Thomas placed Elise on a stool behind him and narrated the scene while he poured pints for all those who leaned against the bar. Conversation was lively, and Elise tried to follow and catalogue the information in the off chance anyone would want her opinion. There was, apparently, a war going on, a king named George, a prime minister, and a stifling upper class system. Elise noted that although the names were different from the American politicians she was familiar with, the outrage against policies was the same. Walk into any bar in Tucson in the early evening and you'd hear the same joy in shared oppression. The only real difference she saw between the watering holes she went to there and the Quiet Woman was that everyone here seemed to have grown up together.

"That one there, the skinny man with the big mouth who's standing up at table two," Thomas pointed out to her. "That's Long Urie. He'll be the first to be snoring on the floor. Best to let me know when that happens and I'll put him out so you don't have to clean up his vomit."

A customer at the bar who overheard guffawed as Thomas refilled his mug. "Urie is always the first to get cut and fuddled."

Mary swooped by the bar holding up four fingers, and Thomas grabbed four mugs from under the bar and started pouring. "Near the hearth you'll always find Boffet and Jones. They've been coming here since before I was born. You just leave them two be and let Mary serve them. That goes for anyone who sits at the bar. You just leave them be, and anyone sitting in any of the armchairs for that matter. The armchair folk are the Old Mr. Ferrington's customers. They've earned those chairs and they've taken to Mary." Thomas paused to place the mugs of beer on Mary's tray and drop the coins she handed him into an open lockbox. "That one over there, the one sitting down with the red waistcoat and the weasel eyes, you watch out for him. Keep your farthings safe when you bend over his lap."

"I'm not bending over anyone's lap." Elise said sharply.

Thomas laughed. "You'll be bending over everyone's lap tonight. You won't even know you're doing it. Just mind what I say and watch yourself." He set a mug in front of Elise and clinked it with his own. "That one's for you. Drink up. I need you to be happy and smiling tonight for a change." He took a carefully tiny sip, his eyes narrowed at Elise. "Don't think that I'm the one wanting you serving tonight. If it was up to me you'd be sitting up in your room, well away from making any trouble. But Richard thinks you can be helpful. Don't make him a fool."

Elise huffed defiantly before taking a sullen gulp of her beer. She turned her head to look at Richard, who was standing in the middle of the dining room scraping a lively jig from his fiddle while stomping his foot.

"Watch Mrs. Ferrington there," Thomas pointed out Richard's mother who was greeting customers. Her smile was wide and practiced. "See how she always takes the money before she leaves the plates? Always remember: customers must open their purses first." Elise only half listened as she watched Mrs. Ferrington perform a curtsy while simultaneously primping her graying updo. Elise was impressed by the woman's grace. The men at the table were eating it up, doffing hats and scraping back chairs to stand in her presence. Apparently Richard came by his charm honestly.

Thomas gripped Elise's arm to get her attention back. "If anyone tells you they've a tab in my book, collect the name and start counting drinks. At the end of the night I'll be checking your apron pockets and whatever other hidden pockets you have, so don't think to keep nothing from the Quiet Woman that's hers.

"Now, finish it," Thomas ordered nodding at Elise's mug. Elise hesitated for one moment, then grinned and slammed back her porter. After she wiped her mouth with the back of her hand, she was handed a full pitcher. "Table three looks thirsty," Thomas dismissed.

With her heart in her mouth, braced by the cool drink, Elise approached the table already crowded with men shoveling down Mrs. Postlethwaite's stew. Six pence, tuppence, a farthing, she had no idea what the currency even looked like until the first man pressed coins into her palm like they were feeding a vending machine. Elise looked at the money and felt a jolt. She was working again, and here was the reward in little metal discs. The intense sense of relief she felt surprised her. Things happened with money – maybe she could buy her way forward in time. Despite Thomas's warning that all proceeds went straight to the pub, tears pricked her eyes. She quickly batted them back with her long lashes and slipped the money into her apron pocket, setting to work with renewed energy and a flirtatious smile.

When all the chairs at the tables were taken, men began to stand around the tables, shoulder to shoulder, leaning in and yelling to be heard. Elise was constantly being flagged down as she tried to keep up with the demands for more of everything. In the kitchen, it didn't take long for Mrs. Postlethwaite's ladle to scrape the bottom of the cast iron pot and when it did, the kitchen closed and the cook went home. Mrs. Ferrington, with Johnny's help, cleared all the dinner plates, then said goodnight and retreated back to her quarters. Richard, quickly noticing the absence of his mother, allowed himself to be pulled into a card game.

When a loud cheer erupted, Elise looked up from pouring ale in time to see Mary leap across the room with both her hands helping her corset support her prodigious flesh. Then, grinning, she turned and leaped in another direction. Mugs bounced on tables when she landed and her breasts nearly spilled out of her dress as she pushed them up and clapped them together. "Got it this time," she yelled, and pulled a coin out from the depths of her cleavage. Another cheer went up and three men stood to toss more coins into the air.

The man Elise was pouring for shook her elbow to get her attention. "Can you do that too?"

His friend scoffed, "You always were a man with special tastes, Jonas, but for me, I'll not toss coins for those useless targets," he said, pointing at Elise's breasts. "Mary," he yelled, "over here lass." He waved to Mary who was bending forward and jiggling to release her cache while coins rained down around her.

"No one cares if they're large, as long as they're soft, warm, and round," Jonas said. "Give us a show. Are your tits round?" Elise jumped forward, surprised by a pinch. "Her arse is round enough," he hooted.

Elise watched her arm move through the air like someone else was carrying it, knowing full well it was her own rage that caused it to move. When she slammed the pitcher against Jonas's chest, he was knocked backwards and onto the floor—a satisfying surprise. She stood over him and tried to hide her smile as the table roared with laughter. Her smile disappeared when she caught a glimpse of Jonas's expression as he pulled himself off the floor, dripping in beer. "Better run, Lass," a man called out. She didn't need the encouragement. She was already mid-stride when she was caught in another man's arms.

"If it isn't the Little Lunatic," Mr. Tilsdale said happily, giving her a squeeze. "Sweet one minute, devilish the next. Don't know what Mr. MacEwan was thinking—you'll never do as a barmaid."

Elise threw her arms over her head and poured out of his grasp like water. When she bent at the knees and shimmied into a squat, she felt a draft of air rush over the top of her head. Instead of hitting her, the chair that Jonas swung crashed into Mr. Tilsdale, one of the chair legs hitting his neck with a sickening crunch. He clutched his neck with wide, frightened eyes, unable to even gasp. Everyone else who saw the attack caught their breath for him in horror and sympathy. Hats were placed over hearts as Mr. Tilsdale staggered from one man to the next, pleading for help with his eyes as he struggled to breathe. Everyone stopped to watch the slow death of a comrade.

"I didn't mean it," Jonas whimpered, breaking the spell. He was still holding the broken chair in his hands. "I swear I didn't mean it."

Elise pushed him impatiently out of the way and cleared the table with a sweep of her arm. "Get him up here," she ordered, not talking to anyone specifically, but expecting everyone to jump. Thomas was suddenly at her side. "I need your knife," she demanded.

"What knife?"

"Give it to me now." It made sense that he would keep a knife hidden in his belt. She knew it was there. She only had minutes to work and wasn't going to argue. The knife was handed over. Pointing to four different men, she gave the order to pin Mr. Tillsdale down on the table. He struggled for a few seconds and then turned blue and fainted.

Working quickly, she untied the man's silk scarf, tilted back his head, and palpated his neck to find the space between his Adam's apple and cricoid bone. She used the adrenaline that surged through her body to concentrate on the task at hand, took a steadying breath and brought the knife towards his neck.

The men around the table roared in unison and the knife was suddenly wrenched away. When the crowd lifted her from the ground to be pulled away, she grabbed Mr. Tilsdale's torso and held on. "I'm saving his life," she screamed over and over, desperately.

She felt, more than saw, Thomas working to push back the men. When her feet touched the floor again, she held out her hand and the knife was replaced into her palm. Quickly, before anyone could object again, she made a one-inch incision and inserted her finger to open the hole. She felt people behind her push forward to watch. She needed a drinking straw, or a pen. She looked up at Thomas. "I need the stem off your pipe."

"My pipe? You can't have my pipe." Thomas looked alarmed.

No, of course not, that was too much to ask. "Get me the beer engine."

It took Thomas seconds to return from the bar. Elise selected the shortest of the black pipes and carefully inserted it into Mr. Tilsdale's neck. Then she blew rhythmically into his lungs to revive him. She stopped and waited. Everyone waited with her, all eyes on Mr. Tilsdale's chest. No one moved. No one spoke. Except Jonas who whispered, "I didn't mean it." He was immediately shushed.

A whistle was heard through the narrow opening of the pipe and when Mr. Tilsdale's chest rose on its own, the Quiet Woman erupted with cheers. Elise slumped in relief and felt a supporting arm slip around her waist. She looked up to see Richard staring at her with his mouth open. "Where did you learn to do that?" he asked incredulously.

She leaned heavily against his side, her ribcage throbbing with a dull ache. With the immediate danger gone, she could see the black pipe sticking out of her patient's neck in a new light. The weight of it caused it to fall distractingly to the left. "That pipe—is it lead?" she asked.

"Yes, of course. Lead pipe."

"Fantastic." Elise made a mental note to never drink beer that wasn't tapped directly from the cask.

ABDUCTED AGAIN

There's nothing like hearing the pitiful whistle of a man sucking air through a pipe in his neck to kill the mood. After a small group of customers helped Elise carry Mr. Tilsdale upstairs to his room, the tone of the Quiet Woman became dour. Even Richard, normally so optimistic, seemed only able to play a long list of soul-wrenching melodies in minor keys until Thomas exasperatedly knocked his fiddle off his shoulder. It didn't help. Most of the men in the dining hall quietly finished up their drinks and left early. With the excitement over, Elise had regained enough presence of mind to roll a torn piece of the front page from *The Morning Advertiser* into a short straw to replace the lead pipe. Then she sat at Mr. Tilsdale's bedside until he'd fallen asleep and stayed there until she was sure his airway was well established.

When she finally went to bed, sleep didn't come easily. She was fairly certain she was staring at the ceiling because her eyes were open and she was lying on her back, but she couldn't be positive. Was there really a ceiling up there in the pitch darkness? Having been unexpectedly thrown back in time, it was now hard to trust that even the most trivial details would conform to expectations of reality. Reality was gone. Expectations were useless.

She knew she had shocked everyone who had seen her save Mr. Tilsdale's life. People weren't supposed to jab others in the neck with knives and then insert objects into the holes. It just wasn't done. The entire scene played over and over in her head as she stared into the blackness above her. There would be more to come, she thought, more distrust, more questions, more sidelong glances. She should have let Mr. Tilsdale choke to death. That was what they'd expected.

When Elise's eyelids slowly drooped, she wasn't surprised to see the black-haired woman behind her lids. This time, the distance between them was too far to feel threatening. The thread between them was gossamer—sticky, but weak. There was a ceiling above her, Elise thought. There had to be.

As she fell asleep, she watched the black-haired woman gather up the thread and roll it into a ball as though she was preparing to knit it into something. As the ball grew, so did her arms, and she seemed to gain a second elbow. Two more arms emerged from her ribcage and she fell onto her stomach as her legs arched out behind her. She brought the ball of goo up to her mandibles and began rolling the entire thing forward towards Elise, scuttling like a beetle as she approached with the sands of the desert slipping under her feet.

Elise pressed her lips together as tight as she could, but for some reason she was frozen to the bed and the beetle pushed its prize straight into her mouth. She felt the goo-ball being rolled down along her tongue, and then the black-haired woman's six legs scratched against the narrow wall of her epiglottis and her glottis before moving into her esophagus. Suddenly unfrozen, Elise sat up and clutched at her neck and dug at her skin to get the bug out, but there was no access hole. There was only one other way to remove the beetle. She swallowed hard and it slipped further down. The sphincter to her stomach opened and then shut quickly.

Elise waited. Her stomach gurgled. Then she felt the beetle again—duodenum, small intestine, large intestine, rectum. She got up and sat on the pot and waited some more, then stood and looked behind her. An emerald scarab, set in glittering gold sat in the bottom of the bowl. It held the moon above its head with the soft wings of time eternal.

The dream was completely erased from Elise's memory the next morning by a pounding headache and a vague sense of urgency which she fought by forcing herself to sit an extra five minutes on the side of the bed to pick boiled beef from her teeth. Knowing she'd only gotten a few hours of sleep, she longed to pull the covers back over her head, but Mary's bed was already empty, and she'd never hear the end of it if she went back to sleep. She rubbed her temples and ignored the nagging feeling that she was forgetting something important; that something, which belonged to her, was missing. She was missing lots of things, she rationalized—her apartment, her car, her cell phone, her job…her life.

She had already tied all the complicated laces of her corset around her chest before she realized someone had left her a basin on the little rickety table with a steaming pitcher of water and a wedge of soap. Elise sighed heavily and began untying her stays. Mary must have decided to reward her, she decided. The plump barmaid was strangely fond of Mr. Tilsdale. The water felt good, but standing naked in the cold room with nothing but a sponge to keep her warm was not the equivalent of a hot shower. And a bottle of shampoo would have been nice.

Once dressed, her first stop was to Mr. Tilsdale's room. He was having difficulty drawing a breath through the paper trach tube that had gotten soggy overnight, so Elise found Mr. Tilsdale's broken pipe, cleaned out as much tar as she could from inside the walls of the stem, and gently inserted it into the incision in his neck. The rattling sound that came through the pipe as he breathed was disconcerting, but his smiled thanks reassured Elise that he would be fine for the next few hours.

After she tied a scarf around his neck to secure the breathing tube, she brushed a spot off his shoulder. She looked closer when the spot scratched the back of her hand. A splinter from the broken chair, as thick as a pencil, had lodged itself in the muscle of his shoulder. She felt her stomach sink. "I'm sorry," she whispered to Mr. Tilsdale. She was sorry for having missed seeing the splinter the night before. If she had done a full assessment he wouldn't have spent the last eight hours with a piece of chair sticking out of his skin. A good nurse always does a full assessment of her patients, she thought, berating herself.

There was enough of the splinter sticking out that she was easily able to take it between her thumb and forefinger, but as she drew it out, it seemed to keep coming. It had to be at least three inches long, assuming the tip hadn't broken off somewhere in his flesh. She pressed the edge of the sheet over the tiny wound, but there wasn't much bleeding. "All better now?" she asked. Mr. Tilsdale closed his eyes. It looked like he would have sighed, if he could have. Elise drew the blankets up and tucked him in before heading downstairs to start her day.

A whispered conversation between Mary and Mrs. Postlethwaite stopped quite suddenly as Elise entered the hot kitchen, and they stared with wide eyes as she moved to find the broom. She was starving, but her desire to get out of the kitchen and away from the puzzled looks was keener. "Don't bother with breakfast. I'm not hungry," she said to no one in particular. She grabbed the broom and an apple from the larder and returned upstairs.

An hour later, wedged into a dark corner of the hallway and propped upright by her broom, she gasped awake from her precariously balanced nap and started furiously sweeping. Thomas's heavy footsteps descended from his room in the garret, turned on the landing to the second floor, and approached her from the darkness to lean against the wall and watch her work with his arms crossed. Already he had his pipe clenched in his teeth, but it was cold and unlit, and he chewed the stem of it thoughtfully as he stood there with his inscrutable, scarred expression. It annoyed Elise. "What?" she asked sharply.

His response was lightning fast, and entirely unexpected. He grabbed her by the elbow and led her forcefully down the stairs. Elise had only enough time and presence of mind to struggle to keep her feet on the wooden steps before she was dragged across the black and white tiles of the entrance hall and into the dining room. As they neared the kitchen, she broke free, but he caught her back up and tucked her into a vise-like grip under his strong arms. He called out over her protestations into the kitchen, "Can you stay a bit later tonight, Mrs. P? I'm off to visit Mrs. Southill."

"Mrs. Southill? Must you see that Sheela na-gig?" Mrs. Postlethwaite asked sharply as she poked her head out of the kitchen. Then she gasped when she saw the furious struggle. "What on earth? You're taking the Queen with you then?"

Thomas yelped his assent as Elise's heel came down hard on his toe. He threw her over his shoulder like a cask of beer and headed towards the front door.

"Let her borrow Mary's coat or she'll catch her death. She's always shivering and huddling near the fire, that one. And you," she pointed at Elise, who glared at her as she hung upside down. "You leave that broom here," Mrs. Postlethwaite ordered. Surprised that she was still holding onto the broomstick, Elise dropped it quickly causing Thomas to stumble over it as it hit his ankles. He recovered enough to grab Mary's coat from the hook.

"Shut the bloody…" The familiar shout from the old man in the armchair was cut short as Thomas slammed the front door behind them.

"Let go of me," yelled Elise as she attempted to shimmy down the back of her captor. Thomas obeyed by pushing her off his shoulder as though brushing off dandruff and she landed hard. The jolt to her ribs created fireworks of pain behind her eyes and she drew her knees up to her chest in an instinctual effort to protect herself. The cobble stones smelled like old piss and vomit.

 Thomas squatted down next to her and turned her chin so that she would look at him. "How did you know to do what you did last night?" His other hand raked his hair back from his forehead.

Elise jerked her chin out of his grip. "I dated an EMT," she said, knowing her words would be meaningless. She rolled over onto her knees to crawl away, but Thomas grabbed her ankle. Elise kicked, but he managed to drag her close so that her face was in range of his fists and he cocked his arm back. She ducked her head under her arms, flinching from his glare.

"You never make any sense when you speak," he said grabbing her shoulders. "And you always slink away like a dog whenever anyone asks you to explain. Mrs. P told me not to push, but I'll not allow it any longer. I'll have your story. How can you know what to do when a man is choking, but not know anything else of use? Why do you speak so strangely?"

"I forgot," Elise said defiantly.

"I suppose you forgot where you put the money you collected from the lads as well? I told you I'd be checking every pocket, didn't I?"

"I swear! I forgot!" Elise flinched from Thomas. His threat felt very real. "It's all on the windowsill upstairs. I forgot all about it until I went to bed."

Thomas glared at her and then sat back on his heels. "You'll be coming with me to see Mrs. Southill now. Will you walk or must I carry you?"

"Who's Mrs. Southill?" asked Elise, still frightened.

"Never you mind." He stood and offered his hand to help her up off the ground, then raised it to his head to tug at his black hair when Elise got up on her own. "Here, at least take this," he said, handing her Mary's coat. "We've got a ways to walk."

"But I don't have any shoes. My feet are cold." Elise lifted the skirt of her dress to show her bare feet and garner his pity.

"Why haven't you washed that off your toes yet?"

Elise looked down, surprised at his reaction. "My toenail polish? It doesn't wash off. It's lacquered on."

"Why would you do that? It makes your toes look bloody."

"No it doesn't. It's pretty," Elise insisted, feeling defensive. The pedicure was growing out and pale moons were beginning to show near her cuticles. "Can you get me shoes?" she asked, shrugging into the coat. It actually felt warmer outside than in. The sun strove to melt away the reeking mist that hovered in the narrow lane.

"Not now, if that's what you're asking. The Missus is looking out for your shoes." The way Thomas said it didn't give Elise much hope for acquiring footwear any time soon. He offered his elbow, which surprised her since he had made it clear he was kidnapping her, and she took it despite distrusting his motives. When she touched his arm, the sincerity of his smile jarred her.

They stepped off the curb and into the street, and although he seemed to try to circumnavigate the larger of the manure piles for her sake, it didn't take long for Elise to feel something ooze between her toes despite her best hopscotch moves. "Oh god," she whined piteously as she lifted her skirt and tried to scrape the bottom of her foot against a cobblestone.

"Don't start, Queen. We don't have all day." The smile was gone. He pinned her wrist painfully between his arm and ribcage to better drag her along, hiding her captivity in a gentleman's posture.

They stayed mostly to the winding back lanes, where the buildings, stacked tightly side by side, made rough walls that locked her in to a dank maze of streets. Children seemed to explode from hidden corners, running and dodging each other as though they had somewhere important to be. Mothers, some looking no more than children themselves while others looked ancient with drawn faces and worry lines, stood in open doorways. Each woman held something as they looked out: brooms, babies, mixing bowls. When Elise and Thomas approached their doorways, many would quickly retreat. Elise felt her loneliness grow heavier with every slammed door. A woman nodded at Thomas, clearly recognizing him. It made Elise wonder. She hadn't given much thought about what his life was like outside the Quiet Woman, but now a part of her was afraid she was about to find out why all the women in the street disappeared as Thomas approached.

Elise shivered under Mary's large coat. The sound of crying babies was incessant background noise. Wet, hacking coughs from behind closed windows were intermittent. The black smoke from hundreds of chimneys hung low and choking, burning Elise's eyes so that she saw London through a watery haze. A buggy turned the corner and approached. She sniffed and wiped her nose on the sleeve of Mary's coat and despite her misgivings about her companion, moved closer to his side to avoid the horse. "How much farther?" she asked. She was pretty sure they'd already gone over a mile.

He slowed his pace and looked down at her, his eyes vivid blue under his black brows. "Are you tiring? We'll continue east, then down. We can rest a bit if you wish."

"I'm okay." She didn't know what "east, then down," meant, but it felt good to walk, even though her heels were bruising where they hit the cobblestones. She had shifted her gait to land more on the balls of her feet, helping her keep up with Thomas's long stride. The exertion wasn't the issue—the light jog was clearing her head even as her sinuses filled. It was the growing distance from the Quiet Woman that made her nervous. There was something about the pub that felt comforting, and seeing the way the rest of London lived made her realize how lucky she was. She could have landed in front of a tenement row. "Tell me again how you found me?" she asked.

Thomas walked to a corner that seemed to mark the border between London city squalor, and London suburban squalor. Beyond the corner, the homes began to spread apart from each other, becoming slightly wider with roofs that clung low to the ground. He stopped and leaned against the wall to study her. "You were full of fever when we found you, to be sure. I believe you wouldn't remember that night."

"I told you I don't."

Thomas nodded and pulled his pipe out of a pocket to fiddle with it as he thought, then tucked it away again. "It was late, near closing time. Not many were in that night, just the few regular lads. Richard found you in the Lane, half froze to death and covered in mud. He had me carry you into the kitchen to warm you by the fire and went in back to get his mother. Mrs. P. hadn't gone home yet, and she took one look at you and started bathing you right there on the hearth."

"Mrs. P.?" That was hard for Elise to believe.

"Aye, and it was a good thing too, because Mrs. Ferrington didn't take to you right away. You could hear she and Richard having words in their quarters." Thomas smiled at the memory. "So it was Mrs. P. who bathed you on the hearth and as soon as that water touched your pelt, you started kicking and screaming like a wild heathen."

"Wait. You watched while I was bathed?"

"I held you down."

Elise stared at Thomas while she processed his words and the look he gave in return was steady and unapologetic. She'd been strong-armed by the bar's Strong Arm. It was nothing personal, a job completed, like stripping an unconscious patient with an abdominal wound. She decided she didn't feel violated, and tried to shake it off. "Why did Richard take me in?" There were plenty of others he could have rescued, all those children they passed earlier, for instance.

Thomas was silent for a long while before he finally replied, as though weighing his words. "The Ferringtons have always cared for strays."

"Stray cats, I get, but stray people?"

"Aye, I was a stray when I was younger than Johnny and it was Old Mr. Ferrington as took me in and gave me a bed in the garret. I'd do the same for Johnny, but we're full up right now. Though when it's horrible cold out he'll sleep in the kitchen." His voice was soft and grumbled low, like his songs.

"But I'm not a kid to be adopted. I'm a grown woman."

Thomas snorted and looked her up and down. "So you say." Then he took her arm to get her attention. "Maybe you don't remember that night, but I'll wager you remember the day before that, and the day before that, and all the days back until the day you were born. You've a story to tell and you're not telling it. Maybe that's why Richard took you in. Maybe he likes a mystery."

He stepped in close, and Elise recognized the gesture as his act of intimidation, only this time she didn't feel intimidated. His eyes were sparking and his scar pulled the one side of his mouth up. Richard wasn't the one who liked mysteries. "Where are you dragging me to again?" she asked, changing the subject.

"To see Mrs. Southill. Not long now." They began to walk again and he tucked her hand under his elbow, this time protectively. They passed a group of men who were sharing a bottle around campfire in the middle of the street. One of them tipped his hat to Elise in a gesture that looked more obscene than polite, but he kept his thoughts to himself after assessing Thomas. In the not so far off distance as the houses fell back away from the road, she saw fields in shades of green and yellow. "We're headed to those trees," Thomas said as he pointed to a dark clump of forested land that Elise hadn't yet noticed. The trees seemed to lean forward over a bordering road as though reaching towards the thin sunlight in fear of what might be deep within their dark midst. There were no homes near the forest's shadow.

Thomas turned down a dirt road that cut across a rocky field no bigger than a schoolyard park where shabby rows of greenery attempted to grow. Turnips? Carrots? Elise had no idea. Directly on the other side of the field, shanty houses began to crowd together again as though huddling for protection against the imposing arms of nature. While it was true that the road was much wider, and the air cleaner, Elise still didn't feel any safer. A person could hide as easily behind a bush as behind a brick wall. And Thomas was just one man.

It was nearly a half hour before they finally arrived at the edge of forest grove. Thomas pointed out a silver line in the distance to show how the road continued past the wooded area to trace the shore of the Thames. Then, he turned to duck under a narrow opening between two arching oaks that was the entrance to a pale and winding trail. Without speaking, he gestured for Elise to walk in front of him but hooked his fingers under her apron strings to pull her back when she got more than three steps ahead. Soon afterwards he seemed to think better of the arrangement and stepped in front to lead the way while glancing suspiciously into the dark branches of the forest above. "Keep up," Thomas ordered unnecessarily, curling his arm around her waist. Branches stretched across the trail and anchored threads of spider webs on either side. Thomas waved at the air in front of them to knock the webs away and lifted the arching branches safely over their heads.

As the light grew ever more dim, the hair on the back of Elise's neck rose. "I don't like this place," she hissed. They had taken so many left and right turns at various forks that she was completely lost.

"Most don't like this forest, but that's what makes it safe. Only idiots and lost souls come here. Not much further." Thomas tucked her more protectively against his side, but she didn't feel very reassured. She wondered which he was—idiot or lost soul.

Finally, when Elise was sure they were completely lost, the trail ended at another archway of oak trees that framed a small clearing filled with sunshine. "We're here," Thomas said with a relieved sigh as he dropped his arm and let her go. Elise took another step forward, and gasped in surprise when he pulled her back sharply by her apron strings. "Watch out!"

Alarmed, Elise stumbled backwards a few steps and ducked. Then looked to see where Thomas was pointing. A low ring of stones outlined the entire clearing, and she had nearly stepped over them. She straightened up in relief. "Seriously? That's all? You scared me."

"Never cross a stone ring without being invited," he looked fiercely at her. "Never."

Elise cocked her head in confusion at her companion, but stood safely on the outside of the stones while Thomas called into the clearing. A door opened to a little shack that she hadn't noticed before and a woman as brown and as crinkled as a dead leaf poked her head out. "Is that you Thomas MacEwan?" she called back. She stepped out of the door and as Elise's eyes adjusted to the glare of the sun, she saw how the building leaned up against four straight trees, forming the four corners to the home. Smoke puffed from a chimney in the back.

"I'll introduce you," Thomas whispered at Elise, "but you must promise to be polite, no matter what she says to you." He seemed very anxious and was tugging at his hair again. "In fact," he continued, "it's best you don't say anything at all. Just let her talk."

"What's wrong with her?"

"Nothing is wrong with her! Why would you ask that?" he snapped as the little woman beckoned them to enter into her space.

The clearing was not very large, but held a few notable items that she'd missed when standing at the edge of the forest. A trestle table and bench, for instance, were set close to a fire pit that held glowing embers. A small pile of bones—mostly small animal skulls - was arranged near a large boulder. Firewood was stacked neatly within steps of a chopping block and the axe leaned against a nearby sapling.

As they walked past the table, Elise picked up the top stone from a small pile of stones that all had a single hole, probably drilled by the constant tapping of a dripping water source. "Put that down," whispered Thomas. "Don't touch anything." Elise put the stone up to her eye and peered at him through the hole. He seemed to glow, bouncing rays of sun from his black hair, making her smile. She swung her head around the clearing with the stone still at her eye and noticed that a low bush near the house was decorated with a garland of colorful scraps of cloth tied around the branches. Thomas snatched the stone from her hand and replaced it on the pile. The garland returned to being trash randomly caught in the underbrush.

"Tommy-boy," the woman said as she approached. "What have you brought me today?"

Thomas pulled from his waist pocket a bulging pouch and offered it to Mrs. Southill, who took it, loosened the strings and pulled out a pinch of tobacco to sniff and roll between her finger and thumb. "I meant that one," she growled, pointing to Elise with her pinky, her crooked index finger being occupied with assessing the quality of the moist leaf.

"Might I introduce to you Miss Elise Duboys," Thomas said, presenting Elise to the old lady. "Elise, this is Mrs. Southill."

"Dubois," corrected Elise.

"Pleased to meet you Miss Elsie," said Mrs. Southill. She curtsied like a little girl. "Would you like to see what's in my hands?" She put the tobacco down on the table and held her empty cupped hands together. She peered inside before offering her hands to Elise.

Thomas abruptly interrupted with a nervous cough. "I brought Elise to be your new apprentice."

Both women turned to stare at the barman with open mouths.

USELESS

"**S**tay here?" Elise asked shocked. "You've got to be kidding me." She looked over Thomas's shoulder to survey her new home and shuddered. Mrs. Southill's shack reminded her of a compost heap. The walls and roof were shedding grass clippings, decaying leaves, lumpy oatmeal, and maybe a dead frog or two, and the entire architectural nightmare leaned dangerously to one side. In contrast to the decomposing house, the stone ring around the clearing might as well have been prison-bars. The forest leaned oppressively over the ring to reinforce her captivity.

"I thought you could use some help," Thomas explained to Mrs. Southill. He refused to look at Elise as she jogged a circle around the small ring like a caged animal.

"Why in god's name would you think that?" the old lady exclaimed.

"Aren't you always saying how you could do with some help?"

"That was almost fifteen years ago, and it was you I wanted. I gladly raised you after your mother died in childbirth. I would have kept you as my own too, but you ran off and got caught by that dreadful kitchen witch Postlethwaite. I don't want anyone now. Certainly not that one." The woman pointed to Elise, who had returned to Thomas's side to grip his arm possessively. "She's too old."

"She's not old," Thomas protested. "She still has all her teeth." He unwound Elise's fingers from his arm, still without looking at her.

"Look at those soft hands," Mrs. Southill countered. "She hasn't done a day's work in her life."

"Her back is plenty strong and her legs and arms are like iron. I've never seen the like on a woman. She knocked a man off his chair last night with just one blow. She'd be a perfect apprentice."

"Then she'll eat too much. I'll starve myself trying to keep her fed." Mrs. Southill reached out to give Elise's upper arm a squeeze, testing the strength of her bicep.

Elise slapped away the woman's probing hand and the gesture slightly restored her dwindling sense of control. "This is a joke, right?" she shook her head and looked up at Thomas in amazement. "Apprentice? What the hell do you think I'd learn from this old bat that I don't already know? How to piss in the woods maybe? How to spit-shine a bone collection?"

Mrs. Southill pale grey eyes pierced through Elise and she seemed to grow six inches. Elise took a couple hasty steps backwards then noticed Thomas had his hand raised and sidestepped him too. His hand continued back to rake his hair in frustration. "All you've done since the day you arrived is stir up trouble," he said. "Another fight like the one last night and the Ferringtons will lose their publican's license. I can't have it anymore."

"You're the one with the perpetual black eye, not me," Elise said defensively.

"You're no good as a barmaid. You're a slothful chambermaid. Mrs. P. is not herself when you're in her kitchen. You can't even stoke a fire without burning your fingers. You're of no use to anyone."

"Then what are you bringing her to me for?" snapped Mrs. Southill. "Just leave her in the streets. I'm sure it wouldn't be long before someone finds something she can do."

"Because," Thomas said excitedly, "last night she saved Mr. Tilsdale's life, and it was an amazing thing. I've never seen anyone do what she did. She's got the gift, I'm sure of it. I believe you can further her skills, hone them."

"This one has skills?" Mrs. Southill scoffed. "I doubt that very much." Her eyes narrowed as she studied Elise. "She does have a strangeness about her," she allowed. "Where did you say she's from?"

Thomas straightened up hopefully at the old woman's interest. "No one knows where she's from. She says she doesn't remember, but if you had seen her last night, you wouldn't doubt that she's a healer through and through. When Mr. Tilsdale went and got his air pipe crushed last night, Elise stepped in without hesitation."

"Mr. Tilsdale's air pipe got crushed?" the old woman looked shocked. "Poor Mr. Tilsdale."

"No, no. He's quite alright," Thomas assured. He got in the way of a chair is all. It was Jonas who swung it at Elise's head. But Elise cut a hole in his neck and inserted the beer engine. Saved his life, she did."

The story seemed to puzzle Mrs. Southill. "Why was Jonas swinging a chair at Elsie? Was there a brawl? Mr. Tilsdale should know better than to be brawling. He's too old for those kinds of activities. Did she really pour beer in his neck-hole?"

"No, not beer. A pipe. Mr. Tilsdale just got in the way of a chair is all," Thomas replied.

There was a long silence while Mrs. Southill seemed to ponder the various threads of the story. "And how is it that she's a healer?"

Thomas threw up his hands in exasperation. "She saved his bloody life, I said!"

"I'm not deaf. I heard you the first time," the old woman snapped. "Stop pulling at your hair, you'll make yourself bald."

When they had finished glaring at each other, both Thomas and the old woman turned towards Elise. She watched their eyes take her in, starting from her toenails that peeked out from under her gown, to her dirty auburn hair that fell around her shoulders. "She's no healer," the old woman finally scoffed. "Mr. Tilsdale is a dead man. Mark my words, this one's merely turned an easy death into a difficult one."

"You might want to get your crystal ball recalibrated," Elise snarled, "because he's breathing right now, no thanks to anyone but me. Everyone else was standing around with their hats in their hands looking stupid."

"Didn't you put a bloody hole in his neck and insert a filthy pipe? Isn't that what Tommy just said? How do you think Mr. Tilsdale will survive that?" Mrs. Southill shook her head sadly, "Poor Mr. Tilsdale. He's a dead man."

It hadn't escaped Elise that infection was a likely possibility; she was just surprised that the old woman thought so too. She was pretty sure Pasteur hadn't yet figured out his germ theory. For that matter, he probably wasn't even born. The idea that saving a life was worse than letting the life go was hard to swallow, so instead of arguing further how she'd done a great thing by saving the Poor Mr. Tilsdale, she kept her mouth shut and ignored Mrs. Southill's raised eyebrow and sly knowing smile.

Suddenly, Mrs. Southill clapped her hands together in front of Elise's nose as though trapping a fly. "Tell me what I'm holding in my hands," she said with a grin. "Look!"

The change in demeanor and subject startled Elise and she leaned forward to peer inside. She noted how the cracks and wrinkles on the woman's cupped hands had become accidental tattoos, inked with black dirt. "There's nothing in there," Elise said.

"You are correct. Isn't that strange?"

Elise clenched her jaw. "You can't leave me here," she hissed at Thomas. Her eyes rolled towards the sky, and then towards old woman with meaning.

"Mother Southill, please. Elise can ease your nights with companionship. You shouldn't be here all alone."

"If I were to cup my hands in water," Mrs. Southill continued, ignoring Thomas's entreaty, "I would catch the water. But when I cup my hands in sunlight," she clapped at the air again and then opened her palms. "Nothing. There's nothing."

Elise stared at the woman. Was she serious? She glanced at Thomas and saw that he was looking at the woman's empty hands with a puzzled expression. "But light is not a thing to be caught," he countered, finally taking the bait. "You can't catch light."

"And why not? I can trap light inside my house at night when I light a candle and draw the curtains. In the day the curtains keep the light outside. So why can't I catch it out of the air?"

"It's energy," Elise said, clarifying nothing. Her legs suddenly felt tired. She wondered if she should just go take a seat at the trestle table by herself, since apparently no one was going to offer her any of whatever they'd been smoking.

"Yes, that is what I thought too. Energy," Mrs. Southill said, gazing softly into the sky. "I was thinking there might be a way to use it, if only I could somehow trap it." She tapped her chin with her crooked index finger, thinking. Then her grey eyes lit up as though suddenly remembering something. "There's something else I'd like to show you,

Thomas. I just have to find it," and she turned to head towards her house.

"Please don't trouble yourself." Thomas called after her receding back. Then he glowered at Elise.

"Let me go back to the pub with you," Elise pleaded, ignoring his look. "I'll be the best waitress. I'll let all the customers grab my ass."

"Don't be silly. There is much Mother Southill can teach you—you'll be glad for the opportunity. Besides, after last night, no one will want you to serve them. You'll just be in Mary's way."

"That's not true. They love me."

"You?" Thomas laughed in disbelief. "You're far too scrawny. You put everyone off their porter just to look at you."

"If I'm so ugly, why did you take me in?" Elise demanded as her green eyes filled with tears.

Thomas looked uncomfortable and shifted his weight from one foot to the other. "You're not ugly," he mumbled at the ground.

"Yes, why?" Mrs. Southill returned, holding a large wooden bowl. She smiled strangely at Thomas, her eyes twinkling. "Why did you take in a girl with such an unfortunate nose? Where did you say she comes from?" Elise touched her nose in surprise.

"I've no idea. As far as I know, she was born from the mud in front of the Quiet Woman," Thomas answered dryly. "She hasn't seen fit to tell me where she's from, or anyone else, for that matter. Richard was the one that wanted to keep her."

"I'm sure you had nothing to do with it," Mrs. Southill said sarcastically. "When did you find her?"

"It's been nearly a fortnight."

Mrs. Southill seemed to take the information very seriously. She nodded slowly. "She does have an interesting manner of speech," the old lady mused.

"One can hardly understand her, most times. We might as well be speaking two different languages."

"What did you say your family name was, dear?" Mrs. Southill asked.

"Dubois."

"French," Mrs. Southill noted. They both looked at Elise, silently, pointedly.

"You've got a problem with that?"

"Of course not. We're merely making the observation that you're a frog," Mrs. Southill said with a smile. Elise was becoming more and more convinced that the old woman's silliness was an act to cover a shrewd intelligence.

"I found what I was looking for," Mrs. Southill said, abruptly changing the subject again as she placed the wooden bowl she'd been holding on the table. Elise breathed out in relief. In the bowl were many small bundles of tied fabric and a single rock, which the old woman removed and placed on the table in front of Thomas. "Take a look at this." The bottom of the rock was rough granite but quartz crystal formations jutted from the grey stone, one of which was faceted and almost two inches long. Thomas smiled at the rainbows that danced against the wood of the table, passing his hand over them so that the colors moved up his arm. "I knew this would make you happy, Tommy-Boy," Mrs. Southill said chuckling. "See? I thought at first the stone was reflecting the light to transform it into rainbows, but it's not. It's capturing the light and it becomes transformed when it's released. It captures the light," she repeated.

"Are you sure?" asked Thomas with a look of awe on his face.

"Of course I'm not sure. Who can be sure of anything? What a thing to ask. But think: if a mere rock can capture and transform light, maybe I can find a way to do it myself."

"The crystal is splitting white light into its component parts," Elise said absently, thinking of the rainbows she used to see in Tucson in the early morning when the sun would angle through her bedroom window.

"Component parts?" Mrs. Southill asked. Both she and Thomas turned to her and stared. "I've heard that before. I just wonder how a woman who comes from mud knows such a thing."

Elise shrugged. She'd opened her mouth again when she should have kept it shut. "Someone else said that? Really? I was just thinking out loud. Because, you know, wouldn't it be cool to split things inside rocks?"

"Cool? Do you mean interesting? Yes, it would be very interesting to split things inside rocks. In this example, you can see that splitting light has an very interesting effect indeed," Mrs. Southill said, smiling at Thomas who was still playing with the rainbow that bounced happily on his forearm. She paused as though weighing her next words. "What if you could split other intangible things into parts, like time? You can't catch time in your hands either, can you?" There was a tiny hesitation in Mrs. Southill's questioning, just long enough for her wrinkled eyes to bore deep into Elise.

"There are no parts to time," Elise said quickly. "It just marches forward in one long line."

"Do you think so?"

"What do you know about it?" Elise asked with suspicion. Her heart was pounding and she was sure the old bat could hear it race.

"Oh, nothing really, only that it's 'cool' to think about." Mrs. Southill paused over the unfamiliar usage of the new word before she pushed the rock out of the way to end the conversation. She pulled the bowl in front of her. "If you're going to be cutting into people's necks, Miss Elsie, you might as well do it correctly. Sit down, I've something to show you too." She pointed to the bench on the opposite side of the table and placed about thirty different pouches in front of Elise. "But you'll have to remember everything I say. Can you do that?"

"Probably not," Elise replied, looking dubiously at all the bundles.

"You'll remember. Otherwise you'll be no better than a farmer who heals their beasts by shoving peeled onions inside them where onions don't belong." She spread out a rough tablecloth. "Oh, you wouldn't believe the things I've seen," she said when she noted Elise's horrified look. "Onions, turnips, garlic in the nostrils, anything that can go into a stew can also go into the holes in a person's body." She nodded to the bowl. "Go on. Take a pinch from one of those bundles and put it here on this cloth. I'll tell you what it is, and how to use it. Every tradesman has his tools. These will be yours, if you want them."

"So you'll take her on, then." Thomas looked relieved.

"I told you already I've no use for a neophyte, but I'll do you the favor of giving her a pinch of knowledge before you take her back to the Quiet Woman. She may be no use to me, but I'll wager she'll be of use to you very soon. You'll see. You're going to need her more than me."

"I can't take her back. There's no money to pay her. And she's horrible, besides."

Elise looked up at the barman in surprise. She'd assumed the custom was to pay chambermaids in room and board and thought of the coins on the windowsill. She felt less inclined to give herself a cut off the top now that she knew the pub was struggling.

"You can take her back, and you will." Mrs. Southill fixed Thomas with a glare until he sighed in resignation, pulled his pipe out of his pocket, and wandered off.

"Here, look at this," Mrs. Southill turned back to Elise and unrolled a bundle. "What do you see?"

"Dried leaves," she responded distractedly. A waft of tobacco smoke passed over Elise. She turned to look at Thomas, who was standing next to the fire ring, lighting his pipe with a glowing twig.

"What color? What shape? What do they smell like, taste like, feel like?"

Elise turned back to the table and tried to concentrate on the task at hand, her teeth grinding with the effort. She lifted the cord that tied the leaves together at the stems and gently brought the delicate packet to her nose. They smelled like fall weather in the Catalina mountains, and tobacco. Another puff of smoke passed between them. The muscle in her jaw twitched as her teeth clenched. "They're brown like dead leaves, dry like dead leaves, and I'm not going to taste them."

Mrs. Southill's eyes bored through Elise's head. "Thomas!" the old woman finally shouted without breaking eye contact. "Come here." When he arrived, she snatched the pipe out of his hands and gave it to Elise. "I wouldn't be sneering over the power of those dead brown leaves when you can't think for yearning to breathe them. Here's one dead brown leaf as already taken hold of you, I can tell." She pressed the pipe into Elise's hands. "Smoke it then and be done with it so we can continue."

Muscles Elise never knew she had been clenching relaxed as the smoke passed into her mouth and filled every neural receptor in her brain. She closed her eyes as tears welled and a sigh broke from her lips.

"For god's sake," Thomas laughed. "Just look at her. She's obscene." He snatched the pipe back, took another toke, and then passed it to Mrs. Southill. The pipe made its way back to Elise, and they let her hold on to it as long as she needed to. The sky seemed very blue as she watched the smoke rise.

The next hours were spent going through every cloth bundle Mrs. Southill had placed in the bowl while Thomas busied himself by chopping and stacking wood. Elise was told to feel and smell everything she unwrapped, some she even allowed herself to be convinced to taste. As she did so, Mrs. Southill described the process to prepare each herb. The inhalants Elise learned quickly because there were only two. The easiest to distinguish was not an herb at all, but a small vial of mercury. It was the ones that were to be steeped or made into poultices that were the most difficult - the ones with multiple possibilities for preparations and multifunctional healing properties. To aid Elise's memory, Mrs. Southill used personal examples of her own patients to illustrate the use of each herb. Case studies were familiar to Elise, and she listened carefully and tried soak it all in.

It was an enormous relief to finally return to a topic she loved without fear. For the first time since her fall through time, Elise felt truly engaged and respected. Finally, she wasn't being handed just a broom or a potato to peel, she was being handed power. Mrs. Southill was a patient and insistent instructor, and drilled her until she could recite the dosages, methods for preparation, route taken, body system affected, ailments healed, possible side effects, combinations, and names of the contents of each pouch in the wooden bowl. It took some hours, but when Mrs. Southill was finally satisfied that her pupil had learned her lessons, she leaned back from the table with a pleased smile. "There," she said. "A pinch of salt and no more—that's what I've given you. Now that you've a taste for it, I've no doubt you'll be wanting salt with every meal."

"Thank you," Elise said, and was surprised at how genuinely she felt it.

"Thank me?" Mrs. Southill laughed. "I've done you no favor. Why do you think I live out here in the middle of the forest? I've no neighbors out here, there's no one but the trees. Out there," she waved her hand towards the path to town, "everyone is ill, everyone is dying. And now you'll be killing yourself to save them all, even if their life isn't decent or kind. In my younger days I ran all over London, day or night. Now, if someone has need of me, they'd better be well enough to come find me. I may live in the forest, but I get a full night's sleep every night." She shook her head and made a rude gesture in the direction of London. "Out there you can't walk two feet without someone coughing and lobbing their sputum on you. Everyone is bleeding or oozing from somewheres on their body. The second they figure out you've got the skills to help, they'll be knocking down your door. Thank me? You'll see. You'll be cursing me by the year's end and hoping to find your own forest clearing."

Mrs. Southill pulled two drawstrings from around the hem of the tablecloth and it gathered around all the herb bundles to become a sturdy sack. To Elise's delight, the old woman handed her the sack before sitting back with a satisfied smile. "Now. You must be hungry."

For a woman well versed in plant and herb lore, Mrs. Southill cooked a remarkably bland stew of indistinguishable meat and limp vegetables. It looked like it had been simmering for days with new water added to the pot with each serving taken out, maybe simmering a full week even, given the pale broth. Regardless, Thomas slurped it down quickly, swiping the liquid from his chin, and even asked for seconds.

Elise was delighted by her gift. Mrs. Southill added a couple needles, silk thread for sewing wounds, muslin for bandages and other items she thought might be needed. When it was time to leave, Thomas offered to help her carry the sack, but she slung it over her own shoulder. It represented for her the one thing from her past that she had been able to keep with her in this new time: her pride in her career. She carried the bag like a trophy.

Back at the trailhead on the edge of the clearing, Elise hesitated, looking as far down the dark path as she could for any strange movements. Evening was setting in, and the forest had gotten darker and more sinister. Even Thomas looked wary.

Suddenly, she felt something slam between her shoulder blades and she stumbled forward into the oppressive green. "Find your courage, girl," Mrs. Southill shouted. The woman had given her as hard a shove as her small, withered body would allow, causing Elise to trip over the stone ring and stumble onto the trail. She chuckled at the surprised and angry curse that erupted from Elise. "That's right," Mrs. Southill said. "Let your anger rise. You've a long journey ahead of you, and you'll need all your courage. Anger simmers in the cauldron nicely with courage, and I hope I've given you enough of both. I hope you don't come back here, Miss Elsie Duboyse. You don't belong here. Find your way home."

"How?" Elise demanded. "How do I go home?"

Mrs. Southill chuckled. "Catch the light, dear. Hold it in your fist and follow the trail back to the road."

June XX, 1808
London, England

> *My Dear Mlle. L.,*
> *I have found your golem. After spending most of a long day with her, I recommend that you forgo your attempt to recapture this quarry. I found her to be profoundly self-centered, unknowledgeable about the things that matter most, and of very little use in any general manner.*
>
> *Since you mentioned in your letter that you were not sure what type of creature you brought forth, allow me to describe her so that you may know her better. Although at the outset of our meeting*

she seemed frail, she is actually powerfully muscular and given to fits of violence. She has already sliced one man's neck, although I was told it was to save his life. I suspect that you have brought her forth from another place, perhaps even another time as she utilized strange idioms in her speech and had an unnatural accent.

I must confess I did consent to give her a smattering of the Knowledge, only a few hours worth, and flatter myself to think that she took to the lessons quite readily. The young man who brought her to me is under the impression that she has considerable talents, so it may be that your continued interest in her is not completely unfounded. Should you still feel it necessary to the Cause to return her to Paris, she currently resides at the Quiet Woman public house in London where she is using her considerable untapped talents to empty chamber pots. Please use caution in retrieving her as the young man I mentioned earlier can be dangerous when provoked.

I did wonder, however, how a golem who calls herself Elise Dubois, a perfectly French name, pulled forth by someone with your esteemed lineage, ended up in a public house in London? I delight in the idea that one day we may be able to meet in person so that I might hear the tale directly from your lips. I am sure that the story will be fascinating.

The last Sabbath was such a pleasant night. If only all our encounters on the astral plane could be so peaceful. I'm afraid it will be a long time before we experience that again as you and I well know the near future will be tumultuous and the war between our nations devastating.

I hope that this letter, so hastily written, will put your mind at ease regarding this matter.

Yours, etc., etc.,

Mrs. U. Southill

La Prison des Fleurs

The clicking of Adelaide's knitting needles divided time as precisely as a metronome. Since her arrival at the prison, she had knit a single stocking, one mitten, and a neckerchief, and had unraveled the yarn in between each creation with deliberate care. The act of organizing a single strand of yarn into a useful object was just as interesting to her as the act of pulling the yarn away from itself to wind into a ball, ready to be knit again. While Adelaide's ball waxed and waned, she spoke her meditation to herself quietly, feeling the words form on her lips, "things that are made, can be unmade." In the dim evening light, she concentrated on the feel of the yarn as it slid through her fingers, her muscle memory taking the place of her vision. She could knit twenty stitches for every one of the pathetic wails that came from a neighboring cell directly across the hall where little Odile was incarcerated. It took five wails for her to reach the end of the row.

"Why? Why? Why?" cried Odile—her own metronomic meditation. The sound resonated in Adelaide's mind like the distant mewling of a baby and she resolutely ignored her instinctual pull to protect. Instead of pursing her lips in a consoling shush, she ground her teeth. She was no mother. She knew no lullabies. And Odile was not a baby.

Earlier that afternoon when they were allowed to take in the sun in the great courtyard of the prison, Odile had wheeled in delighted circles at the relative freedom and joined a game of cache-cache with the other caged kittens while Adelaide had watched under the shade of the old chestnut tree near the wall. In the warm summer sun the young women's oppression temporarily lifted. But now that night had descended, Odile was simple enough to allow her mind to whirl around a single word.

"Why?" sobbed Odile as she railed against the betrayal that caused her to be locked away within the cold, stone walls of the prison. Was she not obedient enough, productive enough, quiet, pretty, smart? Her self-flagellation went on and on into the night. In their dark cells, young women's restless thoughts took torturous paths, bruising against the walls of their cages. The prisoners bit their nails and pulled out their hair one single strand at a time as they agonized over why they were being punished by those that had professed to care for them.

Adelaide wondered if she would have locked away her own children, had she ever conceived. She wasn't sure she'd have been a good mother, her own being but a dim memory. Mostly she remembered how she would be pulled away from her mother's weak embrace whenever the hacking coughs began. She had died when Adelaide was still a small child. Her father had died a few months later, after remarrying. He left his new wife with Adelaide and her sister and brother, but when her stepmother remarried, a new baby quickly became the center of attention and Adelaide and her siblings were sent away. Her brother went to apprentice at the iron foundry where he made cannons for the navy, and Adelaide and her sister went to stay with the Sisters in Alençon. They had been lucky. They could have been sent to prison, like Odile.

Ironically, the prison was a converted convent and brought back memories of a childhood filled with the promise of life everlasting. The wailing paralleled the melismatic tones of the Hours, chanted in unison. The Church had given her the groundwork to not just endure, but to utilize routine and rigidity for maintaining her self-possession and independent thought.

The sound of retching came from Odile's cell. She'd made herself sick again. It made Adelaide think of the first time she had vomited in the hallway of the convent's boarding school. It had been after eating a large serving of *hachis parmentier* for lunch, and then devouring her little sister's portion as well, who had a weak appetite and would helplessly push food around on her plate. To punish Adelaide's gluttony, the Sisters told her she wouldn't be given dinner that night, and sent her straight to bed where she luxuriated in the peace and quiet of the empty barracks. She stole a romance novel from out of a classmate's trunk and read it cover to cover that day while everyone else sat in class. Her classmate had kept the contraband literature for over a month without sharing it, so Adelaide felt justified in helping herself.

The second time she'd vomited was a few months later. The schoolgirls had taken a trip into the country where they picked baskets full of strawberries. The smells that floated through the hallways as the sisters boiled the strawberries for canning was excruciating, so while everyone was memorizing their psalms, Adelaide slipped away to the abbey's great kitchen pantry and ate three *boîtes de confiture au fraises* and an entire *pain de campagne*. For that misadventure, she was made to clean her own mess before being banished to the barracks. That time Adelaide had waited in bed with the covers pulled up to her nose for fifteen minutes, but when no one came to check on her, she slipped away to spend the early evening exploring all of the most shadowed corners of the convent until the Abbess herself, old Sister Marie-Therese, found her trying to pick the lock to an inner garden reserved for the Bishop. The Abbess dragged her by her ear all the way back to Sister Ignatia's classroom and made her stand on a stool in front of all her classmates for the last twenty minutes of class. The students jeered and laughed, ignoring Sister Ignatia's calls to order until one sharp bark from the Abbess got all their heads bowed over their books again.

Two weeks later, a doctor was called for a third bout of vomiting, this time most likely due to the night vapors that had come through a window accidentally left open. The doctor had forced her to swallow a spoon full of thick black syrup that tasted of anise which caused a fourth bout that brought up beef and onion bouillon onto his shiny buckled shoes. The back of her left hand had been slapped for that transgression, but happily the doctor insisted she be quarantined from the other fourth year students. She was given a tiny room all to herself with a window that overlooked the same garden she'd tried to break into two weeks earlier. Despite feeling woozy, she still had the presence of mind to pilfer the bottle of *sirop d'anise* out of the doctor's bag when his attention had been focused on returning his shoes, which Sister Marthe had brought back, clean and polished, to his feet.

One week after she'd recovered, Adelaide sat in the classroom with the little brown bottle tucked deep inside her sleeve, still thinking of the garden. She'd been carrying the bottle with her for the last four days, having taken three days to get the courage to pull it out from under her mattress where she'd hidden it. She was glad she now had the fail-safe tucked into her sleeve as Sister Ignatia droned on at the front of the room, head bowed over her text, reading aloud the steps involved in the set up of an algebraic equation.

She was seated second from the back in a modest sized classroom with twenty other girls all lined up behind little desks in four rows of five. It was moving on towards the afternoon and Adelaide had been in the same position for what seemed like an eternity. Despite her ample supply of cushioning flesh, her bottom hurt from sitting so long on the wooden seat. She stretched her feet forward, threading them between the legs of the chair in front of her, and accidentally bumped the ankles of the girl sitting in front of her. Adelaide caught her breath when Roxane's body straightened from the contact. Keeping her upper body still to hide her movements from the professor, Roxane slammed the heels of her wooden *sabots* into Adelaide's shins in retribution. The loud scrape of clogs against the floorboards that was Adelaide's reflexive retreat from pain caused Sister Ignatia to look up sharply, but since nothing looked amiss, she bowed her head and returned to reciting algebra.

Adelaide put her hand up her sleeve and fingered the smooth glass of the bottle as she considered how she would force its entire vile contents down Roxane's gullet. Her shins throbbed where she'd been kicked as she stared at the part on the back of Roxane's head where her blonde hair was sectioned into two braids. The part was irritatingly straight and white. Adelaide glared at it until another classmate in the next row two desks forward rose to her feet. The movement alerted her to the end of the lecture and the beginning of the drills. Adelaide knew she wouldn't bear the pain of being called upon to do the same—

listening to the girl stumble through the task of solving for x was painful enough. She retrieved the bottle and sunk down in her chair to hide behind Roxane.

As the standing girl coughed and stuttered through her mental gymnastics, a pall had fallen over the classroom. Everyone sat in dread of sharing the mumbling girl's fate, and stared at her as she shifted her weight nervously from one foot to the other. It was the perfect moment, Adelaide decided. She raised the bottle to her lips to drink only as much as would be effective, leaving the rest for future pedagogical emergencies.

"Adelaide, what are you doing?" Sister Ignatia asked sharply. It never took her long to notice when students were marching out of step. "Why are you slouching? Sit up."

Roxane took the opportunity to turn around and give Adelaide a withering smile. Adelaide locked eyes with Roxane while under her desk she hastily corked her bottle.

"You might as well stand," Sister Ignatia said with a sigh. She picked up her ruler, more with resignation than with threatening intent. "Tell me how you would solve the following: The market vendor's basket has potatoes, parsnips, and turnips. He tells you there are forty-nine tubers in all and that there are as many parsnips as there are potatoes, and only three turnips. Solve for the class how many of each tuber is in the vendor's basket."

Adelaide pushed her chair back to stand uneasily in the aisle. She cleared her throat. "We know that there are three turnips," she began nervously. Roxane's snicker was barely a breath, designed to be inaudible to all but Adelaide.

"Yes, that is what I said. Three turnips. How did you manage to stain your frock again?" Sister Ignatia clicked her tongue in consternation at the large brown spot on Adelaide's skirt that had been invisible up until that moment. Everyone turned to look, but Adelaide merely folded her hands over the stain. The gravy from the *pot au feu* they'd eaten that afternoon had been too watery and had spilled from her spoon. Goose bumps stood up along her arms and sweat rolled down her sides. The sweet poison in her little brown bottle was working, and the thought of the *pot au feu* made her mouth water.

"*Et alors?*" asked Sister Ignatia impatiently. "The class is waiting. Shall I repeat the question?"

Adelaide opened her mouth to respond, but saliva unpleasantly flooded over her tongue. She slurped it all to the back of her mouth and tried to swallow, creating exactly the trigger she needed. Adelaide took two lurching steps forwards and then turned to open her mouth over Roxane. Happily, the watery gravy was easier to expel than if it had been cooked to the correct consistency. Beef chunks and bits of orange carrots spilled into Roxane's lap and perfumed her with musk of boiled fat, hints of stomach acid, and a finishing bouquet of anise.

It didn't take long for the classroom to fill with black robed Sisters who set to calming the screaming Roxane. Three took to caring for Adelaide, whose strange smile was proof of her delicate state. Within minutes Adelaide was led to the little room with the pretty window and sweetly tucked under the bedcovers by Sister Marthe. The three Sisters gently stroked her hair and kissed her brow before they left to tend to steaming cauldrons of laundry.

As attentive as the Sisters had been in ensuring her comfort, it still wasn't Adelaide's intention to stay in bed. It was the first day she could remember without rain, and in Normandy it was a crime to not take advantage of every precious warm afternoon. She kneeled at the foot of the bed and threw open the window. Bracing herself with her arms on either side of the window frame, she leaned her body out to take a deep breath of the fresh air but withdrew quickly when she glanced down. The ground looked very far from her third floor vantage, and the vertigo it induced made her stomach clench, a side effect she wasn't prepared for so soon after her earlier gastric adventure. She moved back to the head of the bed where she could see only a slice of the garden wall and the sky above, enough to entice her to return to the window.

The scent of the blooming hedge roses and the possibility of adventure made her breath catch. She welcomed the feeling of blood pounding through her veins, this time experiencing it not as vertigo, as she leaned from the window, but as liberty. The garden was bursting with a promise that made her feel fully alive. *Thank you God,* she remembered to pray, looking up to the sky. *Thank you for saving me from algebra and for punishing Roxane by letting me puke in her lap.* The warmth of the sun on her face felt like a blessing and gave her the courage to lean out again. Faced with so much evidence of the goodness of her guardian angels, Adelaide knew nothing bad would happen.

A thick branch growing in a gentle slope from the trunk of an oak passed under the window ledge. It wouldn't be too difficult to slide from the ledge and straddle the branch, then shimmy down to the trunk and make her way into the garden. The branch seemed sturdy enough, but the distance from the window to the branch was the span of about two of her hand lengths, and seeing the ground far below made her ears buzz with fear. Then there was the length she'd have to crawl down the branch before reaching the stability of the knotty trunk. For at least three meters there would be no stabilizing place to put her hands on either side of her body. She took a deep breath. God was on her side today, she reminded herself.

She left her wooden *sabots* on the floor and stood up on the bed, then took up the skirt of her gown and draped it over one arm. After maneuvering herself to hug the window frame, she peeked down towards the branch and tentatively poked her bare foot out into the air. Just as her big toe touched the rough surface of the branch, she heard the garden gate creak open. Adelaide gasped and pulled her leg back inside and pressed herself against the wall.

Voices rose from below and drifted into her little bedroom like a stray breeze. At first the words were hard to distinguish. A feminine voice rose liltingly in a question. A masculine voice responded with the chesty breathiness of gentle reassurance. The feminine voice circled confusedly like a fluttering butterfly. The masculine voice lengthened and slowed in a more determined response. Eventually, curiosity got the better of Adelaide and she bellied down the length of the bed to poke her nose out the window. Far below, seated on a bench under the hedge roses, a man dressed all in black was talking to a young woman.

Le Père Gregoire, Adelaide breathed. She crossed herself, knowing the priest was practically on par with Jesus himself. Even old Abbess Sister Marie-Thérèse couldn't keep the fire from her eyes when she spoke of him. He was an older man, at least forty, Adelaide guessed, looking at the white that was beginning thread through his thick dark hair. He was speaking earnestly and holding to his chest the pale hand of a plainly dressed woman who had her back to Adelaide. There was an intimacy about them that made her want to sink deeper into the blankets of the bed. She strained to hear what they were saying.

"She knows. I'm sure she knows," said Bishop Gregoire. "She saw us last Sunday."

"So we must not see each other any longer. It cannot be."

"We must, I cannot live without you," the Bishop said. He pulled the woman's hands to his mouth and bent over them and she sighed and put her head on his shoulder. "I've taken care of it," he continued.

"Soon it will not matter if she's seen us or not. It is for God to judge, not the Abbess."

"How? How have you taken care of it? We must stop this. We must confess and atone for our sins." She pulled her hands from the Bishop's grasp and began to weep.

"Don't cry, love. I can't bear it." He didn't seem to know what to do with his hands. He offered them beseechingly and when they were refused he pressed them to his face. Then he pulled the woman into his arms. She melted so quickly against him that her initial resistance seemed like a ruse. She turned to press her cheek against his chest, allowing Adelaide her first glimpse of the woman's face.

It was Claire, the quiet girl in the top class, the one with the soft brown hair and sad eyes. Bishop Gregoire was so *old*, how could Claire possibly be in love with him? The fact that he was also a man of God didn't immediately strike Adelaide as a knock against his eligibility, but when it slowly seeped into her consciousness, past the rush of vicarious romance she was feeling, she couldn't help but lean further out the window. The discovery of two colliding worlds made Adelaide's head reel. She wished she had made it to the oak tree before they had arrived in the garden so that she could have a better vantage.

"Do not worry, *ma petite chou-chou*," Bishop Gregoire said soothingly while smoothing Claire's hair back into the fashionable updo she wore at the back of her neck. "Sister Marie-Thérèse will not be the Abbess here for much longer. I've found a place for her at Caen."

Both Adelaide and Claire sat up straight with a gasp. "You cannot do that. She's lived here for nearly her entire life," Claire protested. To her credit, her eyes were round and shocked at the scandalous idea.

"It's done. Now there's nothing to stop us. Once Sister Ignatia takes her place, you will take the vows so that we can be happy together."

Claire tried to pull away, but was cornered. "Take the vows?" she squeaked.

"Sister Ignatia?" mouthed Adelaide. The idea was horrific.

Suddenly the door to Adelaide's room crashed open and there in the hallway was the Abbess herself, as though conjured by their very thoughts. The great old woman glared at her with her tiny black eyes set much too close together. The wrinkles around her mouth were accentuated by her pucker of disapproval. Adelaide felt her body melt under her glare. Fear of discovery clutched at her throat as she slammed the window shut. "I was only taking in a bit of fresh air."

With a single dismissive wave of Sister Marie-Thérèse's arm, any sense of self-possession Adelaide had gained by the solitude of her little room was removed. She watched as the Abbess pulled the bottle of sirop d'anise from her pocket to hold in front of Adelaide's nose. "Sister Ignatia found this under your desk after you had gone. Tell me how it got there. You have one chance to answer. If you weave the wrong story, you will not be allowed to weave a second. You will be punished."

Adelaide felt herself press back against the wall. The evidence might have been circumstantial, but it was also fairly damning. She had no doubt that the Abbess already knew why the bottle was under her desk and didn't truly require any explanations. "Oh, Mother Superior," she cried as she fell to her knees on the floor like a supplicant. "Thank you so much for coming," she wept, wringing her hands in distress. Adelaide was soothed to see the old woman take a step backwards in confusion. She continued with an inner calm that belied her outer panic. "You've awoken me from the most awful dream, just horrible. God must have known and called you here to intercede."

The pucker around Sister Marie-Agnes's mouth grew tighter in concern and her thick black brows knitted in sympathy. She swooped into the room to wipe the tears from Adelaide's cheeks and help her crawl back into bed. "My dear girl, do not think upon dark dreams. They are from the devil and are sent to draw you down. To dwell upon them is to let them influence your heart."

"But I must tell you what I dreamed. I must," Adelaide insisted. "For I dreamt of you."

The old sister's eyebrows shot up under her wimple in surprise. "Me?" She busied herself by tucking the blanket under the straw mattress. Adelaide could see at once that she was struggling with her curiosity. Finally, the Abbess gave in. "Why on earth would you dream of me?"

"Oh Mother Superior, you were so beautiful in my dream, so that I knew it was you. You were bathed in the holy light of goodness and righteousness and your white cloak glimmered and your beautiful high brow reflected its…" Adelaide paused to find another suitable word, hoping she wasn't laying it on too thick, "righteousness," she said again. "You held out your hand for me to come to you, and I tried, Mother Superior. Truly I tried, but something held me back."

The old woman sat down on the edge of the bed and took Adelaide's hand in her own. She leaned forward with a look of deep concern on her face. "Go on, child. Tell me what held you back."

Adelaide's mind whirled as she tried to pull the threads of her story together. She opened her mouth, then closed it, then opened her mouth again and rolled her eyes up towards the ceiling, thinking. If she could draw the story out long enough, the bottle of sirop d'anise might be forgotten. Thus far, it seemed to be working. "Bishop Gregoire kept me back," she said. "He said I shouldn't go to you, that you were no longer who you said you were—you were no longer Mother Superior. He said Sister Ignatia was to be the new leader of the Abbey. Is it true? I fear it to be true. I couldn't bear it if it were."

The Mother Superior froze as the story came to its finish. She seemed to consider the possibility, then she chuckled. "My sweet child, do not fret so. I have been the Abbess for many years and will remain for many more years to come. It was just a dream, although perhaps it tells of your true protective nature. I appreciate that you do not wish for any harm to come to me." She patted Adelaide's cheek affectionately and then looked at the brown bottle that she'd left on the table beside the bed. Adelaide held her breath, waiting for the punishment to arrive and hoping she'd done enough to be spared from the worst of it.

A soft knock announced someone at the door, extending Adelaide's sentencing a moment longer. "Come," said old Sister Marie-Thérèse. The sweet face of Sister Marthe appeared in the crack. Her expression caused the Mother Superior to rise in alarm. "What is it?" she asked.

"Bishop Gregoire is here. He has asked to speak with you."

Taking Control

As a result of having her prophetic dream come true, Adelaide had been made to leave the convent school. It had been a painful parting, full of fear and misunderstanding. Her talent had not been lauded, as it might have if she'd predicted a happy occurrence. She had not been touched by god, but by the devil and as a result, deemed dangerous to the other students. Just thinking of those months after she'd been cast out made her feel as though rocks were rolling heavily in her heart.

She had prayed every day to be able to return to the convent. Now here she was again, in a convent turned into a prison. There was not much difference. The old saying was true—be careful what you wish for. Adelaide bent her knees and pressed her feet against the far wall of her cell so she could lie flat on her back in the mildewed straw.

Despite the cramped space, she was not uncomfortable. She had always been able to think more clearly in an unadorned room and there was nothing in this one save her knitting and her cards, both of which kept her sharp.

"Why?" came pitiful cry from the cell across the hall. Adelaide rolled onto her side and twisted the end of the yarn idly around one finger, her legs still curled out of necessity. "Because" was the answer. It was the only meaningless answer that could match Odile's meaningless question. Because no one cares about you, that's why. The sooner Odile learned this lesson, the stronger she would become. Adelaide sat back up again and took her knitting into her hands once again. Things that can be made, can be unmade, she thought to herself as she strengthened the yarn by turning it into an ever growing plait of chained loops, like a shirt of mail. She started a pattern of added and subtracted stitches and lace fell from the needles. It made her think of the lace she had learned to make in Alençon.

It had been the kind Sister Marthe who had been brave enough to help Adelaide find a new home. "I've asked all manner of business owners to take you as an apprentice," Sister Marthe explained, "and Madame Sagii was the only one who would consider you." Adelaide was hurt by the confession, but the town's slight faded when she saw her new quarters at the milliner's shop. She'd been given a tiny room just under the roof. Adelaide finally found the privacy she longed for, and from the window of her new bedroom she was able to look out at any number of pretty gardens in the old town.

Madame Sagii was a quiet widow, always busy with the hat forms and the shop books, but she was kind to Adelaide. There was an air of independence about the woman that both attracted Adelaide and intimidated her. In those initial first days, Adelaide slunk around behind Madame Sagii and watched her like a hawk; in the evenings she'd practice moving like her, gracefully, with confident large gestures.

When she began tying her hair up in the same style, Madame Sagii took note and offered her bits of wisdom as a reward for her many hat sales. Her patience had been boundless.

At first, Adelaide was taught to needlepoint lace in the Alençon style. She spent many hours learning the patterns for creating nets of lace to complete the orders for the aristocrats who wished to remain fashionable. She had been promised a good salary for the skill should she endure the seven years to complete her apprenticeship, but the activity and the promise hadn't been enough to keep her interest. She soon veered from following the prescribed patterns and began creating her own strange curlicues. Mrs. Sagii again took note and split Adelaide's time between lace making and sales, to break up her day. Adelaide found she excelled in convincing even the most modest woman to purchase ribbon for her petticoats, and the thriftiest woman to buy a lavish bonnet. When she boasted of this to Madame Sagii, her mentor correctly pointed out that her talent was not in gathering money, but in keeping up a long stream of stories and compliments, a far more profitable skill which could be used in all manner of instances. For her success, Madame Sagii presented Adelaide with a wolf's fang for polishing the filling stitches of her lace.

The moment she realized that creating lace was not just for adorning women and furniture was the moment that Adelaide's true lessons began. It had happened when Madame Sagii had introduced her to three other women, one who delivered babies, one who owned the bakery down the street, and one who had eight daughters who also sewed lace. They all had smiled at Adelaide with sharp eyes, touched her with delicate hands, and radiated a palpable power. Three years after the introduction, she was given her very own leather bound grimoire wrapped in a protective lace shawl.

Adelaide still had the grimoire and the fang, but Alençon was in the distant past. The Revolution had made it a dangerous business to cater to the luxurious tastes of the aristocracy. The lace makers who hadn't fled the town had been guillotined. Now she no longer netted her hopes and wishes into delicate threads. Knitting with thick wool was faster for weaving spells and, Adelaide found, just as effective.

She was a spider spinning a grey web, her spinnerets clicking rhythmically in the gloom of her cell. She'd heard that spider wives ate their husbands for dinner. The thought made her smile. Not all of creation's females mewled in the darkness like Odile. There were women who were spinning webs at that very moment, she was sure of it, creating patterns of cables and knots that bound all foes and warmed all friends. She thought of Mademoiselle Rachlieu, Mademoiselle Languedoux, and Madame Laurier who had received the letter she'd sent and responded with soothing words of sympathy. She was confident that their knitting included a protective pattern designed to keep her safe. Then there was Madame Southill.

Her little maid Agnes had stopped by the prison that morning to bring the letter that had arrived from across the channel. It had pleased Adelaide to see Agnes, but when she read the letter, her company was forgotten. If she had interpreted Ursula Southill's poorly written French correctly, the woman had had the golem within her grasp, inside her own circle even, and still she did nothing, asked nothing, offered nothing in her note but casual advice. At best, the woman was being deliberately useless; at worst, she was simply incapable. Madame Southill's predilection for puttering in her woods and attending the occasional birth of another English whelp was baffling to Adelaide. She seemed to have no aspirations to anything higher than dabbling in the basest of superstitions. Ridiculous woman, thought Adelaide, dreadful woman. What gall to send such a condescending reply!

Adelaide reached into her corset and touched the deck of cards that she kept secret, pressed against her heart. The gesture had become recurrent, the action consoling. At least she now knew where the creature was dwelling. It did seem strange that the golem had landed in London, but of all the infinite possibilities in time and location, London was far from the worst. The creature was retrievable. She merely had to find a method for doing it, and in the meantime, she would let it be known that Ursula Southill was too weak to continue her affiliations with la Société.

The knitting had fallen into her lap where it sagged over her thighs in loose strands, now too slack to contain within it all the protective qualities she had instilled. In its place in her hands, Adelaide held a single card that seemed to have magically manifested itself; she had no memory of pulling it from her cleavage. It was the six of diamonds, a card that demanded prudence in the face of adversity. She studied it in the dimming evening light.

The subject in the center of the card was that of the dauntless mongoose, protected by an armor of dried mud, entering the mouth of the crocodile to tear it apart from the inside. Years ago when Adelaide had created the cards, she had seen fit to draw the pair of animals in a riverside landscape, the Nile perhaps. The river had been meaningless to her initially, but now as she studied the card it took on a new importance. The way the water edged up on the bank opposite from the crocodile made it seem swollen and dangerous, and yet the crocodile was obviously standing on a sandbar, which would only happen when the river receded. The more she stared at it, the more the scene confused her. The mongoose and the crocodile were easy enough to understand—the crocodile represented a hardship that the mongoose was about to dispel. However, should the river sweep them downstream, hardship and hero both, then only the river would matter.

Adelaide slipped the card into her apron pocket, pressed her hands against her eyes, and mulled how she would maintain prudence in the face of adversity. Ministre Fouché's thin face loomed into her mind as her adversity. He was still hounding her nearly every day, just as he'd promised. He still wanted to know the location of the jewel and assumed the golem had it in her possession. With Madame Southill's letter, she could now tell him the location of the golem. He could go and retrieve the scarab, but she feared for her creature. Its punishment would never be as lenient as prison, that much was certain. She must tell him anyway. Telling him would certainly secure her own release. And there was a small chance that he would bring the golem back for a trial. If that happened, she might even be able to retake control. Adelaide's fingers found her temples and gingerly pressed in concentric circles. It bothered her to have to place so much of her own future in Fouché's hands. Perhaps the card was suggesting there was another way to proceed prudently.

The wails from Odile's cell were beginning to give her a headache. The sound wrapped itself around her thoughts so that any spark she might create was extinguished. The girl was casting banishing spells without even realizing it. When a particularly loud whine assaulted her, Adelaide jumped up and screamed, *"Pour l'amour de dieu, cessez de greindre!* Shut up!"* She stood frozen with her muscles trembling, her ears straining for the next sound, her knitting needles clutched in her fist daring Odile to defy her. There was a loud sniff, then silence. Cautiously, Adelaide resettled herself onto the straw. She pulled the card back out of her pocket, ready to try again now that the incessant cries had stopped.

On the bottom of the card, in the center, were sprigs of heather, rhododendron, and strawberry. Even though herbology wasn't a useful method for divination she'd enjoyed the process of illustrating each card with a different flower, despite considering it below her talent as a sibyl. Let the more vulgar practitioners like Madame Southill mess about with poultices for oozing sores and teas for coughs. Adelaide found herself squinting at the card as she remembered how painfully tedious her lessons in botany had been—all memorization without utilization. She was utterly bored by it. How could the medical properties of lichen compete with the story of brave Orion stretching his bow over the heavens, or the proper method of preparing a tincture compete with the nuances in Hermetic philosophy? There was no subtlety in herbal lore. There was only the disease and the leaf, the problem and the solution.

Adelaide rubbed her temples again and forced herself to concentrate. Heather was useful for the promotion of urine. Honey made from the pollen of rhododendrons was lethal, but the leaves reduced the heat of inflamation and protected the liver. An infusion of the leaves of the strawberry plant was excellent for calming anxiety, or for strengthening the weak by clarifying the blood. She had known an herbalist who gargled water infused with strawberry leaves to sweeten her breath, although the remedy's efficacy always came into doubt when she was tête-a-tête with the poor woman.

Heather, rhododendron, and strawberry—neither of the three seemed to have anything to do with each other, or anything else depicted on her card, except they would all be torn up by their roots and swept away to Alexandria when the swollen Nile roared over its banks. Perhaps the crocodile would swim to a quieter tributary and the mongoose would escape drowning by sucking at air pockets in the mud walls of its den. She shook her head. She was finding it difficult to delve beyond literal interpretations. Between the vocalizing of the other inmates and her own deep shame of failure every time she thought of Madame Southill's condescending letter, her only fully formed thoughts revolved around despair.

"Why?" Odile sounded like she had choked on her question in an effort to silence it. Adelaide took a deep breath and then let it out slowly as she tried not to think unkind thoughts about sweet Odile with her thick blonde hair and trusting blue eyes. Why indeed? Absently, Adelaide traced the mortar between the bricks in the wall of her cell with the tip of her index finger. Odile's endless question was asked of those who professed to love her, including her god. This was the commonality between all the women who were sharing her fate – they directed their questions outward and waited for someone to give them answers. The majority of them sat trembling in their cells hoping someone would allow them to leave, yet the only women actually locked in at night were those who had proven to be disruptive. Everyone else had the freedom to walk about. The great wooden door from the courtyard to the street beyond was locked, but that was all. That thought gave Adelaide pause. The rule was to stay in your cell after dinner, but rules were meaningless if they didn't apply to the situation at hand. The new situation was that the location of the golem had been revealed. This changed everything.

For the next three hours, Adelaide tried to sleep but the anticipation of the early morning made the wool blanket scratch excessively. She tried to fold it in half so that it could provide both a barrier from the straw underneath her and a covering to keep her warm, but it wasn't big enough for both tasks. Besides, the lice made her skin twitch. Unable to tolerate the situation any longer, she rose and poked her head out into the hallway, but could barely see a thing in the blackness. The light from a single distant lamp at the end of the hall near the foyer was barely enough illumination for her to set as a goal. She would still have to slide a hand along the wall to safely navigate and just pray there was no one else in the hallway for her to bump into. She caught her breath to listen for any movement and heard the soft sounds of deep breathing from the opposite cell, which was reassuring. Even Odile had finally fallen asleep.

Her excitement carried her down the hallway on the balls of her feet at a run despite the darkness. In the foyer, Adelaide's heart pounded in her neck as she tried the arched door to the courtyard, then despite her effort to keep quiet, her breath exploded from her in relief when it opened. She only dared to open it a crack, enough for her to squeeze through, knowing that the hinges would squeal and the old wood would creak if she threw it as wide open as she longed to do.

A half moon shone down into the courtyard and cast long webbed shadows from the crooked branches of the old chestnut tree that grew against the far wall. Adelaide took a deep breath of the cool night air and felt optimistic for the first time since the conjuring. She stepped to the right and started creeping around the perimeter of the yard. The packed dirt under her feet kept her steps quiet as she slunk towards the tree, whose white spikes of blooms shone luridly in the moonlight. The scent filled Adelaide so that her lungs pressed against her ribs.

Usually, the lower branches of chestnut trees were trimmed neatly, so that growth would be symmetrical, but the nuns who occupied the building prior to its prison conversion had been more interested in allowing God to grow the tree as he willed it. As a result, the lower branches were within reach. Assuming Adelaide's arms, as well as her courage, held strong, she would be able to climb it without trouble. She leaned against its rough grey trunk, feeling protected by its concealing foliage. Not wanting to waste time, knowing that the night was nearing its end, Adelaide bent forward and removed her shoes, then tied them together and slung them around her neck. Taking the back of her skirt, she pulled it through her legs to the front to tuck under her apron strings which both lifted the great swathes of cloth above her knees to give her legs more freedom, and kept her modest if she was unfortunate enough to be seen from below. Then she stretched her arms up above her head.

Even with her feet pushed to the tips of her toes, she still was three centimeters shy of touching the lowest branch. She jumped, and slapped it with the palms of her hands but her weight pulled her back to earth. She jumped again, and this time was able to scramble her fingertips higher so that her palms made right angles to her wrists against the top of the branch. Only now her elbows refused to bend to pull up her considerable weight, so she dangled and kicked until she dropped down once again with a frustrated grunt.

Adelaide leaned against the wall to catch her breath. She heard a carriage approaching outside the courtyard and her heart started pounding. She fell into a crouch and waited, listening for the rhythmic sound of the horses' hooves fade as it continued down the road. The interruption made her feel panicked. The prison was in the heart of Paris, not isolated in the outskirts where no one would care if one woman slipped away. The escape would only be the beginning. She'd have to move fast to leave Paris altogether in order to remain hidden.

The moon was moving towards the other side of the yard and threatened to illuminate the tree. How dare it, she thought in frustration. She pushed her fear down and stood again, knowing there wasn't much time left. On the third jump, she again latched on, only this time she flattened her feet against the wide trunk and walked them up to the same branch her body hung from. With the strength of a lover in the throes of ecstasy, she wrapped her legs tightly around the branch and clung upside down. Her shoes were uncomfortable swinging weights attached to her neck by their laces. It was one thing, Adelaide realized as she dangled upside down from the branch, to imagine climbing the tree, and another thing entirely to actually attempt it.

It took all her strength of body and concentration to pull herself up and around so that the branch was underneath her instead of on top. She trembled as she balanced with the entire length of her torso pressed against the rough bark and started pushing herself backwards until her bottom hit the trunk. The great muscles of her ass clenched pitifully against the trunk like a squirrel without a tail, or a weak third hand. Then she reached behind her. A sigh of relief escaped her lips as she dug her fingertips deep into the crevices of the tree trunk's bark. A sturdy handhold is more reassuring than the most detailed plans, and her plan was less than completely thought through. With some ungraceful maneuvering combined with heavy breathing and pints of nervous sweat, Adelaide managed to pull herself up until she was standing on the branch. Luckily, from there the branches above were much more numerous, providing a relative ladder-like ease of ascent as the canopy stretched higher.

The wall, Adelaide's ultimate goal, was nearly as tall as the tree itself, and as she climbed closer to the top of the wall, the limbs of the tree thinned. When Adelaide heard the branch snap underneath her, she leapt at the top of the wall with a choked cry and draped herself over the very narrow edge, clinging for her very life.

There were no suitable branches on her left to grab onto, so retreating from her plan wasn't an option. To her right, the cobblestoned street shone far below, six meters at least, with no method for a safe descent. She was effectively stuck. A sob rose to her throat but she swallowed it, and pressed her forehead into the cold tile capping the wall. Someone would have to rescue her for her to survive this scrape, and the laughter that would accompany the rescue would be earsplitting. It was enough to feel defeated, she thought, but to also feel so entirely humiliated was even worse. The image of the mongoose walking into the mouth of the crocodile returned to her behind her tightly squeezed eyelids. Prudence in the face of adversity—the irony of it made her feel sick to her stomach. How prudent had it been to try to climb a tree in order to scale a wall? How would she rescue the golem if she couldn't even rescue herself?

Suddenly Adelaide realized the significance of heather, rhododendron, and strawberry. Of course the one card she turned would somehow reflect that which most obsessed her, namely, the golem. Heather, rhododendron, and strawberry had all been used to flavor and preserve beer in past times before hops became the fashion, and the golem was working in a public house. Adelaide wondered if she was unknowingly pulling cards to tell the golem's fortune instead of her own. If that were the case, then the mongoose and the crocodile would have nothing to do with Adelaide at all. The fact that an image of hops was a better representation of beer, and that she'd illustrated the hop vine on another card that hadn't been pulled, wasn't lost on Adelaide. It just added more nuance to an already impossible puzzle. She was so tied in knots over the card's meanings that it took a while for her to hear the insistent hiss from the alley below. She opened one eye and dared to roll her head slightly to the right to look down.

Far below in the street, a pale face peered out from under the brim of a wool cap and looked back up at her. It took her seconds to recognize him, and seconds more to control the emotions that swelled. He was supposed to be in Lille. His presence underneath her was nothing short of a miracle. "Dodo," Adelaide whispered down at the man, "What are you doing here?"

"Adelaide, is that you? What are you doing up there, you fool?" Dodeauvie whispered back.

"Oh please, *pitié*, help me." She tried to control her voice from rising in panic. "I'm stuck." Her voice cracked as the tears finally spilled.

She watched the man hesitate, no doubt weighing the costs and merits. "Wait there," he finally said. She listened to the sound of his boots as he jogged off down the street. She wouldn't be going anywhere, he could rest assured of that.

It seemed like he was gone for hours. She feared her muscles would give out as every single one of them was frozen in its effort to balance along the ridge of the wall. Without daring to move her head, Adelaide's right eye traveled the path of another carriage as it traversed the street. Then a movement in a window directly across from her suddenly drew her attention. A curtain shifted. Had someone seen her? She prayed the chestnut tree had her hidden in the shadows. Just as she'd decided it was too late, the top of a ladder gently touched the wall near her hands. "Come down," Dodeauvie hissed up to her.

Her fear swelled when she hesitatingly touched the tip of the ladder. "I can't," she whispered desperately to herself. It was too high; the ladder would surely tip and fall; her foot would slip. "I can't," she said again in a pitiful wail that sounded, even to her own ears, like Odile. "Come get me."

"Come down, Witch, or I'll leave you to your jailors." The contempt in his voice was familiar and it angered her enough to make a second attempt. This time she slowly pushed her torso up to straddle the top of the wall in a sitting position and was surprised to find she was more balanced. Now she could survey the roof of the prison, the courtyard behind her, and the entire length of the street as well. She noticed a sign for a print shop at the corner and suddenly knew why Dodeauvie had happened upon her. Dodo was too calculating for providential circumstances; he simply had business three doors away. She stretched her right foot to the third rung of the ladder.

CONVERGING FORCES

"You do realize that my involvement here has put me in a very difficult situation. I'm already on house arrest."

"In Lille," Adelaide murmured.

"If I should now be found with an escaped prisoner, can you imagine how that would look?"

Adelaide heaved an annoyed sigh. "How many times must I thank you? Would saying it again help you to feel more appreciated?" She rolled her eyes then turned to look at the massive printing press that commandeered one half of the dark room. When she ran a hand over a tray of letters, they rattled in their individual compartments like dice in a cup.

"Don't touch those, you'll get ink everywhere," Dodeauvie snapped.

Adelaide ignored him and rattled the letters one last time before continuing on her self-guided tour of the print shop. When she reached Dodeauvie's coat draped over the back of a chair, she deliberately wiped her fingers over the shoulders as she passed it, leaving streaks of ink on the boiled wool. There was something comforting about the smell of wood pulp in the stacks of fresh paper on the shelves. The great iron press was like a muscled demon, its machinery was well oiled and ready. Behind it, Dodeauvie stood at a table and was hastily stuffing pamphlets into a large satchel. He tossed a second bag at Adelaide. "Help me with this," he ordered.

"I should really leave while there's some night left. You can stuff your stolen pamphlets into bags by yourself," Adelaide said. "I only came because you said you had a place for me to hide."

"I'm not stealing. The pamphlets are mine. I wrote them."

"Yes Dodo, and that's why we've arrived well before the Printer and charmed the concierge into letting us enter," Adelaide said sarcastically. Nevertheless, she began filling her bag with pamphlets. There was something about the print shop that intrigued her and made her wish to linger, but its location, so close to the prison, was unfortunate. Soon the street would begin to fill with those who might recognize her. Her absence from her cell may already have been noted, and if that were the case, police would be looking for her starting near the prison. As they circled outwards, like dogs on the scent, there was a likely chance they'd find her.

"The faster you fill your bag, the faster we can leave," Dodeauvie encouraged.

The pamphlets were stacked neatly in a corner of the desk so that she had to rub shoulders with her companion as they worked. Two other groupings of different pamphlets and one stack of bound books were also on the table with handwritten invoice statements neatly crowning each stack. Dodeauvie's invoice was conspicuously missing. Curious, Adelaide scanned his title quickly, *Les Instructions de Thoth, Divulguée par M. M. Dodeauvie, Partie IV.* "I see you are pilfering ideas as well as paper," she said with a smile.

"Mind your own business." Dodeauvie snarled. "Zenours is dead, he won't mind. Besides, I've added enough of my own thoughts to make the practical theories my own."

"Ton-Ton Zenours was good to you. He taught you everything, and you spit on his memory by taking credit for everything he did."

"And what are you doing to aggrandize our mentor? You flip cards for ridiculous women and then get thrown in jail. You whore whatever small powers Zenours was able to draw out from you. And stop calling him Ton-Ton. He wasn't anyone's uncle." He snatched the satchel from Adelaide's hand and pushed her further down the table. "Stand aside. I'll do it myself."

Pulling herself up in righteous indignation, Adelaide sputtered, "I am France's most important *sibylle*. My powers have been sought by none other than the Emperor himself."

"Yes, I heard about that. I'm looking forward to hearing more." He pushed the last pamphlet into the satchel and slung both bags over his shoulder. Then he took Adelaide by her arm and marshaled her towards the door, stopping only to pick up his coat. He draped it over her shoulders. "Keep your gown concealed and your head down," he instructed, handing her his hat to wear.

There is a line between night and dawn that is drawn with a subtle difference in smell, detectable even in a city that confuses the senses like Paris. Just before the first birds start to awaken, the air becomes lighter, more floral, and everything that was worrisome just minutes before seems suddenly insignificant. Adelaide felt none of this as she was shuttled into the street. "Where are you taking me?" she demanded.

"First, we will retrieve your grimoire. Then, we'll find a quiet place to discuss our next steps."

"But my grimoire is kept at rue de Tournot. We can't go there – that's the first place they'll search for me."

"Don't be stupid. No one really cares if you're missing. You're just a card reader. Do you really think they'll send out the entire *gendarmerie* to roust you from the shadows? As long as you stay out of sight, you're no trouble to anyone."

Adelaide bristled. "You have no idea. You've never had any idea of my worth."

"To be honest, I've never cared."

Adelaide had no response to that. Never? She tried to push the memories aside and refuse to be surprised—she'd learned Dodeauvie's real nature long ago and it did her no good to revisit those feelings of heartache, especially now when she needed to be sharp. A reminder of his rejection would only lower her. She pulled herself straight and lifted her chin. "All the same, it would be safer to send word to my maid rather than to arrive in person. Ministre Fouché has ears and eyes everywhere. Surely you have a messenger you can trust, perhaps an acolyte? My maid will know where my grimoire is kept."

Dodeauvie paused in his stride to consider, then pulled Adelaide down a side street. "*Comme vous voulez.* I know someone who owes me a favor. We'll stay with Jean-Tout-Simple and he'll go to your maid for the book."

The shadows in the narrow alleys were long as the sun started to rise. They hugged the walls as they hurried along, their heels sounding unnaturally loud against the cobblestones. Adelaide was glad for the coat. Despite being summer, the damp kept the narrow streets chilled until the afternoon when the sun could shine unheeded by shadows.

It wasn't long before Dodeauvie started questioning her as they walked, whispering under his breath. "I've heard through the channels that you conjured a little red man who stole the Emperor's Nile Valley jewel. Tell me that's true. Oh how I'd love for Bonaparte to be taken down a notch or two."

"Be careful about what you say, your royalist leanings are what got you stuck in Lille," Adelaide warned.

"He speaks of the equality of all French born, and yet he places a crown upon his head and sits in a palace. How is that different from anything else we've ever had? We might as well bring back the Bourbons—at least they were legitimate."

"I might feel the same as you," Adelaide said, "but I'm not likely to publish and distribute those words with my own name to identify me as author. That was very foolish."

"Do not speak to me of foolishness. I wasn't the one imprisoned for thievery."

"Fouché imprisoned me for fraud, not thievery," she puffed. Speaking of politics caused Dodeauvie's pace to quicken and she was having difficulty keeping up.

"Of course they would call it fraud. It would not do to have everyone know you swindled Napoleon to steal his finery. Fraud?" Dodeauvie scoffed. "An interesting choice of crimes." He gallantly stopped and pulled her into an alley where she could pause and catch her breath. "So where is this jewel now? Where have you hidden it?"

"The jewel? I don't care about the scarab. It is the golem I care about. No one but me has managed to do what I have done since the great Golem of Prague."

"You don't really think to swindle me too? Tell me what happened in truth—there was no golem, was there? It was merely you and one of those old crones you associate yourself with dressed as some dreadful red creature." He studied her face, then shook his head in amazement. "You're quite serious. A golem?"

"It fell away through a second vortex after I called it forth."

"Fell away? Fell where? You mean to tell me the jewel went with the golem and you've no idea where it is?" Dodeauvie put his hands to his face and shook his head. "Oh Adelaide, you have not changed much since last we knew each other."

His words made her feel small again. There had been a time in her life when she trusted Dodeauvie enough to come to him with all her questions. He had been the first and most promising of a handful of adepts she'd met after leaving Madame Sagii's shop. Smart, confident, and irresistibly handsome, he'd flattered her with his patient attentions, always helping to make any botched experiment right so that she could learn from her mistakes. At least he had seemed that way when she was sixteen, but perhaps he had been laughing at her the entire time. Now, fifteen years later, his strong slender legs were topped with a round stomach, his eyes were framed with fine wrinkles, his hair was graying at his temples, and his cheeks were becoming jowls. However despite his advancing age, he retained much of his allure. Knowledge such as theirs did not change as it aged, and he would always have fifteen years more experience. "I must show you my grimoire," she said. "Perhaps you can tell me what I did wrong."

"Perhaps," he allowed. "You must have been studying the Cabala to bring forth a golem. I myself have not spent much time with that philosophy."

"Why not? It is just as old as the Hermetic texts, and may even be more powerful."

Dodeauvie sighed heavily. "Have you ever considered why we obsess over the age of a book? Why is it that we assume that the oldest pages are the ones most powerful? It undermines the value of our own work." When Adelaide returned his question with a skeptical look, he sighed again. "As you wish. I will look at your grimoire tonight to see where you might have gone wrong. You must also tell me exactly what happened at the ceremony and leave out no detail."

They began walking again, this time with less urgency, and it lulled Adelaide into a more intimate mood. She curled her arm through his elbow. There had been plenty of walks in the past, just the two of them, where everything had been discussed. "I received a letter," she began hesitantly.

"Yes?" he encouraged.

"From a woman I know. She said she found the golem. It's in London residing in a pub called the Quiet Woman."

"A public house? What kind of woman would send you a letter like that? I've never understood why you insist on fraternizing with those hags. They are all simple-minded and toothless. The golem is living in a pub? That's ridiculous."

"They are not toothless. They're my sisters," Adelaide responded defensively.

"Sisterhood," Dodeauvie rolled his eyes. "What do your sisters know of philosophy, or of alchemy, or astrology, or of anything save the weeds that grow in their little circle of influence? Nothing, that's what. All your cronies know is how to pull babes from between the legs of whores and farmer's wives. You are better than they are. You were Zenours's student, although I warned him against bothering with you. He should have listened to me. If he had he wouldn't have been so heartbroken when you left."

"He didn't care one bit about me. I was only a part of his entourage for less than a full year, hardly enough time for him to even learn my name."

"You crushed him when you left—he considered you a daughter. He wished to give you an understanding of the world, but all you wanted was to learn only enough to provide you an income for silk gowns and a house in Paris."

"When I left, he wiped me from the slate. The sisters never did that to me, not before, not after and they still keep me in their arms to this day. It was your betrayal that killed Zenours, not mine. You print and distribute all his ideas as your own. *Ecrit par Dodo Le Magnifique.*"

"Stop calling me that. My name is Dodeauvie."

"What difference does it make what I call you? Zenours's name will be remembered, as will mine, but in time, your name will be lost to the world - nothing more than a shit smear on the paper you keep printing."

His eyes flashed in anger and he dropped her arm with a disgusted flick of his hand. His gait sped up and became heavier in anger until they rounded a corner, whereupon Dodo took a deep breath and stopped. "So, where is this letter?" he asked, trying to calm himself. "Show it to me."

Adelaide patted her apron pocket and slipped her hand inside. A sudden sick feeling washed over her. "The letter? The one from Madame Southill?" she asked innocently, stalling.

"Madame Southill wrote it?" he seemed to recognize the name. "I would like to see it, if you don't mind."

Adelaide pulled her hand out of her right pocket and checked the left. Nothing. She felt her face burn as she slipped a hand down into her cleavage and pulled out her cards to rifle through them for the folded letter. Then she pushed her hand back down her corset to feel for more paper. "Hold these," she said, giving Dodo her deck of cards. His eyes narrowed as he watched her jiggle and squirm to dislodge any hidden document. "It must have fallen out," she finally admitted.

"What do you mean, fallen out? Fallen where?"

Adelaide pictured herself clinging upside down on the great chestnut tree. She had been sure she'd put the letter in her apron pocket. Perhaps it slipped out when she'd flipped her skirt up to free her legs. In that case, it was under the tree behind the wall of the prison. She tried to picture herself replacing the letter into her pocket after having read it the last time in her cell, but all she could remember was picking up her knitting. Did she leave it in the cell? There was no way to know, except by retracing her steps, and that was out of the question. "I don't know," she finally squeaked.

"Oh for the love of god," Dodo whispered fiercely, throwing his arms in the air. "Fouché has the letter now, count on it."

"You cannot know that."

"Yes, I know that for a fact. Fouché has the letter and he no longer has any use for you. He's already on his way to London. I want my coat back, you need not hide any longer and I'm cold." He snatched his cloak off Adelaide's back and put it on.

"You are no gentleman," Adelaide spat. Tears burned her eyes, but she refused to let them spill. Instead, she wrapped her arms around herself to keep warm.

"Don't worry, we'll be at Jean's home soon. You'll warm up if we walk faster." He lengthened his stride to take full advantage of his long legs and Adelaide had to jog to keep up. He was right; she warmed up quickly.

When they finally arrived at the home of Dodo's acolyte, Adelaide found Jean-Tout-Simple to be a corpulent young man with pustules on his red, puffed face. The apartment was very cramped for such a large man, and the food offered was ironically spare. They sat crushed together at a tiny table where they drank red wine, ate slices of *saucisson sec*, and tore hunks from a long baguette. There wasn't even any cheese, Adelaide thought dourly. She herself was no svelte kitten, but at least she came by her weight honestly. She had no idea how Jean had packed it on, considering the meager fare. To make matters worse, he was a man who refused to close his thighs while sitting down, and as a result there was hardly any space for her to fit her knees under the table. She stepped hard upon his foot and he withdrew his leg for a moment with a yelp. "Oh, was that you? Begging your pardon," Adelaide said. She ignored Dodo's glare.

"What do you mean the bookseller on Rue du Temple is gone?" Dodo continued, heaving the satchels onto the table. "I received a letter from him just last week saying he would peddle my pamphlets."

"He's gone." Jean-Tout-Simple unhelpfully repeated with his mouth full of cured sausage.

"If I stay too long in Paris, it will eventually be discovered that I've broken my house arrest in Lille. I don't have time to find a new bookseller. You must find one for me. Can you do that Jean?"

Jean shrugged and took a sip of wine.

"I would not even be here if you had taken the pamphlets last week as I asked. I was quite surprised to receive an invoice."

Jean shrugged again and considered his empty wineglass. "You'd promised I'd become rich from your knowledge," he said quietly. "You didn't mention I'd become your servant."

Dodo pulled himself up off his chair and took a deep and irate breath, expanding his lungs so that he seemed to have the shoulder span of Hercules. His eyes flashed. He ripped his wool cap off his head, making his hair spark with tall green fingers of static electricity that startled Adelaide. When Jean-Tout-Simple pushed himself away from the table to cower against the wall, she considered the possible advantage of knitting a wool cap for herself for the same effect. "If you want my power," Dodo started in a voice twice as deep as it normally was, "you must pay for it with your servitude." Then with a dramatic wave of his arm, he ordered Jean to fetch Adelaide's grimoire.

It would have been best if Jean had gone off then and there, but Adelaide had to decide what to give him to show her maid he was acting upon her authority. A letter was best, but Agnes had never learned to read, so instead Adelaide gave Jean-Tout-Simple a tiny square of Alençon lace from the hem of her chemise. In the meantime, Dodo had collapsed back into his chair in his old, mortal form, while Jean downed three more glasses of wine.

After he was gone, Adelaide made a half-hearted attempt at polite conversation, but Dodo was unable to participate and responded monosyllabically. He had pulled out a sheaf of paper and was busy scribbling away, obviously trying to ignore her. In the face of Dodo's brooding mood, Adelaide finished her second glass of wine and opened a third bottle. She deeply regretted having left her knitting in the prison. She didn't know what to do with her hands, so she placed them palm down on the table and pretended they didn't exist. There wasn't even a window to look out of, so she drained the new bottle as she watched Dodo scrawl his thoughts. The silence and boredom, as Adelaide waited for Jean to return, combined with the previous sleepless night were too much to bear. A jaw-breaking yawn overtook her, causing Dodo to look up in annoyance. She brushed the crumbs from the table and put her head down.

It felt very late when she lifted her head again, and the fog of sleep confused her. Dodo was no longer seated across the table from her. Instead, Jean-Tout-Simple was looking at her. He had a new *saucisson* in his fist, and his bottom jaw slid slowly from side to side as he worked a hunk of the dry meat. "Where's Dodo?" Adelaide asked, rubbing her eyes.

"Who?"

"Dodeauvie."

"Oh," Jean paused to think. "He's gone."

"Gone where?"

"I don't remember."

"Where is my grimoire?"

"He took it."

Adelaide sat straight up in her chair. Her skin tingled in alarm. "When is he coming back?"

Jean rolled his eyes to the ceiling as he thought. Then lifted his finger. "Now I remember," he said. He paused the grinding of his jaws to give her a self-satisfied smile. "He's gone to Calais."

CHORES

"How are you feeling this morning, Mr. Tilsdale?" Elise asked cheerfully. Without intentionally doing so, she had put her happy nurse voice on, a job requirement as automatic as donning hospital scrubs. Time and the anti-inflammatory properties of Mrs. Southill's white willow bark had eased the swelling in his neck considerably and he was now able to breathe normally without the aid of his pipe stem. His voice, however, sounded like sandpaper. Elise had instructed him to keep to whispers if he had to speak at all so that his larynx could continue to heal.

"My back hurts," Mr. Tilsdale complained hoarsely with his lips pulled back in a tense smile that caused the muscles of his jaw to twitch.

"Of course it does—you've been in bed for over a week. Have you tried sitting up recently? It'll help you breathe." As he struggled to prop himself up, she noticed he seemed flushed. Beads of sweat were forming on his upper lip and his nightshirt clung damp against his hollow chest. Elise reached over and placed her palm on his forehead. "You've got a fever, Mr. Tilsdale," she said excessively loudly, another nursing habit she couldn't shake. She pulled the blanket up higher around his shoulders and noted how the tendons in his neck flexed spasmodically at her touch.

As she began to prepare her patient's tea, Elise pondered possible diagnoses. Her first guess was a wound infection, but after her encounter with Mrs. Southill, she had been very careful with her wound care as his neck healed, and the edges of the hole were pink and healthy where a scar was forming. The cut from the splinter had almost healed. If not bacterial infection, then maybe he suffered from a viral infection, she thought. Mr. Tilsdale had lost some weight over the past week, his throat being too sore to swallow much more than liquids, and Elise considered the possibility that poor nutrition had given his immune system a hit. If that was the case, he could have a simple cold. Only he wasn't congested.

A soft tap on the door sounded and Mary poked her head in. "I've brought breakfast," she chirped.

"Don't come in here," barked Elise. If Mr. Tilsdale had the flu, the last thing she needed was for it to get carried around to everyone in the Quiet Woman. Elise was always careful to get vaccinated every year, but no one else would have had that luxury.

Mary entered despite the order. "Why not? Mr. Tilsdale and I are good friends. Aren't we Mr. Tilsdale?" She made a face at Elise as she handed her the tray with a steaming bowl of broth and then left before Elise could retaliate.

As she turned to set the tray on the bedside table, she noticed her patient had begun to drool from the corner of his mouth. She wiped his chin with the sheet. "Drink the willow bark tea first," she instructed, handing him the cup. "It'll bring your fever down."

Elise studied Mr. Tilsdale as he brought the tea to his mouth. Normally he grimaced at the acrid flavor, but today he was grimacing prior to taking his first sip. Something about his strange smile nagged at Elise. As she watched the man struggle to drink, she was reminded of another patient she'd helped in the emergency room. A mother had come in with her baby, cradled in her arms and when Elise had pulled back the soft swaddling blanket, she'd seen the same tight grimacing smile on the babe that she now saw on Mr. Tilsdale's face.

Elise sucked in a breath, now sure of the diagnosis. Despite her intense and sudden pity, she couldn't help but lean forward to marvel at the closed puncture wound in Mr. Tilsdale's shoulder. Things were happening on the inside. Bacteria, hidden deep in his flesh, was releasing toxin that was wreaking havoc on the man's nervous system. Mrs. Southill's words echoed in Elise's mind: *you've turned an easy death into a difficult one.* This was worse than a wound infection, worse than even influenza.

The truth of the old woman's prophecy was suddenly too heavy to bear. She placed Mr. Tilsdale's lunch tray on his lap, handed him his spoon, and quickly left the room.

In the hallway she found Mary bent over at the waist, mumbling at a long trail of whatever she was sprinkling on the floor. Elise groaned, "What are you doing? I already swept the hallway. Now I have to do it again."

"You can't sweep until Mr. Laroque comes back up to his room. He's got to walk on these seeds." Mary smiled conspiratorially at Elise. "It's a love spell. My granny taught it to me. Hempseed I sow, hempseed I sow," she chanted, "the man I love come after me and mow."

"That's the stupidest thing I've ever heard," Elise grumbled. "You can't sow seeds on a hardwood floor." Mr. Laroque was the new tenant everyone, with the exception of Elise, had been hoping for. All Elise could think of was the fact that she now had one more room to clean. The man kept to himself by sitting in dark corners of the dining hall at mealtimes. He peered warily at everyone, spoke only when spoken to, and generally behaved in a way that made Elise nervous. Elise had been dumping his chamber pot for two days before she ever actually saw his face. Mary, on the other hand, swooned over his accent and convinced herself he was a French duke and a refugee from the Revolution. The Ferringtons had come to the same conclusion. As a result, the morning after he had appeared, Mrs. Ferrington had suddenly found a renewed interest in managing the operations of the Quiet Woman, much to Mrs. Postlethwaite's irritation.

Elise raised an eyebrow at the pretty barmaid. "You think he's going to fall in love with you because you made him walk over pot seeds? If he crushes those into the floor it's going to be a pain to clean up."

Mary's smile turned sour. "You sweep that up before he's come and I'll make your life a misery."

"You already make me miserable," Elise sniffed. "Fine. I won't get in the way of your magical seduction, but you can clean your own mess. I'm not doing it." She sidled along the wall to the stairs and was careful not to disturb the trail.

Passing through the dining hall on the way to the kitchen she saw all the usual men eating their breakfasts. Mr. Laroque had seated himself close to the bar and looked up when she entered the room. She felt his eyes follow her as she walked towards the kitchen so she turned and smiled. In return, he gave her a barely noticeable nod before returning to his newspaper.

"That man gives me the heebie-jeebies," Elise said as she entered the kitchen.

"The what?" asked Mrs. Postlethwaite.

"Which man?" asked Thomas. He was sitting on the low stool in his usual corner next the hearth, the ever-present pipe clutched in his teeth.

"That guy, Mr. Laroque."

"I'll have none of your strange talk regarding our tenants," Mrs. Ferrington called from the open door of the larder where she was taking inventory. She didn't seem to notice how the fumes from the basement were seeping slowly into the kitchen. "The Quiet Woman always treats each of her guests with dignified hospitality. That's what makes us renowned in London."

"I suppose that's why I caught Mary scattering seeds in front of Mr. Laroque's door."

"Seeds? Hemp seeds?" Mrs. Postlethwaite laughed. "She'll get no husband that way." She stepped aside to let Mrs. Ferrington stomp out of the kitchen, presumably to check on Mary. "Lord knows I tried it myself when I was young. Does Mary still think he's an exiled duke?"

"Any duke renting a room here wouldn't be any better than the rest of us. It's been at least five years since Nappy gave amnesty to the French noble class." Thomas sniffed.

"You take care as to who's listening to your Republican opinions, Thomas. You'll get into trouble one of these days with your talk." Mrs. Postlethwaite turned to Elise, "Did you check in on Mr. Tilsdale? How is he?"

The reminder of the old tenant caused Elise to reach out to the kitchen table to steady herself. All week Mrs. Postlethwaite had asked the same thing and up to now, he'd been improving. "Not good," she said. "He's taken a turn. I think he has tetanus."

"There you go again with those words. Are you even speaking English?"

"Lockjaw. He has lockjaw." Elise said simply and Mrs. Postlethwaite dropped her knife. "I'm hoping the willow will bring his fever down, but I don't think there's anything else I can do."

The room was strangely silent for a moment as Elise's words soaked in. Then the stool scraped as Thomas stood up somberly.

"You sit right back down again Thomas MacEwan, do you hear me? You aren't to be deciding who lives and dies in this house, so you sit." Mrs. Postlethwaite picked up her knife and waved it at him. "Sit! God may yet choose to spare him. Besides, we just got the house filled. What would Richard think if you made us one tenant short again?"

Thomas blew out a puff of smoke and took back his stool. "Poor bugger," he grumbled.

"You're right, Elise," Mrs. Postlethwaite said. "There's nothing for him now. We just have to wait it out. You might as well go fetch the water, since Mary forgot." She pointed to the empty buckets near the courtyard door.

Despite her excursion with Thomas, the idea of going out into the city was still frightening. "I don't know where the pump is," she said. "Maybe you could show me?"

"Show you? What makes you think I've time for that? Did you hear, Thomas? Our Queen needs to be escorted to the pumps."

Elise rolled her eyes and looked away into the dining hall as she tried to come up with another task she could suggest doing instead of leaving the safety of the pub. Scrubbing the floor or washing the breakfast dishes would require water, she thought. Mrs. Postlethwaite didn't trust her to help prepare the meals, and stoking fires and sweeping was already on her docket. She noticed Mr. Laroque was looking at her through the kitchen door. She smiled thinly and he looked away. Her smile turned more genuine when Richard walked through the door.

"Did you just say Elise needs to be shown the way to the pump? I'll show her," he said cheerfully as he headed towards the larder.

"You, Mr. Ferrington?" Mrs. Postlethwaite seemed surprised. Elise looked over at Thomas when his stool scraped again. He was scowling around the stem of his pipe.

Richard came out of the larder with his mouth full of apple and the jar of pickled eggs under his arm. Mrs. Postlethwaite dutifully stepped to one side to let him place the heavy jar on her table and remove the lid, but as he reached in to pull out an egg she erupted. "For goodness sakes, be careful. You'll stain your cravat." She waved her knife at the young man who was dripping pink brine from his wrists. "At least let me slice that apple for you."

"No time, Mrs. P," Richard said, spraying egg on the table. Miraculously his cravat remained unstained. He grabbed Elise's arm and drew her out into the dining hall, leaving the open jar on the table.

"Take the buckets, you nit-wit," the cook shouted at Elise.

Elise circled back and hauled the heavy yoke onto her shoulders and nearly knocked Mrs. Postlethwaite in the head as she hooked on the buckets. Then she walked sideways through the door behind Richard. In the dining hall, Mr. Laroque's eyes followed them to the front door. "Do you know I haven't fetched water since I was a boy?" Richard said. "My father used to send me out every morning. Then Thomas came around and took over the job." He held the front door open for Elise and she banged the buckets on the doorframe. "It's quite amusing to be carrying water again after so long," Richard called back to her as he walked down the lane ahead, "brings back old memories. We were both boys then, Thomas and I."

Outside, Elise took a deep breath and then coughed from the soot. The temperature was slightly higher from the summer sun than it was inside, which reminded Elise just how gloomy her life had become.

She scurried to keep up with Richard's long stride while the buckets swung awkwardly at her sides. "How long has Thomas been here?"

"Oh, he was just a skinny gutter-boy when he arrived on our doorstep and it was Mrs. P what took him in and fed him up. Why do you think he's such a big man now? It's all Mrs. P's doing. Of course, she was much younger back then too and mothering everyone, her own children as well as anyone else she could feed. I can tell you we all benefitted."

"I think if I had been Thomas, I'd think twice about hanging around a pub with a headless woman for a sign."

"Ah yes, the martyrdom of Saint Juthwara. She just wouldn't pipe down about her religion, so they cut off her head. Either that or it was a jealous lover who took her head. In any case, a headless woman can't keep talking, can she?"

Elise looked at Richard to see if he was serious. He was. "That's awful," she said.

"I suppose it is. Never really thought about it much. It's an ancient legend."

"It must have been fun, growing up with so much going on all the time," Elise said changing the subject. She tried to imagine Thomas and Richard playing together in the great kitchen, getting underfoot and dodging Mrs. P's motherly smacks with the broom.

"Well, there was plenty of hard work for us too. Make no mistake, we were pouring ales and rolling kegs before either of us could read." Richard paused while a cloud seemed to pass across his face. Elise was surprised by the gloomy look and wondered what memory caused it, but it was gone as quickly as it had arrived. "Enough about old Tom and me. Have you been able to remember anything about your own past? I'm most anxious that you heal completely. I'm sure that there is a capital story somewhere in that head of yours and you just need a good rest for it to come tumbling out, but I'm very much afraid we're not allowing you enough rest. Mrs. P. and Thomas can be such taskmasters. I've been trying to get them to stop bothering you about sleeping late in the mornings. You should be allowed to sleep as long as you'd like so that you may fully recover."

It was hard for Elise to argue with that line of thinking. "I haven't remembered a thing yet," she said innocently. "Maybe I do come from a wealthy family. That would explain why it's so hard for me to scrub the floor the way Mary thinks I should scrub it."

"Don't listen to Mary. She was nothing but a costermonger before she came to us. Mrs. P. caught her in the dining hall selling flowers from a basket and figured if she was so good at getting the lads to buy something they didn't need, she'd be excellent getting them to buy more beer. But Mary doesn't know anything beyond enticing men to open their purses, and certainly nothing about scrubbing floors. In any case, we've had no response as yet from the advert mother posted about you, but I'm sure your family will claim you soon."

Elise smiled to herself. He really was a sweet man, she thought. She just wished he wouldn't walk so fast. They had been passing women and boys carrying full buckets of water for a couple blocks, so they had to be getting close. She was now constantly dipping and sidestepping to avoid tangling with others as Richard fell through the crowd like sand through a sieve. Suddenly the street dead-ended in a small square where a line of people with empty urns and buckets all faced a wall.

Elise started to feel anxious as they approached the back of the line. At the bar the only questions she ever got were "Why aren't you as jolly as Mary," and "Where's my beer?" Here, where women gathered every day, sometimes three times a day, Elise knew the conversations would be more personal, more pointed. As she approached, people turned to her in curiosity to view the new girl. Elise braced herself for the questions she felt sure would come, worried she might say the wrong thing, flub her story, or otherwise draw attention to her questionable sanity. She was grateful to have Richard with her to play interference. Having the proprietor of the Quiet Woman join them in line to fetch water wasn't a common occurrence and Richard seemed delighted at the attention as people nodded and smiled. A young girl directly in front addressed them sweetly, "Good morning, Mr. Ferrington. How's Mrs. Ferrington faring?"

"Mrs. Ferrington's faring well," he replied.

Richard was really good at this, Elise thought to herself as she listened to his polite conversation. He seemed to know everyone and could ask about the health of Great Aunt Tilly, or Poor Little Billy. Those he didn't know received his wisdom regarding the weather. In response, the women blushed and tried to reply just as politely without giggling or stammering. Afterwards, they tittered amongst themselves and flicked their skirts like little brown sparrows. She couldn't blame them—for Richard to be able to enquire on the health of so many strangers by name was a compliment. All the nice little things everyone said to each other were so rehearsed it almost seemed sincere. It was as though everyone had memorized their lines and Elise was the only one in the drama club still asking for prompts at the dress rehearsal. It also made her realize how tiny the big city of London really was, which made her feel even more like an outsider.

As their turn at the pump neared, others were still stepping into line at the back. Richard resolutely ignored all the newcomers even though it was clear that a whisper went through to the back of the line he was amongst them. Elise saw eyes linger on Richard, then flit curiously to her. Just before they reached the pump, a woman approached with a baby wrapped in her shawl and a toddler clinging to her skirt. She was nervously and carelessly swinging an empty water bucket back and forth and it just barely missed hitting the top of her little boy's head. "Mr. Ferrington? I've been paid a visit by your man, Mr. MacEwan," she said abruptly.

Richard blushed and smiled. "Have you? I trust you had a pleasant conversation," he quickly turned away while motioning to Elise to step forward in line.

"Mr. Ferrington, Sir, I can't say that I did." Elise caught the woman's toddler when he staggered forward after finally getting clobbered in the back of the head with the bucket. The boy's yowling was earsplitting, but the woman continued as though nothing had happened. "My husband is paid on Fridays and by Sunday morn all his wages have gone to drink. Can you not send him home before the money's gone?"

"Madam, I am not at liberty to tell your husband how to spend his wages."

"We've got five little ones, Sir. All needs to be fed, Sir." The little one at her side was rubbing his head with his tiny hand. His wailing was still loud and as a result, the woman had to be even louder. It was impossible for anyone not to hear the conversation, especially since everyone had stopped to stare and listen. Richard's face was beet red and he shifted from one foot to the other in an embarrassed dance as the woman dropped her bucket to fish coins out of her filthy apron pocket. "Tell your man not to hurt my husband," she pleaded. "If you send him back home to me on wage days, you'll have what he owes soon enough." She pressed the coins into Richard's hand. "You'll give Mr. MacEwan this money? Tell him it's to be put against Robert Elliot's tab."

Richard took the money and pocketed it, "I am sorry that Mr. MacEwan frightened you. Let me assure you that I will speak with him forthwith to curtail his overly enthusiastic methods for helping our customers settle their debts. The Quiet Woman is always happy to help her neighbors. We strive to offer friendly smiles and a warm place to visit."

Mrs. Elliot looked confused at Richard's strangely loud and florid speech, and looked at Elise for clarification.

"Robert Elliot is your husband's name?" Elise asked. When the woman nodded she said, "I'll give Mr. MacEwan your message."

"And give him those coins, if you please?" Tears started to roll down Mrs. Elliot's cheeks. "Don't let Mr. MacEwan hurt my husband, Miss. He's a good man to us, my Robert. He'll pay what he owes."

"Oh look at that! It's already our turn at the pump," Richard said with an artificial smile and a tip of his hat.

She took the hint and picked up her bucket. "I'll just go to the back of the queue then," she said uncertainly. When no one responded, she slouched away with her kid still howling and clutching the back of her skirt.

Richard couldn't work the pump handle fast enough. When the buckets were full, he insisted on carrying them both and somehow managed to grab Elise's elbow at the same time to hurry her away from the whispering crowd, sloshing water as he went. "What on earth was that all about?" Elise asked as she trotted behind Richard.

"I've told Thomas time and time again he needn't threaten people for them to repay the Quiet Woman. He just needs to *remind* them of their debt. A reminder is all they need." Richard was agitated and as a result, more of the precious water sloshed out of the buckets.

"Threaten?" It was difficult to believe Thomas would ever threaten someone as pitiful as Mrs. Elliot. Elise pictured his blue eyes glaring at her through the mantle of his black hair. It was hard to believe others couldn't see through the act.

"I try to remember that he loves the Quiet Woman as much as I do but that he may be more brutish in his methods for protecting her. It all comes from his earliest years I'd wager. A thing like living on the London streets with that dreadful woman can't be wiped from a person's character, not to mention his questionable parentage."

"You mean Mrs. Southill? I don't think he knew his parents."

"Yes. As I said: questionable." Richard slowed to a stop and waited for Elise to catch up. "But one mustn't dwell on such things." He smiled reassuringly as he hung the buckets on Elise's yoke. "I presume you can find your way back to the Quiet Woman from here? It's just two lefts and a right at the haberdashery."

"Two lefts?" Elise pointed hesitantly down the road.

"Quite right." He touched his hat politely. "Until this evening then," he said and took off in the opposite direction, his long legs working too fast for Elise to question him further.

A left and then a left at the dashing habery, Elise thought as she watched Richard quickly receding away. She tried to picture the landmark he'd specified, but had a hard time imagining what a radishabery might look like. The only thing she could think of was a cart of some sort. They'd passed plenty of vegetable carts, but she couldn't remember one that specifically displayed radishes for sale. She'd been too intent on keeping up and not hitting anyone with the wooden bludgeon she had draped across her shoulders to notice the particulars of the sales carts.

The yoke now felt ten times more cumbersome with two full buckets of water swinging from it on her already bruised and sore shoulders. She took a few steps in the direction Richard had pointed and the swinging weight of the buckets caused her to shuffle off balance. She overcorrected to her right and water sloshed down her skirt. With the aid of a stream of profanity, she managed to steady the buckets with both hands. When she began again, Elise walked more slowly and with her legs spaced wide apart in a balanced waddle. Recognizing Mary's solid gait in her own movements, she smiled and headed for the Quiet Woman with a newfound respect for the barmaid.

WHERE IS IT?

This is all Mary's fault, thought Elise grumpily after countless city blocks where she was forced to swing back and forth to avoid smacking people with her load. If it hadn't been for Mary and her stupid crush on that stupid Frenchman, she never would have been asked to fetch water, Richard would never have abandoned her in deepest London, she wouldn't still be wondering what a havershamery was, and she wouldn't now be completely lost. Elise's mind worked over how to exact revenge as she staggered along down the narrow road. Maybe she should scatter a thick layer of sand in Mary's bed, or dunk all her pantaloons in beef broth so she'd attract stray dogs. Replacing her face powder with cinders from the fireplace seemed too obvious.

It had been easier following behind Richard who had easily cleared a path through the costermongers selling parasols, apples, second hand clothing, bits of old iron and other trash, the scullery maids, the bakers, the clerks, merchants, laborers, layabouts, and all the other riffraff of the streets. It felt like the entire population was out walking. Plodding through the crowd, she became more and more tired as the weight on her shoulders pressed her down. With her hands occupied in steadying the buckets, she was unable to lift her skirt when she stepped off the platform to circle around those that formed clots in her way. As a result, the hem of her skirt swished over everything disgusting that pooled along the edges of the road, which then slowly worked its way up her legs. Initially, Elise had attempted to stop people for directions. Three women she asked looked straight through her and gave her a wide berth as they passed and a young man asked for money for the favor. She thought she would finally get the help she needed from a finely dressed gentleman, but when he tried to lead her down a strange alley, Elise thought better of following and hurried back to the main street. The name he'd hurled at her retreating back confirmed Elise's instincts, so she resolved to find her own way back.

A woman who approached on the arm of a gentleman flipped her skirt away from Elise in what was more of a gesture than an actual attempt to get out of Elise's way. The unspoken air of hierarchical self-importance that caused the woman to think a skirt swish was all she needed to move out of the way made Elise's teeth grind. She wasn't accustomed to thinking of herself as near the lowest rung of society, and she didn't like the way it felt. Elise grazed the woman's shoulder with the end of her yoke and the bucket sloshed over the woman's skirt as she yelped in pain. "I say," the woman's escort yelled at her retreating back, "return here this instant or I'll thrash you within an inch of your life."

Elise rolled her eyes. He was obviously posturing. There was no way he'd chase her down. She knew she wasn't worth the sweat it would cause him, but the threat of punishment would be enough to win him his girlfriend's appreciation, and who knows what that could lead to? She just did the guy a big favor. She paused at yet another intersection and peered down the street. It seemed familiar, but in the way that one lane lined with brick buildings and paved in slop looked like any other brick lined slop chute. Elise used Mary's coat sleeve to wipe her escaping tears of frustration and the motion of raising her arm nearly upset the heavy yoke from her shoulders. She barely saved the buckets from being overturned. Choking down her sobs, she slipped away from the London crowds into the empty lane to gather her courage. A huge sigh escaped her lips when she took the torturous wooden board from her shoulders and carefully set the buckets down. Peace, away from the cries of the street vendors, the rattle of the carriages drawn by monstrous horses, and the snobbery of the upper class, was what she needed, if only for five minutes.

She'd never hear the end of it if she got back to the Quiet Woman without two full buckets of water, she thought to herself, and now they were three-quarters full. Elise considered trying to retrace her steps back to the pump. Everyone seemed to know Richard, so not only would she be able to top off the buckets, she'd probably find someone to tell her how to get back to the pub. She thought longingly of Tucson's logical grid of North-South, East-West streets. It was impossible to get lost in Tucson with the sun always so clear in the sky casting shadows in shades of burnt orange and lavender between the soft ridges of the Catalina Mountains directly North of the city. Find the Catalinas and you'll always be able to find your way home. Again, Elise was reminded of Mrs. Southill's words. "Find your way home," the witch had said. If only it was that easy.

The sound of footsteps caused Elise to suddenly straighten up and wipe her tears. A short man approached from the main road. He adjusted his cloak over his shoulders and pulled his hat lower on his brow, but his sallow look was unmistakable. "Mr. Laroque," called out Elise happily. "Am I glad to see you!"

The man glanced to his right and left, surveying the area as he quickly walked to her side and grabbed her elbow. Being newly introduced to the London custom of elbow grabbing, Elise went along as he led her into the shadows and growled at her in his own language.

"I'm sorry, I don't speak French. Did Mary send you? They must be worried about me by now." She continued in her relieved prattle, castigating both Mary and Richard for her current situation, until Mr. Laroque suddenly swung her hard into a stack of empty crates and she fell with her arms and legs inelegantly splayed.

The snarl on Mr. Laroque's face made Elise wish she hadn't looked at him. His expression spoke volumes, but his words were incomprehensible. "No *habla* French," Elise repeated slowly and loudly as she struggled to get back to her feet.

He stood so close she had to turn her head to avoid making eye contact. The sharp corners of the wooden crates pressed against her calves.

"You are a bad liar, Elise Dubois." He said her name in four perfectly accented syllables as if the name itself was proof of her understanding his language. "Where is the Emperor's jewel?"

The question was absurd. The type of person that kept jewelry wouldn't have horse manure caked to her ankles. "What are you talking about?"

"You know perfectly well. The emerald: give it to me."

"Right," she drawled. "Maybe women in France wear emeralds when they're sent to lug water, but here in London we don't find it very practical."

The force of his backhanded slap spun Elise back to the ground. She didn't even have time to scream before he snatched her hair and pulled her to the other side of the alley where he slammed her against the wall, pinning her with a body check and pressing the side of her face against the rough brick with one hand. "You conspired with that *salope* Lenormand. Do not think to fool me. Did you not think we would catch up with you? Fouché finds everyone, no matter where they hide." He switched back to French, speaking it in a low guttural lilt as he grazed the skin of her neck with his lips. Shivers went down her spine. His breath was hot and smelled vaguely sour and sulfuric, like he'd had too many of Mrs. Postlethwaite's pickled eggs. Elise closed her eyes and willed it all to go away—the water buckets, the soupy streets, the choking air, and most of all, the man who was grinding her face against the rough brick. "Tell me!" he shouted, interrupting Elise's prayers, and slammed her head against the wall a second time to add emphasis to his demand.

Time stretched and slowed. She saw nothing that wasn't ringed in red; she heard nothing that wasn't the pounding of her heart. She reached up with both hands and took hold of Laroque's wrist. When his hand came away from her face, she wasn't surprised at her success. She took two steps to the side, like a dancer circling her partner, and carried his arm backwards and up until he howled and bent forward. With his head now close to her waist, it was only natural to lift her knee and slam it into his face before pushing him away.

Her lungs expanded, taking in as much oxygen as physically possible to feed her muscles; her shoulders bent forward with her arms at her sides ready to pump. Run. Run fast. Run like there's nothing in front of you but blue skies and dusty trails. Elise lunged and felt her foot slide forward into her stride. Then, alarmingly, it continued to slide forward and her arms shot out at her sides to wave in wide circles, extended and flightless. *Grand jeté*, she suddenly remembered from her childhood ballet classes. I do know some French, she thought as she fell onto the cobblestones.

Before she could get up again, the Frenchman was against her back. There was no difference, Elise found, between the rough textures of the cobblestones in the street and the brick wall—both were equally unpleasant ground against her face. The only difference was this time the point of a knife pricked just under her jaw. Elise opened her mouth, but didn't know if she should beg for mercy or make up a location for the emerald he wanted so badly. He was speaking French again and when she didn't respond, he grabbed her hair and slammed her head against the ground. He's a one trick pony, she thought as the pain brought stars to her eyes. Her head hit the ground again and the stars sparkled green and flew with golden wings, buzzing pleasantly. If he killed her, maybe she would return to Tucson. The thought calmed her, and she smiled as Laroque's angry face faded from view. A new face took its place, and was scowling just like the old face, only crosshatched with white scars. "Thomas," Elise breathed.

"Move. Now," he ordered.

Elise obeyed. She scurried backwards on the ground like a crab to huddle against the wall while Thomas and Laroque circled each other with knives drawn. Thomas feigned a lunge to the right then spun in a dodge. The Frenchman countered with two jabs and a slice, but it didn't stop Thomas's forward momentum. He dropped his shoulder and sent Laroque skittering into the wall two feet from Elise. "I said move," shouted Thomas as the Frenchman shook off the blow and reached to grab her. She spiraled away just inches from his fingertips. While Laroque's attention was still centered on Elise, Thomas stepped in. He wrapped one massive arm around the Frenchman's head and pulled back, sliding his knife across the exposed neck. A spray of blood arced into the air, then ebbed.

"No, no, no, no, no. Don't scream," Thomas pleaded as the noise poured from Elise. He reached for her, but she flinched from his knife. He slid the knife back into his belt and caught her arm, which she deftly twisted from his grip. "Bloody hell, stop screaming." He grabbed her wrist again and with a jerk, pulled her against his chest and crushed his hand over her mouth. He sank into a squat, clamping down on her struggles and folding her into his lap. "Where are you going to run to?" he whispered in her ear. He pressed his cheek against her hair. "You've nowhere to run. Pull yourself together."

The memory of Mrs. Elliot begging for leniency for her husband loomed fresh in her mind. The woman's fear had confused her then, but now she understood. Thomas had killed without hesitation. Pull yourself together? She'd been barely keeping it together since she woke up a month ago, and now she was sitting in a murderer's lap inches from a pool of his victim's blood. Part of her had still been expecting to wake up one morning back home in her own bed, but there was nothing dream-like about the body sprawled against the wall.

"Please don't cry," Thomas crooned while rocking her. He moved his hand from her mouth and gently tucked her head under his chin and they sat balled like kittens while Elise trembled from the aftereffects of finally submitting to the reality of everything.

"I just want to go home," she whispered.

The world felt much colder when he opened his arms. She unsteadily climbed to her feet and turned to watch as Thomas dragged Laroque by his ankles into a dark niche where two buildings came together. To Elise, the red trail from Laroque's draining jugular looked like a neon sign reading, "Here lies a man with new gills," but Thomas seemed unconcerned. He half-heartedly tried to rub out the blood trail with the toe of his shoe. The action unnerved Elise. He was too casual, as though he'd done it all before.

"We've tarried too long. Can you walk?" he asked.

She took his offered hand and he pulled her close, catching her chin to twist her face up into the dull light. "Look at what that bastard did to you."

Elise was glad for the supportive arm around her waist, but the cupped chin went too far. It reminded her that her cheek stung like hell where the skin had been ground away. "It'll heal," she said, trying to ignore his probing look. The side of her mouth felt thick where her lip had split.

"I hope that doesn't leave a permanent mark."

"Maybe everyone will leave me alone if it does."

"I know how that feels. You wouldn't like it." Thomas pushed his shaggy black hair away from his face to reveal his own scars but all Elise could see were his intense blue eyes, which effectively disproved both of their arguments for and against facial disfigurement.

He led her away through more quiet alleys out of sight of those who might notice the blood on Thomas's sleeve and the bruises on Elise's face. At first, Elise attempted to keep track of where they were going, but since the route was so circuitous and she didn't know where she was coming from, the effort was fruitless. She was surprised when Thomas called a rest on the stoop of a boarded entrance to an old shop. A lopsided sign over the door read, "Miss Mary's Haberdashery." To Elise, the sign was more evidence to prove it was all Mary's fault.

Thinking of Mary reminded her of why she had stepped out in the first place. "Oh no," she gasped, "the buckets." Her eyes well up again when she realized she'd lost them. "Mrs. Postlethwaite will flay me."

"After all that's happened today, you're still frightened by Mrs. P? She'll forgive the buckets when she sees your bruised face, don't you worry." Thomas guided her to sit on the bottom step and stirred a small bonfire that some other wanderer had left smoldering just outside the shop's stoop. When the coals glowed and crackled, Thomas sat back with a hiss and clutched his side.

"You're stabbed? Why didn't you say anything?" Elise cried. She reached out to look under his coat but had her hand slapped away.

"Leave it. It's nothing."

"Just let me look at it."

"No."

Thomas pulled his pipe and tobacco from his pocket and Elise instantly forgot about the possible gravity of Thomas's knife wound. "Will you share that bowl?"

He smiled. "Yes."

There was something calming about watching Thomas perform the ritual of packing his pipe with three pinches of tobacco. "There's rules to filling a pipe," he instructed. "They say the first pinch you push in as if shaking the hand of a baby." He tamped the tobacco into the bowl with his thumb. "The second, the hand of a lady. The last you push in like it's a man's hand you're shaking." He lit the pipe with a splinter of wood from the dying embers and passed it to Elise.

"Someone should hurry up and invent little sticks that ignite on their own," she said as she blew smoke into the air.

"Wouldn't that be something?"

Elise smiled, feeling strangely calm. "I'm glad you showed up when you did."

"It's all Mrs. P.'s doing. When Richard came into the kitchen with you having yet to come back, she started to worry. So, I sent Johnny off to look for you. Well, when he came back shaking his head, I went to look for you myself. But it's Mrs. P. as started the worrying." He took the pipe back from Elise and they sat in silence and watched the little bonfire eat up the last of its tinder. "Who was he?" Thomas finally asked.

"Who was who?"

"The Frenchman."

"You mean Mr. Laroque? You know as much as I do."

Thomas seemed to think about this for a while as he puffed, then asked, "So what did he want from you?"

Elise was about to mention the emerald, but thought better of it. The idea of a missing jewel felt familiar somehow, like trying to recapture a fading dream five minutes after waking up. "I think he thought I was someone else." She reached for the pipe, but Thomas held onto it and puffed thoughtfully.

"Have any of your memories come back?"

"What is this, twenty questions? No. I have no memories."

Thomas turned to look at her and pulled the pipe out of his mouth. "Are you sure?"

"No. Memories."

Elise felt herself wither under his glare. It wouldn't have been so bad if he didn't look so hurt. "I saw what you did," he finally said. "You bloodied the frog's nose. I've never seen a woman get out of a tight spot the way you did. You wouldn't have needed my help at all had you not slipped and fallen." He spat into the fire and shook his head.

"Wait, you were watching me? Why didn't you step in sooner?"

Elise was relieved to see Thomas looked appropriately uncomfortable at having been discovered lurking in the shadows. He had displayed no shame in murdering, but watching a woman getting beaten up, that, at least, seemed to make him bashful. "I didn't want to make a bad situation worse. Look here," he said when Elise rolled her eyes, "how else am I supposed to understand what you're about if you never open your mouth except to say gibberish? Everyone thinks you're touched because half the things you say make no bloody sense. But I know there's more to you than what people think. Watching you fight just now proved it. Where did you learn to do that?"

Elise struggled to find an answer. Where would a 19th Century woman learn to fight? Not one of the pathways she took to learn to defend herself would make any sense to Thomas. "I don't know," she said.

"Yes you do. You know. You know everything. You just won't tell me," Thomas knocked the ash out of his pipe on the step. "You've been nothing but trouble since the day you arrived. We should have swept you out with the Magdalenes when we had the chance, only I suppose it wouldn't have done any good. You strays always come back for feed."

"Strays? Isn't that the pot calling the kettle black? What about you and your secrets? I bet tonight wasn't the first time you slit someone's throat. I met Mrs. Robert Elliot today. For some reason she thinks you're going to hurt her husband; are you going to slit his throat too?"

"I'd never... Robert Elliot?" Thomas pulled his forelock, looking the picture of a guilty man. Then he heaved himself to his feet. "He owes the Quiet Woman quite a bit."

"You've got a lot of nerve calling me a stray. You're nothing but a thug. That woman's got five kids to feed and instead of buying food she's giving Richard—"

"It's bloody Mr. Ferrington to you."

"Whatever. Giving Mr. Ferrington money and weeping in the street because you're strong-arming her husband. Why don't you just stop him from coming in and drinking?"

"Stop him? You stop him. Aren't you the one as serves him? In fact, why don't you stop all the men who come in to the Quiet Woman to get cut and fuddled. That'll be just grand for business. The Dancing Bear would be so sorry to have to serve all our customers."

"I'm just saying if they don't have any money, then they shouldn't get served. No one should be owing us anything."

"And I'm telling you that's just not how it's done. If we don't keep a running ledger for the local lads, they'll take their business elsewhere where they don't have to pay in advance. But if you want to tell Mr. Elliot when he's had his last, you go right ahead."

"I don't know what he looks like," Elise said, feeling defeated. The entire system was stupid, she decided, and rigged against everyone. The pubs lose because they rely on drunks that don't pay up, and the drunks lose because the pubs keep pumping them full of beer. The only winners were the brewers who always got paid.

"That's your problem, Elise. You're so wrapped in your secrets you can't see beyond your own nose. How is it that Mr. Elliot comes in every night and you don't know his face? You don't care to learn about anyone, that's how." Thomas shook his head. "Every night he drinks away his wages with us, and him with five wee ones and a wife at home. How afraid for him do you feel now?"

Not very, that was true. "It's not up to you to punish him for being a bad father."

"Punish him? I'm not punishing him. I don't care how he treats his children; I just want to get what he owes us." Thomas held out his hand to help her to her feet, but Elise ignored it and stood up on her own. "Oh, so it's like that now, is it?" Thomas dropped his hand and snarled. "Then you'd best try to keep up," he called over his shoulder as he started walking away. "I'll not hunt you down again if you get lost a second time."

The Wisdom of Onions

Ahead, in the middle of the block, a pole jutted from the wall of a building to which was attached a familiar sign adorned with the image of a headless woman, only quiet by default. Elise breathed a sigh of relief at having finally reached the pub and felt comforted by the creaking wooden flag. Somehow, in the short time that she'd been living there, the emblem had etched itself onto her identity. Had the bar been in Tucson, she would have bought the t-shirt.

Despite Thomas's parting words, keeping up had been no trouble. What she found hard was maintaining the ten paces she'd deliberately placed between them since the wound in his side had begun to slow him down. He crossed the front of the pub and peered surreptitiously through the windows. Elise followed in a crouch, not really knowing why. She tried to look inside the dining hall, but could only see her own reflection in the soot-caked window. She was truly a mess, with abrasions on her cheeks and a swollen lip. The bun she'd carefully twisted and pinned that morning had exploded into an auburn halo of lopsided frizz after having been pulled and yanked in the fight. Quickly, she tried to flatten it down with the palms of her hands. This, she thought to herself as she longed for her shea butter deep conditioning hot oil hair serum, is why respectable women wear bonnets.

Thomas was already circling around to the back so that they could enter through the kitchen instead of the dining hall. It was a brave thing to do, considering Mrs. Postlethwaite was sure to be standing at the table holding a large knife. Just outside the kitchen door, Thomas paused to take a deep breath and straighten his coat. Then he swung the door wide with conviction. He wasn't even inside before Mrs. Postlethwaite's loud voice poured into the courtyard. "For God's sake Tommy, what's happened to you this time?" Nothing got past the cook's shrewd eye. She could have been a fantastic nurse, thought Elise.

When Elise stepped through the door and around from behind Thomas, the cook nearly dropped her carving knife. "What happened to her face?" she exclaimed looking to Thomas for answers.

"Don't look at me like that," he replied. "I didn't have nothing to do with the state of her."

"I didn't say you did, so don't be pert with me."

"You didn't have to say it to think it," Thomas shouted. Elise and Mrs. Postlethwaite stared at Thomas as he stormed out into the dining hall. He didn't get far. "Do I look like a barmaid?" he snapped at a customer who complained about a delinquent refill. He turned and stomped back into the kitchen. "Where's Mary?" he demanded. "Where are the Ferringtons?"

"Mary's tending Mr. Tilsdale," Mrs. Postlethwaite said.

"Elise, go bring her back down here. We can't be nursing everyone who falls into our path."

"He's got no people, and is doing very poorly," Mrs. Postlethwaite chided. "We can't leave him to struggle on his own. At any rate, Mary's very fond of Mr. Tilsdale and Mrs. Ferrington allowed it wouldn't do to have another room sitting empty if we can help it."

Thomas turned to press his forehead against the wall. When he raised his hands to work them through his hair, Elise caught a glimpse of a growing red stain under his coat. "Mary's fondness for Old Tilsdale cannot be more important than getting Mr. Reims another beer," he said through his teeth.

Elise went to pick up a jug half full of beer that was on the kitchen table, but Mrs. Postlethwaite stopped her. "I'll do that. You're not fit to be seen, and Mr. Reims can just wait. I've been pouring for him all afternoon so he can't be in that much of a hurry now." She took the large kettle off the fire and poured steaming water into an ewer. "Johnny fetched the water when it took you so long to return. I know you'll be wanting to thank him for that," she looked directly at Elise, implicating her in everything.

"But I had the buckets," Elise said, confused.

"Do you really think the Quiet Woman can only afford two buckets at one time?" Her shrewd eyes took note of Elise's empty hands, but said nothing about it. "Johnny's gone to collect pots so we'll have enough for tonight, and I'll have him fill jugs when he returns. We don't need anyone else. So get on with you," Mrs. Postlethwaite said, waving at Thomas, "and take your bad humor away from my kitchen."

"I'll go, but Elise will relieve Mary from Mr. Tilsdale's room so Mary can come down and help. You might not need her now but you'll need her soon enough, and the Queen can do more good up there with Tilsdale. Where's Richard?"

"How should I know? Mr. Ferrington will be here later this evening, I'm sure."

"Aye. He'll drag himself back here from his gaming tables when the work's all done." Thomas turned and left the kitchen. "I'll be in my quarters if you need me."

"I said we won't be needing you Tommy, so don't be coming back down tonight or I'll give you what's what." She turned to Elise and placed her hands on her hips. "And you. I don't want to hear naught about how you've come to be all cut and bruised. Not one word. I've got to think of my own family. I've got my own daughter, you know, my own troubles. I don't need yours. Just look at what your troubles has done to our Thomas."

Instead of looking at the retreating barman, Elise looked deep into the ewer that Mrs. Postlethwaite pushed into her hands. The amount of bath water seemed wholly inadequate for removing the amount of crap that was caked and flaking off her legs. "I need a shower," Elise mumbled, her tears welling again. "I want another dress too."

"A what? A dress? I can't wave my hands and get you a dress. I can't cook one up with potatoes and carrots. Don't look to me for dresses. The only dressing I'll be doing is for this beast," she pointed to the large carcass of unidentifiable poultry with the knife and then brought it down on the neck of the bird. Elise cringed and jumped back. "There's a new Mr. Dodo-something-or-other showed up today who's too fancy to eat plain hen. Mary will perk right up when she sees him. Seems Mary's fond of capons too." Two more chops and the feet were scraped down the table and out of the cook's way. Jacob jumped down from her perch and swiftly made off with one of the feet. When Mrs. Postlethwaite turned her back to fuss at the cat, Elise tucked an apple into her apron pocket and slunk out of the kitchen, keeping her own head down and protected.

It was late afternoon when Elise, scrubbed, but hardly clean, finally entered Mr. Tilsdale's bedroom with Mrs. Southill's medical kit slung over her shoulder. Although the curtains over the window were pulled wide open, it was still dark in the room. Taking advantage of the feeble light, Mary sat on the only chair in the room directly under the window and squinted at her knitting. Opposite Mary, a narrow bed was pushed against the wall where Mr. Tilsdale's labored breathing could be heard behind concealing drapes. A rickety nightstand leaned dangerously to one side under a washbasin full of murky water. Next to the basin, a candle remained stubbornly unlit despite the gloom. "I didn't know you could knit," Elise said, by way of hello.

"I don't have time for it most days," Mary replied without bothering to look away from her project.

Elise pushed the bed curtains out of the way to view her patient. His change in condition from just that morning was alarming. Mr. Tilsdale was a naked potato chip of a man: pale, salty, greasy, and alarmingly thin. "Why are the blankets on the floor?" she asked.

"He messed them the last time he got locked up and arched. I bathed him and he's been sleeping ever since. I think he was overheated."

"Locked up? What do you mean locked up?" Elise couldn't believe the symptoms had turned so bad, so fast.

"You know, locked up." Mary stuck her arms, legs, and tongue out, her impression of a seized body. "That's why they call it 'lockjaw.' Don't you know anything?"

Elise swallowed hard and tried to let Mary's final question slide. "He needs more blankets. He can't just hang out naked like this."

"Why ever not? He's too hot for blankets right now."

"He's got a fever. We need to keep him warm."

"He's already burning up. He doesn't need blankets, he needs cooling off."

"And what happens when his fever breaks and he's left shivering?"

"He'll just mess the blankets again. Will you be doing the washing for all those linens?"

Elise sighed. "At least find the man's coat to drape over him, would you?" She pushed the piled bedclothes further away with the side of her foot. There had always been an objectionable odor in Mr. Tilsdale's room, so the soiled blankets didn't add much color to the bouquet, but all the same she didn't want the pile to sit on the floor right under her nose. Also objectionable was the washbasin. Elise wrinkled her nose and moved it closer to Mary so she could set her medical kit on the cleared table and consider her patient's options. There weren't many. Elise cast her eyes down the length of Mr. Tilsdale's naked body as she thought about whether to continue to use her diminishing supply of willow bark tea or save it, and saw that bulging strips of muslin were tied around the bottoms of his feet. "What's up with that?" Elise pointed.

"Onions," Mary said, looking up briefly from her knitting. She'd made no move to find Mr. Tilsdale's coat, convinced he needed to remain naked.

"Bunions?"

"Onions," Mary said louder. "Why would I be wrapping his bunions?" She shook her head incredulously.

Elise gently poked a bandage and was rewarded with a distinctive smell. "No way. You tied onion slices to his feet?"

"Of course I did. It draws the fever out. My Gran used to do the same when I was feeling poorly. Everyone knows about onions."

"Wasn't it your Gran who told you to sprinkle weed outside the door of the man you want to marry?" Elise thought of Thomas dragging Mary's future bridegroom down the alley, leaving a trail of blood stained cobblestones. "How's that working out for you?"

"It will work, you'll see. My Gran was a very clever woman."

"I'll bet she was." Elise put her hands to her temples and forcefully pushed back the memory of the afternoon.

"You're not staying here, are you?" Mary asked hopefully, putting her knitting down for the first time since Elise arrived. "Mr. Tilsdale likes me better. I should be the one to stay at his side." She squinted in the dim light. "What's happened to your face?"

"Mrs. P. wants you downstairs." Elise ignored the question. Suddenly she really wanted Mary to leave.

"Me? Why not you?"

"Because I'm a better nurse than you." Elise put the willow bark back in her bag. It would be wasted on Mr. Tilsdale.

"So Mr. MacEwan finally gave you the back of his hand, did he? I'm surprised he showed as much self-restraint as he did. You're not a better nurse. You're a know-nothing—didn't even know about onions to the feet. I don't believe Mrs. P. sent for me. You just said that so you could sit idly up here." She picked her knitting back up and sniffed. "I'm staying right here. Mr. Tilsdale needs me."

"Then stay. Whatever, I don't care. But you should know that Thomas is down for the count, so if Mrs. P. has to climb those steps to find someone to help her, or if Thomas has to be dragged out of bed, you might end up with a face that matches mine."

A loud groan drew the women's attention back to the subject of their argument. "Look what you've done," Mary shouted. "You've gone and woken him." She got up from her chair and pushed Elise out of the way so she could take her place at the head of the bed. With a wide swipe of her arm, Mary pushed all Elise's herb bundles onto the floor and replaced the water basin on the nightstand.

"Stop!" Elise cried in horror as Mary extended a dripping rag towards Mr. Tilsdale's face. "You wiped his ass with that!"

Mr. Tilsdale gave another groan, as if to echo Elise's objection. He balled his hands into fists and drew them up towards his armpits to arch himself backwards in a reverse headstand. "He's doing it again. He's locking up," Mary cried. The rag finished its journey to cool Mr. Tilsdale's forehead and he curled his toes in agony.

The sound of Mr. Tilsdale's breathing filled the room, a desperate whistling wheeze as he struggled against the combined constraints of a ribcage that was clenched so tightly it could no longer expand, a frozen diaphragm, and an already compromised larynx. The rag was completely forgotten. All Elise wanted was that red button at the head of his bed, the one she could slam with her fist the second she knew she was in over her head, and have a team of doctors, respiratory therapists, and nurses miraculously arrive to take over his care. "How long does this last?" she barked at Mary.

"It's happened twice before and both times lasted forever." She slopped water onto the pillow and started to cry.

"Get out of my way," Elise said, pushing Mary. The average person can only stay conscious for three minutes without breathing. Elise calculated that if he'd survived two attacks, then they couldn't have lasted more than a couple minutes. It must have felt like a lifetime to Mary, she thought with some sympathy. In the hospital she would have given him oxygen and waited for the crash team to come intubate him. He was so tight she couldn't even reposition him for a better airway. She could grind or mix or steep any herbs she wanted, but anything she made would have to be swallowed, and there was no way she would be able to get anything past his clenched jaw. Even if she had an herb that was powerful enough to act as a muscle relaxant or, even better, a paralyzing agent, she would need direct access into his veins to use it. There was nothing she could do.

"Come back here," she said softly to Mary who was weeping at the foot of the bed. "Talk to him. Tell him how much we'll miss him if he leaves us. Do you know any songs? Sing him a song. Something sweet."

Mary wiped her eyes as she hesitantly approached. Her thin high voice wavered with suppressed sobs as she began a lullaby that could barely be heard over Mr. Tilsdale's gurgled breathing. "*Sleep my child, sleep peacefully. God will send his angels to attend thee,*" she sang.

Elise squeezed Mr. Tilsdale's fist in sympathy, then found his pulse at his wrist. The fever by itself was bad enough, but combined with the overachiever's gym workout forced on him by the tetany, it was no wonder his pulse raced. Elise hoped Mary's song would bring down his heart rate. There were all kinds of medicine, she thought.

The fragile breaths he took fell into rhythm with the song even as his breathing grew weaker and shallower. "*'Tis the hour to stop your weeping. All the world is sleeping.*" Mr. Tilsdale's eyes rolled to the side to look at Mary's tear-stained face. She must have found this encouraging because she wailed more loudly, if not more melodiously, "*A solemn bell sounds the hour for the angels to alight upon your bower.*"

The pulse in his wrist sputtered, then faded, then stopped. Thankfully he had only suffered through a few verses. It hadn't been suffocation that killed him. It was his heart that couldn't take it. "I'm so sorry," Elise whispered to Mary.

Mary took a deep breath, ready to sing some more, then let her breath out in a long sigh. "He's gone, isn't he?"

"Yes, he is. I'm glad you were here for him." Elise dragged the chair from under the window up close to the bed for Mary. Then she gathered up the contents of her medical kit and left quietly, closing the door on the sound of Mary's choking sobs.

In the hallway, Elise tried to force everything that had just happened into insignificance so that she could swallow it more easily. The still air and close walls in the hallway helped as she leaned her head against the door and tried not to cry. Downstairs, the voices in the dining hall were muted. Mrs. Postlethwaite would soon struggle to get everyone served as the dinner hour came on. Elise knew she should go down to help, since Mary wouldn't be in any condition to do so, but she couldn't move. Upstairs, she heard the sound of a door squeaking open, shuffling footsteps, then the door thudded shut as a conversation continued in the hallway.

"You can't just sell it," came Thomas's voice. "It doesn't belong to you."

"She doesn't even remember she ever had it." Richard's voice sounded petulant. "We badly need the money."

"It doesn't belong to you." Thomas insisted. "You should give it back to her. It might help her to remember what happened."

Elise strained to hear more of the conversation, but both men had lowered their voices to whispers. Then she heard Richard say, "Fine. But you must take better pains to tabulate the debts of our customers. I'm certain they all eat and drink much more than gets recorded."

"We can't keep taking the lads at their word and writing it down. I can't keep up with it. They must pay for each drink they order at the time that they order them."

Elise rolled her eyes to hear Thomas repeat her own suggestion as though it was his idea, especially since he had so roundly dismissed it only hours earlier.

"Come now, Tom. We can't do that. They'd leave the Quiet Woman to drink at the Dancing Bear. You know that."

Elise didn't have to see Thomas to know he was running his hand through his hair. "I can't keep up with it," he repeated sullenly. No one said anything for a moment and Elise touched the doorknob to Mr. Tilsdale's room, ready to duck back in the moment she heard footsteps on the stairs. She didn't want to get caught in the hallway doing nothing but eavesdropping. Suddenly, Thomas roared, "For god's sake, I can't possibly chase down all the men on this list. Do you want me dead? Is that what you want?"

Richard laughed in response. "Don't be so dramatic! There are just a few more names than usual. If you go out to hunt them more often, you won't feel the difference because then you'll have less debtors to find per night."

"More often? No. I'll get Cooper to set up another fight for me when I'm healed again. I think he had someone in mind. We can earn more money that way."

"That'll take too long. The brewery needs the money now."

"Look at me, Richard. Look at my gut. How am I to get these men to pay me with my gut torn like this? I'm no bloody cat. I don't have nine lives."

There was a long pause and Elise caught her breath, knowing that Richard was looking at the wound Thomas hadn't let her see. She prayed it was a slice, rather than a deep stab where tetanus bacteria could grow and thrive, buried in his flesh. She couldn't help but picture the barman's body clenched into the same horrifying arch that killed Mr. Tilsdale. She knew the idea wasn't a stretch. It could happen easily.

"You'll heal, Tom." she heard Richard say softly. "You always do."

Which One?

Elise ran downstairs towards the kitchen. The kitchen was where everyone was healthy, the fire was joyous, the food was plentiful, and the cats purred. In the kitchen you didn't need a candle to chase away death and darkness like you did on the upper floors. In the kitchen, it was all love.

"You again?" Mrs. Postlethwaite exclaimed as Elise burst into the room. "I thought we'd agreed that you'd send down Mary and keep your ugly broken mug upstairs."

"Mr. Tilsdale passed away a few minutes ago. Mary's not going to be any help tonight."

Mrs. Ferrington, just returned, was having difficulty slipping the ties of her apron over her head since she'd forgotten to first remove the fancy bonnet that she wore when out calling. "He's dead?" she asked, her voice muffled. "That's a nuisance. He's two months in arrears."

"Just one," Mrs. Postlethwaite corrected.

"Regardless, I think Richard was counting on that money this week. Well, he was a good tenant and a good man, may he rest in peace. I hope we can find another just as steady to take his place, and soon.

"Goodness," Mrs. Ferrington exclaimed when she finally got the shroud away from her face to look at Elise. "What happened to you?"

Mrs. Postlethwaite jumped in before Elise could answer. "She tripped and fell in the street when she was sent to fetch water. She must have slid a good twenty feet face first in the mud." The cook put a plate down on the table and filled it with an enormous ladle of stew while giving Elise a hard look and a hunk of bread. Elise found a spoon and pulled up a stool, feeling more grateful than she had in a long time for the warm food. "I don't think she should serve our customers with her face all scraped up like that. It's not good for business, don't you think?"

"Certainly not," Mrs. Ferrington agreed. "You and I can handle the curs in the dining hall, with Johnny to run for us. Where is that rascal, by the by? You don't mind working late tonight, do you Mrs. P.?"

Mrs. Postlethwaite heaved a sigh. "Would it even matter if I minded? No, I don't mind." She took a bottle of brandy off the shelf and poured it into a small cup for Elise, who threw it back thankfully. "You heard Mrs. Ferrington," she said refilling the glass. "Finish up your dinner and get on to bed. You've had a difficult day."

Despite the promise of an early dismissal, Elise stayed in the kitchen with Johnny who had finally appeared not in a puff of smoke as she half expected, but in a cloud of dust from the cellar with beer on his breath. They worked for over three hours scrubbing the dishes while the two older women moved about the dining hall. The work relieved the chaos in her brain, and the company of the women was reassuring as the night quieted down. Perhaps it was the pall of death in the building, or maybe it was Mrs. Postlethwaite's glares, but Thomas was not needed to control the high spirits of the customers, and Richard's fiddle was not missed.

It was late when Elise finally climbed the stairs to the third floor with her second ewer that day of hot bathwater a heavy luxury in her arms. The tiny flame from a candle she dangled off her index finger from the ring of a candlestick cast eerie shadows against the walls as she moved up slowly, step by weary step. In her bedroom, she rested, elbows on knees, on the edge of her mattress and set both candle and ewer on the floor between her feet. Steam rose from the mouth of the ewer, depositing dew on Elise's face and disguising the tears that rolled down her cheeks.

Across the room, from behind the closed drapes of Mary's bed, a voice called out peevishly. "Close the door, you're letting in the cold." Elise wasn't sure how Mary could feel a draft, sequestered as she was in her bed. She decided the barmaid had an alien sensitivity to any possible irritant Elise could create, accidental or otherwise.

She walked back to the door, and instead of closing it, stood in the open doorway to look down the hall towards Thomas's room. Their walk through London already seemed like it had happened years ago while her first awakening in the Quiet Woman felt like yesterday. She was amazed how time shortened and expanded so unreasonably when the weather was always bleak and no one wore a watch. Time was meaningless now. She didn't even keep track of the days of the week, only knowing what day it was when payday happened along and all hell broke loose downstairs. Not that it was ever payday for her.

"If I have to get up to close that door myself…" Mary threatened loudly from behind her curtain. Elise leaned against the doorframe and ignored her roommate. It was unlikely Thomas had gone out to shake people down, as Richard had asked him to do. Elise imagined him lying in bed slowly bleeding out from the wound in his side. She bit her bottom lip in hesitation. She wanted nothing more than to sit on the edge of her bed and soak her feet in the water she'd lugged all the way up from the kitchen. Finally, she sighed and went to pick up the ewer, throwing her medical kit over her shoulder as she closed the door behind her.

Something felt very wrong about walking up the three stairs in the hallway towards Thomas's bedroom. He's just a guy, she told herself as she stood in front of the strangely small entrance to Thomas's bedroom and fought back her nerves. There was nothing wrong about offering her services, and she wasn't tied to 19th century moralities, she reasoned. She knocked. Her heart raced as she heard his footsteps approach the door. It was a quiet sound, like a man accustomed to sneaking around corners. However, the door banged open with very little stealth.

"Oh. It's you," Thomas said as he ducked under the doorframe for a better look. Looming awkwardly next to the little door of the garret, he seemed much larger than he really was. Elise wondered how he hadn't grown up crookedly, living so near the roof his entire life. He was backlit from the candles in his room, but Elise didn't have to see his face to know he was glowering. "What do you want?"

"I'm here to clean up your knife wound."

"I've already done it."

Elise looked down at his waist. "I don't think what you did there counts." He was still wearing his trousers, but he'd taken his shirt off and twisted it into a narrow bandage to wrap around his side. A large red stain bloomed across the shirt over his right flank and dried blood was smeared on his skin where he'd tried to clean himself up.

"I don't need your tending-to," he repeated. "Just go back to your own room. You shouldn't be here."

Elise's eyes narrowed. There was something about him that seemed off, and it wasn't just blood loss. "Are you drinking?" she asked.

"No."

"Yes you are. The bottle's right there on that table." She craned her head around him to see inside.

Thomas turned and walked back into his room but left the door open. It wasn't exactly an invitation, but Elise chose to interpret it that way.

Though the ceiling was low, sweeping down on one side so that Thomas had to progressively bend over to walk to his bed, the actual room was quite large and fit a surprising amount of furniture. Near his bed, a small table pushed against the wall was a pedestal for a washbasin. A silver mirror was hung just over the basin and soap, razor blade, and brush were all neatly lined within reach. To the right of the mirror, clean shirts and a towel were hung on pegs. Elise set her ewer down near the basin. The room was so infused with his personality that she felt uncomfortable by the intimacy of it. The bed looked like it may have fit Thomas at one time, but no one bothered to upgrade the length as the boy grew into a man. She imagined him curled comfortably at night with one of the books he had stacked on the floor, or stretched out with his feet and ankles dangling off the end. "I guess you like to read," Elise said stupidly, looking at more books that were stacked on a nearby desk. "I thought you were a boxer."

"I can't control the way I was built, or my place in society, but I can control how I use my mind," Thomas replied.

"That's very fatalistic."

"Is it?" He took a petulant swig from his bottle and sat down on the edge of his bed. "I thought I was being radical." He pointed to a chair that was covered in a pile of papers that were flowing to the floor. "Please be seated," he offered, leaning forward to swipe his arm across the seat of the chair to clean it. Paper floated like fall leaves to the floor, and he kicked at them to clear a path. One of the papers caught Elise's eye. It was a long list of names and monetary figures containing tally marks and corrections. She pretended not to notice the list, and instead dragged the chair to place it directly in front of the barman, who looked up at her expectantly. "I forgot to ask," he said with a smile, "Did you enjoy your outing with Richard? You must be the only chambermaid in London to take the elbow of her employer and be so escorted to the water pump."

Elise opened her mouth to respond but nothing came out as she struggled with the idea that being escorted was unusual. "It was nice of him to take me," she finally thought to say, feeling deeply embarrassed. "Did Mr. Ferrington give you Mrs. Elliot's money?"

"So now it's 'Mr. Ferrington'? No. He didn't give me Mrs. Elliot's money. Why would he give me the money? I'm not the one who makes the decisions here."

Elise looked down at the chair, suddenly feeling too shy to sit.

"Stop hovering, you're making me nervous. Either leave," he looked up to meet her eyes, "or tell me who your people are and how you came to be in the lane that night. Why was that Frenchman after you?"

"Let's not do this again. I told you. I don't know anything about that French guy. I'm just a chambermaid."

He scraped his hair back and his blue eyes flashed startlingly from the darkness. "You never were no maid, chamber or otherwise. And you're no lady."

Elise finally sat down. Somehow his anger was easier to take than whatever weirdness he was projecting earlier. "You don't need to do that," Thomas said. He sat up in alarm as she scooted her chair closer to him and prepared to pour hot water into the basin. "I was going to go see Mrs. Southill tomorrow. It won't be the first time I've gone to bed bleeding and I've got the brandy to keep me company."

"Mrs. Southill? That's a long walk and with all the bleeding you've already done, you'll be too weak to make it. Just let me look at it."

"No." Thomas's black eyebrows furrowed dangerously. He leaned forward with a scowl while the muscles in his shoulders rippled with intimidation.

"I see what you're doing," Elise growled. "Stop it. You're not winning this one." When he slumped back down, she couldn't help but smirk. All men were peacocks, she thought as she set to untying the shirt around his waist. After fumbling at the knot, she brought a candle closer to get a better look. It was not a simple granny knot. "What the hell did you do here?" She tugged at what she thought was a loose end.

"Damn it lass, that hurts. Stop pulling and cut it free. Where's your knife?"

Elise thought how she used to keep a pair of scissors that were perfect for sliding under bandages in the pocket of her scrubs. She used to keep lots of things in her pockets—rolls of gauze, rolls of tape, syringes full of saline, pens, medications. Now all she kept in her apron pocket was lint. "I don't have a knife."

"Why not? I'd have thought you'd be smart enough to pilfer one from the kitchen, especially after what happened today."

"What am I going to do with a knife, slit someone's throat?" She yanked again at the knot, but it didn't budge.

"Fight dirty, is what. Stop tugging, I said. I'll do it." He grabbed her wrist and twisted it away from the bandage then reached for something on his bedside table. Elise jumped out of her chair when she recognized the knife he'd used that morning.

"Easy, lass. Easy." He threw his arms wide, one hand holding his knife, the other the bottle of brandy. He shook his head and smiled crookedly. "Don't be such a skittish rabbit." He deftly turned the weapon in his hand so that the blade pointed towards his own body.

"See?" He sliced through the bandage. It dropped away from his skin on the left side, but stuck fast to the wound on the right. What blood Thomas had left drained from his face. "Damn," he whispered.

"Don't worry," Elise pulled the chair back up to sit across from him again. "We can just soak that with water and peel—" Her explanation was interrupted when Thomas, with a stoic grunt, ripped the rest of the bandage away from his body. "—Or we can do it that way too," she finished as the wound welled with fresh blood. At least with all the blood there was little chance of getting tetanus, she thought, knowing the blood would act to clean and aerate the area. When Thomas started shaking brandy on his wound while simultaneously flinching from his own efforts, she snatched the bottle away to tip back a long, steadying swallow. Then she held it up to the candlelight. Most of it was already gone.

"Here," she said. "Finish it." Without something to take the edge off, Thomas was bound to twitch and jerk throughout her entire wound care procedure. Some people, she'd found, could deal with intense pain like jabs to the face and knives in the gut, but the little things, like slowly peeling off bandages and having a wound sewn, would be unbearable. She rummaged in Mrs. Southill's kit for a needle and silk thread and set them on the table, then dipped a square of clean muslin into the water. "Tell me how you found me this afternoon." She hoped a story would distract him.

"I went to the pump and asked anyone who would listen, 'have you seen a skinny lass about so tall? Grey dress, white apron, barefoot, and carrying water?'"

"That describes every chambermaid in London."

Thomas chuckled, then flinched and tried to slap her hands away as Elise started to clean the edges of his wound. "Stop mincing about and just sew me together."

"Drink," Elise ordered.

They glared at each other until Thomas raised the bottle to his lips. "Green eyed and wild looking," he said, wiping his mouth with the back of his hand.

"What?"

"I asked people, 'Have you seen a woman with big feet, a mannish stride, and golden-red hair like a lion's mane?'"

"You did not," Elise said with a smile and finished bathing the dried blood from his skin. The water turned pink in the basin. Its warmth made Thomas's eyes close. She pulled the candle on the nightstand closer to hold the sewing needle in the flame before threading it with silk.

"I did. What's more, I said, 'she'd be the kind of woman that lifts her skirt to scratch an itch on her arse when she thinks no one is looking.' A wee girl knew right away I was talking about you and pointed me in the right direction." He gasped when Elise made her first poke with the needle.

"A wee girl? One look from you and a wee girl would pee her pants and run away."

"You're a wee girl and you haven't run."

"I thought I had big feet and a mannish stride."

"You do."

After finishing her first knot, Elise cut the end of the thread with Thomas's knife and heaved a sigh of relief. She'd watched doctors tie sutures many times before in the ER, but had never done it herself. It wasn't rocket science, but not having a doctor to oversee her work made her nervous. She glanced up to see how her patient was coping. His eyes were now squeezed shut and he was taking long, steadying breaths. "I'll go as fast as I can," she said.

"You do that."

They sat silently as Elise slowly pulled the edges of his oblique muscle back together. Too much tension and the stitches would tear through the skin or pucker the wound, not enough and it would gape and become vulnerable to infection. She tried to align the upper and lower sides to minimize the scarring. He already had enough scars, she thought as she glanced at a jagged line that parted the hair on his chest from his collarbone to his lower ribs. Another white scar bisected the curve of his shoulder. He was no stranger to knives, Elise thought ruefully.

Thomas's hand found Elise's thigh and gripped it with a strength that bruised. The touch helped both of them stay focused as she worked along his five-inch wound. Periodically, she dabbed away blood to better see what she was doing. It took twenty stitches all separately tied in surgical knots. "Done," she whispered, and the grip on her thigh loosened. Without antibiotics, her work was far from a sure thing, but she felt a sense of relief regardless. "You okay?"

"I'm okay." The word sounded strange coming from Thomas, as though he was trying it for the first time for her sake. It was such a simple word. Elise wondered how many times a day she said it at the hospital, at least fifty or a hundred times a shift. Okay. Ok. Finger and thumb together. Now each time she said it she was rewarded with puzzled looks and raised eyebrows. It had taken her days to figure out that the word hadn't been invented yet and was completely meaningless. How could a word she used so thoughtlessly not exist? She dropped the rag back into the basin and pushed it away with her foot. "Cool," she said with a nod.

She realized her hands were trembling when she reached into her bag for a narrow roll of muslin to cover the wound and stretch around Thomas's waist. Her fingertips stumbled over the curve of his muscles as she unrolled the bandage and brushed the hair under his navel. One end of the muslin drifted uselessly to the floor and Elise struggled to gather it back. "You've got to be careful for the next few days," she mumbled. "Those stitches could tear pretty easy," She laid her hand flat against his stomach to trap the bandage under her palm and was brought to a halt when she felt the rise and fall of his breathing. His stomach was like sun-warmed stones on a cold day.

He peeled her hand back and took the bandage. "Let me do it," he whispered as he gathered the muslin back into a roll. Elise couldn't lift her eyes from his stomach, even as Thomas slid the soft muslin over her lips and along the edge of her jaw. She pushed his hand away and finally looked up in time to see him smile at her rejection. He dropped his hand to draw a deep, long line along her thigh from her hip to the end of her knee. His touch made her slide towards him as her body followed his hand.

"You've lost too much blood. You're not thinking straight," she breathed.

"You knew I was drunk the second I opened the door, and you still entered my bedroom. It's you who's not thinking straight." Elise's chair scraped loudly on the floor as he pulled her closer towards him and spread his legs to accommodate her into his space. The smell of his blood mingled with the musked spice of his sweat. Tobacco and brandy sweetened his breath. She drew his scent into her lungs and it invaded her like a virus. Her pounding heart moved him through her vessels, cell by cell, so that she felt the scent of him everywhere, flushed into her flesh. When his hands slid up her arms, she tilted her head back and closed her eyes.

But the kiss, frozen a mere inch from her mouth, never arrived. "What's the matter?" Elise's eyes were now wide open.

Thomas sat back and looked away. "You should go."

"What? Why?"

"I'm sorry. I can't," Thomas stuttered. "Just leave."

"You've got to be kidding me," Elise said, waiting for more explanation with her mouth open in astonishment. When she realized Thomas was going to remain silent and look everywhere but at her, she stood and gathered up her medical kit as fast as she could while she fought back tears of disappointment.

In the hallway, she felt such an urgency to run from her rejection that she missed the three steps that elevated Thomas's bedroom. Profanity ricocheted off the walls as Elise's body launched into the air, thudded to the floor, and slid to a stop outside her bedroom door. She scrambled back to her feet and headed downstairs, her only goal being Mrs. Postlethwaite's kitchen stash of brandy.

Elise's entrance into the dining hall happened with much less dramatic flair. The dying fire cast a red glow across her features and reflected warmly off the polished walnut furnishings. In the empty room, she could hear embers falling from the glowing logs. Before she had started nursing, Elise thought a good bar was supposed to be dark and full of people moving to music so loud that she couldn't hear the man next to her unless he got close enough to brush her ear with his lips. Then a few years later, when she started going to bars in the morning after her night shift, she thought a good bar had to have a shadowed corner to escape the morning sun. As she stood bathing in the warmth of the fireplace, Elise realized her expectations of the Quiet Woman were unreasonable. The pub fed her, clothed her, tucked her in at night, and kept her safe, but Elise would have to shake the Quiet Woman off like an overbearing mother if she ever wanted to return to her own time. "Find your way home," Mrs. Southill had said. "You don't belong here." The old woman's words felt heavy and hard.

Feeling an itch she couldn't scratch, Elise ran from the warmth of the pub into the heat of the kitchen and felt instantly irritated by thoughts of Thomas when she saw his empty stool on the hearth. She had no pathway to anything she wanted, she thought, thinking of their near kiss; it was all out of reach. "Where is it, where is it," Elise whispered to herself as she twirled to scan the shelves. Even the brandy was hidden from her. Then she spied the larder and wrinkled her nose.

After lighting a candle she opened the door and held it high to illuminate shelves packed with containers of sugar, platters of meat pasties, jars of applebutter, strawberry jam, pickled eggs, canned beans, and anything else imaginable. She was sliding aside a basket of onions to reach towards a glimmer of brown glass that promised liquor when she was suddenly pushed deeper towards the bowels of the larder. Elise grunted when her face slammed against the wall near the top of the cellar stairs. Stars of pain flashed behind her eyes when the abrasions on her face opened from the impact. "Don't worry," hissed a familiar voice. Pinned against the wall, Elise felt her skirt being hitched up her thighs. "It's me. I'll be quick about it; it won't hurt but for just a minute."

She turned as much as she was allowed in order to see her assailant. "It's you," she echoed, surprised, and just a little bit disappointed.

Richard's eyes were bleary and the smell of alcohol emanated from his pores to mix with the stench that swirled up from the septic tank below. Elise still didn't have the brandy she wanted, but she quickly decided Richard was an adequate substitute for the time being. She grabbed onto his wrist and twirled under his arm to come around behind him. Standing on her tip-toes, she pulled his arm high between his shoulder blades to sprawl him against the cold bricks, just as she had been seconds earlier. "Damn your eyes," he cried out in pain. "Release me." Elise complied and allowed him to turn towards her.

Even drunk, Richard seemed surprised when she began fumbling with the buttons on the placket of his trousers. They were both breathing hard when Elise managed to get Richard's pants around his knees. She pulled at him until he sat on the ground. "Don't move," she instructed, and lifted her skirts. Delighted to be straddled, Richard spent himself quickly, but Elise bravely continued on, whimpering in the foul air as she worked the wilting stem. Then it was all over. The orgasm she'd pounded out for herself had been necessary, but left her strangely unsatisfied.

"Well," Elise said standing. "Thanks for that." She straightened her apron over her skirt and finally grabbed the neck of the brandy bottle. It was on the shelf towards the front, so obviously placed that she'd overlooked it. "I didn't hurt you, did I?" She pointed to his wet penis, curled against his thigh.

Richard hid his crotch behind his hands and looked befuddled. "No, no, of course not. It's just… Now we'll have to marry, for the sake of your honor, and what's yours will be mine."

"Yeah," Elise sniffed and wiped her nose on her sleeve. The cold coming from below was making it run. "Sure. Marriage." She pulled the cork out of the bottle and took a long swig as she surveyed her employer. Then she turned to walk out of the larder with a half-hearted wave goodnight. She was beat; it had been a long day and now she was finally ready for bed.

THE BEGINNING OF THE END OF IT ALL

It was late when Elise woke. She had finally figured out how to distinguish the early morning weak light from the late morning weak light by ignoring the light altogether and listening to the sounds coming from the street. For instance, at that moment she could hear Johnny's young voice calling to a vendor. If Johnny was present at the pub, and alert enough to be shouting in the lane, it was late. Elise rolled onto her side and curled her finger around the bed's drapes to peer out into the room. A drab apron, attached to a grey skirt wrapped around a wide ass blocked her view. Elise raked open the curtain to reveal Mary standing over her holding an empty brandy bottle. "You're so creepy. How long have you been standing there?" Elise asked.

"I was just about to wake you. You must come down to the kitchen at once. Mr. Ferrington is asking for you."

Elise rubbed her eyes. "Richard? What's wrong with Richard?"

"I think he's completely lost his mind. Mrs. Ferrington is crying her eyes out, and Mrs. P. is chopping a whole basket of turnips that don't need chopping."

Elise sat straight up in her bed then slapped her hands to her pounding head as the bed started twirling. "You should have gotten me up earlier," Elise moaned as she fought back her nausea. "Why don't you ever wake me up when you get up? You sneak out of here like a bandit every morning and I end up missing everything. I bet you do it on purpose too, just to mess with me."

"If you would just go to sleep at a reasonable hour, you wouldn't need me to wake you. And you should thank me for the favor of telling you: you fart in your sleep when you're drunk. That'll never do when you're married. You've got to start thinking on how to keep your husband faithful and true." Mary tossed the empty brandy bottle on the bed for emphasis and shook her head. "I've no idea how you did it. Did you use the hemp seeds like I showed you? You know, I don't think Mr. Laroque slept here last night." Her face clouded in frustration.

"What are you talking about?"

"Your engagement."

"My what?" Elise's brain scrambled to put together the events of the previous night. She swallowed hard when she remembered, trying to calm the panic that began to rise with her returning nausea. "I never agreed to anything," she said quietly. Then, feeling defeated, said, "I'll be down as soon as I'm dressed." Elise couldn't imagine why Richard would go and tell everyone in the kitchen. The silly Mrs. Ferrington was bad enough, but the idea of facing Mrs. Postlethwaite was horrifying.

"I laid out one of my dresses for you. It'll hang on you like a dishrag, but no one wants to see you in that muddy thing you were wearing yesterday. Maybe if you tighten your apron strings real tight and keep your stays loose you can cut a neater figure."

Elise looked past Mary to see two dresses draped across the foot of the other bed, one large and crisp, the other dress small, wet, and stretched to dry flat. "You washed my dress," Elise exclaimed delightedly.

"Mrs. P. let me take the time to do it this morning—we both knew you'd make a mess of it if you washed it yourself. I have no idea what happened to you yesterday, but if the condition of your dress is any indication, your day was quite a trial. Your face already looks better," Mary reassured. "I don't think it will leave a scar."

Elise blinked back the pricks of tears from the corners of her eyes. "You really didn't have to go to all that trouble," she said with a sniff.

"I did it for Mr. Tilsdale. I know he would have wanted someone to repay your kindness."

"Here she is," Mrs. Ferrington said when Elise stepped into the kitchen. Her eyes were red and puffy, and her mouth was pinched in a resolute line. "Give it to her now, Richard. Let's see if she remembers."

"Not now, Mother. Later. After." Richard's eyes were clear and bright. Elise resented his energy, knowing he too had been less than sober the night before.

A pile of carrots, turnips, and potatoes was rising in mountainous proportions in front of Mrs. Postlethwaite as her knife kept up its productive rhythm. The cook kept her eyes down at the table, and her mouth shut. Elise found it disconcerting. "Give me what?" Elise asked. She was still hoping for a pair of new shoes. Mrs. Postlethwaite glanced up long enough to shoot daggers at Elise with her eyes.

"I'd like for you to take a turn with me outdoors," Richard said pulling Mary's coat off the peg by the courtyard door to hold out for Elise.

"Oh my poor boy," Mrs. Ferrington cried out. Tears resumed rolling down her cheeks as the rhythm of Mrs. Postlethwaite's knife sped up. Richard draped the coat over Elise's shoulders and offered his arm, which she took reluctantly. There didn't seem to be another choice.

They strolled for a long ways, in a different direction from the water pump, without either of them speaking. As they entered wide, tree-lined boulevards, Richard's pace slowed and he tucked Elise's hand tighter against his elbow. They seemed to be joining a parade of other men and women who were also strolling with very little purpose. The women's dresses were gauzy under pashmina shawls wrapped about their shoulders. Their gentlemen escort's cravats were tied in complicated flounced knots while their breeches squeaked under the strain of being too tight. "Where are we?" Elise asked.

"Mayfair. Everyone who's anyone lives here." He sounded wistful as he launched into a steady stream of commentary for each person they passed, as though he was flipping through the pages of a celebrity gossip magazine. The detail with which he wove the relationships between each character rivaled that of the winding melodies he played on his violin. "Think back, Elise," he instructed. "Do any of these stories, any names I mention, ring a bell? Are any of these faces recognizable to you? Surely none of them would recognize you, dressed as you are, but perhaps you might see a glimmer of familiarity?"

Elise took a moment to pretend to study a mother walking with her two teenaged daughters on the other side of the street. She sadly shook her head and heaved a sigh. "It's useless. I don't think I know any of these people."

Richard nodded, "It'll yet come to you. I've a theory and I'm anxious to prove myself right."

He led her into a park with a long and narrow expanse of lawn. Encircling the park on one end was a low wall covered in a weathered vine of pink roses. Richard slid Elise's hand from his arm and seated her on a garden bench just under the wall. A willow tree arched nearby. Its branches, covered in delicate pale green leaves, formed a protective curtain around them. "Elise," Richard started, taking up her hand. He paused to smile at her nervously before starting on a lengthy rehearsed speech. Elise watched as his lips moved, but could barely take in the words. Her palm felt slimy in his. She pulled it out of his grasp and wiped it on her skirt, then realized he had stopped speaking and was looking a little worried. "My feelings for you can not be a surprise," he said. "I have done nothing to hide them from you."

"Your feelings?" Elise shook her head, trying to clear it. "Richard, I had no idea. Is this because of last night? I mean it was fun and all…"

"Don't be coy with me, Elise. I have never doubted that you returned my affections. Last night only proved it."

"Wait. No. You got this all wrong. I'm okay, you're okay, no one's under any obligations here."

Richard looked surprised. "Wouldn't you like to be my wife? I thought you'd be happy. I've felt the way you touch my arm; listened to the way you address me so casually. You gave me every reason to think you'd be happy as my wife."

"I did? No, I didn't. I didn't give you any reasons. None." Elise shook her head.

"I don't understand."

"I'm not getting married. Seriously, why would you want to do that?" Elise couldn't help feeling like Richard was making fun of her. She could think of no possible reason for him to want to marry her, unless he truly felt morally obligated. "If this is about last night, don't worry. I wont tell anyone." That was one promise Elise felt positive she could keep.

"Then it's too late. You have remembered who you are and now you think you cannot marry me. I understand. I'm below you."

"What the hell are you talking about?"

"Why else would you deny me? No, it's no use my darling. I won't hear your excuses when I know in my heart that you love me. I know this to be true because you told me yourself countless times in the way you address me, look at me, smile at me. The only reason you would not have my hand is to keep from dishonoring your family." Richard shook his head sadly. "Star crossed lovers—that is what we are."

Elise studied Richard. Could he be serious? It would be so easy to just make up a wealthy family to get him to abandon the idea of marrying her. But if she did, everyone would expect her to leave the Quiet Woman. But if she didn't leave the Quiet Woman, everyone would wonder why she didn't marry the proprietor when she had the chance. She was damned either way. "I just don't want to, Richard. Why is that so hard to understand?"

"You must marry me," he whined. "I've already purchased the license. Besides, I can't possibly take the King's shilling without knowing you were here, waiting for me to come home."

"Take what? The king's what?"

Richard took Elise's hands in his own and looked at them thoughtfully. When he swept his thumbs across the backs of her hands and drew them to his lips, she felt hair rise up on her arms in response. Elise faltered slightly in her resolve. Despite how ridiculous she felt the situation was, he was still proposing, and that kind of thing didn't happen every day. "Elise," he started, "I've must join the army, and if you won't marry me, I'm sure I will die on my first battlefield."

"The army? Why? Why would you leave the Quiet Woman?"

Richard looked at the grass under his feet, then over his shoulder. "You see, it's the damnedest thing: the Brewery decided, all of a sudden, that they cannot continue. That is," Richard scratched his head and began again. "You see if I cannot come up with a rather large sum of money, as of this evening, the Quiet Woman will no longer be mine. The Brewery has taken possession of our pub, and Cooper will be operating it."

Inexplicably, Elise felt the need to fight back tears. She didn't care about the fate of the Quiet Woman, she thought as she sniffed loudly. There was no reason for her to cry about it.

"So, you see," Richard continued, "now there's nothing left for me in London. There's nothing left but to travel with the regiment to America."

"America," breathed Elise. Her eyes dried instantly as her world shifted. "Where in America?"

"I'm not sure; they didn't tell me."

"North or South America?"

"Why does it matter? I'm as easily slaughtered near the one pole as the other if you don't marry me."

Elise looked up at the sandy blonde hair that curled at Richard's brow, at his strong shoulders, then into his light brown eyes. It wouldn't be the worst thing in the world to have him as a husband, she thought. At least he was nice to look at. She gave him a smile she hoped looked dreamy. There was no way the British government cared about Brazil or Argentina. Wasn't it the colonies that gave them headaches, Plymouth Rock, and all that? "Could I go with you? To America?" she asked.

Richard looked surprised. "Some wives do follow their husbands, but I think you'd be much better off staying at the Quiet Woman with my mother. The Brewery's allowed us to keep our apartment."

How would she get from the East Coast back to Tucson? Elise's mind whirled with the possibilities. She pictured wagon trains, gunslingers with spurs on their heels and bandanas at their necks. She just needed to cross the Atlantic and then she could snag some cowboy to be her guide. Elise looked at Richard's tight waistcoat and her hopes fell slightly, realizing it would be at least fifty years before John Wayne. Briefly, she considered the idea that her beloved city may not even be part of the United States. She tried to remember what year the Gasden Purchase happened, then took a deep breath and pushed away her doubt. It didn't matter. She'd worry about the details later. "Find your way home," Mrs. Southill had instructed. This was her way. If she could just get back to the foothills of the Catalina mountains where it had all started, she was certain she'd have a better chance to return to the 21st Century. "Of course I'll marry you," she said sweetly. "I'd follow you to the ends of the earth."

"My darling, you have made me the happiest man." Richard pulled Elise's hands back to his lips.

"I'm so glad for you."

"Let's do it right now."

"Now?"

"Yes." Richard stood and drew Elise up with him. "I'll be shipped out in two days, so I really can't wait."

"You mean, 'we'll' be shipped out." Elise corrected.

Richard's smile faltered slightly. "If it comes to that," he said enigmatically.

"If I can't go with you, then I won't marry you."

Richard shrugged and pulled Elise along by the hand. "Vicar Harris has been marrying couples *en masse* for the last week, what with the surge of recruitments. If we hurry we can get there before noon for the ceremony." Hesitatingly, Elise took a step towards Richard and froze, still unsure. With a grin, Richard tugged at her. "Come along," he coaxed. "Won't we be quite the pair?" When Elise took another step forward, he tucked her hand under his arm and took off across the park towards a church conveniently located on the other side of the green.

When they stepped inside, the heaviness of the building caught Elise off guard, as though the building itself was adding weight to her impending marriage. Light streamed through the tall stained glass windows from the great vaulted ceiling and spilled onto the stone paved floor in warning reds. The chill of disapproval she felt was only slightly warmed by the spiced smell of incense that wafted down the aisles of pews.

They were shuttled by a sour looking crone to a chapel within the church where five other couples waited. Another young bride holding a small bouquet of blue forget-me-nots and dressed in a simple grey gown impetuously clutched Elise's arm when she got too near. "Our lives will never be the same," she said breathlessly. Her eyes were wide and clouded with joy. Elise disengaged as politely as she could, thinking how her life was already nothing like the one she left. Marriage to Richard would be an easy transition in comparison. "Aren't they so handsome and brave, to be so willing to die for their country?" The rhetorical question triggered the beginning of a headache. Elise gave the girl a tight smile before desolately slumping as the vicar began to drone.

The words were incomprehensible; Elise was completely unable to process the vicar's words over the growing panic she felt. Then suddenly it was too late to change her mind when the vicar pronounced everyone wedded with a bored wave of his hand. A few nervous cheers went up. Three couples kissed quickly. When Richard bent down to do the same, Elise turned her head away. Her heart beat a drum roll against her chest while she told herself over and over that it wasn't real, it was all some sort of bad dream. Nothing that was happening would matter when she woke up. She felt Richard slip a ring on her finger and she glanced at the simple golden band. She was surprised by how prepared he was—the argument for marriage, the church, the license he mentioned purchasing, now the ring. She was even surprised that she had fallen for it all. She barely knew she was moving forward in a line with the crowd until she reached the front. "I don't believe we've met. Are you not from this parish?" Vicar Harris asked, surprised. His quill was poised to write down her information in a large tome. Elise opened her mouth but her jaw hung slack and no words formed on her lips.

"She doesn't remember her parents yet, but I'm fairly certain they're French. Her name is Elise Dubois. That's spelled D.u.b.o.y.s.e." Richard watched while the vicar carefully wrote down her name. "Would it be alright if we were to return later today? Something tells me she'll remember in an hour or so." Richard winked at Elise.

The vicar merely nodded as he shuffled through papers to find the correct document and handed Elise the quill to sign the license. Elise could feel herself breathing faster. Red pin dots obscured the peripherals of her vision. "I need to sit down," she whispered to Richard. He wrapped a protective arm around her waist and nearly carried her to a quiet spot off to one side of the church.

Taking the little wooden chair Richard offered, Elise looked up at a stained glass window high above. In a mosaic made from sharp shards of glass was a woman wearing calm blue and pale ivory robes. The sun came through the window in such as way as to make her head invisible. Elise knew the artist had most likely given the woman a serene expression, but couldn't help but imagine a face with sparking eyes and a mouth wide open to deliver an angry, finger-wagging lecture.

"I've a wedding present for you," Richard said softly, drawing a chair up next to her.

"I don't want anything," Elise said quickly as she glanced at the band on her finger. It was a simple narrow ring with no stones or adornments, but it completely changed the feel of her left hand. It didn't seem to belong to her body anymore.

"Don't be silly, of course you want a wedding present." Richard reached into his waist pocket and pulled out his handkerchief. A thick gold chain slipped out from the folds of the linen square and caught Elise's eye. "What's that?" she asked.

"I thought you didn't want it?" Richard teased, jerking his hand away. When Elise's eyes narrowed in warning, he carefully unfolded the little package to reveal an enormous emerald cut into the shape of a beetle and set in gold with outstretched wings. "Do you recognize it?" Richard asked.

The jewel gleamed and winked with a luminescence that rivaled that of the windows above Elise's head. She felt compelled to touch the scarab to feel its smooth surface. Its warmth was as soothing as the desert evening sun. "Why would I recognize it?" Her voice sounded hollow to herself as she asked the question. She had no doubts about having seen the jewel before.

"Think, Elise. I thought it would help you remember your family."

Elise shook her head to clear the dazzle. "My family? Why do you think it'll help me remember my family?" She thought fleetingly of her mother in the mid-West, then tried to remember her ancestry beyond the scope of Richard's question. There was something about the jewel that drew her to it, but it frightened her too. "Where did you get this?"

"Look at it, damn it. Think."

The intensity in Richard's voice startled Elise. She took the scarab out of the handkerchief and placed it in her left hand where it spanned the entire length of her palm. When she spread her fingers apart, the links of the broken chain drooped heavily between them. She closed her fingers back up and the loops became three separate circles of chain attached distantly to each other. Tucson, London, there had been a third place, Elise suddenly realized. She felt an echo of the same intense fear that had paralyzed her that first night. Even though it was cold in the church, sweat formed beads on her upper lip. She absently wiped them off with the cuff of her sleeve as images of faces crowded her senses—faces with surprised looks intensified by garish makeup and lit from underneath by countless candles.

A man with black eyes had kicked her viciously. Then he lifted her by her collar and squeezed. The more helpless she became as her breath failed, the angrier she grew so that when the scarab manifested itself she snatched fiercely at it and twisted until it gave way.

Elise felt her heart pulsing in her open palm and the scarab moved up and down with her heart's rhythm. "You're returning to me what is already mine," she said coldly. "How is that a gift?"

"I'm giving you the gift of your memories," Richard said with relief in his voice. "It worked. Tell me about your family. Our family. Where are they?"

"I don't remember anything."

"But when I found you, your entire body was limp except for your fist. I had to pry your fingers apart to save that jewel for you. You obviously treasured it beyond your own well-being, even while unconscious. I'm sure it is a clue about your family legacy."

"Legacy." Elise paused, thinking it over. "Is that what you're hoping for? A legacy?"

"Of course I am. Your family must be frantically searching for you at this very moment. Just think how relieved they'll be when I bring you back. No one's responded to the many adverts Mother posted in the papers, so I'm sure your family must be in France. Your parents must have gone back after Napoleon granted amnesty, and somehow you were lost. That would explain your name, wouldn't it? That jewel must be the key to discovering who you are."

"Are you really that stupid? Can't you think of at least one other way a woman could snag a golden bug?" Richard looked blank. "Emphasis on snag," Elise drawled. "Why do you think the chain is broken?"

Elise watched Richard's smile freeze as he slowly processed the information. "I'll take that back then," he said, holding out his hand.

"What?" Elise closed her hand over the jewel and drew it to her chest. "No. It's mine. I don't know why you had it in the first place."

"I was keeping it safe for you. It could have easily been stolen during those days you were convalescing. And then later, when you were so confused, it would have been completely irresponsible of me to give it to you then. And now," Richard shrugged and looked at the floor. "If what you suggest is true, and you have no family, then there's no point in you continuing the charade. Give me the jewel and I'll find a better use for it. For the future of the family we will create together."

"Better use for it?" Elise repeated in outrage. "Who the hell do you think you are?"

"I'll be able to pay off the Quiet Woman's debts with a jewel that size, and have money left over."

Elise stared at Richard, trying to understand. "Isn't it too late? You told me you'd joined the Army. I thought I had to marry you or you'd die on the battlefield."

"I never said I'd joined the army. I said that I was unable to pay my debt to the Brewery, and because of that my only choice was to join or go to debtor's prison. But now that I've married you, together we can pay off the Brewery. So be a good girl and hand me that beetle." The volume of his voice vacillated strangely as he struggled to keep his voice down in the echoing church. He grabbed her hand and tried to peel back her fingers. "What's yours is now mine."

Elise neatly twisted her arm and broke Richard's grip, then pointedly placed the jewel in her apron pocket. When Richard lunged at it again, her hand flew out and caught his cheek in a slap. Stunned, he stared at Elise with his mouth open. "Where were you last night before we met up?" Elise demanded. "I bet you were sitting at some poker table—or whist table, whatever you guys play these days— getting more and more drunk and desperate until you went all in on a bad hand and lost the Quiet Woman. You totally deserved that slap. I hope it hurt." She looked around, suddenly self-conscious. The church had emptied out after the ceremony and they were alone. She turned back to Richard and considered slapping him again.

"Elise, don't be so selfish. Think of how many people depend on the Quiet Woman. Mary, Thomas, Mrs. P., my own mother—all of them need the public house to maintain their living. If you give me the jewel, we can help them." Elise slumped back down into her chair and put her head in her hands. "You must give it to me." Richard insisted. "We've only a short amount of time left before Cooper takes over." He lifted her chin up and smiled into her eyes. "Don't you want to run the Quiet Woman with me?"

Elise pulled her face out of his grip. "Why did you have to show it to me? Why didn't you just sell the damn thing? I never would have known the difference."

"It wasn't mine until today."

"It's still not yours."

"It is mine now." Richard's brown eyes turned flinty. "We're married."

Elise suddenly remembered the conversation she'd overheard in the stairs. Thomas knew. Thomas knew all along Richard had the scarab, and in the stairway he all but accused him of stealing it. This was Richard's stupid contrivance to honorably acquire the jewel through sex and resultant marriage. All along Richard had been keeping her in his back pocket, just in case he needed a final weapon against the bankruptcy he must have known was coming, and hoped that it would also bring entrance into a wealthy family.

Elise felt her eyes burn with tears. She'd been played. Despite her contempt for the man, she couldn't help but feel rejected when she realized he had to get drunk before setting his plan in motion in the larder.

THE CHASE

In Adelaide's dream, the golem was nearly within reach, close enough to distinguish features she'd never noticed before. She had a lovely black freckle just under her left eye. Laugh lines creased the tops of her cheekbones like extensions of the thick golden-red lashes that framed her demonic green eyes. The effect of her full, pouty mouth was not overshadowed by her sizeable nose, but was marred by the bruise on her jaw. The patchy red wound on her cheek detracted from the appeal of her cloud of auburn hair.

"Whatever that has happened to you will never happen again. No one shall beat you again. Come to me," Adelaide beckoned. "Come, *ma petite fille*, and I will protect you from all that you have endured." She spread her arms wide in a show of love to entice the creature to enter her embrace. The golem had only to take three steps; three steps and the bond between them would be repaired and strengthened.

There was a longing in the golem's eyes for the comfort that Adelaide promised. Sure of her success, Adelaide was about to breathe a sigh of relief when the creature opened her rosy mouth. "Like I told the other guy: I don't speak French," she said adamantly, in French.

The golem's voice, as loud and as lovely as a church bell choir, was startling. "What other man?"

"What did I just say? I don't speak French," she repeated and put her hands on her hips. "You people just don't get it." She turned on her heel and walked out of Adelaide's dream.

When the hackney cab rattled to a stop, she woke with a start. "The Quiet Woman, Miss," announced the driver from his bench in front. Adelaide waited for him to open the door and place the steps before she gathered her satchel and descended into the dark street.

It had been a long and tedious trip, starting with machinations for funding that included an embarrassing entreaty to a certain wealthy client who hadn't yet abandoned her, and a disguised visit to her banker's home. Once the ticket was bought, the coach trip to Calais hadn't been too terrible. On the contrary, it had been a relief to put Paris, and all of Fouché's police force, behind her. It was the passage across the channel that had left her green and swooning. As to be expected, the weather at sea was tumultuous and her stomach, ever since her schoolgirl days, was sensitive.

She stayed overnight in Dover at an inn to recover. The innkeepers spoke a little French, it being nearly a requirement for them to do so for the sake of their business, and after dinner helped her to create an itinerary for traveling the rest of the way to London. Despite the relief of having specific plans for the rest of her voyage, it had been difficult to fall asleep in the little room she rented. When she closed her eyes that night, she physically felt the memory of the rising and falling sea as she listened to the surf that made its way in through the cracked open window. The salty air calmed her spirit while the English food she'd been served earlier frothed in her already roiling digestive tract. The next morning she bravely took the carriage to London, hoping to put the heaving shoreline as far behind her as possible.

Adelaide pressed a coin into the outstretched hand of the hackney driver, who looked at it in distaste. He said something in English and waved the money at her in anger. She raised her hands in the universal gesture of, "take it or leave it," and in response he spat in the gutter before climbing back to his bench. Although unfamiliar with the driver's language, Adelaide was still able to recognize some of the more colorful English words he was sputtering as he drove away.

She looked across the lane to the front of the building with the squeaking wooden sign as she carefully lifted her skirt over the mud. A man finished urinating against the wall next to the door and tipped his hat. Her nose wrinkled in distaste and she pulled her handkerchief out of her pocket to hold over her face. It wasn't that English urine smelled any worse than French urine, it was just that English men seemed to be able to produce so much more than French men.

When she opened the door, she paused at the threshold to let her eyes adjust to the darkness within. An old man, huddled deep in a chair by the fire, shouted something at her in an insistent and angry voice that cut through the dining hall so that all eyes lifted and fixed on her. She shut the door behind her.

A plump barmaid with a halo of blonde curls escaping the intricate braids she had pinned to the back of her neck rushed to her from a nearby table. She said something to her in English, lilting the sentence upwards in a question. Adelaide looked at her blankly. The barmaid repeated her question and Adelaide told her in French that she didn't understand. A frown passed over the maid's face and she pointed to the door before stomping over to it and holding it open. She then made a sweeping gesture out the door, indicating Adelaide should leave. The old man in the armchair near the fireplace started yelling again and the barmaid yelled back. Her voice reminded Adelaide of the unpleasant chills that come from grinding sand between your teeth.

"Shee eez my seestair. Shee weell eet zee deenair weef mee." A tall, thin man stood from a table located near the bar and gestured to an empty chair beside him. Adelaide squinted. She couldn't see his face through the smoky room, but she knew exactly who he was.

The barmaid smiled widely. "Seestair?" she repeated with the same accent, as though it made her more easily understandable. With raised eyebrows, she pointed to Adelaide, then to the man, who, with theatrically long legs, stepped away from his table. Dodo, she thought as he approached. *Quel connard.* Adelaide wasn't sure what relationship she had just confirmed with the barmaid, but doing so seemed to put the pretty woman in better spirits.

"How do you expect to do get anything accomplished in London if you cannot speak the language?" Dodo grumbled. He led her back to his table and pulled the chair out for her.

"What have you done with my grimoire?" Adelaide demanded as she sat. "You will return it to me this instant."

"Wouldn't it be more pleasant to have dinner together first?" The maid returned without having been called to take his order. It was obvious he had placed some sort of enchantment on her—her eyes were outrageously round when she looked at him, she wet her mouth with her tongue before replying to any of his questions regarding the menu, and curtsied exaggeratedly to better display her deep décolletage. If Dodo noticed any of the barmaid's contortions, he wasn't moved to respond. He dispatched her to the kitchen with a callous wave.

It took mere minutes for her to return with the steaming bowls, which Adelaide found suspicious. If the food was already ready to serve, how long ago had it been prepared? Had it been sitting over the fire for days or weeks? Her stomach had calmed a little from her passage over the channel, but the long carriage ride, followed by the tiny hackney cab had set her bowels on edge. She peered into the brown sauce and sniffed hesitantly at the floating nourishment. The smell was sweet and turned her suspicion into hope. It had been an interminable time since she'd last eaten.

"The food here is horrible—nothing but boiled beef and turnips," Dodo said. Adelaide felt her stomach rumble disappointedly. "What I would do for a simple *poireau*, you've no idea," he continued. "Yesterday I begged for a roast capon in lieu of the regular fare. *La Grosse* in the kitchen stuffed it with apples, onions, and eggs. Can you imagine?"

Adelaide shook her head sadly and spooned a slippery thread of the beef from her stew. "One cannot expect the British to be as well versed in the culinary arts as the French."

"Perhaps not, but really," Dodo made a languid and irritated gesture over the bowls in front of them, "culinary arts? I think not. This food is only fit for English barbarians."

"The food fits the fortunes." Adelaide indicated a group of men at the next table, who were thin in body, clothes, hair, and, apparently, thin on soap as well. One noticed her looking and broke from the lively banter of his comrades to salute with his knuckle to his forehead and give her a saucy wink.

The sound of Dodo's spoon clanking down on the table drew her back to the conversation. "I cannot accept the excuse of poverty for this pig's slop," he said in disgust. "I have seen a farmer's wife do more with a basket of onions, stale bread, and a bit of broth. But, of course, that was in France. I say it is a poverty of mind, not of material."

Adelaide nodded absently as she spooned the stew into her mouth. Startled by the flavor, she looked up past the bar where *La Grosse* was perfectly framed by the kitchen door. She was gesturing with a butcher's knife to someone hidden behind the wall. Adelaide spooned more of the stew into her mouth and felt it spread across her tongue and slide down her throat in a way that made her eyes close and her chest heave in a sigh. Whatever the cook had done in her cauldron was magic. The beef was no longer beef. The turnips were no longer turnips. They were something other, something never before classified but wholly better. When she picked up her pot of beer and swallowed a chasing sip, the flavor rolled like melting butter. She broke a corner off the slice of bread she'd been given to slow the pleasure and reconnect with the conversation at hand. "As I recall, the last meal we shared was less than satisfying," she said, dunking the bread into the sauce.

"If you are referring to our stay with dear Jean-Tout-Simple, I must apologize. It was imperative that we initiate a rescue of the golem at once so that Fouché's men would not find her first. I sacrificed the completion of my own projects and acted immediately, without thought. I should have made you aware of my plans and found you a more suitable place to stay while I attempted to retrieve our quarry, but there was no time. I hope you will forgive my hasty departure. As you can see, it was advantageous. I believe I arrived much earlier than any of Fouché's agents."

Adelaide looked at Dodo warily, unwilling to accept his apology. He obviously thought she was still a naïve young woman, just starting her life. She wondered briefly if he pictured her as a sixteen year old when he looked at her. That would have its advantages. "Have you seen our quarry?"

"Yes, as a matter of fact, I saw her yesterday. She walked through the dining hall with her head down, trying not to draw attention to herself. Of course, everyone looked. She was all anyone talked of for the next hour. 'Bloody spindle-shanked lass,' they called her."

"What does that mean? Is that bad?"

"It means she has not made many friends. Someone had treated her face very roughly I'm afraid, and other parts as well, judging by the condition of her habiliments."

Adelaide nodded, thinking of how the golem looked in her dream. The poor creature had been treated poorly the second she fell through the vortex, so it was likely she would be desperate to find a friend.

"She's been accompanied by the two hulking publicans, *Le Blond et Le Brun* ever since I've arrived," Dodo continued, as though reading Adelaide's mind. "Those two hover over her like new mothers. Then there's *La Grosse* in the kitchen. Between the three of them I've not had the chance to speak to her yet." He leaned forward, looking suspiciously around at the clientele at the next table and put his hand to his mouth to hide his words. "I have not seen her wear the scarab. I've no doubt it has been stolen from her."

"She still has it. I've dreamed of it." Adelaide cleaned the bottom of her bowl with the last bit of her bread before eyeing Dodo's untouched meal.

"You do not reassure me. We all dream of jewels."

"What does it matter anyway? The jewel is not important. It is the golem we need."

Dodo laughed and shook his head. "Is that what they told you when they sent you to conjure the golem? *Ma jolie petite imbecile*, your knowledge of the political maneuverings of *La Société* could fit inside a thimble."

"I know more than you."

"No, you do not."

"Your own thimble of knowledge is sized to fit a child," Adelaide spat.

"And yours fits a mouse."

"You are the mouse, Dodo."

"No, you are."

Their argument was suddenly halted by a commotion from the kitchen. Everyone in the dining hall stopped what they were doing to watch two men, wrapped in a dramatic embrace, cross behind the frame of the kitchen door from right to left, then back from left to right, then tumble through the doorway. One of the men slammed the other against the edge of the bar and grabbing a fist full of blond hair, pinned his opponent's face onto the hard wood as he shouted the same thing over and over. "Why did you do it? Why did you do it?"

The cook came roaring out of the kitchen, as though mise-en-scène with the thunder of rattling sheet metal, and began to beat the two men indiscriminately with the head of a broom. From the back of the room, the barmaid came running to tug at the men's clothing. Great clouds of dust rose as the cook swung her weapon down on everyone's backs until, coughing and choking, the combatants untangled themselves from each other and stepped apart.

When the fighting turned to yelling and finger-pointing, most men in the dining hall returned to spooning their stew and sipping their brews, watching the drama from behind the steam of their meals in the most surreptitious manner. At the next table, one man attempted to insert his own opinion, but La Grosse roundly shouted him down. "What are they saying?" Adelaide asked Dodo breathlessly.

"It seems to be a lovers' quarrel."

"Over the barmaid?" She was quite lovely, with dimples and rolls that jiggled pleasingly.

"Over a quiet woman. No, wait, I am mistaken. It's a business quarrel."

"Yes, but what about our golem? Where is she?"

Adelaide jumped when Dodo brought a fist down on the table in an expression of irritation. "I can't hear what they are saying over your shrill voice. Do you want me to translate or not?"

"By all means, continue," said Adelaide as she slid Dodo's bowl nearer to herself. His bread was untouched too, so she reached across him again and was rewarded with a slap on the back of her hand.

"The man with all the hair—"

"They both have lots of hair," Adelaide interrupted.

"The brown haired one—the smaller man."

"Smaller? Are you blind? *Le Brun* is much bigger."

"Yes, but *Le Blond* is taller. Please stop interrupting. *Le Brun* keeps asking 'Why did you do it?' and *Le Blond* is making excuses. He says that it was a sure bet, that he had the better hand but that he was cheated. They needed the money. He swears he did it for the Quiet Woman. 'You told me I couldn't sell what wasn't mine.' *Le Blond* says. 'So I made it mine,' he says. 'I was sure she had more; that we would be able to end our debt.'" Dodo looked puzzled. "I think he's speaking of two different things," he said.

"'So where is it?'" Dodo translated *Le Brun's* question.

"'I'm afraid that's where my plan went a little awry...'"

"'Your plan?'" Dodo paused a moment while *Le Brun* resumed attacking *Le Blond.* As they careened towards a nearby table, the clientele stood and gracefully moved out of the way, taking their beers to some other area where spills were less imminent.

"'Did you even tell her?'" Dodo resumed his translation after the combined efforts of *La Grosse* and the barmaid pulled the overwrought *Le Brun* away.

"'Tell her what?'"

"'Tell her that the Quiet Woman is gone.'"

"'Of course I did. She acted like she didn't care. She was ready to follow me all the way to America.'"

Dodo fell silent as they watched *Le Brun* sink into a chair. He raked his dark hair away from his face. Two deep long scars that sliced through his features startled Adelaide. "'What are you looking at?

Who let another bloody woman in here?'" Dodo turned in surprise to Adelaide and she quickly looked down at the second empty bowl in front of her. "Shee eez my seestair," Dodo said quickly. *Le Brun* snapped something in reply, which Dodo didn't translate. The scarred man's blue eyes lingered on them both for so long that Adelaide's stomach began to churn again while Dodo played nervously with his slice of bread, rolling the soft white dough between his fingers into long snakes until the barman finally looked away. Soon the rest of the conversations in the dining hall came back into focus. Most of the others were finished with their meals. Some were lighting pipes. The barmaid was busy pouring, and attention had turned to her smiles, to politics and war, to factory unrest, to rights for Catholics, to the strange cold weather, to my wife's ailing mother, to nothing but normal neutral. Even *La Grosse* returned to the kitchen, sweeping the floor with her weapon as she went.

"'Elise is yours now, and so is the jewel' says *Le Brun*." Dodo resumed his translation. "'I suppose if you can find a buyer for the emerald, you'll be able to pay off the brewery, even if there's no dowry.'

"'That's the trouble. She wasn't very happy when I told her I needed it. She refuses to give back the jewel. You must talk to her and make her see reason.'"

"'Me? What makes you think she'll listen to me? I pull no weight with that one.'"

"'Then you must take it from her!'"

"'I will not.'"

Le Blond looked surprised at so brusque a response. *Le Brun* smiled wryly, "'So it seems you're still joining the King's Army, the Quiet Woman is still going to the Brewery, Elise sells the jewel and goes where ever she wants, and the rest of us will go to hell. You gambled and lost. Again.'

"'You'll be coming with me, won't you?'

"'Oh, aye. Don't you worry—we'll be together 'till the sorry end, even if that be hell. I've still my shackles. Where is your new bride? Did she bolt off already?'" Dodo pushed his chair back and half rose, awaiting the answer.

"'Actually, she's not well. She said she was feeling terrible, something about headaches and a black-haired woman. I didn't press her about it. She's retired to her room.'"

"She's alone upstairs," Dodo whispered and pushed back his chair, his eyes bright with excitement. As casually as possible, Dodo started to move across the dining hall towards the entrance to the inn. He had gotten as far as two tables away when *Le Brun* leapt to his feet. "Get that bloody Frog!" he yelled with a finger pointed straight at Dodo's back. The sound of scraping chairs reverberated as everyone stood in unison. Adelaide screamed in horror when *Le Brun* advanced with the sleek lope of a wolf. A mastery of the English language was unnecessary to know that she needed to run for her life. She turned towards the door, but a grinning *Rosbif* stuck his leg out and sent her sprawling onto the filthy wooden floor. The jeering patrons of the Quiet Woman quickly surrounded her.

Elise rolled the thin gold band around and around her finger as she sat up in bed. It didn't matter, she told herself. She could be married in this time, but single in her own time. What happened here had no bearing on what was happening there. Nevertheless she couldn't help but wonder how her decision was going to change her circumstances. Attaching herself to Richard, in retrospect, seemed less than ideal, even if it did get her a free ticket back to the States.

Still wrapped in Richard's handkerchief, the emerald was a heavy lump in her apron pocket. He had been livid when she wouldn't return it to him, but there was no doubt in Elise's mind that the scarab belonged to her. That Richard had been keeping it, that he showed it to her only after having married her, that he still claimed it as his own, was unforgiveable. Elise gambled that he wouldn't fight her for it, and luckily she'd assessed him correctly. Fighting was okay for Thomas, but not something he himself would stoop to doing.

Her head throbbed. Having no energy to even bother to make tea, Elise chewed willow bark rhythmically to get rid of the aching pain. It tasted horrible, but seemed to help push the visions of the black-haired woman from her mind. She remembered it all: the man, the bug, the dark candlelit room with all the strange people, everything. And she was sure the black-haired woman was the key to why it happened. With the emerald in her pocket, the visions and memories seemed much more vivid, as though the black-haired woman was no farther away than the front door.

A loud crash from the dining hall below startled her. Then a muffled roar from the crowd worked its way through the walls of her bedroom. Elise remembered that first night she'd heard cheers coming from the pub and how she had been sure it was a football game on television. The sound had reassured her then. But now, the sound of screaming made her think she should go below and see what was going on. Yelling was typical; screaming was unusual. Was that Mary? It didn't sound like Mary. Elise closed her eyes. She should go down, she thought as she pressed her fingers to her temples. She shifted the wad of bark from her right cheek to her left and sunk lower in bed. She'd go, just as soon as her headache went away.

The End of the End of It All, Which is Really Just the Beginning

It was late in the evening when Elise finally stumbled back downstairs. She had fallen asleep in her room with the willow bark tucked into her cheek. Now her head hurt less, but a painful sore had developed where the woody pulp had rested against her gums. It seemed as though her face just wasn't going to catch a break.

She expected Thomas would be at the bar and was thankful when he wasn't. A few of the regulars sat at the best tables near the street side windows sipping foam from their mugs. There was no sign of having been any commotion. Cooper was leaning over the bar rearranging the pots and making tally marks in a little book. He nodded at her and smiled with evasive eyes and thinned lips when she slipped past him. His presence made her chest tighten painfully, a reminder of impending changes.

"Well if it isn't the New Mrs. Ferrington, come to grace us." Mrs. Postlethwaite called out as soon as Elise entered the kitchen. She was sitting at the end of the kitchen table. There was a red mark in the middle of her forehead where she had been resting it against her arms and her eyes were swollen and wet. No one else was there.

Elise was sure she'd never seen the cook sitting at her own table. She felt her heart sink. "Did Richard tell you already?"

Mrs. Postlethwaite raised her arms dramatically towards the ceiling as though making a big announcement, "Today a simple chambermaid married a handsome and wealthy publican. No, Mr. Ferrington didn't tell me. Mr. Ferrington didn't have to tell me. You've given hope to chambermaids all over London."

"Look on the bright side," Elise snapped. She was already getting tired of feeling guilty for not sacrificing her own life for everyone else's benefit. "Now I'll be out of your hair. That's what you wanted, isn't it?"

Mrs. Postlethwaite's mouth opened and closed, as though censoring herself. "I rue the day you ever fell into our laps," she finally spat. "You've been nothing but heartache and trouble, dividing everyone up. You're worthless." Two enormous tears splattered on the table and she took a great, shaking breath and buried her head back into her arms.

"This is not my fault," she answered hotly. "I was not the one who gambled everything away. Where's Thomas?" she demanded. "At least he'll stay here for you, right? Now he can do whatever he wants without Richard undermining him."

"You don't know your head from your arse, do you?" Mrs. Postlethwaite studied Elise with a sad look on her face. "He'll be going too."

"I don't understand. Who's going? Where? Thomas?" This was not part of the plan, she thought. "Thomas has to stay here and run things. He can't leave."

"Thomas stay here with the Brewery owning the business?" Mrs. Postlethwaite shook her head. "You must be daft." She wiped her eyes and pulled another stool up next to her. "Sit down. I don't know why you did what you did. You could not have done it for love because we both know our Mr. Ferrington is a dolt. And you did not do it for money because you've seen Thomas with his black eyes and surly manner. You must have seen the way of things." She paused and looked at Elise narrowly and waited. When Elise didn't explain she sighed. "You've got your reasons, I'm sure.

"This place has been in the Ferrington family for many generations. I've known only two of those generations, but from the stories I hear they've all been grand. All but this last one." Mrs. Postlethwaite sniffed wetly and shook her head. "He's your problem now, bless him.

"Oh Richard was a sweet boy back in the day, to be sure. Always bringing kittens to his mother and tugging at my skirt looking for sweets; looking for affection. But he never showed much in the way of having savvy for anything except how to make people like him. Now, as a barman, that's a good thing. It's always good to have people enjoy your company. It brings them in; makes people want to stay around and buy more ale. But it was always Thomas that had the head for business. It was Old Mr. Ferrington as saw the value in Thomas. It was he that taught Thomas to read, then made him promise to protect Richard as payment. After Old Mr. Ferrington passed, things were fine as long as Thomas and Richard was working together. But lately," she looked down at her hands thoughtfully, then reached for her knife, touching it, but letting it rest on the table.

"Tom's always liked clever girls. Never had much use for the pretty ones. And you're clever, that's sure. I'd seen it the second you walked into my kitchen. 'There's a clever girl,' I said to myself, I did. I knew you'd be trouble when I saw your nasty green eyes." She started coughing. "Bring me some water. My mouth's gone dry."

Elise got up to get them both some water. Then watched as Mrs. Postlethwaite drained her mug. "More?" she asked.

When the cook shook her head, Elise sat back down. Mrs. Postlethwaite sighed deeply. It didn't seem right to see her so tired. "Now it's all gone," the cook finally said. "None of this matters anymore. The Quiet Woman is going to change for good. I'm not worried about myself, nor Mary neither. Cooper offered me and Mary good wages to keep working, but it won't be the same, will it? Not with Tom gone. It's Thomas I worry about. And Johnny. Poor Johnny."

Elise gently touched Mrs. Postlethwaite's shoulder in sympathy, but put her hand quickly back into her lap when she felt the cook stiffen. "Thomas is gone? Where did he go?"

"He's not gone yet, fool. He's out back in the yard waiting for you. Go ask him his plans. Maybe it's you he'll tell. He's not told me, although I can guess."

When Elise hesitated, Mrs. Postlethwaite shoved her off the stool. "Go on. Get out of my kitchen. I've had enough of you for a lifetime."

Elise stepped through the door into the courtyard and squinted in the darkness. Behind a screen of empty casks came a flickering glow of a trash fire. "Thomas?" she called. When no one replied, she shuffled in the darkness towards the fire. Midway to her destination, Elise stumbled over a loose cobble. A deep and irritated sigh came from behind the casks as Elise cursed and danced on one foot in pain. "For pity's sake, can't you just leave me alone?" Thomas yelled.

He was perched on an empty cask near the woodpile, whipping woodchips at Mrs. Ferrington's cats when Elise found him. The small trash fire burned nearby within a stone ring, casting feeble warmth and sending a billowing plume of black smoke up between the buildings to mix with the rest of the charred air over London. "How's your side?" Elise asked, holding her hands over the fire.

In reply, Thomas hurled another woodchip with a perfectly aimed sidearm at the throng of cats. There was a bloodstain welling on his shirt, but since he showed no sign of pain, Elise decided not to press the issue. When the stinking smoke curled around in a breeze and into her eyes, she moved and settled next to Thomas on her own empty cask. She stole a longer look at the sullen barman. He had been tugging at his hair again. Most of it had been pulled out of the queue at the nape of his neck, and stood up straight off his head in clumps. "Jesus," Elise breathed. "What happened to your hands?" His right hand was swollen and his knuckles were bloody and raw. The left wasn't as bad, but Elise could tell it too had been recently used as a battering ram.

"That's no business of yours, is it?" Thomas snapped. He slipped his hands under the coat he had draped across his lap.

"Richard made you do it, didn't he? He's been sending you out to gather money from everyone with a tab. You went back out last night, didn't you?"

"That's not what happened."

"What's he got over you? Why don't you just leave?"

"And what of you? Why did you do it? Why did you marry him?" Thomas demanded. His eyes were startlingly hollow when he turned to look at her and his voice cut deeper than the wound bleeding from his gut. "Do you love him?"

"I did it because he said he was enlisting and being shipped to America. He said wives sometimes go with their husbands."

"Then you love him."

"No, I don't."

"I don't understand. Why would you want to become a camp follower if you don't love him? The King's Army is no place for a woman. If you don't love him, why wear that ring on your finger?"

"This?" Elise waved her left hand in the air. "This is meaningless. It's nothing, just a tool he used to try to get what he wanted, and now it's a tool I'm using for the same reason."

Thomas shook his head. "You're cold-hearted to call that a tool. You can deny it all you want, but that ring has power. Even now, it constricts, does it not? You've been twisting it and picking at it since you sat down, like trying to give yourself a little more space underneath it. Like it or not, that ring is just as powerful as that golden insect you're carrying in your pocket."

Thomas's shirt opened slightly at his neck and Elise noticed a blue vein under his skin that traced a crooked path like a shadow across his collarbone. It made her think of how she'd felt his pulse under her palm just the night before. She looked away quickly. "Richard gave me the scarab today. He said it was in my hand when you guys found me." She didn't question how he knew it was in her pocket. Thomas just seemed to know things.

"Aye, that's true."

"You could have told me he had it."

"It wasn't for me to say." Thomas began throwing woodchips in a high arc and the cats leaped in the air, paws extended. Jacob collided with Jericho and fell onto his side. When Magdalene objected to being disturbed, Jacob bunny-hopped out of the way of her flashing claws. The antics made Thomas smile as he stood to dig his pouch of tobacco out of his pocket. Sitting down again, he settled into the routine of packing his pipe. Elise watched the tendons in the backs of his hands rise and fall, the wounds on his knuckles having no effect on the grace of his movements.

"Mrs. Southill was right, you know," Elise said. "Smoking is going to kill you someday." Thomas lifted the pipe stem to his mouth and sucked in as he touched a glowing rag pulled from the fire to the bowl of his pipe. Then he handed the pipe to Elise. It was still wet from his mouth when Elise touched it to her lips. She closed her eyes as she pulled the smoke.

"I'm not surprised you married him," he finally said as Elise settled back against the stack of kegs behind her. "I'm just disappointed."

"How can you be disappointed by something you expected?" Elise smiled and handed the pipe back. As usual, she felt herself relax as the nicotine rushed through her bloodstream.

"Any woman would marry Richard, so I'm not surprised. I'm just disappointed to find out you're like any woman." Thomas pointed to the lump in her apron pocket with the stem of his pipe. "I knew about the insect, to be sure, but I never thought you'd marry him for it."

"I'm not like any woman," Elise said defensively.

"You are. You're just like any woman." Thomas passed the pipe back over and Elise ground her teeth on its stem as she puffed. "All you need is a nice compliment and a flashy jewel and you're lost."

"For your information, he gave me the scarab after we were married. He wasn't so secure in my affections that he would give me the jewel without ensuring his own possession of it." She passed the pipe back and changed the subject. "So what will you do now that the Quiet Woman's gone? Mrs. P. says you won't stay at the pub."

Thomas shrugged. "I'll follow Richard to war. There's nothing left for me here."

"What? Are you serious? You're a great bartender. You could stay here and work for Cooper."

"Even army life would be better than working for Cooper. Cooper'd have me killed fighting every single night of my life, and against hardened men. At least in the army I'll only fight every fortnight, and even then, it'd be against some poor farmer with a belly full of brandy holding a musket. I can't blame Cooper. You can make a good deal of money setting up a boxing match." Thomas shook his head. "But my odds are better fighting for King and Country. I've no longer the spirit to fight for money."

"What about that other pub everyone keeps talking about? The Bear and Snare, the Dancing Hare, whatever. You could go work there, couldn't you? There's got to be other pubs you could work for. Or you could open your own. You know the business better than anyone."

"Open my own? With what money?" Thomas looked surprised.

"Haven't you been working here your whole life? You must have some savings. Or maybe you could go to the bank and get a business loan."

"A business loan? From a bank? Me?" Thomas snorted.

Elise frowned. "It's not funny. You could, you know."

"Tell me," Thomas smiled. "How much do I pay you?"

"Nothing."

"That's not true. I pay you in hot meals and a warm bed. That's what strays get paid. We're two peas in a pod, you and I, both living on the charity of the Ferringtons. While it may be that Mrs. Ferrington pays better attention to clothing and feeding me than she does to you, we're still both strays. No banker in his right mind would forward me a loan."

Elise stared at him with her mouth open, horrified at the idea that such a capable person would settle to such a life. "But I bet you could get a job at another pub, and get paid too."

"No one would hire the likes of me as a publican. Not with my reputation. I'd be fighting the rest of my life—those with a chip on their shoulder just looking to best me, and those who I'm sent after, with nothing in their pockets but lint." He shook his head. "The army will be a nice holiday compared to what I've been doing. And I'll not do factory work either, so don't you bother asking. That would break me faster than anything else. The only thing those poor sots are good for after a day in the factory is walking through the Quiet Woman's doors… no, the army is best."

"So I could have married you instead."

Thomas looked at her sharply. "Would you have?"

Elise remained silent and twisted her ring. It felt like a rhetorical question. What did it matter who she married if her goal was to go back home? Still, there was something oddly comforting about knowing Thomas would be getting on the boat with her. She lingered with his pipe as she contemplated the passage with both Richard and Thomas in the confines of a warship.

"Mrs. P. told me I ought to give this to you." Thomas leaned over and picked something up from the other side of his cask and offered it for the return of his pipe.

"My running shoe!" Elise cried out excitedly. She recognized it right away and pulled it lovingly to her chest, leaving red dust stains on the lace of her chemise. "Where's the other one?" She slipped it onto her foot and her toes fell into all the familiar indentations, luxuriating in cushioning.

"There was only the one."

Tears came quickly. "Really? Only one?" she asked, sucking air over her rattling bottom lip. Weeks of having to walk barefoot had given her hardened black heels, cracked and flaking toenails, and now, a stubbed toe. And there was only one shoe. "Where were you hiding it? In your room?"

Thomas looked somewhat abashed. "It's a strange shoe," he said, by way of excuse. "I've never seen its like and Mrs. P. was most perplexed."

"They're better when they come in pairs," Elise pouted. She looked at her foot in the firelight. Encased in nylon and rubber, it certainly looked alien. The neon pink stripes were garish. "I think this sole is made from petroleum products," she mused. Not wood, not leather, not steel, but made from an indecipherable chemical recipe of ingredients.

"Elise," Thomas said, trying to get her attention back. "Where did you get that shoe? Once and for all, tell me how you came to be in the lane that night."

Elise sighed. "I'm from America. That's why I want to go back so badly. But, you have to believe me. I have no idea how I got here. I don't remember."

"You don't remember the passage? The ship?"

"There was no ship. I just," she paused to try to think of how to describe what she'd gone through. "I just fell."

"What do you mean, fell?"

"Arrived. I just arrived in the street. From the future."

Thomas knocked the ashes of his pipe out on his heel and shook his head. He took some time cleaning out the pipe stem before tucking it back into the folds of his coat. Elise watched nervously. She hadn't expected to tell him anything.

"I know you think to get on that boat with Richard," Thomas finally began, "but you'll not do it. You'll keep the jewel until you can find someone reputable to sell it to. I asked Mary to look out for you. She's wily, that one. You can learn a thing or two from her. Mrs. P. will come around eventually. Just stay out of her way for the time being."

Elise's green eyes flashed dangerously. That Thomas would have the audacity to make arrangements for her didn't sit well. "I'm going with Richard."

"You most definitely are not."

"Yes I am. I married him to get to America. I'm going. Didn't you just hear me? I'm from the future. 200 years ahead."

"I heard you, and I'll not allow you to follow the regiment, no matter what ridiculous story you concoct." Thomas's brow was furrowed, insistent.

"I don't think you understand what I'm going through here." Lack of understanding was an understatement, thought Elise. She wanted to rope him into the same contortions of understanding she herself was fighting though. "I had friends in the future. I had a job—I was a real healer. I was needed. When I showed up to help people, people were glad to see me. Relieved, even. That's what I had. That's who I was. But I've got nothing here." Tears started rolling down her cheeks. She was exhausted. "What've I got now? Nothing. I've got a broom, Thomas. That's what I've got: a broom. And if I don't show up in the kitchen, no one cares. Someone else sweeps up. Johnny gets the water. This life here is worthless." She sniffed hard. "I've got to go back there. When Richard said he was deploying to America and that I could go along if I was married to him," Elise shook her head. "I suddenly had hope. He gave me hope."

Thomas raked his hair back from his face with his bloodied hand. He looked as though he was fighting his own thoughts. "That shoe is the strangest thing I've ever seen," he said. "I've studied it many a night, trying to make sense of it. Just like how I've studied the words you use and the way you use them and they make no kind of sense either. Maybe you were hit on the head, or maybe you really do come from the future. All I know for certain is that you're lost, and that the Frogs seem to keep coming for you. Maybe you're right and I just don't understand. But the way I see it, you don't seem to understand anything either. You complain about what it smells like here in London? You drag yourself to lift just one pitcher of beer? Don't you know it takes at least a month to cross the ocean? And that's with good seas. What do you think it'll smell like on the ship? What kind of work do you think you'll be asked to do in the army?"

"For free passage, I can deal."

"No Elise." Thomas stood in front of her and gripped her shoulders. He had the same fierce eyes; the same set mouth as he did the first time they had met. "I won't let you. There's nothing free about the King's Army. You'll starve. You'll get sick. And you'll be shoulder to shoulder with other starving, sick people."

"I'm going. You can't stop me. Only my husband can do that, and you're not my husband."

The sound of Thomas's back-handed slap echoed in the narrow courtyard. Elise was knocked off the cask and onto the hard packed dirt, narrowly missing the fire. Her jaw burned from the blow. Her green eyes sparked in anger. She looked at Thomas and seethed.

"If you can't take a slap like that one, you won't last two seconds as a camp follower." Thomas's eyes filled as he looked down on her sprawled at his feet. "It will be constant humiliation, the likes of which you've never experienced. You won't survive that. It will break you." He hastily wiped his eyes then wiped his hand on his trousers before offering it to Elise to lift her back to her feet. When she flinched, he turned away.

In his profile, she saw the muscles of his jaw flexing as he pushed back his hair. Watching him make that movement made her chest ache even as her stomach clenched in anger. She climbed to her feet. "Don't come with us. Don't come, Elise," he pleaded quietly. "Stay here where you'll be safe."

"Fuck you." Elise touched the corner of her mouth with her tongue and tasted blood. She turned to walk back to the kitchen with all the grace of a woman with only one tennis shoe on, holding her shoulder where she'd landed on it.

"I promised Old Mr. Ferrington I'd protect Richard," Thomas's deep voice stopped her in her tracks. "I never said nothing about protecting Richard's wife." When Elise turned back to look at him she saw that his eyes had become cold. "If you come, you'll be on your own. You'd better hope Dick has the strength to make you happy and keep you safe. God knows you've tested my own strength."

"I don't need him to protect me, and I don't need you," Elise spat. "I'm strong enough on my own."

Elise watched Thomas as he walked away. His back was stiff and resolved, his gait smooth.

There was a warm summer wind that crossed the Thames. It found Adelaide and Dodo sitting against the thin plank wall of a riverside warehouse where they'd taken shelter. She herself was bruised and sore, but she hadn't suffered anything like what Dodo had endured. *Le Brun* had beat him mercilessly with fists that glowed golden with power as they made contact again and again. She'd watched horrified, screamed for it to stop but was helpless to end it. *Le Brun* had only stopped when he was spent, crumpling in a heap to the floor so that both men had to be helped to their feet to be led away. Since then, she'd set Dodo's broken arm, but there was nothing she could do for his broken ribs or face. His brow, his jaw, his bleeding ears, his missing teeth – he'd never be the same man. Dodo had been able to walk with her for a while, far enough away from the Quiet Woman to feel safe. But now he could walk no longer. Adelaide was afraid he was bleeding inside, which was a condition she was helpless to cure. In the face of this worry, she felt the urgency of her situation all the more strongly. "Where's my grimoire?" she whispered in his ear.

"The golem," he lisped through his broken teeth. "The golem…"

"The golem has it?"

"No, you imbecile. Your ridiculously useless grimiore is at the Dancing Bear. The golem…"

"Yes? Yes?"

"… is married. She's leaving England with her husband tonight."

Adelaide was astonished. Married? Certainly she would have felt the ritual as it occurred and the resultant transformation of the golem. "How do you know she's married?"

"Everyone in London knows a chambermaid married a wealthy publican brought low by gambling debts. I heard the story only an hour ago from a beach comber shouting to a ferryman."

Adelaide sighed and wished she spoke English. "An hour ago? Why didn't you tell me? Where are they going?"

"America," Dodo lisped.

"Are you sure you want to follow your husband?" Corporal Wiffle asked. "Think hard Mrs. Ferrington, it's one thing to live near a garrisoned army, and entirely different to follow a regiment on campaign."

Elise had finally reached the front of the line that formed on the dock. Corporal Whiffle sat behind a table on which ledgers were spread to record the names of the new recruits who were climbing aboard H.M.S. *Valiant*. The breeze coming off the Thames was light and warm, but carried the unfortunate smell of all of London's sewage. The delicate pings, creaks, and moans that came from the moored tall ships that rocked in the river's current were sounds that soothed.

"I'm staying with Richard," Elise responded heatedly.

"We'll see about that," the corporal replied. "The lottery will be tonight."

"Lottery?" She echoed. Elise turned around to look at her husband with astonished eyes and reddened cheeks. "What lottery?"

Richard adjusted the bag on his back and a violin string twanged. "The one that determines if you can win a place on board. All the wives names get thrown in a hat."

"I thought marrying you was as good as a ticket. Do you mean that I might not get to go?"

"You've got outstanding odds, my darling."

"You'd be better off telling your wife the truth of the odds," Corporal Wiffle sniffed and smiled at Elise. "You've approximately a six percent chance."

Elise felt her ears burn as she stared at her sheepish husband. Those were decidedly not excellent odds. She turned back to the corporal in desperation. "Trust me: you want me on that boat."

"If truth be told, I don't want any women on our troopships. But I'll allow we'll all be glad to have our laundry done. The King's Army wants only stout and hearty women of good moral character. Do you have good moral character? You certainly don't seem very stout. You look as though a light wind might blow you over."

Richard bristled. "How dare you, Sir. How dare you question my wife's moral fiber."

Corporal Wiffle's reaction was swift. He stood, knocking back his chair, and leaned over his desk. "I'll do as I please, Private," he yelled. Although considerably shorter, his authority in all matters over Richard was unmistakable. He calmly took his chair back up and sat down again. "You'd best accept that now."

"You have to take me," Elise begged. "I'm a nurse. I can help on the battlefield. I'll be your medic." Elise felt the words leave her mouth even as her mind shuffled to rationalize the lie. She knew she would take off as soon as she stepped on American soil. As far as her moral character was concerned, that was none of the corporal's business.

"A medic you say?" The man's squinty eyes thinned to slits as he paused to think. "The regimental surgeon is always looking for help, that's sure, but you're a tiny little thing. I can't see how you'd be much use. But perhaps if you've got soft enough hands," he leered, "the men could find other uses for your nursing skills. You wouldn't happen to have a letter of introduction?" he asked.

"No. Do I need one?"

"The surgeon would be wanting a letter."

Elise felt her stomach drop with a sick thud. "Look, let me talk to the surgeon. I'm sure I can convince him to let me onboard. I don't have a letter and I'm not throwing my name in any hat."

"The surgeon's not here." Corporal Wiffle stood and waved his arm for the next man in line to approach. "Move aside. I've said my peace," he dismissed.

"You're making a mistake," a gruff voice called from the crowd. Elise looked up quickly and saw someone pushing his way to the front.

"Who the hell are you?" Corporal Whiffle asked.

"Private Thomas MacEwan, Sir." He lifted his shirt to show his knife wound. "This woman is a healer. She saved my very life." He turned to the other men in the crowd to display the neat sutures that held his flesh together. Men strained to see what was happening.

Elise couldn't believe Thomas was drumming for her to be signed. She tried to catch his eyes, but he looked everywhere but at her.

"Sign the lass up," someone yelled. A murmur of approval moved through the crowd. Not one of them wished to be sliced with a saber and have no one around to sew up the pieces.

The corporal surveyed restless men. "Fine, it's your funeral," he said to Elise, "but Private MacEwan must stay. He's not fit to serve with that wound."

Richard's eyes nearly popped out of his head. "He must come," he insisted.

Again the corporal stood. "I make the rules, Private,"

"Don't you know who he is?" Richard demanded. "He's one of London's champion pugilists. You'd be daft to not want him in the regiment."

Slowly, the corporal lowered himself back into his chair after glowering at the menacing crowd. Then he dipped his quill. "I don't give a damn who he is. You're all cannon fodder as far as I'm concerned."

"You won't be sorry," Elise said. "I can guarantee I'm the best nurse this army has ever seen. It's Mrs. Richard Ferrington. Two 'r's." She punctuated her words by jabbing with her finger on the open page of the roster.

The corporal stared at her for a moment, then shrugged and wrote her name down with the word "nurse" behind it, underlined three times. "It's no skin off my nose, I can tell you, but I've done you no favors, believe me." He looked over at Richard. "You'd best learn fast to keep your wife in check or the captain will have her lashed over the barrel as quickly as he would any man. He doesn't take kindly to anyone questioning his orders or stirring up trouble. Take a firm hand with her now, that's my advice. It's bad for morale to see a woman flogged."

"That's it?" Elise asked excitedly.

"That's it then," Corporal Wiffle replied.

"So I'm going to America?"

"America?" he laughed. "Is that what you think? No, not anymore. America was yesterday's problem, a momentary Parliamentary dalliance. Haven't you heard? Nappy is stirring trouble in Spain, so tonight we'll be under weigh for Lisbon's harbor."

*à suivre *

𐤀 𐤔𐤓𐤀𐤉

A PREVIEW OF
THE NEXT BOOK
IN THE GOLDEN
SCARAB SERIES,
THE BRAZEN WOMAN

ישראל

PREVIEW

After ten days of enduring the misery of temperatures over 100, Elise was only too happy to leave the dusty town behind and head into the mountains for a long weekend with her friends. She held a lighter to the end of her cigarette and rolled down the window. In the Tucson valley, escaping the heat usually meant heading to the mall, or the movie theater. But Elise had enough of air conditioning and the stale smells of people. She was looking forward to camping under the stars.

In the driver's seat next to Elise, Anita started flapping one hand in the air. "Do you have to do that now?" she asked. "You're letting all the AC out."

"Seriously? This is the fanciest Wrangler I've ever been in. Aren't you supposed to leave the doors off these things or something? Don't you just want to feel the wind in your face for once?"

Anita shot Elise a dirty look. "The wind I'm feeling smells nasty, thanks to you."

"Fine, I'll just smoke half," Elise consoled. "Keep both hands on the wheel, please," Elise said clutching the dashboard while trying to keep the cherry of her cigarette from blowing out the window. Anita reached under her seat for an old catalog and used it to vigorously fan away the smoke. The Wrangler wove in its lane. "Okay! Okay! I'll put it out."

"Damn it, Elise. Not in my ashtray. You'll stink up my car."

"Do you really want me to throw it out the window and start a grassfire?" Elise slammed the tray back into the dashboard. "I didn't think so." All three fumed as they headed up Catalina Highway—the two friends, and the cigarette still smoldering in the ashtray.

Now, two hundred years in the past, which inexplicably was Elise's forward trajectory on her timeline, she found she missed Anita with a full-body ache. Even the arguments were precious memories as the wind howled and the waves broke against the side of the three-masted troopship with sickening regularity. Dreaming of intense desert sunshine, she sat shivering in the humid darkness with nearly five hundred soldiers in her regiment, three decks deep inside the ship's hull. While the ship pitched over the waves, she breathed with pursed lips, in through the nose, out through the mouth, concentrated, regulated, steady, as her stomach tumbled into knots and cold sweat beaded on her forehead.

It had been exciting at first. When the white sails snapped open with the crisp wind of the English Channel, Elise wanted nothing more than to climb to the top of the main mast and look out over the sparkling blue water. Just being able to breathe sea air instead of choking on London smoke was exquisite freedom, but the feeling was stolen from her the second she grabbed the ratlines to ascend past the rail for a better look at the horizon. A sailor who had no patience for "the playful frivolities of women" tore her from the ropes. So Elise left to watch the men in her company line up in ranks to be drilled by their sergeant. She carefully stood behind a cannon to protect herself from any accidental firings, since a few green soldiers would swing their muskets wildly when the ship rocked unexpectedly and their boots slipped on the slick deck. It had been entertaining to watch, unfortunately, her freedom ended that evening when the weather changed. All women and children were banished the decks below. The rest of the regiment joined them an hour later when the storm gathered strength and the seamen rushed to action.

On the third day of rough seas, there were not many left that could stand and walk. There was one person, however, who seemed immune to the motion. In the dark, far aft of where Elise was sitting, someone cursed. "Get off me you fiddle-scraping blockhead!"

"Begging your pardon," was the reply.

Then, closer, "Look out! Damn your eyes—you've trod on my satchel."

"Your pardon." The sound of protests from various soldiers got louder as the man eliciting the ugly curses made his way up the center of the narrow corridor. "Pardon. Begging your pardon. Whoops, pardon me." Elise sighed resignedly.

"What are you doing up there?" Richard asked when he finally reached her side. His face twisted into a look of annoyance, which was not unusual. "Come down. It isn't seemly to have you crawling all over the cargo. You'll hurt yourself."

Elise ignored him and looked across to the starboard side and saw the shadow of O'Brian against a wall of stacked crates. He was retching into a bucket. Before the storm had gotten bad, Elise had been happy to use the waves as an excuse to fall into the arms of the young soldier. O'Brian's slow grin revealed he wasn't buying the frail damsel routine. "Steady on, Mrs. Ferrington," he'd said to her. "You ought not be walking about in this weather." The hand that had caught her elbow slid up Elise's shoulder to linger at the bare spot on her neck – not long, but long enough.

Elise felt Richard grip her ankle as the floor dropped out from under them. The ship was falling into a deep trough in the waves. She clung to the chains that anchored her packing crate to the curved wall and held on tight as Richard pulled. "Get down here at once. This entire nightmare is your fault you know."

Elise weakly kicked her leg to dislodge Richard's hand while her mind floated back to Tucson. "Slow down," she had said to Anita. "If I get sick in your car it'll be your own fault."

"Seriously?" Anita protested. "I'm not going all that fast."

"Just around the curves," Elise said as g-forces slammed her stomach against her ribs. "Slow down around the curves."

The way to the top of Mount Lemon was normally a pleasant drive on a twisting two-lane road. The air cooled as the miles melted away behind them. Elise rolled the window down again and felt the wind slip under the sleeve of her shirt when she hung her arm out of the car. It raised goose bumps on her skin, smoothed away the sweat, and brought the tingling smell of piñon as they moved out of the low desert and into the coniferous forest.

This time, however, Elise leaned out of the car window for a purpose other than to enjoy the view into the deep canyon dotted with saguaros. Instead, she stared at the horizon to steady herself and hoped the wind would slap her back to normal. "Oh god," she moaned. "For fuck's sake, Anita. Slow down." Her words were blown away, unheard.

Her stomach surged again as her friend whipped around yet another hairpin. The tires of the bouncing Wrangler were barely clinging to the asphalt.

Elise would have given anything to be back in Anita's tidy silver Wrangler. That anyone would blame her for present situation was hurtfully ironic. "None of this is my fault," she snapped at Richard. "None of it." She finally kicked Richard's hand from her ankle and looked at the slick floor. All cargo and provisions were smartly tied, chained or netted so that they'd stay in place in the case of bad weather. Everything was battened down but the people on board, and the people's buckets. The rule was to do your business at the ship's head, but in weather like this, the rule didn't apply. A bucket rolled across the floor from aft to fore. There was no way she'd get down off the crate in her bare feet.

Instinctively she touched her dress where her emerald was tucked under her corset. She felt it pressed against her flesh by the tight strings of her bodice, warm and hard. It was her only clue to how she might have traveled through time, but the scarab was enigmatic. Until she could figure it out, she followed along through the adventure like an attached barnacle. It didn't improve her mood to be so submissive to the flow of her life, but for once, Richard seemed grumpier. "Did you lose your shirt again?" Elise asked as Richard gave up trying to pull her off the crate and sunk to his blanket. His sullen silence confirmed her guess. Elise sighed.

As a camp follower "on the strength", she was entitled to one half of the rations of a soldier and none of the liquor. This meant either she drank water from the barrels, which was questionably fresh even before they set sail (a possible reason the "bung-hole" on a barrel is a synonym for something else), or she shared Richard's beer. However, Richard tended to gamble away his beer rations. In the ship's galley was a stove that kept water boiling for the officers, and once she managed to sneak past the cook to get at it with the result of a nearly scalded hand when the ship suddenly lurched over a rogue wave. Hydration was an issue, especially now that she felt seasick. She needed Richard's beer. On the other hand, beer wasn't going to help an already churning stomach.

A moan rose in the damp air. The sound, a waveringly long note, came from behind a blanket that had been raised to allow privacy for another married couple—a convenience Elise and Richard hadn't bothered to attempt. Despite her own misery, Elise still had enough strength to roll her eyes. They had no business being that happy.

"It is your fault," Richard pouted. "Our being here is entirely your fault. You should have let me sell that stone. We could be tucked safe in the Quiet Woman had you done so. Look at you—you're pitiful," Richard turned to survey Elise and his eyes took in her greasy hair, and her dress that she'd been wearing since it had been given to her a month ago. "You are content to remain slattern and unpleasant when wealth could have at least given you the veneer of social acceptability. It was most definitely you who brought me into this position. I blame you."

When they'd first boarded the ship, they hissed their arguments at each other. Now they no longer bothered to keep their voices down. The tight quarters made it difficult for others to politely move away when they began to bicker, although most still tried. A positive result of their marital spats was acquiring more space in the confined orlop deck than had any others. Elise saw the shadow of O'Brian recede.

"It's not just me you damned to this fate," continued Richard. "Tom blames you too. He told me so himself."

Thomas. The name was like a hammer on Elise's chest, subduing all further argument. She knew he was close. He'd probably set himself up with a direct line of sight to them, but she'd barely seen him since they'd first set sail. Elise doubted Thomas actually blamed her, but knew he resented her. The thought made her stomach rise. She felt her mouth fill with a swell of saliva and she swallowed hard. Stop the boat. Roll the windows down. Pull over.

"Oh my god, Anita. Pull over."

"Hang on for just another minute. We're almost there."

"PULL OVER."

Elise remembered she had the car door open before the Wrangler came to a complete stop. It had been a strawberry and mango smoothie that created the vibrant orange line against the roadside sage. Anita stepped out of the car and came around while looking at her watch impatiently. "We're going to be late," she said.

"Late for what? You can't be late to go camping!"

"Everyone's waiting for us at the trailhead." Anita sighed when Elise bent over a second time. "Okay, okay. Get it all out," she said, catching up Elise's hair in her fist to hold it back.

Elise pointed weakly to the car and wiped her mouth with the back of her hand. "I'm not getting back in there."

"Walk up to that tree and back. Then you drive."

"No way."

"You can't get carsick when you're in the driver's seat."

You can't get seasick when you're unfurling the sails. Elise imagined the men three floors above her on the main deck happily stomping their feet in the puddles while the Captain pumped a jig from a squeeze-box. She could hear the slashing rain on the side of the ship. She knew the men were clinging to ropes and skittering across the wet deck in bare feet. But she imagined them all smoking pipes and swallowing hunks of salted beef with swigs of hard liquor. The thought of rum made Elise's stomach muscles ripple in an uneasy clench. No wonder the captain had confined the army to the depths of the dank, dark hull. Why have a bunch of vomiting landlubbers spoil their fun?

Another moan from behind the curtain cut through the gloom. Richard climbed up onto the crates next to Elise and she scooted over to give him space. Despite their marriage, there was little chance Elise would be emitting her own full-throated moans any time soon. She wasn't adverse to the idea, just indifferent, despite the fact that Richard was the least rumpled of all the soldiers. While the entire regiment was soaked in the sweat of nausea, Richard's skin took on a healthy sheen from the humidity and his cheeks remained rosy. When everyone else had turned inward in their misery, Richard thought nothing of pulling out a deck of cards from his pack to seek out the ship's old carpenter and purser for a game and a conversation. Those men lucky enough to still have their hair kept it matted and slicked over their skulls, but Richard's blonde waves looked as though he had applied a leave-in conditioner. It didn't seem fair. His beauty was wasted, Elise thought as she surveyed his profile. Richard was the perfect example of attractive without attraction.

"Shouldn't you look in on Mrs. Collins?" he asked.

"What for? She sounds a little busy right now." Elise had exchanged few words with Amanda Collins in the past four days. There were five women in their Company, about twenty on the ship, not including herself or the Major's wife. All of them had more personality than Amanda Collins, who rarely emerged from behind her marital curtain.

Richard shrugged. "You know your own business." He reached down to his knapsack and pulled out his fiddle. The squeaking sounds his instrument made as he rotated the tuning pegs and plucked the strings were a welcome distraction. When he drew out a long note with his bow, nearby soldiers, suffering from their own thoughts and fears for the future, heaved a sigh of relief. Elise scooted to the edge of the crate to avoid Richard's sharp elbows and settled back against the wall.

The melodies he pulled from his fiddle meandered without pause from one song to another. Elise was beginning to recognize the more common refrains that circled back around in various keys and rhythms. The way people would join in making music without any kind of showmanship was one aspect of her new world that she truly appreciated, and she loved it when someone was moved to stand and sing. Only once had Thomas emerged from the shadows to join in with his earthy baritone, and there was barely a man in the company that hadn't wiped tears from his eyes when he sang, "Man to man, the world o'er, shall brother's be for a' that."

A sudden choked, gasping sound burst from behind the blanket curtain, causing Richard to play four atonal notes in rapid succession as his bow fell off the fiddle. "I can't think why you shouldn't be calling upon Mrs. Collins," he insisted.

"Why are you so concerned abo—" Elise's words trailed off. She felt her stomach clench again, but this time it wasn't from nausea. It was caused by sudden fear. She sat up straight. "She's not pregnant, is she?"

"Good god, woman. Didn't you know?"

Private Collins poked his head from behind the curtain. Even in the gloom Elise was able to detect his wild-eyed look. He walked towards her like a drunken man, careening from side to side. Other soldiers caught him as he passed, thumping him on his back, giving words of encouragement, and keeping him on his feet.

"Some nurse you're turning out to be," Richard laughed ruefully. "You can't even tell when a fellow female is nearing her time of confinement."

"How was I supposed to see her condition with all these stupid skirts we wear?" She flicked her own and reached for Mrs. Southill's medical kitbag. "I thought pregnant women weren't allowed on board?"

"Yes, quite right," Richard agreed. He took her elbow to steady her as she descended from the crate to the floor. "But no one could bear to see the couple torn asunder. She was weeping so prettily."

The ship began rising up a swell which created a slick ramp for Elise to surf down with one bare foot in front of the other. Private Collins caught her mid way. "How far apart are her contractions?" she asked as they made their way towards the curtained corner. Collins shook his head, not understanding. "Her pains! How many minutes between her pains?"

"She's in a great deal of pain," he agreed. "It's her first."

Elise ducked behind the curtain and discovered Mrs. Collins hovering in a squat over a single blanket with her skirt hitched over her knees and her palms braced against two casks. Her face, pale as a boiled turnip, was streaming in sweat.

"Private Hobert's birthed plenty of lambs," Collins noted. "Shall I fetch him to help?"

"No. God, no," Elise said in horror. Hobert, formerly a shepherd, was so used to having only his sheep as company that he felt no compunction in sending snot-rockets in all directions whenever his sinuses felt clogged, which was all the time. Elise considered any area within a ten-foot radius of the man a hazard zone.

Amanda half stood on trembling thighs as she let out another cry. In two long strides, Elise reached her and offered her shoulder. "I'm so thirsty," Amanda whispered. "If you please," she begged, "send someone to get me a drink. Tea perhaps? Peter's got nothing but beer."

Elise froze while ideas tumbled all over her brain. She eased her shoulder under Amanda's armpit, hoping to steady them both as she worked out a way to get everyone hydrated. "Hey Collins?" she started, sounding hesitant. "It's Peter, right? Peter Collins? I'll help your wife but you need to pay me half your beer ration for the next two weeks."

Collins's mouth dropped open. "My beer? Half?" he stuttered.

"I can call in Hobert if you prefer." Elise slipped her hand under Amanda's dress and worked her palm along her belly, feeling both for the baby's heartbeat and position. "He probably won't ask for payment, except for maybe, here and there, a favor from Amanda. After she's recovered of course. What do you say?"

Amanda Collins squeezed her eyes shut. Her wail took on an edge of panic....

Acknowledgements

Many people helped me conjure this novel into the world and I'd like to take a page to thank them for their part in the ceremony.

I would like to thank Tracy Ertl, Karen Hughes, Megan Trank, and the publishing crew at Beaufort Books. Their knowledge, skill, and enthusiasm for this project kept me going when I started to doubt myself.

To my writing group, Serena Le, Carrie Ritter, Katie Harper, and Trista Mallory—thanks for the coffee, the friendship, and setting the timer when the work needed to get done.

A very special thank you to my beta readers, Kristin Rabosky, Julie Steiner, Trista Mallory, Chris Glazowski, Dan Ellerbroek, Margaret and Jean-Alex Molina, and Kate Chase, who all played various important parts in the process either by calling out plot inconsistencies, correcting my French, red-lining my errors, and being, in general, wonderful.

Finally, I wish to thank my very patient and good-humored husband Kevin, who gently pulls me back when he sees me fall into the vortex.

About the Author

With a French father and a mother from New Orleans, Anne Gross's interest in the Napoleonic era was inevitable. Currently, she lives in San Francisco with her husband and beloved chihuahua, where she's working on the continued adventures of her recalcitrant heroine.

CPSIA information can be obtained at www.ICGtesting.com
Printed in the USA
LVOW11s0520050516

486464LV00001B/1/P

9 780825 307980